The Army Times

Generals in Muddy Boots

The Army Times

Generals in Muddy Boots

A Concise Encyclopedia of Combat Commanders

Dan Cragg
Sergeant Major, U.S. Army (Ret.)

Edited by Walter J. Boyne

BERKLEY BOOKS, New York

GENERALS IN MUDDY BOOTS

A Berkley Book
Published by The Berkley Publishing Group
200 Madison Avenue, New York, New York 10016

Book design by Irving Perkins Associates

First edition: February 1996

Library of Congress Cataloging-in-Publication Data
Cragg, Dan.
   Generals in muddy boots : a concise encyclopedia of
combat commanders / Dan Cragg ; edited by Walter J.
Boyne. — 1st ed.
      p. cm.
   Includes bibliographical references.
   ISBN 0-425-15136-0
   1. Military biography—Encyclopedias.   I. Boyne,
Walter J., 1929– . II. Title.
  U51.C747   1996
  355′.0092′2—dc20
   [B]   95-20089
                             CIP

Printed in the United States of America

10 9 8 7 6 5 4 3 2 1

Acknowledgments

I owe special debts of gratitude to a lot of people who gave a lot of their time to helping me with this book.

Colonel John R. Elting, U.S. Army, Retired, the ideal of an officer, a gentleman, and a scholar. No one writes better about soldiers than John because he *is* a soldier, bred through and through, as Robert Burns wrote of Captain Francis Grose:

> *It's tauld he was a sodger bred,*
> *And ane was rather fa'n than fled;*
> *But now he's quat the spurtle-blade*
> *   And dog-skin wallet*
> *And taen the—Historian trade,*
> *   I think they call it.*

Lieutenant Colonel Michael Lee Lanning, U.S. Army, Retired, who knows about command in combat from firsthand experience. Lee has the instinctive incisiveness of the born infantryman and never calls a spade a spade if he can call it a goddamned shovel.

Both John and Lee have written extensively and well on military subjects, and while I would never presume to classify myself as one of their historian colleagues, I am honored to call them friends.

First Lieutenant Peter C. Joannides, U.S. Army, Retired, whose background as a classical scholar includes family from both Athens and Sparta. Pete has also seen infantry combat as close as any man can and still live to tell about it.

Dr. Thomas M. Carhart, III, scholar, soldier, boulevardier, who can always find time for sergeants. Thanks, too, for all the coffee, Tom—and get your feet off my desk!

Mr. J. B. Post, who as the Secret Master of Mapdom, always gives timely and accurate directions.

Mr. Walter J. Boyne, the only editor I've ever known who gets the job done simply by issuing "mission-type orders." Walt, thanks for the "hand," and it was a free one.

Mr. Bill Lang and Mr. Richard Wysocki, of the Free Library of Philadelphia, who gave me some breaks when I really needed them.

And finally, Mr. David Sherman, without whose help my work could never have been done. That is not an exaggeration. David thinks for himself, speaks the truth, and takes pride in his work. He's also a superb teller of war stories, and knows what it's like to carry a rifle. Men don't come any better than David.

Where I have gone astray in what follows, it is my fault entirely, and not theirs.

Foreword

The title *Generals in Muddy Boots* is an absolutely perfect one for Dan Cragg's delightful compilation of biographies of the world's fighting generals. It also captures Cragg's style, which is at once scholarly and humorously insightful; one can imagine the generals themselves reading their biographies and smiling.

One of the great incongruities of human experience is that we continue to be utterly fascinated by warfare, even as we disavow its horrors and destruction. War has been with us since the beginning of time, and the experience of the twentieth century suggests that we poor humans never tire of it, despite the misery it causes. Whether it is a great world war, pitting coalitions of nations against each other, or a Bosnian or Rwandan tribal conflict, the world records the events with an avid interest, not least of which is the recognition of new generals with muddy—and too often bloody—boots.

The fascination stems perhaps from the fact that war brings out the best and the worst in human nature. Young men—and now young women, too—are pulled from their homes and forced into situations more horrible than they could ever have imagined. In the process, they learn things about themselves they never knew before. Each one must ask, before the battle, "Can I take it?" Each one must demonstrate during the battle that he or she can, or else face the ultimate penalty, the censure of their comrades.

If the ordinary soldier must reach into his or her soul to discover fundamental personal truths, how much more difficult is the task of the general who commits thousands to battle? For some, isolated from the battlefield in a comfortable staff headquarters, the task is easy, for the death and the pain are remote. But for the generals Cragg has chosen to write about, the task is much more difficult, for these are the fighting generals, in the front lines with the troops, standing with them amid the whine of shell and whistle of bullet, seeing their friends fall and die. They are aware not only of their own mortality, but also of the mortality of the thousands whose lives they have placed at risk.

Generals in Muddy Boots deftly outlines the lives of great men as seen through the lens of war, 300 commanders selected from ancient times to Vietnam, and representing every great nation. Some are immensely famous and others are less well-known, but all are connected by a single thread, for, be they conqueror or liberator, they all have triumphed over adversity.

The fighting general has always captured the affection both of his nation and his men. Stonewall Jackson, a muddy boots general if there ever was one, drove his troops harder than anyone. He threw them into battle time and again when they were underfed, unshod, and dead tired, yet they loved him for it. Fighting generals like Jackson share another characteristic: they almost always have a genuine concern for their troops, making sure that they are not committed to battle without having obtained every possible advantage for them.

One can read *Generals in Muddy Boots* straight through, but one can also dip into it at random; it is especially interesting to pick two generals from widely different eras and compare them. Cragg has been able to define their basic military characteristics along with their human foibles; in doing so, he makes it clear that these are a special type of human being, able to reach within themselves for that last ounce of strength necessary to prevail.

As warfare becomes more scientific, as the generals perforce become remote from the battlefield, there will be fewer generals with muddy boots. It will be a loss to history and an even greater loss to the troops who will remain in the field at the cutting edge of combat.

—Colonel Walter J. Boyne, USAF (Ret.)

Introduction

The primary purpose of this book is to provide concise, readable, and useful portraits of the lives and accomplishments of some of history's greatest military commanders. It is not intended as a definitive work of military biography, although I hope it will inspire readers to find out more about some of the figures included, and for that I invite their attention to the extensive bibliography that follows the main entries.

Secondarily, it will, I hope, answer the question "What makes a good commander?"

One criterion for selecting individuals was used: they must have successfully and directly commanded men in combat at some time in their lives. Thus Dwight Eisenhower and George C. Marshall—two of America's greatest soldiers in many ways—are not represented here because neither ever directly commanded troops under fire.

Not all these commanders were generals or admirals either. John Rouse Merriot Chard was never more than a colonel and he was only a lieutenant of engineers when he organized the defense of Rorke's Drift in the Zulu War of 1879. Chard knew how to fight, yet he was an officer to whom mothers could safely trust the lives of their sons, and that is one mark of a great commander—in our modern Christian environment, that is.

The operative word here is *commander*. We in the West of the twentieth century think of a *general* (this also includes admirals) as a professional military officer ranking above the grade of colonel or the equivalent. But throughout much of recorded history these terms have had no meaning, as men of great natural abilities with no formal training or rank led armies and navies to great victories.

I have included only the salient aspects of each commander's career and I have not bothered to explain the political and military developments that influenced and shaped the times they lived in. Such information is beyond the scope of this book.

Where applicable, I have used the standard U.S. Army organizational designations: company, battalion, regiment/brigade, division, corps, army, i.e., Company A, 1st Battalion, 26th Infantry Regiment, 2nd Brigade, 25th Division, IX Corps, Fifth Army.

Finally, with any compendium such as this, someone's hero inevitably will be missed, and for that I apologize and most humbly offer ignorance, not lack of appreciation, as my only excuse.

So what makes a good commander in war? It is not always success, because two of history's greatest generals, Robert E. Lee and Napoleon Bonaparte, were ultimately failures. Experience and education in the profession of arms are important, but Joan of Arc, Oliver Cromwell, and Nathan Bedford Forrest, to mention only three examples of many you will find here, likely never had a military thought in their heads before they won lasting fame on the field of battle.

It is good if soldiers love their commanders, but this feeling must be based on solid leadership qualities. George B. McClellan's troops loved him as commander of the Army of the Potomac, and they called him affectionately "Little Mac," but he was arrogant, dilatory, and easily frightened, one of Abraham Lincoln's greatest disappointments as a general. Those same soldiers felt little affection for stolid, unemotional Sam Grant, aptly called a butcher in his day, but it was he who led them to victory.

And how to define *leadership?* Military historian John Elting has noted that it is the ability to influence and move others, and consists partly of character—courage and decisiveness—taking care of the troops' welfare, and professional competence, which may be instinctive or learned, but "soldiers will follow an officer who knows what he's doing—even if he's hard to live with."

One commander who was not "hard to live with" was Robert E. Lee. While he never hesitated to fight, he realized the human cost of war. And at Gettysburg, after the failure of Pickett's Charge, Lee's veterans refused to accept his apology for the disaster and clamored to be sent back to try it again.

Bravery under fire is an important characteristic for a commander as well. No one had more of it than George Armstrong Custer, who during the American Civil War had no fewer than eight horses shot out from under him, yet today he is known largely for his disaster on the Little Big Horn in 1876. Self-confidence is vital in a general as well. Custer had that, too.

Thomas Jonathan Jackson—"Stonewall"—wrote of Turner Ashby after his death in action, "His daring was proverbial, his powers of endurance almost incredible; his tone of character heroic, and his sagacity almost intuitive in divining the purposes and movements of the enemy." It is not surprising that Jackson admired these qualities in Ashby because, with the exception of physical endurance—Jackson was almost useless when deprived of sleep—they were his own, and few soldiers of any era in history have possessed them in the same measure as did Jackson. But Ashby lacked the discipline that characterized Jackson, who was as strict with himself as he was with his men.

Within a year of writing those words in praise of Ashby, Stonewall himself was dead—shot accidentally by one of his own men. Good luck is another attribute of the successful battlefield commander, but it involves more than just staying alive amid shot and shell. Napoleon recognized this and defined *luck* as the ability to recognize and exploit the unexpected breaks and accidents that proliferate on the battlefield.

Great commanders must believe in their cause. Joan of Arc thought the saints spoke to her and she was so successful communicating her zeal to the demoralized Frenchmen around her that she was able to lead them in a string of spectacular victories against the English invaders. But John Hawkwood, the fourteenth-century English mercenary who served Italian princes and city states, never fought for anything but money and he died a prosperous and honored old man.

There is much to be said for common sense in generalship. The mercenaries of Hawkwood's day, for instance, realized that earning one's pay and loyalty to one's employer were very important virtues—so long as the pay kept coming. That is just another way of saying a good commander has the ability to estimate the situation and choose the best course of action consistent with his abilities and means.

The will and courage to keep trying against all odds is most important. Examples of men who accomplished this include Alfred the Great, Robert Bruce, William of Orange, George Washington, and Nathaniel Greene.

We love commanders who are humane and magnanimous in victory, as was that great general U. S. Grant. But at other times and in other places, terror and destruction worked well, too, as the career of Genghis Khan demonstrates. Withal, a good general must be able to look dry-eyed upon a battlefield and put the horror of war aside so it does not affect his judgment, because war is killing, pure and simple, and every general at one time must bloody his army. The general who can win at the least cost of life should be praised above all others, but he who balks at the thought of sacrificing his men courts disaster.

It helps to be something of an actor, too. George Patton, Jr., and Napoleon understood this and had a flair for dramatically underscoring their solid abilities as battlefield commanders with good theater, exploiting their own mythology to encourage belief in their bigger-than-life images. Similarly, Admiral Ernest King was delighted that he had such a reputation for toughness people could joke that he shaved with a blowtorch. And when everybody else around him is losing his head, the good commander, no matter how he really feels, must be able to pretend calm and project this onto others.

The best commanders are plainspoken, especially in the face of the enemy, as was the Spartan Leonidas at Thermopylae when he told the Persian Xerxes, "If you want it, come and get it." Bluntness is another desirable quality in the good commander, but as much as we may admire Marshal Lannes, who told Napoleon's foreign minister, Talleyrand, to his face that he was a "stocking stuffed with shit," it should be exercised prudently.

Those are only some of the qualities that make a good commander. Add to them: the courage to accept responsibility for failure; the ability to make decisions quickly and to issue clear and concise orders; a shrewdness in picking reliable subordinates and, having done that, the confidence to trust them; attention to every detail required in the running of an army, from the adjutant to the quartermaster; and possibly a firm resistance to the allure of success and power, although any commander who claims not to care for promotion is probably a mountebank.

All those qualities have never been bestowed upon a single person, even the greatest leaders, but in the 306 biographies that follow are individuals who had enough of them enough of the time to win at least some of the time.

A

Abdelkader or Kadir

1807/8–1883

Born in the province of Oran, Algeria, into a family of marabouts (holy men), Abdelkader received an excellent religious education in a strict Muslim environment. It is doubtful he received any instruction in military affairs, but he was a skilled horseman from an early age.

In 1832, two years after the French occupied Algeria, Mahi ed-Din, his father, declared a holy war against them. As a military leader, Abdelkader displayed great organizational ability and sound tactical judgment, taking advantage of French mistakes while securing for himself French recognition of his leadership at the Treaty of Tafna in 1837. In October 1837, declaring the treaty violated, Abdelkader took the field again, with an army of 60,000 cavalry. With this highly mobile force he waged a successful campaign against the French until he was defeated by **Bugeaud** at the Battle of Isly on August 14, 1844. Nevertheless, Abdelkader held out until December 1847. After a time in prison, he settled in Damascus, where, in 1860, he used his influence to save thousands of Christians from a mob of Muslim fanatics. For this act he was awarded the *grand cordon* of the French *Légion d'Honneur*. He died in Damascus, May 26, 1883.

Abdelkader was the first national hero of Algeria. He was a skillful and tenacious fighter, an effective civil administrator, and a resourceful leader in adversity. His greatest feat was uniting his people and organizing them into the first serious threat to French military authority in Algeria.

Abd el-Krim or Muhammad Abd al-Karim al-Khattabi

1881–1963

Son of an Islamic schoolteacher, Abd el-Krim was born in Ajdir in the Riff mountains of Morocco. He acquired a knowledge of European culture and language such that by 1906 he was editing the Arabic supplement of a Spanish newspaper, and in 1907 he was appointed a secretary in the Spanish Bureau of Native Affairs.

Imprisoned during World War I for protesting the presence of foreigners in his country, Abd el-Krim took to the mountains upon his release. With his father and younger brother, he began organizing armed resistance among his people, the Beni Uriaghel Berbers.

At the Battle of Anual on July 21, 1921, Abd el-Krim's tribesmen routed a Spanish army under General Fernandes Silvestre. At least 12,000 Spaniards, including Silvestre, were killed and another 4,000 taken prisoner. Abd el-Krim used the modern weapons captured at Anual to equip an army of 20,000 men. He seized the initiative and launched a series of successful attacks against French outposts between Taza and Fez. It

1

took a combined army of more than 200,000 men, including a French column of 160,000 under Marshal Pétain, to defeat Abd el-Krim's Berbers.

After twenty years in exile on Reunion Island, Abd el-Krim took refuge in Egypt, where he died on February 6, 1963. A splendid tactician and strategist, he was also a capable civil administrator. With no shortage of courage, brains, and initiative, Abd el-Krim was defeated ultimately by superior European organization and numbers.

Creighton W. Abrams, Jr.

1914–1974

Born in rural Massachusetts, Abrams was appointed to West Point in 1932, graduating 185 out of 276 in the Class of 1936. Commissioned a cavalryman, he commanded the 37th Tank Battalion under **Patton** in WWII. He emerged from the war with two Distinguished Service Crosses and the deserved reputation of, as Patton called him, "the world's champion" tank commander.

Abrams rose steadily in rank after WWII, serving with quiet competence in a variety of assignments before serving for three years as army vice chief of staff, then going to Vietnam as deputy commander in 1967. In July 1968 he succeeded General William Westmoreland as commander of U.S. forces there, emphasizing security for the Vietnamese population instead of the big-unit "search-and-destroy" operations favored by Westmoreland. Many believe Abrams's tactics would have won the war if they had been applied earlier, but by the time he took command, the U.S. political leadership was already determined to withdraw. As chief of staff of the army, 1972–1974, he oversaw its difficult transition to an all-volunteer force and laid the groundwork for the revitalized army of Desert Storm.

Known as "Abe" throughout the army, Abrams was a blunt, no-nonsense commander who, like Grant before him, eschewed the trappings of command. As a four-star general, he would pop into an infantryman's foxhole in Vietnam and ask how things were going. He knew his duty, he followed his orders, and he was scrupulously honest with his superiors. His untimely death from cancer was universally mourned by an army he loved.

Gustavus II, Adolphus

1594–1632

Eldest son of Charles IX of Sweden, Gustavus Adolphus was introduced to public life at a very early age. He succeeded to the throne in 1611, beset with problems that would have destroyed a lesser man, but at his death he left Sweden one of the most powerful countries in Europe.

While he borrowed freely from commanders like **Maurice** of Nassau, Adolphus was the first to integrate the operations of infantry, cavalry, and artillery on the battlefield. He introduced a standing army that honed its skills through maneuvers and training, and reorganized its formations into permanent brigades composed of three squadrons of four companies for greater battlefield flexibility. At Breitenfeld, Germany, September 17, 1631, the superior mobility of the Swedish professionals turned defeat into decisive victory.

In the fog and smoke at Lützen, November 16, 1632, Adolphus, who was nearsighted and would not wear body armor because it irritated old wounds, blundered into a cavalry melee and was killed.

Gustavus Adolphus was a shrewd judge of character and appointed good men to run his government. He was a religious man who believed in honor, duty, and hard work. He dressed simply and in the field shared hardship with his troops. He was methodical but could be spontaneous, to the confusion of his enemies. He left an indelible stamp on his age.

Scipio Africanus [Publius Cornelius Scipio Aemilianus Africanus Numantinus]

185? B.C.–129 B.C.

Sometimes called Scipio the Younger (Scipio Minor), Scipio Africanus was adopted by the son of Scipio Africanus the Elder (Scipio Major), hence the name by which he is known today, although his true father was Aemilius Paulus Macedonicus. He was given the surname Numantinus after the capture of Numantia (near modern Soria), in Spain (133 B.C.).

At the age of eighteen Scipio accompanied his father to Macedonia, where, with some distinction, he participated in the Battle of Pydna (168).

Scipio is remembered principally for the capture and destruction of Carthage (146). Even before he arrived in Africa, his valor and resourcefulness were well-known from his service in Spain, but at Carthage he demonstrated exemplary courage and skill. It is said that while watching the city burn, he was moved to tears and that he protested the senate's order to obliterate the place. After a time as a censor at Rome, where he won renown for his eloquence, Scipio returned to Spain as consul (134), where he further distinguished himself during the fifteen-month siege of Numantia.

A friend of poets and philosophers and the Greek general/historian Polybius, Scipio Africanus was not only a brilliant commander but a cultured man, respected for his honorable conduct in public life and exemplary virtue as a private citizen.

Alaric

370?–410

Born on an island in the mouth of the Danube about the year 370, Alaric (*Ala-reiks* or "All-ruler") is remembered chiefly as the first Teutonic leader to sack Rome. He was a Goth of the western branch of that nation, known as Visigoths, and descended from a noble family. He served as the commander of Gothic mercenaries under the Roman emperor Theodosius, upon whose death in 395 he sought his fortune by invading Greece, sparing Athens but ravaging Corinth and Sparta. Outmaneuvered by an army under the Roman general Stilicho and placated by the eastern emperor Arcadius, he withdrew (397).

Alaric invaded Italy in 401 and again in 403, but was forced to withdraw both times by Stilicho, who was murdered in 408, allowing Alaric to invade a third time. His advance on Rome was halted by the payment of a huge bribe, but in 410, impatient at the failure of negotiations to win further concessions from the Romans, he besieged the city, capturing it on August 24, 410.

He died in December while preparing to invade Sicily.

Alaric was driven more by motives of profit than conquest. While he was ruthless, he was also a Christian and spared the churches when he took Rome. He sacked the city as a last resort, and the damage his men inflicted was not total. His defeats by Stilicho in 402 and 403 were not total, and that he kept his Visigoths together during extensive campaigns in Greece and Italy speaks highly of his character as a leader.

Afonso de Albuquerque

1453–1515

Born near Lisbon into a family of the minor nobility, Albuquerque was educated at the royal court. After military service in Africa, he was appointed chief equerry to John II. He first went to India in 1503–1504, and again with Tristão da Cunha in 1506.

In 1507 Albuquerque seized Hormuz Island, the principal spice distribution center in the Persian Gulf, from the Arabs. In 1509 he superseded the viceroy at Cannanore in southwest India, on the Malabar coast, and in March 1510 captured Goa. Expelled in August, he retook the place in November. In 1511 he took Malacca and established a base to control trade from the East Indies and China. Shipwrecked in 1512, he survived to suppress a revolt in Goa that same year.

These were hard-fought actions, and Albuquerque was severely wounded before Calicut in 1510. His siege of Aden in 1513 was unsuccessful, but he became the first European to sail a fleet into the Red Sea. After retaking Hormuz in 1515, he was recalled to Portugal but died at sea that December.

Albuquerque was a just governor whose strategy of securing bases for naval operations permitted Portugal to control trade in the Indian Ocean. Nicknamed "the Great" and "the Portuguese Mars," as a soldier he was hardy, bold, and resolute. For years after his death Muslims and Hindus visited his tomb at Goa to invoke his protection against the injustice of those who followed him.

Alexander the Great

356–323 B.C.

Alexander III, King of Macedon, son of **Philip II**, was born at Pela in 356 B.C. He was a pupil of Aristotle for three years, and the Greek philosopher prepared for him a volume of Homer's *Iliad*, which became the future conqueror's favorite book.

Upon the assassination of his father in 336, Alexander, with the support of the army, became King of Macedon. He thereafter forged a Panhellenic league through treaty, threat, and force. From 334, when he invaded Persia, to his death from a fever in 323, he spread his empire from Macedonia to India and Egypt and all the lands in between—the entire civilized world, less China. **Napoleon** called Alexander the greatest general in history. His battles may be studied with profit today, among them Issus in 333 B.C.; Tyre in 332; Arbela in 331, where he charged the Persians at the head of his cavalry; and in India, which he invaded in 326. The army with which he invaded Asia was small by later standards, maybe 40,000 men organized into light- and heavy-infantry and cavalry units, but highly professional, with excellent logistics and siege weapons. Also, this army was devoted to its commander, despite a brief rebellion in 324, which he quelled by the force of his personality and the swift execution of the ringleaders.

Alexander was a careful planner who always made sure his operating bases and lines of communication were secure, and he used military intelligence to good effect. Alexander was magnanimous in victory and tried to cement ties with the Persians, but only he could hold his fragile empire together and it dissolved upon his death. But Greek culture influenced every country where he went and his life influenced the course of history.

Edward Porter Alexander

1835–1910

Born at Washington, Georgia, Alexander entered West Point in 1853 and graduated third in the class of 1857 with a commission in the engineers.

When Georgia seceded he resigned his commission in the U.S. Army to accept one as a captain in the CSA on June 3, 1861. At First Manassas (July 1861) he was chief of **Beauregard's** signal service and later was appointed chief of ordnance for the Army of Northern Virginia. In November 1862 he switched to the artillery, and at Fredericksburg (December 1862) it was his guns that broke the Union assault on Marye's Heights. He fought at Chancellorsville (May 1863) and Gettysburg (July 1863), where his cannon pounded Cemetery Ridge in preparation for **Pickett's** charge. Promoted to brigadier general in February 1864, he commanded **Longstreet's** artillery at Spotsylvania (May) and Cold Harbor (June). He was wounded during the siege of Petersburg and surrendered with **Lee** at Appomattox (April 1865).

Alexander was a man of much energy and talent. After the war he taught engineering at the University of South Carolina and went into the oil business in 1869 and into railroading in 1871. He sat on many boards and commissions throughout his life and was a friend of Grover Cleveland. His critical analysis of the operations of the Army of Northern Virginia and the Army of Tennessee, *Military Memoirs of a Confederate*, published in 1907, is still a highly regarded commentary.

Harold Rupert Leofric George Alexander, 1st Earl Alexander of Tunis

1891–1969

The third son of the 4th Earl of Caledon, Sandhurst-educated Alexander fought with distinction in WWI. In France he was wounded three times, mentioned in dispatches for valor five times, and awarded the Distinguished Service Order and the Military Cross. At war's end he was a battalion commander.

As a major general, Alexander commanded the 1st Division in France in 1940, where he commanded the rear guard at Dunkirk during the evacuation (May 28–June 4, 1940). He went next to Burma, where he arrived in time to preside over a difficult withdrawal into India (March–May 1942). Promoted to full general in April, in August he was given command of the forces in the Middle East. He got on well with

General **Montgomery,** who commanded the Eighth Army under him during the successful campaign to defeat **Rommel**. He then commanded the 15th Army Group in the invasion of Sicily (July–August 1943), directed the invasion of Italy (September), commanded the difficult advance on Rome (October 1943–November 1944), was promoted to field marshal and supreme allied commander, Mediterranean Forces (December 1944), and accepted the German surrender in Italy (May 2, 1945).

Alexander displayed a great talent for leadership under difficult conditions. He was a man of great personal modesty who was able to transmit his confidence and calm to those around him, and he got people to work together, a priceless talent in an allied army. As a general, he kept his enemy off balance until he was able to deliver a knockout blow, and then he followed up tenaciously. He believed in saving both time and men's lives.

Alfred the Great

848–900

Born at Wantage, in Berkshire, Alfred was the fourth son of King Ethelwulf of Wessex. Just as Alfred was entering manhood the Danes, who had conquered most of England, were pushing southward into Wessex. With Ethelred, his last surviving brother, Alfred fought nine pitched battles with the Danes in 870–71. They won a skirmish at Englefield in December 870, lost the battle at Reading in January 871, and then achieved a brilliant victory at Ashdown four days later. When Ethelred died in April, Alfred succeeded him. Peace was made with the Danes in May.

In January 878, with his army scattered for the winter, the Danes attacked Alfred at his winter quarters at Chippenham, but he escaped with a few followers and, according to an ancient chronicler, "moved under difficulties through woods and into inaccessible places in marshes." From a hideout on the lake island of Athelney in Somerset, he reorganized his forces and decisively defeated the Danes at Eddington in May 878. At the peace of Wedmore, the Danes agreed to withdraw from Wessex.

Alfred was a fine general and superb organizer. He divided the militia into two parts to provide continuity when one relieved the other, built fortified posts throughout the land, and enforced the obligations of thanehood on all landowners, providing a cadre around which to form his militia. These reforms enabled him to defeat a second Danish invasion, 892–896.

Ethan Allen

1738–1789

Born at Litchfield, Connecticut, eldest son of a prosperous farmer, Allen saw service at Fort William Henry (1757) during the French and Indian War, and by 1769 was living in the New Hampshire Grants, as Vermont was then known. Allen took New Hampshire's side in the dispute

with New York over control of the "Grants," and organized a group of irregulars known as the Green Mountain Boys to harass New York officials sent to enforce its claims. So successful was Allen that in 1774 Governor Tryon of New York upped the reward for his capture to 100 pounds.

On May 10, 1775, accompanied by **Benedict Arnold,** he captured Fort Ticonderoga. This was no great feat since the garrison was severely understrength, but its guns, transported overland to Boston, were instrumental in forcing the British to evacuate the following year. In September, as a volunteer in General **Schuyler's** army, he went to Canada, where, in an unauthorized raid on Montreal, he was captured. Released in 1778, he played no further role in the Revolution and negotiated with the British for a separate peace, if they would recognize Vermont as a separate state.

Self-confident, shrewd, of imposing physical presence and courageous, Allen typifies that breed of American military leaders who won fame on its frontiers, where command depended more upon the rough-and-ready use of force than on military discipline and science. He was an educated man who published several books, and he endowed the University of Vermont in 1789.

Robert Anderson

1805–1871

Son of an officer in the Continental Army, Anderson graduated from West Point in 1825, commissioned in the artillery. Before the Civil War he fought Indians and served in the War with Mexico (1846–1848), where at the battle of Molino del Rey, September 8, 1847, he was wounded.

But Robert Anderson's finest moment was in defeat: he commanded the garrison at Fort Sumter in Charleston Harbor, South Carolina, which he surrendered after an intense bombardment (April 12–13, 1861), the opening shots of the Civil War.

An expert artilleryman, Anderson was picked to command the forts in Charleston Harbor partly because of his proslavery, pro-Southern sentiments. Convinced that hostilities were imminent, he shifted his garrison from indefensible Fort Moultrie to Fort Sumter on the night of December 26, 1860, but when reinforcements were fired on by shore batteries, January 9, 1861, he did not support them, for fear it would provoke war. But called upon to surrender April 11, 1861, he refused until Fort Sumter had been reduced to rubble after a thirty-four-hour bombardment. Lowering the Stars and Stripes, April 14, 1861, he ordered a fifty-gun salute. As a major general in the Union Army, he personally raised that same flag over Sumter again, April 14, 1865.

It is said he always regretted that the war started on his "watch," but as a man of honor, he had no choice but to hold his post. While his sentiments were with the South, Robert Anderson knew where his duty lay and he did it.

George Anson

1697–1762

Born in Staffordshire, England, Anson entered the navy in 1712. In 1718, as the second lieutenant of the *Montagu,* he saw action at Cape Passaro (July 31) off Syracuse with Admiral Byng's fleet against the Spanish during the War of the Quadruple Alliance. Advanced to captain in 1724, he commanded a frigate off the Carolinas and remained on that station until July 1730.

In December 1737 he was appointed master of the *Centurion* and on September 18, 1740, was sent with a squadron of six vessels to harass Spanish shipping in the Pacific. He did not return to England until June 1744. Of the more than 900 men who set out with him, all but 200 died of sickness and all the ships were lost but *Centurion.* Nevertheless, *Centurion* became the first British ship to visit China, and Anson captured a Spanish galleon with a treasure worth more than 500,000 pounds and returned home a national hero. Commanding a squadron off Cape Finisterre in May 1747, Anson defeated a French fleet, capturing fourteen vessels and 300,000 pounds' worth of specie. Serving in the admiralty, Anson effected many needed naval reforms. The articles of war he got passed in 1749 remained in effect until 1865, and the permanent corps of marines he created in 1755 has lasted until this day. He was first lord of the admiralty, 1751–1756, and 1757–1762.

Anson was a careful, intelligent, and hardy seaman who earned his sea commands through ability. Many men who served under him later rose to distinction and his organizational ability served the Royal Navy well.

Arminius

17? B.C–21 A.D.

The son of Segimer, a prince of the German tribe of the Cherusci, Arminius is the Latinized form of the name Hermann, or possibly Armin. About 1 A.D. he entered the Roman service, serving as an auxiliary with some distinction and earning himself Roman citizenship.

Returning to his native Germany, he found his people suffering under the rule of the Roman governor, Quintilius Varus, and secretly began organizing the Cherusci and neighboring tribes in a revolt. In September or October of 9 A.D., somewhere not far from modern Detmold, Arminius ambushed Varus as he marched with three legions plus auxiliaries, perhaps as many as 20,000 men, through an area known as the Teutoberger Forest. Surprise was complete. Varus rallied his men and attempted to reach a Roman outpost on the North Sea. As they hacked their way through the trackless woods in very bad weather, continually harassed by the Germans, and encumbered by a huge baggage train, their column was eventually broken and the legions were annihilated. Varus and his officers committed suicide and the noncombatants in the train were slaughtered. When word of the defeat reached Rome, near panic ensued. In 21 Arminius was assassinated by a rival tribesman.

Fighting by his own rules on his own territory Arminius inflicted such a defeat on Rome that Augustus had to abandon his plans to colonize Germany, which had a profound and lasting impact on the future history of Europe.

Lewis A. Armistead

1817–1863

Born into a distinguished Virginia family and related to the George Armistead who commanded Fort McHenry against the British assault in 1814, Lewis Armistead entered West Point in 1834 only to be expelled in 1836 when he broke a plate over the head of future Confederate general **Jubal Early**. In 1839 he obtained a direct appointment from the state of Virginia as a second lieutenant in the 6th Infantry.

Armistead saw service in the Seminole Wars

and the War with Mexico, being wounded at Chapultepec (September 13, 1847) and winning two brevet promotions for heroism. In 1861 he was appointed colonel of the 57th Virginia Infantry and in April 1862 was promoted to brigadier general and served with distinction at Seven Pines. He was wounded again at Antietam (September 1862).

During the Gettysburg Campaign he commanded a brigade in **Pickett's** division. On July 3, 1863, he led his brigade in the climactic assault against Cemetery Ridge that has become known as "Pickett's Charge." With his hat raised upon the point of his sword and shouting encouragement to the handful of men who had survived the charge with him, Armistead is said to have placed his hand upon the barrel of a Union cannon and shouted, "Give them cold steel!" before being shot down. He died in a Union field hospital on July 5, 1863.

No doubt Armistead would have obtained high command had he lived, but duty compelled him to share the fate of his men.

Benedict Arnold

1741–1801

Born into a prominent Connecticut family, Arnold lived a life that has all the aspects of classical Greek tragedy.

At the age of fourteen he ran away from home to fight in the French and Indian War, but he deserted. By 1775 he had become a successful businessman and an officer in the Connecticut Militia. In May 1775 he accompanied **Ethan Allen** to Ticonderoga and in September led a column in the invasion of Canada; in the assault on Montreal (December 31, 1775) he was wounded in the leg. He then fought two naval battles on Lake Champlain (October 1776) and played a crucial role in defeating Burgoyne's army at Saratoga (September–October 1777), where he was wounded yet again. Arnold was angry at his slow promotion and his hot temper earned him enemies who accused him of incompetence and profiteering. Although found not guilty by a court-martial, Congress directed **Washington** to reprimand him for improper conduct. In addition, Arnold was in desperate financial straits. In May or June 1779 he began to deal with the British, and in September 1780 plotted to betray the fortress at West Point for 10,000 pounds.

Benedict Arnold's oath of allegiance to the United States

He spent the rest of the war a lackey of the British and died in London, despised by his countrymen and, worse for a man like him, completely forgotten by the British public.

As a battlefield commander, Arnold was almost without peer among Washington's officers. Bold, decisive, resourceful, and utterly fearless, he led his men from the front, always in the thick of action.

Turner Ashby

1828–1862

Born in Farquier County, Virginia; Ashby's father fought in the War of 1812 and his grandfather in the Revolution.

Upon hearing of John Brown's raid at Harper's Ferry (October 16, 1859), Ashby gathered some men and rode to Charlestown, but was too late to participate in the action. When Virginia seceded in April 1861, Ashby again rode to Harper's Ferry with a company of horsemen and offered his services to the Confederacy.

As a lieutenant colonel in the 7th Virginia Cavalry, Ashby rode with **Stuart** in the cavalry screen at First Manassas (July 1861), fought under **Stonewall Jackson** at Kernstown (March 23, 1862), fought at the battle of McDowell, Virginia (May 8, 1862), and Winchester (May 25, 1862). At Kernstown, Ashby badly underestimated the enemy's strength, which led to a Confederate defeat, but redeemed himself by checking the federal pursuit after Jackson's retreating army. Promoted to brigadier general, May 27, 1862, he was killed in a skirmish near Harrisonburg, June 6, 1862.

Ashby was a natural leader, but he had no military training. He has been faulted for his poor intelligence gathering and as a poor organizer, but he made up for it in enterprise and courage. Like many other men in the Civil War, he learned to soldier as he went along, and had he lived, he would have made a fine battlefield commander. His horse shot out from under him at Harrisonburg, he was leading an attack on foot when he was killed.

Mustafa Kemal Atatürk

1881–1938

Born in Salonika, Greece (which was then part of Turkish Macedonia), son of a Turkish customs official, Atatürk graduated from Monastir Military Academy in 1899, after which he attended the war and staff colleges in Istanbul.

Atatürk was commissioned in the general staff in 1905. In that same year he was arrested for political agitation against the Ottoman sultanate and banished to Syria, where he organized a secret society, Vatan (fatherland) among his fellow army officers. He saw action in Libya during the war with Italy (1911–1912) and in the Balkans, where he served as chief of staff to the army on Gallipoli. A colonel and military attaché in Bulgaria when World War I broke out, he quickly rose to prominence as a field commander. As commander of the 19th Division at Gallipoli in 1915, he realized the importance of keeping the Commonwealth forces bottled up on the beaches, which he did, leading by personal example. Next he commanded the Second and Third Armies in the Caucasus in 1916 and at war's end was commanding the 7th Army in Syria. He defeated the Greeks at the Battle of Sakarya in 1921 and reoccupied Izmir. On October 29, 1923, Atatürk proclaimed a republic and became its first president.

Atatürk was an honest and energetic soldier and politician who eschewed the ceremonial trappings of office. At Gallipoli he personally led his men in the attack, inflicting a costly and embarrassing defeat upon the British.

Claude John Ayre Auchinleck

1884–1981

Born at Aldershot, England, Auchinleck was educated at Wellington and Sandhurst and commissioned in the Indian army. During World War I he fought the Turks and ended the war a lieutenant colonel with the *Croix de Guerre,* the D.S.O., and the O.B.E.

Promoted to major general in 1940, he commanded the ill-fated Narvik expedition to Norway (May). He then returned to India as commander of the British forces, but was recalled in June 1941 to command in the Middle East. Initially, his troops made advances against the Axis forces that resulted in the relief of Tobruk. When **Rommel**'s well-prepared counterattack came, Auchinleck's forces, weakened by the transfer of units to other theaters, at the end of an overextended supply line, without adequate naval or air support, and armed with inferior equipment, were driven back. Taking personal command, Auchinleck finally stopped Rommel at El Alamein (June 1942). In July 1942 Auchinleck was replaced by **Alexander,** and **Montgomery** was selected to command the Eighth Army. Auchinleck spent the rest of the war as commander in chief in India. He was promoted to the rank of field marshal in 1946.

Auchinleck was overmatched in the Middle East. Given that his opponent was one of the foremost experts in desert warfare, he did well to avoid being wiped out. He deserves full credit for stopping Rommel and stabilizing the front at el-Alamein, thus saving Egypt and making it possible for a British comeback.

Pierre-François Charles Augereau

1757–1816

Born in Paris, a son of the lower classes, Augereau enlisted in the Royal Cavalry in 1774, afterward serving in the Prussian army and possibly others. He joined the French National Guard in 1790 and by December 1796 was a major general. He served with great distinction under **Napoleon** in Italy.

Augereau retired in 1801 but was recalled in 1803 and made a marshal of France in 1804. He led the VII Corps at Jena (October 14, 1806) and Eylau (February 1807), where he was badly wounded and so ill before the battle, it is said he had to strap himself into the saddle. He served in administrative assignments until 1813 when he commanded the XI Corps and later the XVI Corps, which he led at Naumburg (October 9) and Leipzig (October 16–19), when he fought and commanded with the vigor he showed in Italy. But in 1814, given command of the Army of the Rhone, he defected to the Bourbons and was rewarded with a peerage by Louis XVIII. When Napoleon returned from exile (the Hundred Days) Augereau offered him his sword, but it was refused. At **Ney**'s court-martial he voted for acquittal and Louis in anger stripped him of his titles and cashiered him.

Augereau had a mind of his own but he was a mass of contradictions: wildly brave in combat but ungrateful to Napoleon; a notorious looter at times and at others generously openhanded. He trained and disciplined his men thoroughly but always looked to their welfare, and in the end sacrificed everything in an act of fairness to an old comrade.

B

Bābur (Zahīrud-Dīn Muhammad)

1483–1530

Bābur was born at Farghana in Turkestan and claimed descent from **Tamerlane** and **Genghis Khan**. Upon his father's death in 1494, he became ruler of Farghana, a backwater that proved too small for his ambitions. Despite his tender years, he managed to survive attempts to unseat him as well as an unsuccessful bid to rule in Samarkand and Bukhara. In 1504 he settled in Kabul. After his invasion of Transoxiana to take Samarkand and Bukhara (1511–1512) was repulsed, he conducted raids into the Punjab (1515–1523).

Attracted by the political unrest in northern India and the success of his raids, Bābur occupied Lahore in 1525 and at the Battle of Panipat (April 20, 1526) defeated and killed the sultan of Delhi, which he took on the twenty-seventh, and then Agra. At the Battle of Khanua (March 26, 1527) he destroyed a large Rajput army, and in the three-day Battle of Gorga (May 1529) put down a revolt of Afghan nobles. All of north India was now under his thumb, but before he could extend his empire to the south, he died at Agra on December 26, 1530.

Bābur's early reverses taught him endurance and generalship in the raw, so that in his Indian campaigns he could outfight forces consistently larger than his own. He was an honest and open-minded man, also cultured and literate. He loved gardens and he died in his favorite one. The Mogul empire he founded endured until the British established themselves in India, and the library he established at Delhi lasted until 1857.

Robert Stephenson Smyth, 1st Baron Baden-Powell

1857–1941

Born in London, the son of a mathematics professor at Oxford, Baden-Powell entered the army in 1874 and was sent to the 13th Hussars in India in 1876. While there, he developed his talent for field craft and scouting that was to make him famous. He served in Zululand in 1887 and participated in the Fourth Ashanti War (1895–1896).

Returning to Africa in 1899, on the eve of the Boer War, he was sent to command at Mafeking in Bechuanaland. When war broke out in October, he found himself with a garrison of 900 irregulars, 250 miles from help, and besieged by 6,000 Boers.

Baden-Powell and his tiny garrison of police, militia, and gentlemen volunteers held out for 217 days until relieved in May 1900. He organized defenses consisting of barbed-wire entanglements, strong points, trenches, and surprise sorties. Baden-Powell lost about 200 men while inflicting at least 1,000 casualties on the Boers, who had artillery. He was promoted to lieutenant general in 1907 but left the army in 1910 to devote himself full-time to the Boy Scout movement, which he founded in 1907.

There is a question of just how serious the Boers were about taking Mafeking from Baden-Powell's ragtag garrison, but they were not the Keystone Kops. Baden-Powell held down nearly a fifth of the Boer forces and a quarter of their artillery for more than six months and gave British morale a badly needed boost in a war that had been going badly up to then.

David Beatty

1871–1936

Born in Ireland, the son of an officer in the Royal Navy, Beatty entered the navy as a cadet in 1884. He saw active service with the naval brigade in the Sudan (1896–1898) and during the Boxer Rebellion in China (1900). His skill and courage during these campaigns earned him rapid promotions, and by 1900 he was a captain.

Promoted to rear admiral in 1910, in 1911 he became private secretary to Winston Churchill as first lord of the admiralty. In this capacity he earned Churchill's respect and, in 1913, was appointed to command the battle-cruiser squadron of the home fleet. At the outbreak of World War I, he sank three German cruisers and a destroyer on a raid into Helgoland (August 28, 1914), and in August 1915 sank the *Blücher,* which had been bombarding towns along the English coast. At the great naval battle of Jutland (May 31–June 1, 1916) he commanded the battle cruisers and a squadron of fast battleships. Upon sighting the enemy, he attacked at once, without waiting for the main fleet to come into action, losing two of his cruisers but luring the German fleet into the guns of the main English force. As commander of the Grand Fleet in 1916, Beatty encouraged the use of convoys and technical innovations and, as first sea lord after the war, was a determined proponent of a strong navy.

Beatty was a bold and resourceful commander who earned his stripes at sea and understood the need for technological development and its impact upon naval tactics.

Pierre Gustave Toutant Beauregard

1818–1893

Descended from early French settlers in Louisiana, P.G.T. Beauregard attended West Point, where he graduated second in the class of 1838. An engineer, he served in Mexico, where he was twice wounded. Appointed superintendent of the U.S. Military Academy in 1860, he served in that position only five days (January 23–28, 1861) before resigning to accept an appointment as a brigadier general in the CSA.

Beauregard commanded the forces at Charleston that fired on Fort Sumter (April 12, 1861), had a horse shot out from under him while leading the Confederate left at First Manassas (July 21, 1861), was second in command at Shiloh (April 6–7, 1862), conducted the successful defense of Charleston (January–April 1863), blocked the advance of the Army of the James upon Richmond (May 12–16, 1864), and constructed the defenses around Richmond and Petersburg (May–June 1864).

An early hero of the war, Beauregard was promoted to general on August 31, 1861, enjoying a higher rank for longer than many who were to become more famous than he. Known as "The Little Napoleon," Beauregard held a high opinion of his own ability not always shared by others. His abrasive personality led to clashes with Jefferson Davis that denied him an important independent field command where he might have shown what he could really do. A master of fortification, he was calm and capable under fire and notably courageous in an army noted for its courageous leaders.

Barnard E. Bee

1824–1861

Bee was born in South Carolina but grew up in Texas, where his father had moved in 1835. Graduating from the U.S. Military Academy in 1845, he was commissioned just in time to participate in the Mexican War, where he saw action at Palo Alto (May 8, 1846) and Resaca de la Palma (May 9, 1846), Cerro Gordo (April 18, 1847), where he was wounded, and Chapultepec (September 13, 1847). After the war he served on the frontier. Bee resigned in 1861 to accept an appointment in the CSA, was promoted to the rank of brigadier general in June 1861, and commanded the 3rd Brigade of **Johnston**'s army at First Manassas (Bull Run) (July 21, 1861). Bee is remembered today as the man who gave **Stonewall Jackson** his nickname. The irony in this is that nobody knows if Bee meant it as a compliment or an insult. At about two P.M., having fallen back to the Henry House, Bee was forming the remnants of his brigade into line of battle, determined to hold there against the advancing federals, when, observing Jackson's brigade to his rear and not yet committed, he said, "There is Jackson, standing like a stone wall." Was he extolling Jackson's steadfastness or complaining that he was not coming to his support? A few moments later Bee was mortally wounded.

Bernard E. Bee

Free Library of Philadelphia

Bee's steadfastness helped save the day. Having lost many of his field officers earlier in the fighting, Bee recklessly exposed himself to keep his raw troops in line, thereby halting the federal attack on Henry Hill and turning the tide of battle.

Belisarius

505–565

Born in the Balkans, Belisarius first saw military service in the imperial bodyguard, where he rose quickly in rank. His first major independent command, in the early years of the Emperor Justinian's reign, was during the war with Persia (524–532), where he acquitted himself with distinction. At the head of an expeditionary force of 15,000 men, he achieved a stunning victory against the Vandals in North Africa in 533.

Dispatched to Italy in 535 at the head of an army of 8,000 men, he took Palermo in September, Naples in the summer of 536, and Rome on December 10, 536. He then defended Rome against the Goths, breaking their siege (March 537–March 538) and forcing their surrender in 539. In 541 he was sent to Mesopotamia to fight the Persians again. When a truce was declared in 545, he went back to Italy to recapture territory seized by the Ostrogoth king Totila, retaking Rome and holding it, but unable to advance because the emperor refused him reinforcements. He was recalled to Constantinople in 549 and went into retirement. When the Huns threatened the capital in 559, he sallied forth at the head of his household retinue and drove them off.

Belisarius fought successfully on every front in Justinian's empire, but swayed by Belisarius's enemies, the emperor distrusted him, despite the fact that when the Goths asked the general to be their emperor at Ravenna in 540, he refused the honor. Belisarius was always loyal to Justinian, whom he served faithfully, despite good reason to do otherwise.

Frederick W. Benteen

1834–1898

Born at Petersburg, Virginia, Benteen stayed with the Union at the outbreak of the Civil War and was commissioned a first lieutenant in the 10th Missouri Cavalry. He saw action at Wilson's Creek, Pea Ridge, Vicksburg, and Tupelo. At war's end he was a lieutenant colonel, twice brevetted for valor, and afterward was appointed brigadier general of the Missouri Militia. In 1868 he was commissioned a captain in the regulars with the 7th Cavalry under **Custer**.

Benteen won another brevet promotion for action fighting Indians on the Saline River in Kansas (August 13, 1868), and at the Battle of the Washita (November 27, 1868), he again distinguished himself in action. Afterward, in an unsigned letter published without his consent in the newspapers, he accused Custer of abandoning a detachment that was wiped out by the Indians. When Custer announced that he would beat up the letter writer if he knew his identity, Benteen admitted his authorship and Custer let the matter pass. At the Little Big Horn (June 25, 1876), Benteen's detachment joined with Reno's after Custer's annihilation and held out until rescued. Benteen showed great coolness and courage in this desperate situation. Later he was given a brevet promotion to brigadier general for action against the Nez Percé in Montana (September 13, 1877).

Benteen's hatred of Custer became an obsession and late in life he turned to drink, but in the saddle, he was a valiant, competent, and respected professional who was instrumental in saving what was left of the 7th Cavalry after Custer's debacle.

Frederick Benteen (standing, right)

William Carr, 1st Viscount Beresford

1768–1854

The illegitimate son of the 1st Marquis of Waterford, Beresford entered the army in 1785 and by 1795 had become commanding officer of the 88th Foot, the Connaught Rangers. He served in France, Egypt, Africa, India, and South America on various expeditions and campaigns. Then, in February 1809, **Wellington** recommended him for the task of reorganizing the Portuguese army.

Beresford realized that the Portuguese soldier was of sturdy material but badly led, badly paid, badly supplied, and badly treated. With astonishing energy and dedication he reformed every aspect of the rotten Portuguese military system; British officers and NCOs were brought into Portuguese units, and at Bussaco Ridge on September 27, 1810, they acquitted themselves with dis-

tinction under repeated assaults by Marshal **Masséna's** forces. Thereafter, Anglo-Portuguese units became a permanent part of Wellington's army in the Peninsular War.

At Albuera, May 16, 1811, commanding an independent Anglo-Portuguese corps, Beresford may have lost control of the situation in the fierce fighting with **Soult's** army. The French were beaten, but the British suffered 4,000 casualties. Beresford, who could be a terror when he had to be, was truly shattered by the enormity of his losses.

Beresford was a superlative organizer and administrator and personally courageous—at Albuera he fought hand-to-hand with a Polish lancer—but he was at his best as a subordinate.

Louis-Alexandre Berthier

1753–1815

Born at Versailles, the son of a lieutenant colonel in the topographical engineers, Berthier entered the French army as a cadet at the age of twelve. He was a lieutenant of infantry by 1772 and a captain of cavalry in 1777. He served with **Rochambeau** during the American Revolution, where he was promoted for bravery. He was **Napoleon's** chief of staff for eighteen years, from 1796 to 1814.

Berthier became the quintessential staff officer under Napoleon, working with self-effacing efficiency in the emperor's shadow, carefully mastering the myriad details required to run his staff on campaign. He translated Napoleon's general commands into the specific, lucid directives his field officers required. He was unquestionably brave: at Lodi (May 10, 1796) he charged with Napoleon across the bridge into the Austrian muskets; he was wounded at Marengo (June 14, 1800); and during the Grande Armée's disastrous retreat from Moscow (November–December 1812) it was Berthier, sixty years old, exhausted, sick, who kept it together despite the fact that he was the butt of Napoleon's unfair outbursts of bad temper. At Bautzen (May 20–21, 1812) and Leipzig (October 16–18), he distinguished himself, but during the 1813 and 1814 campaigns he was ill most of the time. He died June 1, 1815, two weeks before Waterloo.

Although Napoleon treated Berthier unfairly, it was the emperor who paid him the highest compliment: "If Berthier had been there [Waterloo], I would not have met this misfortune."

Robert Blake

1599–1657

Born at Bridgewater, Somerset, England, Blake attended Oxford as a young man and was later a successful businessman, until he joined the parliamentary army during the civil war. His brother commanded a company in Blake's regiment. Informed of his death in an accidental skirmish, Blake remarked, "Sam had no business there."

Blake proved such a good fighter on land that in 1649, at age fifty and with no previous experience in command at sea, he was appointed a "general at sea." In November 1650, at Cartagena, Spain, his squadron chased a division of royalist ships into port and destroyed all but three. In May 1651, he captured the strongly fortified royalist privateering base in the Scilly Isles, off Land's End. At the outbreak of war with Holland in May 1652, he took command of the channel fleet, where, off Dover on May 19, he attacked a much larger Dutch fleet. Reinforced during the engagement, Blake drove the Dutch off. Mauled and forced to withdraw in another unequal engagement off Dunge Ness on November 30, 1652, the next February Blake was severely wounded in a running two-day fight with Dutch convoy escorts. After recuperating, he went to sea again, and on his way home after destroying a Spanish fleet off Cadiz, Blake died at sea, August 7, 1657. In 1661 royalists disinterred and mutilated his corpse.

Blake's men followed him readily and fought well under his command, and while sometimes outmaneuvered by his Dutch opponents, he made up for this in enterprise and audacity.

Gebhard Leberecht von Blücher

1742–1819

The son of a cavalryman, Blücher was born at Rostock in the Prussian state of Mecklenburg. He was commissioned in the Swedish army at the age of sixteen, and participated in three campaigns against the Prussians and had risen to the rank of captain when captured in 1760. Changing sides, he served in **Frederick the Great's** army until 1770, when he resigned or was dismissed. Upon Frederick's death in 1786, Blücher got his commission back.

At age fifty-two Blücher was promoted to major general and to lieutenant general in 1801. At the outbreak of war between France and Prussia in 1813, he was promoted to field marshal and given command of a Russo-Prussian army. His aggressiveness earned him the nickname "Marshal Forward." At Lützen (May 2, 1813), he personally led a cavalry charge, had a horse shot out from under him, and was wounded after spending eleven hours in the saddle. He commanded troops in five more battles before Waterloo (June 18, 1815). At Ligny (June 16) he was beaten by **Napoleon** and wounded again, but thanks to the work of his brilliant chief of staff, Gneisenau, his army managed to withdraw from the battlefield intact, and on June 18, with 67,000 men, attacked Napoleon at Placentoit, permitting **Wellington** to launch the counterattack that won the battle.

Blücher was rough and poorly educated but endowed with great common sense, courage, and vitality, and he chose his subordinates with care.

Simón Bolívar

1783–1830

Born of aristocratic Creole parents in Caracas, Venezuela, Bolívar was educated abroad, principally in Spain, but he traveled widely, including a visit to France, and admired **Napoleon**. By his early twenties he had formed the idea of South American independence that was to earn him the title of *El Libertador*, the Liberator.

Upon the collapse of the Venezuelan republic in (July 1812), Bolívar, enraged at the junta's willingness to seek peace with the Spanish, fled to Colombia. There he organized an army of volunteers, returned to Venezuela, and seized Caracas (August 6, 1813). In the civil war that followed, he was defeated at La Puerta (July 1814) by royalist forces and compelled to flee again. By 1819, however, his ceaseless organizing had secured him a base of operations at Angostura in northeastern Venezuela, along the Orinoco River. On June 11, 1819, at the head of 2,500 men, including Irish and British veterans of the Napoleonic Wars, he marched on Bogotá, crossing the Andes and catching the Spanish by surprise, defeating them decisively at Boyaca (August 7, 1819) and taking Bogotá on August 10. With the defeat of a Spanish army at Ayacucho, Peru, on December 9, 1824 (at which Bolívar was absent), Spanish rule in South America was effectively ended.

Bolívar survived serious military reverses to achieve ultimate success with decisive battlefield victories. His march over the Andes is an epic of endurance and courage and stands as the best testament to Bolívar's charisma and tenacity.

Louis Botha

1862–1919

The son of a poor farmer, Botha was descended from Voortrekker (pioneer) and Irish stock. In 1884 he participated in the Zulu Civil War on the side of Dinuzulu, **Cetshwayo's** son, who crushed the rebels. For this aid, the Boers were given three million acres of Zulu land out of which they formed the New Republic, and after its annexation to the Transvaal Republic in 1887, Botha was elected to Parliament.

Upon the outbreak of the Anglo-Boer War in 1899, Botha joined the Transvaal army as a cornet and within two months had risen to command the forces besieging Ladysmith. He defeated three British attempts to relieve the city at Colenso (December 15, 1899), Spion Kop (January 24, 1900), and Vaal Krantz (February 5–7). At Colenso the British had 21,000 men to Botha's 6,000. Boer marksmanship and use of the terrain won the day. At all three battles the Boers lost about 150 men killed and wounded to about 3,200 British killed, wounded, and missing. Outmaneuvered at Tugela (February 17–18), Botha fell back and Ladysmith was relieved on February 28. Defeated at Bergendal (August 27), Botha undertook guerrilla warfare against the British until peace was concluded May 31, 1902. As the first president of the Union of South Africa, he sought conciliation with the British.

Louis Botha was poorly educated but a natural leader who mastered enough of tactics and strategy that it took 500,000 British soldiers more than two years to subdue him.

Henry Bouquet

1719–1765

Born at Rolle, in the canton of Berne, Switzerland, Bouquet saw much service in the Swiss Guards before accepting a commission as lieutenant colonel of the Royal American Regiment in 1754, which was then being raised to fight the French in the English colonies.

From the beginning of his service in North America, Bouquet showed himself remarkably free of the usual European prejudices against the colonists and their special political and military situation. His consideration toward the Americans impressed them very favorably. When Bouquet faced a new situation, such as how to negotiate with Indians, he consulted people who knew about such things. At Bushy Run (August 4–6, 1763), as Bouquet led a column of British regulars and American light troops from Carlisle, Pennsylvania, to Fort Pitt, he was ambushed by a force of Indians. Forming a redoubt of flour bags on a small hill, Bouquet held out all night. Sensing victory, the Indians rushed Bouquet the next morning, but Bouquet counterattacked their flanks with his light companies and cut them to pieces. In 1764, at the head of 1,500 men, Bouquet marched into the land of the Shawnee and Delaware, securing the release of more than 300 whites taken prisoner during Pontiac's War. Promoted to brigadier general, he died of a fever contracted while commanding troops in Florida.

Bouquet was a careful and skillful commander and a man of great patience, integrity, and firmness who earned the admiration and respect of the men who served under him.

Omar N. Bradley

1893–1981

Born in Clark, Missouri, the son of a schoolmaster and a seamstress, Bradley graduated forty-fourth in his West Point class of 1915. While Bradley did not see combat in World War I, between the wars he served with distinction in a succession of staff and teaching assignments, coming under the eye of George C. Marshall, who made him assistant secretary of the army general staff and commandant of the Infantry School, where he earned his first star in February 1941.

He replaced **Patton** in command of the II Corps and led it through North Africa and Sicily. In January 1944 he was appointed to command the First Army in preparation for the Normandy invasion. After the St. Lo breakthrough (July 26, 1944), he commanded the Twelfth Army Group, which became the largest field command ever assembled by the U.S. Army (First, Third, Ninth, and Fifteenth Armies). Bradley clashed with **Montgomery,** supporting Eisenhower's strategy of a broad advance with no overall ground commander. After the Bulge (December 1944) Eisenhower gave Montgomery command of some of Bradley's troops, and while Montgomery was to have the lead in the drive into Germany, Bradley crossed the Rhine before him, linking up with the Russians on the Elbe in April 1945. Bradley earned his fourth star in March 1945, and his fifth in September 1950.

General Omar Bradley

A quiet, modest man, Bradley was a cool and competent commander under fire. While Patton complained that whenever Eisenhower and Bradley got together they "turned timid," Bradley was always genuinely concerned for the welfare of his men.

Joseph Brant

1742–1807

Born in the Ohio Valley, the son of a Mohawk sachem, Brant's Indian name was Thayendanegea ("he who makes two bets"). He took his English name from his Indian stepfather. At the age of thirteen he came under the protec-

tion of Sir William Johnson, the British Indian agent, and at nineteen he was enrolled in Moor's Charity School in Lebanon, Connecticut, where he was converted to Christianity. For the rest of his life he was torn between adopting European culture and fighting the encroachment of whites on Indian lands.

During the American Revolution, Brant knew an American victory would result in the end of the Mohawk way of life. Commissioned a captain by the British, he commanded Indians at the Battle of Oriskany (August 8, 1777). Later Brant led a series of raids throughout New York and Pennsylvania, sometimes in cooperation with Tories. At Cherry Valley (1778) and Wyoming (1779) his men committed terrible atrocities, but he always denied participating or that they were done at his orders. After the war he retired with his people to a reservation in Canada and in 1785 persuaded the British to indemnify the Iroquois for the loss of their lands to the Americans.

Brant fought courageously for his people. Because he picked the losing side in the Revolution and because of Cherry Valley and Wyoming, he has been vilified by history, but on the frontier of his day, getting Indian warriors to fight according to European rules taxed even the greatest commanders.

Brian Boru

941–1014

Born near Killaloe on the Shannon River in Ireland, Brian was the younger son of a petty king, Cennedig or Kennedy, who ruled a region known as Dal Chais.

In 978, avenging the murder of his older brother, Mathgamain or Mahon, who had become king about 951, Brian became king of Munster. He unified the tribes of Munster and Leinster and attacked the invading Danes, building a fleet of ships to harass them. In 1000 he defeated an uprising of Leinstermen supported by the Danes and took Dublin, forcing the Danish king to swear allegiance to him. Brian then turned on Maelsechlainn or Malachy, the chief king of Ireland, forcing him to submit, and in a short time so did all the other Irish chieftains. Brian's surname may derive from an Irish word, *boroma*, "tribute," and certainly, by the year 1001 Brian was high king of Ireland and collecting tribute from the Irish tribes. In 1013 the Leinstermen in Dublin and their Norse allies again revolted. On April 23, 1014, Brian's army met them at Contarf, now a residential suburb of Dublin on the north shore of Dublin Bay. Too aged to take the field himself, Brian directed the battle from his tent while his sons, Murchadh and Donchadh, commanded on the field. A band of Norsemen, fleeing their defeated army, stormed Brian's tent and killed the old king.

Brian was a hardy and skilled leader and a good king who, in the words of an old Munster chronicler, "released the men of Erin and its women from the bondage of the foreigners."

John C. Breckinridge

1821–1875

The son of a distinguished lawyer and politician and grandson of Jefferson's attorney general, Breckinridge was born near Lexington, Kentucky. After brief service in the Mexican War as an officer in the 3rd Kentucky Volunteer Regiment, he entered politics. He served two terms in the U.S. House of Representatives and at the age of thirty-five became the youngest vice-president ever when elected on the ticket with Buchanan in 1856. He was later elected to the Senate for the term beginning in 1861. When Kentucky embraced the Union cause, Breckinridge went South.

In November 1861 he was appointed a brigadier general under **A. S. Johnston** and at Shiloh (April 6–7, 1862) commanded the reserve. As a major general he defended Vicksburg briefly before commanding a division at Stones River (December 31, 1862–January 31, 1863), fought at Chicamagua (September 19–20), Chattanooga (November 23–25); New Market (May 15, 1864), where he won a clear victory over 6,500 federals; Cold Harbor (June 1–3), and Early's Raid on Washington (July 11–12). He then commanded the Department of Southwest Virginia and was appointed Confederate secretary of state in February 1865. After the war he practiced law in Kentucky.

Breckinridge had a natural talent for military command and was an excellent administrator. He was aided in this by his charismatic personality and the ability to improvise.

John C. Breckinridge

Jacob J. Brown

1775–1828

Born in Bucks County, Pennsylvania, Brown was descended from the earliest settlers in the colony, all of them Quakers. Brown was a schoolmaster, surveyor, and journalist until 1799, when he purchased land on Lake Ontario, near Watertown, New York. His commercial ventures prospered thereafter and in 1809 he was given command of a militia regiment and, on the eve of the War of 1812, was appointed brigadier general of militia.

At Sacketts Harbor (May 29, 1813), his force of 400 regulars and 500 militia met a somewhat smaller body of British regulars, and although his militia ran—which Brown anticipated—his regulars held and checked the British with heavy casualties. Promoted to major general in January 1814, Brown was given command in western New York. One of his brigadiers was **Winfield Scott,** whom Brown put in charge of training the troops. Crossing into Canada in early July 1814, Brown's force of 2,600 met 3,000 British at Lundy's Lane (July 25). Both Brown and Scott were wounded in the fierce fighting, which resulted in a tactical victory for the Americans. Retiring to Fort Erie, Brown was besieged there, but in a daring sortie (September 17) he disabled the enemy's cannon and forced them to withdraw. After the war Brown became general in chief of the U.S. Army, a post he held until his death.

Brown was a natural leader, a determined fighter, and a good judge of character. He was one of the most successful American combat leaders of the War of 1812.

Robert Bruce, Robert I, King of Scotland

1274–1329

The eighth of his line to bear the name Robert, scion of a Norman family, Bruce became the heir to a lengthy and complicated controversy over who would become king of Scotland. In 1290 Bruce's grandfather, also named Robert, put forth a claim, but this failed when Edward I, king of England, claimed it for himself. Edward's surrogate revolted, **Wallace** rose up to restore him, and by 1306 there was a power vacuum in Scotland that needed filling. After killing his nearest rival, Bruce was crowned king of Scotland on March 25, 1306.

Edward moved quickly to crush Bruce and defeated him at Methven (June 19, 1306) and Dalry (August 11). Almost all of his retinue was captured at Dalry, but Bruce escaped to return in February 1307 to win the Battle of Loudon.

Bruce's fortunes improved upon the succession of the inept Edward II in 1307. In 1313 he captured Perth, and on June 23–24, 1314, he smashed the English at Bannockburn. Bruce's army consisted of not more than 10,000 men with fewer than 1,000 cavalry against 20,000 English foot and 3,000 horse, but the English arms were poorly coordinated and at the critical moment Bruce committed his reserve to rout them. On the first day Bruce was challenged in single combat by Henry de Bohun, whom he killed with his battle-ax. Bruce kept his throne until his death.

Undaunted by severe reverses and personal loss (three of his brothers were executed after Dalry), Bruce gained and kept his throne by his wits and courage proved in battle.

Aleksey Alekseyevich Brusilov

1853–1926

Born in Tiflis (Tbilisi) in Georgian Russia, the son of a Russian general of noble birth, Brusilov graduated from the Corps of Pages, a military academy for the sons of the Russian aristocracy, in 1872. Assigned to a cavalry regiment, he was decorated for heroism in the Russo-Turkish War (1877–1878) and then served at the cavalry school in St. Petersburg until 1906, when he was promoted to general.

At the outbreak of World War I he commanded the Eighth Army in Galicia and then the central army group, which he launched on an offensive against the Austrian forces in June 1916. Brusilov used simultaneous surprise attacks, coordinated infantry and artillery assaults, and exploited breakthroughs by secretly

concentrating his reserves near the points of attack. Brusilov's aggressive and innovative tactics caught the Austrians by surprise, but he was not supported by the other front commanders, and while he inflicted a serious reverse on the Austrian forces, capturing 375,000 men, they stabilized the front by August. The 1917 offensive (July 1–17), despite some initial success, faltered due to lack of supplies and other factors beyond Brusilov's control. After October 1917 Brusilov supported the Bolsheviks, but they never trusted him. He died in Moscow on March 17, 1926.

Brusilov always understood and identified with the frontline soldiers and prepared his attacks with great care and intelligence, demanding competence and efficiency of his staff.

John Buford

1826–1863

Born in Woodford County, Kentucky, John Buford graduated sixteenth of thirty-eight in his West Point class of 1848. He saw service on the frontier and in Kansas. He accompanied the 2nd Dragoons to Utah during the Mormon troubles, an 1,100-mile march in winter through the wilderness in which he distinguished himself as the regimental quartermaster.

Promoted to brigadier general, July 7, 1862, he participated in the Second Manassas Campaign. At Thoroughfare Gap (August 27) his brigade alone confronted **Longstreet's** corps, foreshadowing Buford's finest moment at Gettysburg. Covering Pope's withdrawal across Bull Run, he was severely wounded. He commanded a division at Brandy Station (June 9, 1863). Reconnoitering ahead of the main body of the Army of the Potomac, he was the first to arrive at Gettysburg. On the morning of July 1 elements of his division engaged two divisions of **A. P. Hill's** corps approaching the town from the west. Realizing the strategic importance of the road junction at Gettysburg, Buford ordered his men to hold at all costs until reinforced by infantry. Fighting dismounted and armed with Spencer repeaters, the cavalrymen withstood two infantry attacks, delaying the Confederate forces until relieved by **Reynold's** I Corps. He died in Washington, D.C., of typhoid on December 16.

Buford was an experienced, out-in-front cavalry commander. Without his quick action on July 1, 1863, Gettysburg might not have developed into one of the decisive battles of the war.

Thomas-Robert Bugeaud de la Piconnerie, Duke of Isly

1784–1849

Born at Limoges into a family of the minor nobility, Bugeaud was raised among the Dordogne peasants after his family was ruined by the revolution, and both his parents died while he was still young. At the age of fifteen he enlisted in the Imperial Guards and was a corporal at Austerlitz. Commissioned in 1806, he saw some hard fighting in Spain, where he rose to the rank of colonel and learned the principles of guerrilla warfare. He resumed his military career after the revolution of July 1830.

In 1836 Bugeaud was sent to Algeria, where he negotiated peace with **Abdelkader**. He was appointed governor-general in February 1841 and returned with the mission of putting down the revolt Abdelkader started two years before. Bugeaud did this by fighting like a Berber. He organized his units into flying columns, equipped his troops with only the bare essentials, gave them mule-borne mountain guns for artillery support, and scorched the earth wherever he went. This wreaked great hardship upon the Algerian villagers, but once an area was pacified, Bugeaud took pains to spare the people further hardship. Created a marshal of France in 1843, at Oued Isly in August 1844, Bugeaud smashed the Moroccans, thus denying Abdelkader their protection, which eventually brought him to bay.

Bugeaud was ruthless in war and a strict disciplinarian. But his men adored him because he was fair with them when they met his exacting standards, knew their lot from personal experience, and gave them victory.

Smedley D. Butler

1881–1940

Born in West Chester, Pennsylvania, of a prominent Quaker family, but at the outbreak of the Spanish-American War, he lied about his age to get a commission in the marine corps. Although he saw no action then, he was wounded twice during the China Relief Expedition of 1900 and, just shy of his nineteenth birthday, was awarded a brevet promotion to captain for heroism under fire.

From 1909–1914 he commanded a battalion reaction force based in Panama, and during interventions in Mexico (1914) and Haiti (1915) he earned two Medals of Honor, one of the few Americans ever to win such a distinction. He established the Haitian gendarmerie and served as its commandant until 1918. In World War I he commanded the major embarkation camp at Brest, France, and although he saw no fighting, was promoted to brigadier general at the age of thirty-seven. Among other activities after the war, he was director of public safety for the city of Philadelphia and commander of the Marine Expeditionary Force in China, where he proved he could be a diplomat. He retired in 1931 after being passed over for the post of commandant of the marine corps and spent the rest of his life an outspoken antiwar, anti-imperialist radical.

Butler was a man of great honor, courage, and integrity, a fighter, not a politician. Controversial and outspoken, he made many enemies, but his radicalism was based on moral, not political principles. He was authoritarian but intensely loyal to his subordinates and a superb organizer.

C

Gaius Julius Caesar

100–44 B.C.

Born into a patrician but hardly distinguished family, Caesar was educated at Rome and in Rhodes, and throughout his life was a persuasive orator and a lucid writer. His first military success came in 62, against some native tribes in Spain, but in 76, captured by pirates on his way to Rhodes, he raised a fleet upon his ransom, and pursued, captured, and crucified them.

Appointed proconsul in Gaul (58), he pacified the tribes in a number of campaigns and invaded Britain (55–54). He was the first to build a bridge across the Rhine (55) and defeated Vercingetorix (52). Recalled to Rome to face charges for alleged crimes, he took his army across the Rubicon (the border between Gaul and Italy) instead, and initiated civil war (49). He defeated Pompey at Pharsalus in Greece (48) and pursued him into Egypt. After disposing of the pharaoh, Ptolemy, who had disposed of Pompey, Caesar installed Cleopatra to rule Egypt and had a child by her. He then turned to Africa, where at Thapsus (46) he defeated a republican army, and returning to Spain (45), he crushed the sons of Pompey at Munda. After Munda, Caesar was appointed dictator for life and an aristocratic clique in the senate, wishing to restore the republic, assassinated him, March 15, 44 B.C.

A skilled administrator, an accomplished politician, a brilliant strategist, and a soldier of great personal courage and endurance, Caesar was one of history's greatest commanders. Today those who know nothing of history know Caesar.

Marcus Furius Camillus

440–365 B.C.

A Roman patrician, Camillus was four times honored with triumphs for his military victories, five times named dictator, and honored with the title "Second Founder of Rome."

As a young man, Camillus distinguished himself in the war against the Aequi and Volscians (429), where, wounded in the thigh by a javelin, he plucked it out and continued fighting. Made censor in 403, he passed an act compelling all bachelors to marry, since Rome's wars had created so many widows. He took the city of Veii (an Etruscan stronghold a few miles north of Rome) in 396 by undermining its walls, thus ending a ten-year siege. Although the Romans honored him with a triumph for this victory, they were appalled at his arrogance when he entered the city in a chariot drawn by white horses, an honor heretofore accorded only to images of Jupiter. Also, his soldiers accused him of unfairly dividing the spoils captured at Veii. Angered by this and other disagreements, Camillus voluntarily exiled himself only to be called back precipitously when the Gauls under Brennus invaded Italy and sacked Rome (390). Discouraged by the destruction wrought by the Gauls, the Roman citizens wanted to migrate to Veii, but Camillus induced them instead to rebuild the city. He then put down a revolt by the Aequians, Volscians, and Latins (389) and, in his seventies, repulsed a second Gallic invasion at Anio (367).

A brilliant commander, Camillus was also a loyal patriot who served Rome well throughout his long and eventful life.

Evans Fordyce Carlson

1896–1947

Son of a Congregationalist minister, Carlson left home at the age of fourteen to work as a farmer and a laborer, and he never completed high school. He joined the army in 1912 and served in the Philippines. Recalled in 1916, he was an artillery instructor before being commissioned a second lieutenant in the 13th Field Artillery. In France during World War I he served briefly on **General Pershing's** staff. He quit the army in 1919, a captain.

In 1922 Carlson enlisted as a private in the marine corps. In 1923 he was commissioned again as a second lieutenant. In 1930 he was awarded the Navy Cross for heroism in Nicaragua. Carlson formed a friendship with President Roosevelt while serving as a member of his guard, and corresponded with him when he went to China as an observer in 1937. He admired the Chinese Red Army and opposed the sale of American goods to Japan. He resigned his commission in 1939, to be free to speak and write on these matters. Recalled in 1941, he was given command of the 2nd Raider Battalion, which became known as "Carlson's Raiders." He trained his men in mobile warfare based on what he had learned in China, and while operating behind the lines on Guadalcanal in 1942, they suffered only 34 casualties while killing nearly 500 enemies. He was seriously wounded on Saipan, rescuing an enlisted man. Carlson retired in 1946 as a brigadier general.

Carlson's unconventional methods did not please his superiors, but his egalitarianism, personal courage, and unpretentious manner earned him the undying loyalty of his men.

Adna Romanza Chaffee

1842–1914

Born at Orwell in Ashtabula County, Ohio, Chaffee was descended from a long line of New England Yankees. In 1861 he enlisted as a private in the 6th U.S. Cavalry, where he was soon promoted to the rank of sergeant. In September 1862, after participating in the Battle of Antietam (September 17, 1862), he was promoted to troop first sergeant and then to second lieutenant on May 12, 1863. He was wounded at Gettysburg.

Chaffee stayed in the army after the war, rising to captain in October 1867. He served with the 6th Cavalry, fighting Indians in the southwest, until June 1897, when he was appointed lieutenant colonel of the 3rd Cavalry Regiment. He was appointed a brigadier general of volunteers on May 4, 1898, and went to Cuba in command of the 3rd Brigade in the 2nd Division. His brigade bore the brunt of the heavy fighting at El Caney (July 1) and later that month he was promoted to major general of volunteers, but reverted to colonel after the war. In 1900 he commanded the China Relief Expedition, again as a major general of volunteers, where he distinguished himself by his competence and humane treatment of the Chinese. Promoted to major general in the regulars in 1901, he earned a third star in January 1904 and became the first Chief of Staff of the U.S. Army. He retired from active service in 1906.

In his forty-five years of army service Chaffee learned the soldier's trade from the bottom up. He rose from private to chief of staff through merit alone.

Joshua Lawrence Chamberlain

1828–1914

Born at Brewer, Maine, Chamberlain was a professor of rhetoric and modern languages at Bowdoin College when the Civil War broke out. He accepted a commission as lieutenant colonel of the 20th Maine in August 1862, and became its colonel in May 1863.

On July 2, 1863 at Gettysburg his regiment held the extreme left of **Meade's** line, on Little Round Top, where his men beat back repeated assaults. Almost out of ammunition, he ordered them to fix bayonets and charge, driving the enemy back and saving his position. Had the Confederates turned Meade's flank, they might have won the battle. In 1893 Chamberlain was awarded the Medal of Honor for this action. Altogether, Chamberlain participated in twenty-four engagements, among them Antietam, Fredericksburg, Chancellorsville, Gettysburg, Spottsylvania, Cold Harbor, Petersburg, and Five Forks; he was wounded six times, so badly at Petersburg he was given up for dead; and he was picked to receive the Confederate surrender at Appomattox. He ended the war a major general. Afterward he was governor of Maine (four times) and president of Bowdoin College.

Chamberlain was called "the knightliest soldier of the Federal army." He never asked any private to do what he would not do himself; shared every hardship with his men; and accepted the responsibility of command, asking

Joshua L. Chamberlain

Free Library of Philadelphia

for himself only to serve. He shared with **Washington** and **R. E. Lee** the highest ideals of honor and devotion. Many believe with justification that his valiant stand at Little Round Top altered the course of world history.

John Rouse Merriot Chard

1847–1897

Born at Boxhill, Near Plymouth, England, Chard attended the Royal Military Academy at Woolwich and was commissioned in the Royal Engineers in 1868. Sent to Africa in 1878, Chard was placed in charge of the station at Rorke's Drift, near Ladysmith, to protect the river crossing there. He had command of about 130 men, 80 of the 2nd Battalion, 24th Foot, and 30 sick and wounded.

Upon being informed that the Zulus, victorious at the Battle of Isandhlwana (January 22, 1879), were descending upon him, Chard determined to hold his post until reinforcements could arrive. He barricaded and loopholed an old church and the hospital, and constructed breastworks out of wagons and bags of grain. On the afternoon of January 22, about 4,000 Zulus attacked. They mounted six all-out assaults against Chard's fortifications, eventually carrying the outer defenses and the hospital building, fighting for it hand-to-hand, room by room. The men then retreated to a stone kraal (a kind of corral), where they continued to repulse further Zulu attacks throughout the night of January 22–23. Leaving 250 dead behind, the Zulus withdrew on the morning of January 23. Chard lost seventeen killed and ten wounded. Chard, his second in command, Gonville Bromhead (1856–1891), and nine enlisted men, were awarded Victoria Crosses, the most ever for any single action. The defense of Rorke's Drift prevented the Zulus from crossing into Natal Province.

Thrust into desperate circumstances by chance, Chard rose to the occasion and gave the British army one of its most epic actions.

Charlemagne

742–814

Born on April 2, 742, the son of Pepin and Berta, Charlemagne is said to have been educated by the abbot of St. Dénis. On the death of his father in 768, Charlemagne and his brother, Carloman, were selected jointly to rule over the Franks. In 771 Carolman died and Charlemagne became king.

Charlemagne's early military campaigns were conducted against the pagan Saxons (772). In 773–774 he invaded Italy on the side of Pope Adrian I and defeated the Lombards. His invasion of Moorish Spain was repulsed at Saragossa in 778. During the withdrawal, his rear guard, under his nephew, Roland, was massacred by Basques near Burguete. This minor disaster, highly romanticized, became the subject of one of the most famous and enduring medieval *chansons de geste, The Song of Roland.* Returning to his campaign against the Saxons, Charlemagne defeated them at the battles of Detmold and Hase in 783, finally subduing them in 798 and then annexing Saxony and converting the Saxons to Christianity in 804. Between 791 and 795 he defeated the Avars along the upper Danube and annexed their lands. On Christmas Day, 800, the pope crowned Charlemagne holy Roman emperor. His domain extended over all the western provinces, except Britain, that had been part of the Roman empire. He died at Aachen, January 28, 814.

Charlemagne was a large, physically imposing man. A bold and imaginative commander who understood strategy and logistics, he was also a great patron of the arts and learning. His reign was a bright light in the Dark Ages.

Charles XII, King of Sweden

1682–1718

The son of Charles XI of Sweden and Ulrica Leonora of Denmark; young Charles's father prepared him assiduously for the throne, giving him a grounding in the military sciences and many other subjects as well; it is said he learned to ride before he was four. Upon his father's death in 1697 the fifteen-year-old Charles became king.

In April 1700 the Danes precipitated the Great Northern War by invading Schleswig, Sweden's ally, thinking to take advantage of the adolescent king. Denmark was supported in this by Russia and Poland, which had leagued themselves to break Sweden's power in the Baltic. By August, with Charles leading them in a seaborne landing, the Swedes were advancing on Copenhagen and the Danes sued for peace. At Narva (November 30, 1700), 8,000 Swedes defeated the Russian army of 40,000 that was besieging the place. Between 1701 and 1706, in one of the most brilliant campaigns of history, Charles won every battle he fought, overturned the Polish throne, and forced **Peter the Great** to ask for peace, but on January 1, 1708, he invaded Russia. The following June at Poltava, weakened by hard fighting and lack of supplies, the Swedes were defeated, losing 9,000 dead and 18,000 captured. Charles was killed defending his borders in December 1718.

A brilliant and determined soldier, Charles was forced to go to war. He has been seen as foolishly stubborn, and while his invasion of Russia proved a costly mistake, it was his premature death that caused Sweden's decline.

Cheng Ho

1371?–1433?

Born in central Yunnan Province, Cheng Ho was recruited as a court eunuch when about ten years old. As a young man he accompanied the future Ming emperor, Chu Ti, on various military campaigns and is said to have distinguished himself in the civil war that placed Chu Ti on the throne in 1402, when he assumed the royal name of Yung Lo. His reign lasted until 1424 and was characterized by a successful foreign policy backed by strong land and sea forces. In 1405 he selected Cheng to command naval expeditions that gained control of the waters around Indonesia and the Indian Ocean.

Between 1425 and 1433, Cheng led seven overseas expeditions that visited thirty-seven different countries from Cambodia to east Africa (Vasco da Gama did not circumnavigate Africa to find the passage to India until 1497). Cheng's first expedition, to Sumatra (1405–1407), consisted of more than 27,000 men and over 300 vessels, the largest a four-decker said to have been more than 500 feet long. Cheng Ho forced the Malays and Indonesians to pay tribute to his emperor. He then commanded a sea-and-land force in the conquest of Ceylon (1408–1411), sailed to Hormuz (1412–1415), and visited Mecca on a voyage up the Red Sea (1431–1433). All told, it is estimated the Chinese built over 1,100 ships to outfit these expeditions.

Cheng Ho's voyages were magnificent feats of organization and seamanship undertaken almost a century before the great Western mariners began their explorations.

John Churchill, see Marlborough

George Rogers Clark

1752–1818

Born near Charlottesville, Virginia, elder brother of William of Lewis and Clark fame, George received little formal education, although he was well-read. At the age of nineteen he began the study of surveying, and by the outbreak of the American Revolution, he had conducted several exploring expeditions and served as a scout during Lord Dunmore's War (1774) against the Indians along the Ohio.

Apprised by agents in 1777 that the British garrison at Kaskaskia in modern Illinois had been withdrawn to Detroit, Clark conceived a plan to seize it and thereby gain a foothold for the Americans on the Mississippi and the Ohio. He sold this idea to Patrick Henry, governor of Virginia, who authorized him to raise seven companies for the purpose of defending Virginia's western borders, but secretly to capture Kaskaskia, which he did, with about 175 men, on July 4, 1778. He then seized Cahokia and Vincennes, but a British force of 500 men under Henry Hamilton retook Vincennes in December. With 200 men, Clark left Kaskaskia on February 6, 1779, and after a grueling midwinter march, fording the icy waters of flooded rivers and marshes, exhausted and starving, they reached Vincennes on February 23. His garrison depleted, and fooled by Clark into thinking his force was much larger, Hamilton surrendered the place February 25, 1779.

Clark was one of the most remarkable leaders to emerge from the American frontier. With a handful of men, Clark's daring and enterprise ended the British threat in Ohio and Illinois.

Mark W. Clark

1896–1984

Born at Madison Barracks, New York, son of an army officer, Clark graduated from West Point in time to serve with the 5th Infantry Division in the Aisne-Marne Offensive (June 1918), where he was wounded. He was assigned to the First Army staff for the Saint-Mihiel (September 12–16) and Meuse-Argonne (September 26–November 11) Offenses and then served with Third Army during the occupation of Germany.

Promoted to lieutenant colonel in 1940, he was made a brigadier general in August 1941, bypassing the grade of colonel. He was appointed commander of U.S. forces in Britain in 1942 and, as a lieutenant general, was Eisenhower's deputy in North Africa and commanded the Fifth Army during the landing at Salerno (September 9, 1943). Although given a fourth star and command of the 15th Army Group (December 1944), Clark considered Italy a "forgotten front" after the Normandy invasion. His dash to capture Rome (June 4, 1944), excluding the British and French, may have allowed German forces to escape encirclement and fight on longer. After the war he advocated a get-tough policy with the communists. He later succeeded General **Ridgway** in Korea (May 1952) and stayed through the armistice (July 27, 1952). He was not pleased to sign an "armistice without victory" or to fight a war with limited objectives and resources, but he did his duty.

Dubbed the "American Eagle" by Churchill, Clark was a tough, strong-willed commander who beat his German opponents and saw it through to a truce in Korea.

Karl Maria von Clausewitz

1780–1831

Born at Burg, near Magdeburg, Germany, the son of an impoverished army officer, Clausewitz entered the Prussian army in 1792 and was commissioned at the siege of Mainz in 1793. Poorly educated, Clausewitz studied on his own in garrison so successfully that in 1801 he was admitted to the Berlin academy for officers. While there, he attracted the attention of the great Prussian military reformer Scharnhorst, who got him an appointment as adjutant to Prince August on the general staff.

Clausewitz fought at Auerstädt (October 14, 1806) and Prenzlau (October 28), where he was captured by the French. Upon his release he assisted Scharnhorst in his reorganization of the Prussian army and was an instructor to Crown Prince Frederick William. On the eve of Napoleon's invasion of Russia, von Clausewitz resigned his commission in protest over Prussia's subservience to Napoleon. He subsequently served with the Russians during the French invasion, and at Waterloo saw action at Ligny (June 16, 1815) and Wavre (June 18). Promoted to major general in 1818, he began writing his great military treatise, *Vom Kriege* (*On War*), which he never finished. He died of cholera contracted while serving as chief of staff to a Prussian corps on the Polish border in 1830.

Clausewitz is remembered for his writing on the art and science of war. But having learned to soldier from the bottom up, he was no scribbling armchair theorist, which is one reason his writings have withstood the test of time and experience.

Patrick R. Cleburne

1828–1864

Born in County Cork, Ireland, Cleburne trained to be a druggist but upon failing an examination, he enlisted in the 41st Regiment of Foot. Purchasing his discharge, he emigrated to America in 1849, eventually settling in Helena, Arkansas. In 1860 he helped organize and later became captain of the Yell Rifles, a local militia company.

Cleburne was appointed colonel of the 15th Arkansas Regiment, and in 1862 (March 4) was promoted to brigadier general. He fought at Shiloh (April 6–7, 1862), was wounded twice at Richmond, Kentucky (August 29–30), and was at Perryville (October 8). He was promoted to major general in December 1862 and commanded a division at Chickamauga (August–September 1863), where he distinguished himself covering the Confederate retreat. He repulsed **Sherman** at Missionary Ridge (November 25, 1863). In 1864 he and some others suggested in a letter to Jefferson Davis that the Confederacy free slaves to be used as soldiers. Although the government did just that after Cleburne's death, at the time it was made, the suggestion was held against him. He fought under **Hood** at Atlanta (July–September 1864) and retreated with him into

Tennessee, where at Franklin (November 30, 1864), he was killed leading a forlorn attack.

Cleburne has been called the "Stonewall Jackson of the West," and Lee thought highly of him. Had he not written the slave letter, he and not Hood might have replaced **Johnston** at Atlanta.

Robert Clive, Baron Clive of Plassey

1725–1774

Born in Shropshire, England, Clive proved a difficult youngster, and at the age of eighteen he was sent to India as a clerk for the East India Company. Moody, depressed, and self-destructive, Clive would probably not have survived long in India were it not for the outbreak of war with France in 1746.

Captured at Madras (September), he escaped and the following year was appointed an ensign in the volunteers. When war broke out again in 1751, Clive volunteered to lead a diversion against the city of Arcot. At the head of 500 men he seized the place in September. He then withstood a fifty-three-day siege and, after being relieved, conducted a very successful guerrilla campaign against the French until he returned to England in March 1753, with a small fortune.

Back in India in 1755, he rescued the Europeans in the infamous "Black Hole" of Calcutta (January 2, 1757). In March, at the head of 1,100 Europeans and 2,100 Indian troops, he marched against the French-supported Sirāj-ud-Dawlah and his army of 50,000. At the Battle of Plassey, June 23, 1757, this tiny force routed Sirāj-ud's army, mainly because Clive's men kept their powder dry during a rainstorm and Sirāj-ud's did not. Clive was twice thereafter governor of Bengal, returning at last to England in 1767. He was later exonerated of charges of corruption, but on November 22, 1774, depressed and ill, he committed suicide.

Clive was a bold and courageous commander who thrived on action. His guts and determination established the British in India.

Clovis I

465–511

Son of Childeric I, a Germanic king who ruled a people known as the Franks in northeastern Gaul and the Rhineland, Clovis became king of the Salian Franks (a tribe along the IJssel River in the Netherlands) upon his father's death in 481.

In 486 Clovis attacked Syagrius, a Roman general who ruled south of the Somme, and defeated him at the Battle of Soissons, where Clovis afterward established his capital. His marriage in 493 to Clotilde, a Burgundian princess, cemented his relations with the Romanized Gauls and also introduced him to Catholicism, to

which he was converted in 496. Thereafter his campaigns against the pagans took on the nature of crusades, assuring him the support of orthodox Christians. His long war with the Alamanni, a tribe living between the Vosges and the Rhine, ended with their conquest at the Battle of Tolbiac (modern Zülpich, near Cologne) in 506. Next he took on the Visigoths, defeating them at Vouillé, near Poitiers in 507. It is said that Clovis personally slew Alaric II, king of the Visigoths, at this battle. Afterward, he moved his capital to Paris, where he ruled until his death.

Clovis is recognized as the founder of the

French nation. He ruled over the Salian Franks by hereditary right and extended his kingdom through shrewd alliances and outright conquest. While he protected and encouraged the church, he was not ruled by it and his codification of Salic Law provided a legal framework for the unification of his kingdom.

Cochise

1812–1874

Born into the Chiricahua Apache tribe in Arizona, Cochise was the scourge of the territory for a decade in revenge for the treachery of an army officer. So successful was he at mobile warfare that Cochise has been dubbed the "Apache Napoleon."

Cochise was friendly toward the first Americans to arrive in Arizona in the 1850s. Unjustly accused of kidnapping a white child in February 1861, Cochise was summarily arrested by Lieutenant G. N. Bascom when in good faith he went to Bascom to clear his name. Cochise escaped, but several of his people were taken hostage and later executed, whereupon Cochise executed his own hostages and went on the warpath.

In July 1862, at Apache Pass in southeastern Arizona, Cochise with about 600 men ambushed a large column (eleven companies of infantry plus cavalry and artillery) on its way to relieve federal forces in Arizona and New Mexico. His warriors withstood repeated charges and were driven off only after coming under artillery fire. Cochise continued a vicious and highly successful guerrilla war against the settlements until President Grant sent a special commissioner to secure peace in 1872.

Cochise admired courage in others, most notably Thomas J. Jeffords, who rode unarmed into his camp to secure safe passage of the U.S. mail through Apache territory. They became good friends. Unjustly treated by people he considered friends, Cochise unleashed upon them the violence his people reserve for those who betray them.

Thomas Cochrane

1775–1860

Born at Annsfield in Lanarkshire, England, on December 14, 1775; Cochrane's father, the 9th Earl of Dundonald, purchased a commission for him in the 104th Regiment while he was still a child. At the same time his uncle, Captain Alexander Cochrane, to hold open a commission for him in the Navy, placed his name on the books of several ships he commanded, so that when Thomas chose a career in the navy at age seventeen in 1793, he had already "served" five years.

Appointed captain of the brig *Speedy* in March 1800, Cochrane successfully preyed upon Spanish shipping. This was no mean feat, since the crew of the *Speedy* has been referred to as a "burlesque on a ship of war." Always his own man, in February 1801, Cochrane, dressed as an ordinary English seaman, crashed a fancy subscription ball in the Maltese port of Valletta. Ordered to leave, he knocked a French officer down and later dueled with the man, putting a pistol ball through his leg. Cochrane distinguished himself at sea during the Napoleonic Wars, but after 1809 he was denied further command because of his outspoken criticism of his superiors. He continued badgering the government from his seat in Parliament, from which he was removed and imprisoned on trumped-up charges of fraud in 1814. Between 1817 and 1823 he commanded the Chilean and Brazilian navies in those countries' wars of independence, and in 1825 served the Greeks in their war with Turkey. He was reinstated in the British navy in 1832 and promoted to admiral in 1851.

Cochrane was a brave and resourceful commander who showed what he could do in South America.

Joseph Lawton Collins

1896–1963

Born in New Orleans of an Irish-born father, Collins graduated 35th of 139 in his West Point class of 1917. While he did not see combat in World War I, he served in the occupation army in Germany.

Between wars he served in a variety of command, staff, and teaching assignments. In 1940 he was the chief of staff of the VII Corps and after Pearl Harbor he became chief of the Hawaiian Department, where he was promoted to brigadier general. In May 1942 he took over command of the 25th Division and led it on Guadalcanal and in the New Georgia Campaign. His penchant for quick movement and the lightning bolt on the 25th Division's shoulder patch earned him the nickname "Lightning Joe." He then led VII Corps in the invasion of France (June 6, 1944), captured Cherbourg (June 18–27), Aachen (December), and Cologne (February 1945), and was the first to link up with the Russians in April 1945. In France, when **Omar Bradley** informed Collins at one point that he'd given his corps all the support he could except his own pistol, Collins held his hand out for the pistol. From 1949–1953 he was U.S. Army chief of staff and from 1954–1955 President Eisenhower's special representative in Vietnam.

The 1917 West Point yearbook said of Collins, "first, concentration and decision, second, rapid and hearty action." Those are the basic characteristics of good generalship and Collins had them before he was even commissioned a second lieutenant.

Louis de Bourbon, Prince de Condé

1621–1686

Son of Henri Bourbon (second cousin of Louis XIII), and Duc d'Enghien from birth (he became Prince of Condé on his father's death in 1646); Louis Condé's early education began with the Jesuits and was completed at the Royal Military Academy in Paris. At the age of seventeen he was appointed governor of Burgundy and from 1640–1642 he served as a volunteer in the war against the Spanish, seeing action at Arras (1640), Aire (1641), and Salces (1642).

In 1643, Cardinal Richelieu, impressed by the twenty-two-year-old Louis's ability, gave him command of the army in Flanders (about 23,000 strong), and at Rocroi (May 19), northwest of Sedan, he decisively defeated the Spanish Netherlands army of 27,000 men, turning the flank of the Flemish cavalry and smashing the veteran Spanish infantry, the most formidable in Europe at that time—when they formed squares, Louis massed his cannon and blew them apart, killing 8,000 and capturing 7,000. Louis never lost this bold spirit. At the Battle of Senef (August 1, 1674), during the Dutch War (1672–1678), he attacked the invading allied army with only half his force and no artillery. The next day the rest of his army arrived and the allies withdrew, thus ending the invasion. He died in his bed.

Condé has been unfavorably compared with his cousin, **Turenne,** who beat him at Dunkirk (June 14, 1658), a battle undertaken against Condé's advice. But swift and decisive, few have ever matched his sustained battlefield success.

Constantine I (Flavius Valerius Constantinus)

274?–337

Born at Naissus in modern Yugoslavia, Constantine began public life as a tribune at Diocletian's court (293). He joined his father in Britain in 305, and when his father died in 306, his troops proclaimed Constantine caesar (successor designate).

When Emperor Maximian died in 310, Constantine invaded Italy to seize the throne from Maxentius, Maximian's son. He defeated Maxentius's armies at Turin and Verona in 312 and killed Maxentius at the Milvian Bridge near Rome later that year. Just before this battle, as Constantine later told the historian Eusebius, he saw in the sun a cross inscribed *In hoc signo vinces* ("in this sign you shall conquer"), which led to his conversion to Christianity. Constantine then clashed with his co-emperor, Licinius, whom he

defeated at Adrianople (July 3, 323) and Chrysopolis (September 18). In 330 he transferred his capital to Byzantium and renamed it Constantinople. In 332 he personally took the field to rout the Goths at Moesia in northern Bulgaria. Constantine created a mobile, central standing army that could be quickly deployed to trouble spots, and he placed his infantry and cavalry under separate commanders.

Constantine was an audacious and intelligent commander. He could be harsh, as when in 326 he executed his eldest son and his nephew (after his death the army completed the job by lynching the rest of his relatives), but his conversion to Christianity, regardless of how consistently he practiced it, had a profound effect on the subsequent history of the Western world.

Gonzalo de Córdoba

1453–1515

In 1466 Córdoba was sent to the court of Henry IV of Castile to serve as a page, first to the pretender Alfonso, and later to his sister, Isabella. In 1474, during the war to determine who would succeed Henry, Córdoba supported Isabella and her husband, Ferdinand. After their joint reign commenced, he saw service in the war against the Moors of Granada, and was one

of two commissioners who negotiated their final surrender in 1492.

In 1495, at the head of 2,100 men, Córdoba was dispatched to Italy to support the King of Naples against the French. At Seminara (June 28) he was defeated, but regained the lost territory over the next three years by conducting a vigorous guerrilla campaign, taking advantage of the terrain and his enemy's long supply lines. At Cerignola (April 26, 1503), his well-drilled pikemen and arquebusiers defeated the French cavalry and Swiss pikemen by luring them into close quarters, where they were cut down by his firearms, the first instance in history of a battle won by the use of handheld firearms. On December 29, Córdoba's army of 15,000 launched a surprise attack against 23,000 Frenchmen across the Garigliano River using pontoon bridges built under the cover of bad weather. The French were driven back to Gaeta with heavy losses. Córdoba died in Granada of malaria, December 1, 1515.

Called *El Gran Capitán,* Córdoba was the first to design tactics to take advantage of infantry firearms, and for the next 100 years the Spanish infantry dominated European battlefields.

John Murray Corse

1835–1893

Born in Pittsburgh, Pennsylvania, Corse grew up in Iowa, where he was a partner in his father's stationery business and was later admitted to the bar. On July 13, 1861, he was appointed major of the 6th Iowa and became its colonel in March 1863. Made a brigadier general of volunteers in March 1863, he was at Corinth (April–June 1862) and Vicksburg (October 1862–July 1863) and Missionary Ridge (November 25, 1863), where he was badly wounded in the head.

In October 1864, **Sherman** ordered Corse to hold Allatoona Pass, twelve miles northwest of Marietta, Georgia, against **Hood,** who was marching north to cut his communications. Corse arrived there October 5, 1864 with about 2,000 men. Opposing him was the division of Confederate major general Samuel French. When he demanded Corse's surrender, "to avoid needless effusion of blood," Corse replied, "We are prepared for the 'needless effusion of blood' whenever it is agreeable to you." In the fighting Corse lost fully a third of his men and was badly wounded. The following day he sent this message to Sherman: "I am short a cheekbone and one ear, but am able to whip all hell yet." The fight inspired Philip B. Bliss to write the song "Hold the Fort," which in turn led to that expression becoming current in the English language. After the war, Corse became a successful businessman and politician in his native Massachusetts.

Corse was a brave and determined soldier, a bright star in that galaxy of gifted amateurs who performed so well as field commanders during the American Civil War.

Hernán [Hernando] Cortéz

1485–1547

Cortéz was born at Medellín, in Estremadura, Spain, and for a time studied law at the University of Salamanca. But in 1504 he settled as a farmer on the island of Santo Domingo, and in 1511 joined Diego Velázquez on his expedition to Cuba, where he was appointed *alcalde* of Santiago.

In 1519, with eleven ships and 500 men, Cortéz set out for Mexico, where he founded the city of Vera Cruz in May and declared himself captain general. In August he set out for the Aztec capital of Tenochtitlán (Mexico City), first defeating and then making allies of the Indians he met on the way. At first the Aztecs thought the Spaniards might be gods and treated them with deference, but to ensure his safety, Cortéz seized their ruler, Montezuma, and held him hostage. Returning to Tenochtitlán after defeating an expedition sent to replace him by Velázquez, Cortéz found his garrison besieged by dissident Aztecs. Montezuma was killed in a riot and on the night of June 30, 1520, Cortéz evacuated the city, every step of the way fiercely contested by the aroused Aztecs. After seventy-five days of desperate street fighting, Tenochtitlán fell to him, August 13, 1521. He then razed it and built Mexico City. Cortéz died on his estate near Seville, December 2, 1547.

Cortéz's conquest of Mexico stands as one of the boldest deeds in history. Unlike other conquistadores, Cortéz treated the Indians with respect. He was a brilliant tactician and an audacious, fearless leader.

Hernando Cortéz

Crazy Horse (Ta-sunko-witko)

1840–1877

Born into the Oglala Sioux tribe on Rapid Creek, South Dakota (near present-day Rapid City), Crazy Horse became an implacable enemy of the white man and his reservation system. While little is known about his early life, it is probable that as a young man he participated in Red Cloud's raids against settlers in Wyoming between 1865 and 1868.

By 1876 Crazy Horse had risen in prominence as a war leader of the southern Sioux, and since he was related to the northern Cheyenne by marriage, many warriors of that nation also followed him. Ordered onto reservations by government edict in 1875, Crazy Horse refused. While camped near the mouth of the Little Powder River on March 17, 1876, Crazy Horse and his people were surprised by a detachment of 450 soldiers who destroyed their lodges and captured their horses. In the running fight that ensued, the Indians were able to retake most of their mounts. His band swelled to about 1,200 warriors by the addition of some Cheyenne.

Free Library of Philadelphia

Crazy Horse

Crazy Horse dealt General **George Crook** a costly defeat at a battle on the upper Rosebud (June 17), and then joined with **Sitting Bull** on the Little Bighorn River, where on June 25, 1876, they defeated the 7th Cavalry Regiment under **Custer**. Relentlessly pursued and attacked, Crazy Horse surrendered on May 6, 1877, and while attempting to avoid arrest, was killed on September 5.

A brilliant tactician and a dogged and determined leader, Crazy Horse has come to symbolize the desire all men have to live free.

Oliver Cromwell

1599–1658

Born into an English country family, Cromwell was pursuing the life of a small farmer when he was elected to the House of Commons from Cambridge in 1640, where he joined a clique of Puritan country gentlemen and lawyers who advocated curbing the power of the king and the Anglican Church.

When Parliament and king finally went to war in August 1642, Cromwell, with no previous military experience or training, distinguished himself, conducting quick raids into royalist territory. He further distinguished himself as a cavalry commander at Marston Moor (July 2, 1644), where he led the left wing of the parliamentary army. At Naseby (June 14, 1645) Cromwell smashed the royalists, and within a year they surrendered. In 1648 he defeated a royalist up-

rising backed by Scots, and in 1649 he conducted a harsh campaign in Ireland, where at Drogheda (September 11) his army massacred both soldiers and civilians. That year he also signed a warrant for the execution of Charles I. In 1650–1651, he defeated first the Scots and then Charles II's forces at Worcester (September 3, 1651). In 1653 he became lord protector, virtually a dictator, and when Parliament could not agree on a constitution, he dismissed it, April 20, 1653 with the words, "You have sat long enough!" In 1661 the royalists exhumed his body and hung it on the gallows at Tyburn.

A superb organizer and brilliant tactician, Cromwell had more power and abused it less than many other leaders. He left England far stronger than he found it.

George Crook

1829–1890

Born near Dayton, Ohio, Crook graduated thirty-eight out of fifty-six in his West Point class of 1848. In September 1861 he was appointed colonel of the 36th Ohio Infantry and brigadier general of volunteers in August 1862. He fought at South Mountain (September 14, 1862) and Antietam (September 17) and served under Sheridan in the Shenandoah (August 1864–March 1865), ending the war a major general.

Crook reverted to lieutenant colonel after the war but stayed in the army, fighting Indians in northern California and the northwest. In 1871 President Grant sent him to deal with the Apaches in the southwest, which he did so successfully he was promoted from lieutenant colonel to brigadier general in the regular army. Sent to command the Department of the Platte in 1875, he spent the entire year of 1876 in the field against the Sioux and Cheyenne, sharing the hardships of the campaign with his men. Outmaneuvered by **Crazy Horse** at the Rosebud (June 17, 1876), he pursued him relentlessly after the Little Big Horn (June 25, 1876) until he was brought to bay. In 1883 he followed the Chiricahua Apaches into the wild Sierra Madres of Mexico, where he induced them to surrender, and he conducted the final campaign against **Geronimo** in 1885–1886. He was promoted to major general in 1888.

Called "Gray Fox" by the Apaches, Crook was an extremely modest man but one of great physical and moral courage. He made friends easily,

George Crook

National Archives

understood the Indian character, and sympathized with them in their unequal struggle with the white man. Far ahead of his times, he believed Indians should have equal rights.

Robert E. Cushman, Jr.

1914–1985

Born in St. Paul, Minnesota, Cushman graduated 10th of 442 in the class of 1935 at the U.S. Naval Academy. Commissioned a second lieutenant of Marines, Cushman saw his first overseas service with the 4th Marines in Shanghai, China, in 1936.

As a captain, Cushman was commanding the marine detachment onboard the battleship *Pennsylvania* at Pearl Harbor on December 7, 1941. Unhurt during the bombing, he lost about a third of his men during the attack. He commanded the 2nd Battalion, 9th Marine Regiment at Bougainville (November 1943), Guam (July–August 1944), and Iwo Jima (February–March 1945). At Guam he won the Navy Cross for valor. After the war he served in a series of command and staff assignments, including assistant for national security affairs to Vice-President Nixon, 1957–1961. As a lieutenant general, he commanded the III Marine Amphibious Force in Vietnam (June 1967–April 1969).

Believing that mobility was the key to success in Vietnam, General Cushman learned to fly a helicopter. He was deputy director of the CIA from 1969 to 1971, becoming the twenty-fifth commandant of the Marine Corps and a four-star general in January 1972.

General Cushman was a no-nonsense marine who proved his mettle in combat. He believed the war in Vietnam should have focused on protecting the population, was uncomfortable with the static defense role assigned the marines there, and openly disagreed with army general Westmoreland on this. As commandant, he provided firm leadership to the corps during an era of social tension and fiscal retrenchment.

George Armstrong Custer

1839–1876

Custer was born in New Rumley, Ohio. Although his ambition was to be a soldier, he graduated last out of thirty-four in his West Point Class of 1861.

Assigned as a second lieutenant to the 2nd Cavalry, Custer was in time for First Manassas (July 1861). He was an aide to McClellan in 1862, and then at Aldie, Virginia (June 17, 1863) he so distinguished himself that he was recommended for brigadier general and given command of the 2nd Brigade (Michigan) of the 3rd Cavalry Division, which he commanded with distinction at Gettysburg (July 1–3, 1863). This brigade sustained the highest casualty rate of any in the Civil War. Custer participated in every battle of the Army of the Potomac save one and had eleven horses shot out from under him. He ended the war a major general of volunteers. After the war Custer fought Indians on the frontier as commander of the 7th Cavalry Regiment, which was organized in July 1866. At the Little Bighorn (June 25, 1876), he split his command of 650 men into three columns and, taking ten companies (266 men), boldly attacked the Sioux camp along the river. Custer and all his men

George Armstrong Custer

National Archives

were killed when they were overwhelmed by about 3,000 warriors. Why he did this instead of waiting for reinforcements is still debated.

Custer's brilliant service during the Civil War has been totally overshadowed by the Little Big-horn debacle. He was a *beau sabreur,* with boundless self-confidence, but no experience in combined operations, which ultimately may have led to the disaster in Montana.

D

Louis Nicholas Davout

1770–1823

Born at Annoux in Burgundy, the son of an impoverished officer in the Royal Champagne Cavalry, Davout graduated from the Brienne Military School and was commissioned a sub-lieutenant in his father's old regiment in 1788.

Although a noble, he supported the revolution but suffered the vicissitudes of the military and political confusion that followed until he joined **Napoleon**'s army in Egypt, where he fought at the Pyramids (July 12, 1798) and Aboukir (July 25, 1799). He returned a devoted follower of Napoleon, who appointed him a division commander (July 1800) and marshal of France (May 1804). He commanded a corps brilliantly at Austerlitz. At Auerstädt (October 14, 1806), his army of 27,000 fought a Prussian army of 63,000 to a standstill and then counterat-tacked. For this victory he was given the title of Duke of Auerstädt in 1808. At Eckmühl (April 22, 1809) he held an isolated position until reinforcements permitted him to attack. Davout led the I Corps of the Grande Armée into Russia in 1812 and was wounded at Borodino (September 7, 1812). His defense of Hamburg (May 1813–May 1814) was a masterpiece. He was appointed minister for war and commander in chief of Paris (March–July 1815). Exiled after Napoleon's abdication, his rank and titles were restored in 1819.

Davout was never defeated and he won his greatest victories on his own. From Austerlitz to Borodino he played a decisive role in Napoleon's campaigns. His troops were the best trained, disciplined, and cared for in the Grande Armée.

Moshe Dayan °

1915–1981

Born of Ukrainian Jewish parents in the kibbutz of Degania, Palestine. In the 1930s he received rudimentary military training in the Haganah defense organization and trained under **Orde Wingate**. After serving time in a British prison for weapons violations, Dayan joined British units in operations against the Vichy French in Syria. On one raid with Australian troops in June 1941, he was wounded in the head and his left eye was destroyed. Unable to wear a glass eye because of extensive bone damage, he wore instead a black eye patch for the rest of his life.

During the Israeli War of Independence (1948–1949) he commanded the Jordan Valley sector and at Degania (May 19–21, 1948) successfully defended the settlement with a tiny force. He distinguished himself as the commander of the 89th Commando Battalion, particularly in daring raids like those against the Arab Legion at Lod and Ramallah (July 9–19, 1949). Promoted to major general in October 1949, he instituted professional training courses for officers of the IDF, demanding realistic exercises and getting rid of incompetents, thus laying the foundation for the modern Israeli army. He planned and directed the Sinai Campaign against Egypt (October–November 1956). He held various posts in the Israeli government until appointed defense minister (1967), a post he held except for a brief period until 1974.

An unorthodox soldier who believed in leading from the front, Dayan was a forceful, outspoken individualist who did not tolerate fools.

William F. Dean

1899–1981

Born at Carlyle, Illinois, the son of a dentist, Dean was commissioned in the army from the ROTC in 1923, after having failed to gain entrance to West Point. In World War II Dean commanded the 44th Infantry Division through Germany into Austria. He was awarded the Distinguished Service Cross for gallantry in action near Echenberg, France, in December 1944, leading an infantry platoon through enemy fire.

In October 1949 Dean took over the 24th Infantry Division, part of the Eighth Army, which was then in Japan. When the Korean War broke out (June 30, 1950), he was ordered there with his division, arriving on July 3. Asked to defend the city of Taejŏn long enough to allow reinforcements to deploy, Dean went to the front. Because of poor communications and low morale among his frontline troops, Dean decided to remain with them better to control the battle and bolster their spirits. To prove to his men that it could be done, he personally took up a 3.5-inch rocket launcher and used it to take out enemy tanks. He ordered the city evacuated on the night of July 20 and, as he was fetching water for some of his wounded, fell, broke his shoulder, and was separated from his party. He wandered behind enemy lines thirty-six days before being captured. He spent three years as a prisoner of the North Koreans, never breaking faith with his country. On September 30, 1950, he was awarded the Medal of Honor in absentia.

Dean saw that his place was at the front, led his men heroically, and earned his pay as a general the hard way.

Stephen Decatur

1779–1820

Born at Sinepuxent, Maryland, where his mother had gone to escape the British occupation of Philadelphia, Decatur was raised in Philadelphia. During the naval war with France (1798–1800), he obtained a commission as a midshipman, making two cruises and rising to the rank of lieutenant.

During the Tripolitan War (1801–1805), sailing under Commodore Preble, he captured the ketch *Mastico* (four guns), renamed *Intrepid,* and proposed to use her to destroy the frigate *Phila-delphia,* which had fallen into the hands of the Tripolitans. This was done with one American casualty on the night of February 16, 1804. During subsequent engagements Decatur led boarding parties wielding a cutlass and a pistol, emerging from these actions a national hero. During the War of 1812, commanding the *United States* (forty-four guns) he took the British frigate *Macedonian* (thirty-eight guns) on October 25, 1812, and in command of the *President* (forty-four guns), engaged three British frigates in a running fight off the coast of New York on the night of January 14, 1815. He dismasted the *Endymion* (twenty-four guns), but with many of his crew wounded, among them himself, and his ship shot to pieces, he was forced to surrender. Commanding a squadron of nine ships, he was sent to Algiers (May–June 1815), where he forced the dey to desist from harassing American shipping. He died fighting a duel using pistols at eight paces.

A commander of great courage and honor, Decatur inspired devotion in his crews and fear in his country's enemies.

Charles De Gaulle

1890–1970

Born in the city of Lille, France, De Gaulle was the proud descendant of a long line of French patriots and intellectuals. One ancestor was at the Battle of Agincourt (1415), and his father, a teacher of mathematics and philosophy, was a veteran of the Franco-Prussian War (1870).

Admitted to St. Cyr in 1909 (where one of his nicknames was "The Big Asparagus"), he was commissioned in 1912. De Gaulle led an infantry company in World War I, being cited thrice for valor. He was so severely wounded at Verdun that he was left for dead. He revived while being carted off to the graveyard and was interned by the Germans, who put him into maximum confinement after he made several escape attempts. Between wars he was an outspoken advocate of mechanized armored warfare, which ran counter to the prevailing defensive strategy of the French high command at the time. At the outbreak of World War II he was a brigadier general. He led the 4th Armored Division against the Germans with some local success, but when France capitulated, he refused to surrender and fled to England, where he established the Free French movement. He returned to France in June 1944 and a triumphant entry into Paris on August 26. Elected president of the Fifth Republic in 1958, he remained the supreme political figure in France for the next eleven years.

A brave and capable combat leader and a superb politician, De Gaulle was a difficult ally and an implacable enemy who always put his country's interests first.

Demosthenes

?–413 B.C.

Little is known of Demosthenes' early life except that he was the son of Alcisthenes.

In 426, during the Second Peloponnesian War (432–404 B.C.), he was elected one of ten generals. In late 426 he inflicted a severe defeat upon the Spartan general Eurylochus at Olpae and a reinforcing army at Idomene, after which the surviving Spartan commander accepted a truce that ended the Spartan threat in north-western Greece. Left in command of a garrison established at Pylos (modern Navarino in the southwest Peloponnesus), he was besieged by the Spartans, who were outraged at this violation of their own soil. Astonishingly, he contrived the surrender of 292 of them, an unheard of event in Greece up to that time (425). Having failed in his invasion of Boetia (424), Demosthenes remained out of favor until recalled in 413 to reinforce the Athenian army under the cowardly and indecisive Nicias, which was besieging Syracuse in Sicily. Demosthenes, sizing up the Athenian situation as hopeless, advised Nicias to withdraw while he could, but Nicias waited too long, lost his fleet, and trying to extract his army by land, was wiped out. Both he and Demosthenes were executed by the victorious Syracusans.

Being picked to serve under Nicias at Syracuse was the worst luck, and had Athens accepted the Spartan peace proposals after Demosthenes' victory at Pylos, it would have won the war. On his own, Demosthenes could be a brilliant general, but teamed with a lesser commander, he is remembered for a terrible defeat.

George Dewey

1837–1917

Born at Montpelier, Vermont, Dewey was descended from a long line of New England patriots who first arrived in Massachusetts in 1634. He graduated five out of fifteen (but sixty started!) in his Naval Academy class of 1858.

In **Farragut's** attack on New Orleans (April 24–25, 1862), as executive officer on the *Mississippi*, Dewey successfully navigated her past Forts Jackson and St. Philip in the dark and engaged the Confederate ram *Manassas,* which was forced to make for shore, where she was burned. At Port Hudson (March 14, 1863), when the pilot ran his ship aground, Dewey was commended for his valiant but futile attempt to save her under enemy fire. As executive officer on the *Monongahela,* Farragut's flagship, Dewey studied that great admiral closely. After the war Dewey served with distinction in a number of commands and rose steadily in rank. Promoted to commodore in 1896, in November 1897 he took over the Asiatic squadron. He studied the Spanish dispositions in the Philippines thoroughly. At the outbreak of war with Spain (April 1898) he sailed for Manila with six light cruisers. Running the potent Spanish shore batteries in the dark, he caught their fleet by surprise. At 5:40 A.M., May 1, 1898, he told his flag captain, "You may fire when ready, Gridley." By noon he had sunk the fleet with a total of only eight Americans wounded.

Cool and decisive under fire, Dewey planned

George Dewey

Free Library of Philadelphia

for action carefully and then attacked aggressively. At Manila Bay he asked himself what would Farragut do, and then went and did it.

James H. Doolittle

1896–1993

Born in Alameda, California, Doolittle grew up in Alaska. He completed pilot training for duty in World War I, but saw no combat. Doolittle stayed in the air corps after the war, earning advanced engineering degrees and national prominence setting flight records, but he resigned in 1930 to work for Shell Oil.

Recalled to active duty as a major in 1940, Doolittle helped plan a retaliatory attack on Japan after Pearl Harbor. On April 18, 1942, now a lieutenant colonel, he led eighty men in sixteen twin-engine B-25 bombers from the deck of the carrier *Hornet* against Tokyo and other targets in Japan, 650 miles away. Fifteen planes flew on to China while the sixteenth ditched in Soviet territory; eleven crewmen were killed or captured. The "Doolittle Raid" was one of the most daring enterprises of the war and earned its commander promotion to brigadier general and the Medal of Honor. Although the actual damage inflicted was minor, compared with what would ensue before war's end, the raid gave American morale a tremendous boost and may have led the Japanese to expand their defensive perimeter in the Pacific, resulting in their decisive defeat at Midway (June 1942). Later Doolittle commanded the Twelfth Air Force in North Africa, the Fifteenth in Italy, and in 1944, the Eighth in England, which he led until V-E Day.

During WWII Doolittle *led* in the literal sense,

James H. Doolittle

whether from the cockpit of a bomber or from his headquarters. As brilliant at planning and organizing as he was at leading combat missions, he was one of the most effective commanders of World War II.

Andrea Doria

1466–1560

Born in Genoa, Italy, of an old patrician family and orphaned early in life, Doria became a professional soldier—a *condottiere*—serving various Italian nobles and Pope Innocent VIII. He rose to prominence in his native Genoa in 1507, when he was sent to suppress a revolt on Corsica.

Appointed captain general of the Genoese navy in 1510, Doria led it against the Barbary pirates before taking service with Francis I of France in 1522, where he was appointed admiral of his Mediterranean fleet. Recognizing that the French cause was doomed, Doria wisely changed sides and in 1528 restored the Genoese republic. While he refused to accept any official position in the government, his control of the fleet entitled him to great influence in its councils, especially since it was he who reformed the constitution, giving political power to the rule of an oligarchy of nobles. In 1535 he commanded **Charles V**'s navy on an expedition to Tunisia, and in 1541, his seamanship permitted much of the emperor's army to escape destruction after its ill-fated expedition against Tunis. Back home, he ruthlessly crushed revolts against his power in 1547 and 1548. Well into his eighties, he led with some success an expedition to recover Corsica from the French (1553–1555).

Andrea Doria was a product of his times, ruthless, dictatorial, and unprincipled. But as a naval commander, he was an intelligent strategist, an excellent tactician, and a bold and fearless seaman.

Francis Drake

1545–1596

Born near Tavistock, Devonshire, the eldest son of a yeoman farmer who later became a Calvinist lay preacher, Drake first went to sea with John Hawkins, a relative, who took him on a slave-trading expedition to the Gulf of Mexico in 1566. Ambushed by the Spanish in the harbor of San Juan de Ulloa, they lost most of their men and ships.

In 1570 and 1571 Drake sailed again to the Spanish main, this time on a privateering expedition. His success embarrassed Elizabeth I, who hoped for peace with Spain, and forced Drake to take service with the Earl of Essex, who was busily suppressing the Irish. In 1577, Elizabeth sent him on his famous circumnavigation of the globe. He was the first Englishman and only the second seaman of any nation ever to perform this feat. After a stint as the mayor of Plymouth, in 1585 Elizabeth again sent Drake to sea against Spain. In May 1587, in a daring raid, Drake captured thirty-seven Spanish vessels gathering at Cádiz as part of the great armada Philip of Spain was sending to invade England. As vice admiral of the English fleet, Drake played a prominent role in repulsing the armada in the English Channel in May 1588. Sailing against the Spanish again in 1595, Drake died of fever in the Caribbean on January 28, 1596, and was buried at sea.

Francis Drake was the quintessential English sea dog of his day, never long comfortable on land, at home only far from home, surviving on his wits and courage. His voyage around the world was one of history's greatest feats of seamanship.

Van Tien Dung

1917–

Born a peasant in Ha Deng Province in Tonkin (formerly North Vietnam), Dung worked as a young man in a textile factory in Hanoi. He joined the Indo-Chinese Communist party in 1936. His revolutionary activities landed him in a French prison in 1939, where he remained until he escaped in 1944 and fled to the mountainous Bac Viet region on the Chinese-Vietnamese border, where he joined Ho Chi Minh.

In 1946 he became head of the party's military political department, and when the 320th Division of the People's Army (PAVN) was formed in 1953, he was given its command and led it against the French garrison at the siege of Dien Bien Phu. At the age of thirty-six, in 1953, he became the PAVN chief of staff, second only to **Vo Nguyen Giap**. In July 1954, he led the North Vietnamese delegation to the International Control Commission in Saigon, where it is said he worked to undermine the peace process and prepare the way for the eventual communist insurgency in South Vietnam. He is credited with having modernized the PAVN as a fighting force in the 1960s. He was promoted to senior general rank in 1974 and on April 8, 1975, took personal command of the blitzkrieg that forced the capitulation of South Vietnam on April 30. He replaced Giap as minister of national defense in 1980.

Dung has been called competent but "unimaginative," yet with no formal military training, he rose to high command and played an important role in the defeat of the best military minds France and the U.S. could bring against his peasant army.

E

Edward I, King of England

1239–1307

Born at Westminster; his first military campaign was fought when he was sixteen against Llewelyn ap Gruffydd in an attempt to impose English rule upon the Welsh. Young Edward was beaten soundly. At Lewes (May 14, 1264), fighting with his father, Henry III, against his rebellious barons led by **Simon de Montfort,** he precipitated defeat by rashly following a part of the baronial army away from the field. Edward was captured but escaped.

Edward learned quickly from his mistakes and at Newport (July 8, 1265) he beat Montfort, turned on 30,000 reinforcements led by de Montfort's son and beat them at Kenilworth (August 2), and went back to finish Montfort off at Evesham (August 4), and rescued his father. In August 1274 Edward became king and in 1277 he invaded Wales with coordinated land and naval forces; by 1294 had subjugated the Welsh. In 1301 he created the title Prince of Wales, borne by all male heirs to the English throne since. Next he turned to Scotland, where, outnumbered 30,000 to 23,000, he defeated **William Wallace** at Falkirk, principally through the use of the deadly English longbow, which wreaked havoc upon the sturdy Scottish phalanxes. On his way to deal with **Robert Bruce,** he died of dysentery at Burgh-on-Sands, July 6, 1307.

Edward I was as good a king as he was a soldier, and he was a very great soldier—a brilliant tactician, decisive in battle, leading by example. He centralized control of the militia and established the longbow as the principal English infantry weapon.

Edward III, King of England

1312–1377

Grandson of **Edward I,** at age fourteen Edward was crowned king upon the abdication of his father, Edward II. His mother and a baron, Roger Mortimer, ruled in his name until 1330, when he had Mortimer executed, thereby defanging his mommy.

Edward first saw battle before he was fifteen in a campaign against the Scots, but in July 1332, leading his forces against David II of Scotland, he defeated them at Halidon Hill. Sailing for France to support his pretensions to the French crown, Edward and his fleet of 140 vessels met 190 French ships at Sluys, a port on the Dutch-Belgian border (June 12, 1340), capturing or destroying 166 of them. With 20,000 men, 12,000 of them archers, he marched to Crécy-en-Ponthieu, near Abbeville, where he made his dispositions to meet an advancing French army of 60,000 (12,000 heavy cavalry). He positioned his men in three divisions, two forward on the flanks and one in the center, which he commanded personally. The archers of each division he deployed to the front as a screen. The French launched more than a dozen waves of infantry and cavalry against Edward, all of which were repulsed by the English bowmen.

France lost 15,000 men at Crécy, including 1,500 knights and lords; the English lost two knights killed and about 200 met-at-arms, killed and wounded. It would not be until World War II that heavy cavalry (in the form of tanks) would again be decisive on a European battlefield.

While Europe slept, Edward perfected the infantry tactics, discipline, and organization that gave him victory at Crécy.

Edward Plantagenet, Prince of Wales

1330–1376

Edward Plantagenet saw his first combat action under his illustrious father, **Edward III,** at Crécy (August 26, 1346), where he commanded (nominally; the Earl of Warwick commanded in fact) the right wing. He distinguished himself in that battle, winning his knight's spurs. Tradition has it that he also won the name "Black Prince" at Crécy because he wore black armor that day, but the sobriquet appears to date only from the late 1500s.

After Crécy, Edward participated in his father's military campaigns in France. Leading an independent command consisting of about 12,000 men across France, Edward met a French army under John II at Poitiers (September 19, 1356). Like his father at Crécy, Edward picked a good defensive position and awaited the enemy,

some 35,000 strong. He repelled three assaults on his lines; the fourth, personally led by King John, was beaten and John taken prisoner; he was later ransomed for three million gold francs. Edward's aggressive tactics and English bowmen were successful again at Najera, Spain (April 3, 1367), inflicting over 12,000 casualties on the Castilians. His rule as Prince of Aquitaine was so mismanaged, however, that he gave it up and in 1371 returned to England, where he lived the remaining years of his life in obscurity, predeceasing his father by a year.

In his political role and personal life Edward Plantagenet was a failure; however, no one knows what he might have done had he become king. But as a soldier he was bold and brave, twice defeating armies much larger than his own.

Robert L. Eichelberger

1886–1961

Born at Urbana, Illinois, the son of a Union Army veteran and a southern girl who could remember the siege of Vicksburg, Eichelberger graduated 68 out of 103 in his West Point class of 1909.

During World War I Eichelberger served with the American Expeditionary Force in Siberia in 1918–1920, where he learned to respect the ability of the Japanese soldier. Between wars he served in China and the Philippines and distinguished himself in staff and school assignments.

Promoted to brigadier general in 1940, he was named superintendent of the U.S. Military Academy. At the outbreak of WWII he commanded the 77th Division and then I Corps, when he joined **MacArthur** in Australia in August 1942 for the New Guinea Campaign. Told by MacArthur to "take Buna, or not come back alive," he took it (November 1942–January 1943), winning the first Allied victory over the Japanese. He led his I Corps through the New Guinea–New Britain campaign and then led the

Eighth Army ashore at Leyte in the Philippines (December 1944), liberating Manila (February–March 1945). After the war he was appointed commander of all the ground forces in occupied Japan. He retired in 1948.

Eichelberger was a low-key, competent, thoroughly professional soldier. He arrived in New Guinea and got the allied effort there going again. He defeated a determined enemy in the jungle and mountains with the minimum cost in lives of his own soldiers.

Epaminondas of Thebes

?425–362 B.C.

Born of a noble but impoverished family, Epaminondas kept aloof from politics in his youth, studying philosophy and music to relieve his poverty. He came to prominence as a military leader after the liberation of Thebes from Sparta in 379.

Commanding an army at Leuctra (July 371), Epaminondas faced a superior army under the Spartan general, Cleombrotus. The Spartans, who up to then had enjoyed a reputation of invincibility, drew up their conventional battle lines—phalanxes in line with a reinforced right wing. Epaminondas, however, formed his men into deep columns and personally led his left in a charge upon the Spartan right wing, refusing to commit his center or the cavalry on his flanks. The column of attack and refused flank (the first known use of these tactics) confused and overwhelmed the Spartans, who lost 2,000 men, including Cleombrotus, to the Thebans' casualties of fewer than 100. This defeat shattered the Spartan influence in Greek affairs that had obtained since their victory in the Peloponnesian War some thirty years before. At Manitea (362), Epaminondas confused his opponents through feints and false maneuvers and then attacked obliquely in column, as he did at Leuctra. Epaminondas was wounded pursuing the defeated enemy and died a short time later.

Modest and not personally ambitious, Epaminondas was a brilliant tactician whose battlefield innovations changed the nature of warfare in Greece. **Alexander the Great** studied his tactics and imitated them.

Eugène Prince of Savoy

1663–1736

Born at Paris, the fifth son of a disgraced French nobleman, Eugène was a sickly youth and ugly. Humiliated at court and refused a commission in the army of Louis XIV, Eugène took service with the Austrians in July 1683, where he distinguished himself at the Battle of Vienna (September 12, 1683) during the war between the Hapsburgs of Austria and the Ottoman empire of Turkey for the control of Hungary. By 1687 he held the rank of lieutenant general and was promoted to field marshal in 1693.

During Turkey's renewed attempt to conquer Hungary (1688–1699), Eugène was given command of the army on the Hungarian front. Having completely reorganized the army, he met the invading Turks at Zenta (September 11, 1693) and nearly wiped them out. During the War of the Spanish Succession (1701–1714), Eugène allied himself with the great English commander **Marlborough,** and at Blenheim (August 13, 1704), they combined forces to beat the French. Sent to Italy in April 1706, Eugène lifted the siege of Turin (September 7), inflicting nearly 10,000 casualties on the French. By December Eugène had swept them out of Italy. Eugène again joined Marlborough and was present at the victory of Oudenaarde in the Netherlands (July 11, 1708). He continued active in Austrian military and political affairs until his retirement in 1735.

Eugène was a genius of maneuver and surprise attack, who inspired his troops by personal example; he was a capable administrator and a faithful ally.

Richard S. Ewell

1817–1872

Born in Georgetown, District of Columbia, Ewell was commissioned a lieutenant of dragoons after graduation from West Point in 1840. He served on the frontier, was brevetted for gallantry at Contreras and Churubusco during the Mexican War, and fought Apaches in New Mexico in 1857.

Ewell resigned from the U.S. Army in May 1861 and accepted a colonelcy in the CSA. In June 1861, he was promoted to brigadier general and at First Manassas commanded the 2nd Brigade in **Beauregard's** army. In October 1861, Ewell was made a major general and given command of a division under **Jackson,** going on to distinguish himself in the Valley Campaign. Although he lost a leg in August 1862—a wound that would have incapacitated most men—Ewell returned to duty the following May and as a lieutenant general commanded Jackson's old II Corps after Chancellorsville. He was at Gettysburg, was wounded again at Kelley's Ford (November 7, 1863), and finally incapacitated when his horse fell on him at Spottsylvania Court House (May 1864). Later he commanded the defenses of Richmond and was captured at Sayler's Creek in April 1865. He died of pneumonia at Spring Hill, Tennessee, January 25, 1872.

Ewell was a colorful, profane, aggressive commander, known affectionately to his men as "Old Baldy." He has perhaps been unjustly criticized for indecision as a corps commander, but he was an indomitable fighter after the manner of Jackson and **Robert E. Lee**.

F

Alessandro Farnese

1545–1592

Born in Rome, the son of Ottavio Farnese, Duke of Parma, and Margaret of Austria, natural daughter of Emperor Charles V, Alessandro was sent to the court of Philip II of Spain at the age of eleven. At that time Philip's court was at Brussels, and Belgium and the Netherlands had been under Spanish rule for some time.

Farnese served under **John of Austria** at the Battle of Lepanto (October 1571) and later in the Netherlands, when Don John was sent there to quell an uprising in 1577. At the Battle of Gembloux (January 31, 1578), Farnese's cavalry defeated the Dutch army amid great slaughter. When Don John died in October 1578, Farnese was appointed regent of the Netherlands in his place. In May 1579, he concluded the Treaty of Arras, which removed the Catholic opposition to Philip's rule, leaving Farnese free to deal with the Union of Utrecht under the Prince of Orange. By the summer of 1585, he had pacified the southern part of the Netherlands. He might have completed the task had Philip not withdrawn 25,000 men in preparation for his disastrous invasion of England. A campaign against Henry IV of France further diverted Farnese from the Dutch, and during his absence, **Maurice of Nassau** won a series of victories against the Spanish. Farnese was fighting a difficult two-front war with some success when he died of wounds in December 1592.

Farnese was an expert field commander, administrator, and diplomat, although his troops often ran amok. He failed to conquer the Dutch only because Philip did not support him.

Elon John Farnsworth

1837–1863

Born at Green Oak, Michigan, Farnsworth was a student at the University of Michigan during the winter of 1857–1858, when he left school to join **A. S. Johnston's** expedition against the Mormons as a forage master.

At the outbreak of the Civil War, Farnsworth joined his uncle's regiment, the 8th Illinois Cavalry, where he was appointed first lieutenant, regimental adjutant, and, in December 1861, captain. Over the next two years he participated in forty-one skirmishes and was commended for gallantry. He became chief quartermaster of the IV Corps of the Army of the Potomac and then aide-de-camp to General Pleasanton. On June 28, 1863, he was promoted from captain to brigadier general of volunteers and given command of the 1st Brigade, 3rd Division, Cavalry Corps, Army of the Potomac. On July 3, 1863, his brigade held a position near Little Round Top on the left flank at Gettysburg. Ordered to charge across open, broken ground against Confederate infantry well protected behind fences and stone walls, Farnsworth protested, but Kilpatrick, his division commander, overrode him, so at the head of the 1st West Virginia Cavalry, Farnsworth attacked. He penetrated the enemy line and forced a partial Confederate withdrawal, but lost a quarter of his men and was himself hit five times and died on the field.

Farnsworth took to soldiering naturally. He was given command because of demonstrated ability and courage under fire. A good soldier to the bitter end, he died obedient to orders.

David Glasgow Farragut

1801–1870

Born James Farragut at Campbell's Station, near Knoxville, Tennessee, Farragut was adopted by then commander **David Porter** in 1810, from whom he took his first name. During the War of 1812, Farragut sailed with Porter on the *Essex*.

Farragut was promoted to commander in 1841. During the Mexican War he commanded the sloop *Saratoga* on blockade duty. In the years before the outbreak of the Civil War, Farragut earned a reputation as a naval ordnance expert. When informed by friends in April 1861 that a man of his pro-union sympathies "could not live in Norfolk," he replied, "Well, then, I can live somewhere else," and he moved to New York. Appointed to command the West Gulf Blockading Squadron in January 1862, Farragut captured New Orleans on April 24, after a daring run under the Confederate shore batteries. He received the thanks of Congress and President Lincoln for this and was promoted to rear admiral, July 30. After opening the Mississippi and running the defenses of Vicksburg, he returned to New Orleans. On the morning of August 5, 1864, his flagship leading a flotilla of eighteen vessels, Farragut steamed into Mobile Bay. Informed that mines ("torpedoes") lay ahead, he shouted, "Damn the torpedoes!" and then proceeded to disperse the Confederate fleet and capture the shore batteries. Later that year he was promoted to vice admiral and, in 1866, became the U.S. Navy's first full admiral.

David Farragut

Already in his sixties in 1861, Farragut proved his mettle in battle and earned the sobriquet "the American Nelson."

Gaston de Foix

1489–1512

A nephew of King Louis XII of France, Foix was descended from an old French noble family that flourished between the eleventh and fifteenth centuries. In 1507 he exchanged his viscountcy of Narbonne with the king for the duchy of Nemours, and as Duke of Nemours he took command of the French army in Italy, which was not making much headway against the Spanish-Neapolitan forces under **Gonzalo de Córdoba**.

During the winter of 1511, he relieved the French force besieged in the city of Bologna by leading his men on forced day and night marches through the snow, taking the Spanish and papal forces by surprise and forcing them to abandon the siege hastily. In February 1512 he marched on Brescia and took the town by storm. Foix did not tarry there but moved at once against the Spanish at Ravenna. On Easter Day, 1512, he attacked the Spanish camp. Foix's infantry, reinforced by 8,500 German mercenary pikemen, was battered by the Spanish artillery but held firm. In turn, the French artillery bombarded the Spanish trenches and Spanish discipline broke; their cavalry charged prematurely and dashed itself to pieces against the French pikemen. In the ensuing infantry battle, casualties on both sides were enormous but Foix's army prevailed. Leading a cavalry detachment against a small Spanish rear guard, Foix was killed.

Foix understood the use of maneuver and speed on the battlefield; he was courageous and daring and, had he lived, may have become one of France's greatest generals.

Andrew H. Foote

1806–1863

Born in New Haven, Connecticut, Foote was appointed an acting midshipman in December 1822. During the next thirty-nine years Foote attained a solid reputation as a naval commander.

In command of the sloop *Portsmouth* at Canton, China, in November 1856, he successfully led a contingent of sailors and marines in storming four Chinese forts—with a total of 176 guns and 5,000 defenders—in retaliation for attacks against American ships. A deeply religious man, Foote was chiefly responsible for abolishing the grog ration in the U.S. Navy. During the Civil War he commanded the naval force operating on the upper Mississippi, where he was under the orders of Brigadier General **U. S. Grant** during the Henry and Donelson campaign in February 1862. Foote's small flotilla, assembled despite incredible difficulties, actually pounded Fort Henry into submission before the army arrived on the scene, but Foote worked well with the army, and the capture of Fort Donelson, February 14, 1862, was a smoothly coordinated land-riverine operation. At Island No. 10, in April 1862, he ordered two gunboats to run the batteries, hastening the position's surrender, April 7. In ill health and still suffering from wounds received at Fort Donelson, Foote turned over his command in May. Promoted to rear admiral, July 16, 1862, he spent that winter on shore duty. He was on his way to assume command at Charleston when he died, June 26, 1863.

Energetic, confident, and determined if somewhat vain, Foote always saw his duty clearly, especially if it involved fighting.

Nathan Bedford Forrest

1821–1877

Born near Chapel Hill, Tennessee, Forrest made a fortune farming, trading horses and cattle, and dealing in slaves. Denied formal education, he taught himself to read and write.

At the outbreak of the Civil War, Forrest enlisted in the 7th Tennessee Cavalry, CSA, as a private, but since he was able to raise and equip his own cavalry regiment, he was commissioned a lieutenant colonel in August 1861. At Fort Donelson in February 1862, he refused to surrender and escaped with his entire command. A full colonel at Shiloh, April 6–7, 1862, he was wounded. Promoted to brigadier general in July 1862, he was given a brigade under Braxton Bragg; he began a series of daring raids and sorties and earned a reputation as a brilliant cavalry commander. Shot by a disgruntled subordinate in June 1863, Forrest held the man with one hand, drew a penknife with the other, opened its blade with his teeth, and stabbed his assailant to death. Forrest's exploits during the Atlanta Campaign caused **Sherman** to refer to him as "that devil Forrest." His handling of the rear guard after the Army of the Tennessee's defeat at Nashville (December 1864) further enhanced his reputation, but the massacre of Negro troops at Fort Pillow the previous April has since stained his memory. After the war he helped found the Ku Klux Klan.

Nathan Bedford Forrest

Free Library of Philadelphia

Forrest was a man "born" to fight and this might account for his brutality, but he was without peer in either army because he followed this simple maxim: "Get there first with the most."

Frederick I ("Barbarossa")

1123–1190

The eldest son of Frederick II of Hohenstaufen, Frederick, as the young Duke of Swabia, participated in the Second Crusade (1147–1149). Upon the death in 1152 of his uncle Conrad, he was elected emperor and crowned at Aachen.

As emperor, Frederick secured peace at home by conciliating his nobles and obtaining alliances through marriage—his own to Beatrice of Burgundy in 1156 and his son's to Constance, heir apparent to the kingdom of Sicily in 1189—and diplomacy. In 1154, ostensibly at the invitation of Pope Adrian IV, Frederick marched into Italy and executed Arnold of Brescia, a religious reformer who had seized power at Rome. Unwilling to submit in any way to papal authority, in 1158 Frederick was back in Italy, this time at the head of a huge army ready to challenge the pope. Between 1154 and 1183 he conducted six expeditions to Italy. In 1162 he captured and razed Milan, and in 1166 he stormed Rome. On May 29, 1176, at Legnano, near Milan, Frederick was defeated by the Lombard League when he attempted to fight with unsupported cavalry. His horsemen were repulsed by the Italian infantry and then crushed by the counterattacking Lombard cavalry. Frederick made peace with Pope Alexander III in 1177. During his Italian campaigns he gained his nickname, "Barbarossa," after his red beard. On June 10, 1190, on his way to the Third Crusade, he drowned while crossing the Goksu River in southern Turkey.

Frederick was a brave and determined soldier and a tireless campaigner who wisely came to terms with his Italian ambitions.

Frederick II ["The Great"]

1712–1786

The son of Frederick William I of Prussia and Princess Sophie Dorothea of Hanover, Frederick II was born in Berlin. He was a rebellious youth who preferred to be a dilettante instead of a soldier like his father. When at eighteen he was caught trying to flee to England, his companion was executed and Frederick was imprisoned for six months, until he asked his father for a pardon.

Given command of a regiment in 1732, Frederick studied hard to be a soldier, and when he became king upon his father's death in 1740, he inherited an army of 80,000 men. One of his first acts as king was to seize Silesia from Austria, launching the First Silesian War (1740–1741). After very nearly being defeated at Mollwitz (April 10, 1741), Frederick realized the need for army reforms. During the War of the Austrian Succession (1740–1748) Frederick first fought Austria, then withdrew, but reentered to prevent Austria from defeating Bavaria and France. During the Seven Years War (1756–1763) he took on Austria, France, Russia, and Saxony. Greatly outnumbered, Frederick kept the allies at bay with a series of lightning-quick campaigns that prevented their armies from uniting. But by 1762, exhausted and on the defensive, Frederick was saved from total defeat by Russia's withdrawal, and at the Treaty of Hubertusburg in January 1763, he was able to guarantee his borders. Frederick died in bed on August 17, 1786.

Known as "Old Fritz" (*Der Alte Fritz*), Frederick was sometimes overconfident and careless of strategy, but when he was in form, he was a master of the eighteenth-century battlefield, consistently defeating armies much larger than his own. He distilled what he had learned about soldiering in his *Instructions,* published in 1747, which may still be read with advantage by today's would be commanders.

Bernard Freyberg

1889–1963

Born in London but raised in New Zealand, Freyberg joined the New Zealand Army in 1909. In 1914, he joined Pancho Villa in Mexico but returned to New Zealand to participate in WWI, where he was promoted to brigadier general at age twenty-seven, earning the Victoria Cross on the Western Front in 1917, ending the war commanding the 29th Division.

In 1939 Freyberg was appointed to command the New Zealand forces abroad. Forced to withdraw from Crete (May 1941), he inflicted heavy losses on the Germans and got off with most of his men. Fighting **Rommel** in Libya and Egypt, he was severely wounded at Mersa Matrūh. He returned to duty in time to lead his men in **Montgomery's** breakout at El Alamein (October–November 1942). Freyberg commanded the New Zealand division during the Winter Line Campaign in Italy (November–December 1943). As a corps commander at Monte Cassino, he ordered the bombing of the ancient Benedictine monastery because he believed it was a German observation post. He led the final push on Trieste, which he entered on May 2, 1945. Appointed governor general of New Zealand in 1946, he was made a baron in 1951, and deputy constable and lieutenant governor of Windsor Castle in 1953, where he died, July 4, 1963.

Freyberg was wounded in action a total of thirty times during the First and Second World Wars. Personally fearless, he instilled the "spirit of the bayonet"—a weapon he admired—in his men.

Louis de Buade, Comte de Frontenac

1622–1698

Born at Saint-Germain-en-Laye, France, the son of a distinguished military family, Frontenac entered the army at an early age and served with distinction in Holland and Italy. Promoted to colonel of the regiment of Normandy in 1643, in 1646 he was promoted to the equivalent of brigadier general for service at the siege of Orbetello in Tuscany, where he was wounded.

Appointed governor of New France, Frontenac arrived in Quebec in September 1672. Almost from the beginning, Frontenac quarreled with everyone in New France, particularly the clergy, who wanted to subordinate the state to the church. These frictions led to his recall in 1682, but during his tenure as governor, he strengthened the colony's defenses and maintained peace with the Indians, principally by dealing diplomatically with the Iroquois Confederacy. Recalled in 1689 to deal with the worsening crisis in relations with the Iroquois, in October 1690, he successfully marshaled the colony's forces to repel an English invasion under the command of Sir William Phipps, who sailed away without giving battle. In July 1696, at the age of seventy-four, he personally took the field against the Iroquois. He laid waste to the land of the Onondagas and soon the Indians sued for peace. He died at Quebec, November 28, 1698.

Fearless and decisive, Frontenac was also an autocrat who understood neither politics nor economics, but he successfully defended New France against the Indians and the English, the major threats to the colony's existence.

Mitsuo Fuchida

1902–1976

Born in Japan's Nara Prefecture, Fuchida graduated from the Japanese Naval Academy in 1924, after which he was trained as a naval aviator.

Fuchida served aboard the carrier *Kaga* in 1929. He gained combat experience as a pilot in China before attending the Japanese naval staff college in 1938. In August 1941 he became flight officer onboard the carrier *Akagi,* flagship of the First Carrier Strike Force, where he was given the responsibility for training the flight crews for the Japanese attack on Pearl Harbor. Fuchida personally led the first wave of attack planes against Pearl Harbor on December 7, 1941, and it was he who transmitted the famous message, *Tora, Tora, Tora* ("Tiger, Tiger, Tiger") that signaled the fact that the surprise attack on the U.S. Pacific Fleet was a success. Fuchida remained over Pearl Harbor after his flight departed to observe the effects of the bombing, and upon his return to the *Akagi,* he urged Vice Admiral Nagumo, strikeforce commander, to launch a second strike, which he refused to do. Later Fuchida commanded air attacks in fighting in the Dutch East Indies, was wounded at Midway when the *Akagi* was sunk in action, June 4, 1942, and was a fleet staff officer at the Battle of the Marianas in June 1944, ending the war a captain. After the war he traveled often to the U.S. and Canada.

Fuchida was a dedicated and fearless professional who, ironically, having led the raid that brought the U.S. into WWII, died an American citizen.

Frederick Funston

1865–1917

Born in New Carlisle, Ohio, the son of a Civil War veteran and Ohio politician, Edward ("Fog Horn") Funston, Frederick was a rover and adventurer as a young man, wandering from Alaska to the Gulf of Mexico. During the Cuban Insurrection (1895–1898) he fought as a volunteer against Spain.

At the outbreak of the Spanish-American War he was offered command of the 20th Kansas, which was deployed to the Philippines, where, at the Battle of Calumpit on April 27, 1899, he won the Medal of Honor and promotion to brigadier general of volunteers. Commanding the Fourth District of Luzon, he carried out a successful counterguerrilla war. In March 1901 he received intelligence of the whereabouts of the *insurrecto* leader, Emilio Aguinaldo. Pretending to be a prisoner of loyal Filipino scouts posing as recruits for Aguinaldo's forces, Funston penetrated his camp and captured the guerrilla leader, effectively ending the insurrection. For this he was commissioned a brigadier general in the regular army. In temporary command of the Department of California, he rendered major assistance to the civil authorities after the San Francisco Earthquake of 1906. Promoted to major general in 1914, he commanded troops at Vera Cruz, and in 1916 commanded the forces sent to pursue Pancho Villa in Mexico. He died of a heart attack at San Antonio, Texas, February 19, 1917.

A colorful figure but capable, vigorous, and resourceful, Funston was destined for very high command when his life was cut short.

G

Adolf Galland

1912–

Born at Westerhold near Wilhelmshaven, Germany, Galland learned to fly gliders in the 1920s, attended airline pilots' school in 1932, and joined the Luftwaffe in 1934.

During Germany's intervention in Spain, 1937–1938, Galland flew over 300 combat missions with the Condor Legion. During the Battle of Britain he was credited with 103 aerial victories while commanding Fighter Group (*Jagdsgruppe*) 26. In November 1941 he became head of the Luftwaffe Fighter Arm and Germany's youngest general. In this position he constantly argued for better equipment, always taking the side of the fighter pilots and representing their interests in his councils with the high command. He was a strong advocate for development of the jet fighter. His aggressive, outspoken style led to confrontations with his superiors, especially Reichsmarshall Hermann Göring, head of the Luftwaffe. Göring relieved him of command in January 1945 but let him go back to flying fighters. In command of an Me-262 jet-powered fighter squadron, he was shot down over Munich, April 26, 1945 and captured. After the war he went to Argentina, where he advised that country's air force and later served as a consultant to various German aerospace companies.

One of Germany's top aces, Galland was a superb pilot and an excellent aerial combat tactician. A poor administrator and politician, he worked hard to improve Germany's fighter force. Once asked by Göring what he needed, Galland replied, "Spitfires."

Roy S. Geiger

1885–1947

Born in Middleburg, Florida, the youngest of four sons in a family of seven children, Geiger worked his way through school, earning a law degree in 1907. That same year he joined the marines and spent fifteen months as an enlisted man before obtaining a commission in 1909.

After service in the Caribbean, the Philippines, and China, Geiger volunteered for pilot training in 1916 and was the fifth marine ever to win pilot's wings. During World War I he commanded a squadron in the 1st Marine Aviation Force, and during October and November 1918 he led fourteen combat missions over France, earning the Navy Cross. After graduating from the Navy War College in 1941, he was promoted to brigadier general and assigned to command the 1st Marine Air Wing, Fleet Marine Force, which he led in combat from Henderson Field on Guadalcanal. As a major general he led the I Marine Amphibious Corps (later redesignated III Corps) in the invasion of Guam, at Peleliu Island, and at Okinawa. When General Buckner, commander of the Tenth Army, was killed, Geiger, as his deputy, took over, the only marine officer ever to command a field army, albeit for only five days, until **Stillwell** relieved him. He fell ill in November 1946 and died the following January.

An aviator and an infantryman, Geiger was a self-confident, aggressive, and personally fearless commander who led his men with distinction through some of the fiercest fighting in the Pacific Theater in WWII.

Genghis Khan

1167–1227

Born Temu-jin, eldest son of Yekusai the Strong of the Kiut clan of the Borjigin Monguls in what is today the Mongolian People's Republic, Genghis Khan spent his early years in a precarious state of exile after his father was killed by Tatars and the family was refused support by their clan.

Still in his teens Temu-jin assembled a small band of warriors, and over the next thirty years, through raiding, negotiation, alliances, and treachery, he built an empire consisting of over thirty tribes, which by 1250 his sons and grandsons had extended from Poland to Korea, from Siberia to Vietnam, and included such capitals as Kiev, Moscow, Baghdad, and Peking. In 1204 he proclaimed himself Genghis Khan, or supreme emperor. His army consisted of cavalry organized into divisions of 10,000 men, subdivided into regiments and companies, down to squads of 10 men. Each man had a spare pony and carried only the equipment he would need to maintain himself and his horse in the field. About half his army was "heavy" cavalry whose main weapon was the lance; the remainder were archers who also carried light javelins. These men were not a massive horde of screaming brigands, but a highly mobile, disciplined, and superbly trained military organization well led by reliable generals who could act independently but who adhered to the Khan's overall strategy. To reduce fortifications, the Mongols carried siege weapons on packhorses, and when engineering skills were required, they were supplied by local experts. The khan developed an excellent intelligence organization, and by using feints and diversions and lightning maneuver, he kept the size of his own force hidden. His enemies often thought they were vastly outnumbered by the Mongol armies when just the opposite was the case. It is estimated that the largest Mongol army the khan ever deployed, when he invaded Persia, was only 240,000 strong. In 1219, at the Battle of Jand in Russian Turkistan, his sons, with only 30,000 men, fought an army of 200,000 to a draw. The Mongols let nothing stand in their path, took no prisoners, and were utterly ruthless to conquered peoples. In 1227, on campaign in China, he fell ill and died in August of that year.

Genghis Khan was one of the most remarkable conquerors in history. He effectively organized his nomadic people into a highly disciplined, superbly coordinated mobile force that was not seen again in history until the blitzkrieg of mechanized spearheads employed during World War II.

Geronimo (Goyathlay or Goyakla)

1829–1909

Born in No-doyohn Canyon near present-day Clifton, Arizona, Geronimo was the son of Taklishim, "the gray one," and a mother known as Juana. Although born into the Nednis tribe, Geronimo became the most famous warrior of the Chiricahua Apaches. The name by which we know him is from the Spanish for Jerome, but his Apache name means "one who yawns."

After his mother, wife, and children were murdered in 1858 by Mexican bounty hunters looking for scalps, Geronimo swore revenge, and over the next fifteen years of reprisal raids, he gained a solid reputation for leadership. Forced onto the San Carlos Reservation in 1876, Geronimo took up farming, and intermittent raiding. But in May 1885, fed up with being cheated on rations and reservation rules infringing tribal customs, Geronimo fled with a band of renegades. He surrendered in March 1886, but before he could be transported to Florida, he escaped with fewer than 40 warriors and about 100 dependents. During the next four months his band eluded capture by a pursuing force of 5,000 soldiers. He finally surrendered on September 4, 1886. Confined in various places, in 1894 he was interned at Fort Sill, Oklahoma, where on February 17, 1909, he died in the post dispensary, of pneumonia.

Although he became an object of curiosity in his later years, "displayed" at various fairs and expositions, in his prime Geronimo was a much-feared master of guerrilla warfare in which he displayed great courage, endurance, and intelligence.

Vo Nguyen Giap

1912–

Giap was born in An Xe Village, Quang Binh Province near the 17th Parallel in the northern part of what is now the Socialist Republic of Vietnam. Son of an impoverished mandarin of the second class, Giap's early education was obtained at the Lycée National in Hue, where, despite the strong anticolonial disposition of his father, French became his second language; later he studied law in Hanoi, where subsequently he taught history at Thanh Long School. Giap was an assiduous student of **Napoleon's** campaigns.

Giap's nationalism turned to communism and in 1930 he became a founding member of the Indochinese Communist party. In 1939 he fled to China, where with Ho Chi Minh, he helped organize the Vietnamese Independence League (Viet Minh). In 1944 he returned to Vietnam, where he directed a guerrilla war against the Japanese, becoming defense minister in the government formed by Ho in 1945. He led the Viet Minh during the subsequent war against the French, at first with some notable successes, but overestimating his capabilities during the Red River Campaign of 1950–1951, he was badly defeated. Learning a lesson, Giap then reverted to a strategy of small-scale operations, denying the French forces setpiece battles where they could bring their superior firepower to bear. This culminated in a decisive victory at the siege at Dien Bien Phu, November 1953–May 1954, which in effect ended the war. After the 1954 partition of Vietnam, he directed the reunification war against the Republic of South Vietnam and the United States. After the Chinese cross-border attack in 1979, for which

Giap's purported unpreparedness was criticized, he gradually fell out of favor. Today he is in semiretirement, occupying essentially insignificant honorary government positions.

Giap's campaign against the French, particularly his victory at Dien Bien Phu, reflects one of the most brilliant military careers in modern Asian history. With no military training himself, he led the Vietnamese communist forces to victory over two modern Western armies, one on the battlefield, the other by default.

John Gibbon

1827–1896

Born in Holmsburg, then a suburb of Philadelphia, Gibbon grew up in North Carolina and was commissioned in the artillery upon graduation from West Point in 1847.

Gibbon arrived in Mexico too late to see any action in that war, but he fought Indians in Florida in 1849. At the outbreak of the Civil War, he stayed with the Union although three of his brothers served the Confederacy. Appointed a brigadier general of volunteers in May 1862, he commanded the famed Iron Brigade at Second Manassas (Bull Run) in August and Sharpsburg (Antietam) in September. Commanding a division at Fredericksburg (December), he was severely wounded, but he recovered in time to get wounded again at Gettysburg, where his division bore the brunt of **Pickett's** Charge (July 1863).

He commanded a division of the Army of the Potomac at the Wilderness and Spotsylvania (May 1864), Cold Harbor and Petersburg (June 1864). Promoted to major general in June 1864, he ended the war commanding a corps of the Army of the James. Gibbon stayed in the army after the war. In 1876 he commanded the expedition that rescued the survivors of the **Custer** massacre on the Little Big Horn, and in 1877 he fought the Nez Percé Indians under **Chief Joseph,** whom he afterward befriended. Promoted to brigadier general in the regular army in 1885, Gibbon retired in 1891.

John Gibbon was a courageous, tough, and tenacious commander who led by personal example.

Charles George Gordon

1833–1885

Born at Woolwich, England, the fourth son of a lieutenant general in the Royal Army, Gordon was commissioned as an engineer upon his graduation from the Royal Military Academy in 1852.

Gordon saw action in the Crimean War in 1854, where he was wounded and decorated with the French Legion of Honor. Promoted to captain in 1859 and sent to China in 1860, he distinguished himself in operations against the Taiping rebels. In 1863 he entered the service of the governor general of Kiang Province, where he took a force of 4,000 disorganized Chinese and molded it into an army that defeated the Taiping rebels. His China service earned him the name "Chinese Gordon." After doing engineering work in England, Gordon went to Africa in 1874. Between 1877 and 1880 he was governor general in the Sudan, where he ended the slave trade; reappointed in 1884, he was given the task of withdrawing the garrison at Khartoum, which was threatened by a Mahdist revolt. Besieged there in March 1884, Gordon defended with minefields, barbed wire, frequent sorties, and "iron-clad" gunboats made out of converted river steamers. He held out until January 26, 1885, when the garrison fell and he was beheaded.

Even without his stand at Khartoum, Gordon's military career would still have been remarkable. He proved his leadership, organizational, and administrative abilities in China, but his 317-day resistance against tremendous odds at Khartoum assured him immortality in the annals of military heroes.

John Brown Gordon

1832–1904

Born in Upson County, Georgia, Gordon attended the University of Georgia but failed to graduate with the Class of 1853. He studied law, was admitted to the Georgia bar, and practiced for a short time in Atlanta. In 1861 he was trying to develop coal mines in the far northwestern reaches of the state.

At the outbreak of the Civil War, Gordon was elected captain of a company of mountaineers called the "Raccoon Roughs," which was accepted into the service as Company I, 6th Alabama. He was colonel of the 6th Alabama at Seven Pines (May 31–June 1, 1862) and of a brigade at Malvern Hill (July 1862). He fought at Sharpsburg (Antietam; September 1862) and was promoted to brigadier general in November. He commanded a brigade at Chancellorsville (May 1863), Gettysburg (July 1863) and in the Wilderness (May 1864), and a division at Spotsylvania (May 8–18, 1864). As a major general in June 1864, he was with Early in the Shenandoah Valley, the raid on Washington, Winchester (September 19, 1864), and Cedar Creek (October 19, 1864). A lieutenant general commanding the II Corps of the Army of Northern Virginia, he surrendered with **R. E. Lee** at Appomattox. Gordon was wounded eight times during the war. After the war he resumed his law practice and entered politics. He was elected to the U.S. Senate in 1873, and governor of Georgia in 1886. Fort Gordon, Georgia, is named in his honor.

With no previous military experience, Gordon proved himself a valiant and capable soldier on the battlefields of the Civil War.

James Graham

1612–1650

Graham was born in Scotland, son of the 4th Earl of Montrose. He became the 5th Earl of Montrose upon the death of his father in November 1626.

A signer of the National Covenant in 1638 that opposed the extension of English Anglicanism into Scotland, Montrose suppressed the anti-Covenanters, which he did mostly through negotiation and conciliation. Although cool toward Charles I initially, Montrose joined him in the First English Civil War (1642–1646) and the king appointed him a marquess and lieutenant general for Scotland in February 1644. With 2,000 men he captured Dumfries in April but was forced out by a larger army. In August he defeated an invading force from Ireland near Blair

Atholl, and in September, with 3,000 men, defeated an army of 7,000 at Tibbermore. Between September 13, 1644, and August 15, 1645, he won five pitched battles, four against armies that outnumbered his. But his strength much reduced by desertion, he was defeated and nearly captured in September 1645, and took to guerrilla warfare. He surrendered in May 1646 and went to Norway in September. Montrose returned to Scotland in March 1650, where, failing to raise the clans for Charles II, he was defeated at Carbiesdale, April 27. When Charles refused to intercede for him, he was hanged at Edinburgh, May 21.

Constantly outnumbered, Montrose fought a brilliant campaign in Scotland, winning most of the country for Charles I before diminished numbers and betrayal defeated him.

Ulysses Simpson Grant

1822–1885

Born Hiram Ulysses at Point Pleasant, Ohio, Grant grew up at Georgetown, Ohio, where he worked in his father's tannery. Upon being accepted at the U.S. Military Academy in 1839, he discovered that his name had been erroneously listed as "Ulysses Simpson" and, unable to get it changed, accepted that as his name for the rest of his life.

Commissioned in the infantry upon graduation, Grant served first in Gen. **Zachary Taylor**'s and later **Winfield Scott**'s armies during the Mexican War, distinguishing himself several times for bravery under fire. He emerged from the war a brevet captain of infantry. Promoted to captain in the regular army in 1853, Grant was transferred to duty in California, where, lonely, separated from his family, with little to do, he became disillusioned with the army and resigned his commission in 1854. For the next six years he tried farming, worked as a real-estate agent, a customs clerk, and finally as a clerk in his father's leather-goods store—all with notable lack of success. When Fort Sumter was fired on, Grant offered his sword to the Union and was appointed colonel of the 21st Illinois in June, and promoted to brigadier general in August 1861. In February 1862, with about 17,000 men, Grant captured first the Confederate positions at Fort Henry on the Tennessee River, and then Fort Donelson on the Cumberland, giving the Union control on those rivers and winning him promotion to major general. At Shiloh, April 6–7, 1862, Grant's army drove off the Confederates under **A. S. Johnston,** but it was a close call and casualties on both sides were heavy. In April 1863, Grant initiated a bold and imaginative plan to take Vicksburg, which he did, July 4, 1863, thus cutting the Confederacy in two. In November he broke the Confederate hold on Chattanooga. Appointed lieutenant general in March 1864, Grant initiated a series of bloody battles—Wilderness, Spotsylvania Court House, Cold Harbor, Petersburg—that ended in the surrender of **Lee's** army at Appomattox in April 1865. Grant was promoted to full general in July 1866. Elected president in 1869, he served two terms in office, but he was a better general than a president.

U.S. Grant was a great general because he knew that to win in war one has to fight, and that's what he did, dry-eyed and tenaciously. In this he emulated the greatest captains of history. Plagued by rumors of drunkenness during the war and criticized for the terrible casualties his army took in Virginia, Grant was a bold and brilliant tactician when circumstances permitted and a ferocious bulldog when they didn't. Personally modest and unassuming, Grant was a magnanimous victor who left his country two enduring monuments: a reunited Union and his *Personal Memoirs,* which he finished on his deathbed.

François-Joseph-Paul De Grasse

1722–1788

Born at Bar in the French Maritime Alps in 1722, De Grasse was descended from an old French noble family. He attended the naval school of Toulon in 1733, entering the navy of the Knights of Malta in 1734.

De Grasse entered the French service at the outbreak of the War of the Austrian Succession in 1740. He was captured at the Battle of Cape Finisterre in May 1747 and interned. Before the French alliance with the fledgling United States in 1778, De Grasse served off India, in the Caribbean, and Mediterranean; he was promoted to commodore in June 1778. Promoted to rear admiral in January 1781, he commanded a squadron of twenty ships-of-the-line, three frigates, and 150 troop transports sent to the Caribbean, where, during April–August 1781, he was victorious over British Admiral Samuel Hood. He arrived off Yorktown on August 30, 1781, to support the armies of **Washington, Rochambeau,** and **Lafayette,** maneuvering against the British general Cornwallis. At the battle of the Virginia Capes, September 5–9, 1781, he drove off the British fleet, thus sealing the fate of the British army at Yorktown. Back in the West Indies, De Grasse captured St. Kitts and defended it against British. Captured at Martinique on April 12, 1782, De Grasse fell briefly out of royal favor. After the French Revolution his children settled in the U.S.

De Grasse was a capable naval commander who worked well with allies. His success against the British fleet sent to relieve Cornwallis was a decisive event in the American Revolution.

William S. Graves

1865–1940

Born in Mount Calm, Texas, the son of a Baptist minister and rancher who had been a colonel in the Confederate Army, Graves was commissioned in the infantry upon graduation from West Point in 1889.

Graves missed field service during the Spanish American War, but as a captain commanding a company of the 20th Infantry in the Philippines, he was cited for gallantry in action against the *insurrectos*. Promoted to major general in June 1918, Graves was given command of the 8th Division, which was training for service in France. In August 1918 he was given command of the 10,000-man American Expeditionary Force being sent to Siberia to protect Allied supplies along the Trans-Siberian Railway and to aid a Czech army that had deserted the Austrians. He arrived at Vladivostok in September. Before he left, the secretary of war told him: "You will be walking on eggs loaded with dynamite. God bless you and good-bye." President Wilson forbade Graves from interfering in Russian domestic affairs, so he kept American soldiers out of the fight against the Bolsheviks, for which he was severely criticized by the Allies, the U.S. State Department, and the American press. He would not be intimidated, even refusing orders to deliver arms to the White Russians because he feared they would be used against his own men.

A man of solid integrity and high personal standards of conduct, Graves refused to give in to pressure and stood by his orders, avoiding a potentially disastrous foreign involvement.

Nathanael Greene

1742–1786

Born in Potowomut, Rhode Island, Greene worked in his father's iron foundry as a young man. He served in the RI General Assembly in 1770, 1771, 1772, and 1775.

Appointed a brigadier general of RI Militia in 1775, he participated in the siege of Boston. He commanded the left wing of **Washington's** army in the attack on the Hessians at Trenton on December 26, 1776. He distinguished himself as a division commander at the battles of Princeton (January 1777), Brandywine (September), and Germantown (October). Appointed quarter-master general in February 1778, Greene nevertheless led the right column at the Battle of Monmouth in June and fought at Newport in August. Although he performed his duties as QMG with great efficiency, Greene resigned in August 1780 over what he saw as congressional interference. In October. Washington gave him command in the south, and except for Charleston, within a year he had forced the British out of the Carolinas and Georgia. Although technically defeated at the battles of Guilford Court House (March 1781), Hobkirk's Hill (April), and Eutaw Springs (September), it was the British who called for reinforcements while Greene harassed them with a skillful guerrilla campaign. In retreating into Virginia, the British fell into the trap at Yorktown, which led to the end of the war.

An efficient administrator and a man of great personal courage, Greene's Carolina Campaign was a strategic success that contributed to Great Britain's defeat.

Benjamin Henry Grierson

1826–1911

Born in Pittsburgh, Grierson was educated in Ohio and taught music before entering business in Illinois.

In 1861 he enlisted in the Union Army and in October was commissioned major in the 6th Illinois Cavalry and promoted to colonel in April 1862. He was given command of a cavalry brigade after distinguishing himself pursuing Confederate raiders in Mississippi. On April 17, 1862, on the orders of General **Grant,** he commenced what has become known as "Grierson's Raid." To divert enemy attention from his plan to move against Vicksburg, Grant wanted to send a mounted force deep into Confederate territory to cause as much damage and confusion as possible. With 1,700 men, Grierson departed La Grange, Tennessee, and for the next sixteen days spread havoc behind Confederate lines, covering 600 miles and coming out with most of his command intact at Baton Rouge, May 2, 1863. For this feat he was commissioned a brigadier general of volunteers in June. He served with distinction throughout the rest of the war, winding up a major general in commanding 4,000 cavalrymen in the Military Division of West Mississippi. After the war Grierson stayed in the army, commanding the 10th Cavalry on the frontier for many years, rising to brigadier general of regulars in 1890.

With no previous military experience or training, Grierson became one of the finest Union cavalrymen of the Civil War and went on to earn a solid reputation as a commander in the post-war west.

Heinz Guderian

1888–1954

Born in Poland, the son of a Prussian army officer, Guderian was commissioned in the infantry upon graduation from the Gross Lichterfelde Military School in 1907.

Guderian served in staff positions during World War I and afterward stayed in the much-reduced postwar army, serving in signal, transportation, and staff assignments. Early in his career Guderian realized the necessity for tank forces supported by mobile infantry and artillery units, and in the 1930s he became a leading exponent of mechanized warfare, maintaining that armored forces should be used as spearheads to penetrate deeply into enemy lines. He distilled these theories in his book, *Achtung! Panzer,* published in 1937. Hitler was receptive to Guderian's ideas. He commanded the XVI Corps of three tank divisions during the Austrian annexation in March 1938, and the XIX Panzer Corps during the Polish campaign in 1939. His corps spearheaded the invasion of France in 1940. Guderian commanded the 2nd Panzer Group, Army Group Center, during the invasion of Russia. Stalled before Moscow as the winter of 1941 closed in, Guderian repeatedly asked permission to withdraw, and when he did so against Hitler's orders, he was relieved, December 25, 1941. He was reinstated in 1943 and when next dismissed by Hitler, in March 1945, was army chief of staff.

Guderian was blunt and outspoken soldier who led from the turret of his tank. That he dared to stand up to Hitler says much for his moral courage.

H

Douglas Haig, Field Marshal, 1st Earl of Bemersyde

1861–1928

Born in Edinburgh and educated at Oxford before entering the Royal Military Academy, he graduated first in his class at Sandhurst in 1885.

Haig saw service in South Africa during the Boer War, ending the war as a colonel. He was promoted to lieutenant general in 1910. In 1914, as a full general, he commanded the I Corps as part of the British Expeditionary Force sent into France, where he fought at Mons (August) and the Marne (September). He became British commander in chief in December 1915 and he planned and executed the British Somme Offensives, June–November 1916, which relieved pressure on the French at Verdun, which it was supposed to do, but resulted in terrible British casualties. Promoted to field marshal in 1916, Haig was by now stuck in a bloody war of attrition. Although he anticipated the German offensive of 1918, he was denied the reinforcements he requested, which nearly led to defeat March 21–April 5. He stopped **Ludendorff's** attack at Lys, April 9–17, mounted a successful counterattack at Amiens in August, and directed the final Allied offensives in Flanders. After the war he devoted himself to improving the welfare of veterans.

Haig has an undeserved reputation as an incompetent and heartless commander, but he was a dedicated and determined soldier who could keep his head in a crisis, and between August and November 1918, he defeated the main forces of the German army in Flanders.

William F. Halsey, Jr.

1882–1959

Born in Elizabeth, New Jersey, the son of a navy captain, Halsey graduated from the U.S. Naval Academy in 1900.

During World War I Halsey commanded destroyers operating out of Ireland against the German fleet. For this wartime service he was awarded the Navy Cross. In 1935, at the age of fifty-one, he qualified as a pilot and later commanded the carrier *Saratoga*. On December 7, 1941, when the Japanese attacked Pearl Harbor, Halsey, now a real admiral, was in command of a carrier force 150 miles west of Oahu. His first WWII combat action came when his carrier task force struck the Japanese in the Marshall Islands. He then carried Colonel **James Doolittle's** bomber force to within striking distance of Japan. During the Guadalcanal Campaign (November 1942) he maintained the naval initiative against the Japanese, telling his carriers, "Attack—repeat—attack." As commander of the South Pacific Force, he pursued a strategy of bypassing enemy strong points while moving his own forces closer to Japan. Halsey has been criticized for leaving the Leyte beachhead exposed during the Philippine invasion as he chased some Japanese carriers, but he justified this based on his estimate that the approaching enemy task force had been too badly hurt by his planes to do much damage. He was promoted to five-star rank in December 1945.

Nicknamed "Bull," Halsey was an aggressive commander who took calculated risks with the enemy and the weather, but his mobile, fast-attack tactics sank enemy ships.

Wade Hampton, III

1818–1902

Born in Charleston, South Carolina, the eldest son of a great South Carolina landlord, Hampton was living the life of a prosperous planter and politician when the Civil War broke out.

Although Hampton opposed secession and doubted the economic viability of slavery, he offered his cotton for sale in Europe to buy arms for the Confederacy and raised his own unit, the Hampton Legion, partly at his personal expense. Wounded at First Manassas (Bull Run) and Seven Pines, Hampton was appointed brigadier general in May 1862 and in July was given command of the 1st Brigade of Cavalry, Army of Northern Virginia. He was under **J.E.B. Stuart's** command at Gettysburg, where he was wounded a third time. Appointed major general in August 1863, he took command of **R. E. Lee's** cavalry upon Stuart's death in 1864. Hampton was or-

dered to cover **Joe Johnston's** retreat in South Carolina in 1865. When Johnston surrendered, Hampton wanted to join President Jefferson Davis and continue resistance in Texas, but Johnston insisted his command was not free to go, so Hampton followed Davis alone. Unable to overtake Davis, he returned to South Carolina. After the war Hampton supported President Johnson's reconstruction plan and advocated civil rights for the freed slaves.

Like many men of his class, Hampton was an expert horseman and hunter, which inclined him to duty in the cavalry arm, and he soon learned on the battlefield the military skills required for high command. A man of imposing physical presence, he was a brave and resourceful commander.

Winfield Scott Hancock

1824–1886

Born in Pennsylvania, Hancock graduated eighteenth in the West Point class of 1844 that also included such future luminaries as **Thomas Jackson** and **Longstreet**.

After service in Texas, Hancock won brevets for valor in Mexico at Contreras and Churubusco; he also fought at Molino del Rey and Chapultepec. Made a brigadier general of volunteers in September 1861, he led a brigade

on the peninsula and at South Mountain; at Sharpsburg (Antietam) he became a division commander in the II Corps and was promoted to major general in November 1862. He fought with distinction at Fredericksburg and was promoted to command of the II Corps after Chancellorsville. It was Hancock's corps that held the center of **Meade's** line at Gettysburg on the final day of the battle, repulsing **Pickett's** Charge. For this, in 1866 he received the thanks of Congress. He was also seriously wounded in this action, but returned to duty in time to lead his corps at the Wilderness, Spotsylvania Court House, Cold Harbor, and Petersburg in 1864. Recalled to Washington in August 1864, he ended the war in command of the defenses of Washington. He stayed in the army after the war, fighting Indians in Kansas. After running for president and losing to Garfield in 1880, he returned to active duty.

Hancock was one of the finest field commanders of the Union Army, the "most conspicuous" of them all, according to **Grant**.

Hannibal

247–183 B.C.

Eldest son of Hamilcar Barca, as a youngster Hannibal served with the Carthaginian army in Spain. Upon the death of his father, Hasdrubal, Hannibal's brother-in-law, succeeded to command, and when he was assassinated in 221 B.C., Hannibal, at the age of twenty-six, was elected to command.

In 219 B.C. Hannibal laid siege to and then captured the city of Sagunto, near Valencia in modern Spain. The Romans, who were allies of Sagunto, protested and demanded that Carthage hand Hannibal over to them. They refused and Rome declared war. Hannibal took the offensive, and with an army of about 40,000 men and 38 war elephants, crossed the Pyrenees and, in October 218, crossed the Alps into Italy. About half his men and most of his elephants perished in the crossing. In December Hannibal's army defeated the Romans at the Ticino River and at the Trebbia, giving him control over the Po Valley. Reinforced by tribesmen from Gaul, he crossed the Apennines and, deciding not to attack Rome, laid waste to the countryside. In the summer of 216 B.C., at Cannae, near modern Barletta, in southeast Italy, he encircled a much larger Roman army of about 55,000 men in a maneuver known as a "double envelopment," and cut it to pieces. Hannibal continued to campaign in Italy for the next several years. When a reinforcing army under Hannibal's younger brother, Hasdrubal Barca, was defeated on the Metaurus River in east-central Italy, Hannibal retreated into the mountains in the south, where he held out for the next four years. Recalled to Carthage in 203 B.C., he was defeated by **Scipio Africanus** at Zama, near Carthage in North Africa, northeast of modern Tunis, in 202 B.C. In 195 B.C., having fallen out with the Carthaginian nobles, he fled to Syria and then to Bithynia, in modern Turkey. In 183 B.C., when the Romans demanded that Prusias, King of Bithynia, turn him over, Hannibal committed suicide, reputedly by taking poison.

Hannibal was one of those great generals whose career ended badly. His worst mistake was in not taking Rome after his victory at Cannae, but his crossing of the Alps and his victory at Cannae remain two of the most brilliant feats in military history.

William Joseph Hardee

1815–1873

Born on the Hardee estate in Camden County, Georgia, Hardee graduated from the U.S. Military Academy in 1838. Assigned to the 2nd Dragoons, he served briefly in the Seminole War of 1835–1843 and was promoted to captain in 1844.

During the Mexican War, Hardee saw action at Vera Cruz, Contreras, and Molino del Rey, earning two brevets for gallantry. In 1855 he published *Rifle and Light Infantry Tactics,* which was adopted as a standard textbook by the army. In 1856, as a senior major in the 2nd Cavalry, he served with **Albert Sidney Johnston, Robert E. Lee,** and **George H. Thomas**. In January 1861 Hardee resigned from the U.S. Army to accept a colonelcy in the CSA. He was promoted to brigadier general in June 1861 and raised a brigade in Arkansas. In the fall, now a major general, he moved to Kentucky. He commanded a corps at Shiloh (April 1862), where he was wounded. He fought at Perryville (October 1862) and was promoted to lieutenant general. He led a corps at Stones River (December 1862–January 1963) and fought at Chattanooga (November 1863). After the fall of Atlanta in 1864, he commanded at Savannah, which he evacuated successfully on December 18, 1864, in the face of **Sherman's** advance, retreating to Charleston. Forced to withdraw into North Carolina in February 1865, his last fight was at Bentonville (March 19, 1865), where his only son was killed.

Nicknamed "Old Reliable," Hardee was known for the skill, gallantry, and vigor he displayed on the battlefield. Like all good fighting generals, he communicated his courage to his men.

Henry Havelock

1795–1857

Born at Ford Hall, Bishop Wearmouth, Sunderland, England, the son of a shipbuilder, Havelock wanted to enter the law, but in 1815 he accepted a commission in the 95th Foot.

Havelock distinguished himself in the British colonial wars in Burma, India, and Persia. Promoted to major in June 1843, he was appointed quartermaster general of the British army in India in 1851 and adjutant general and a brevet colonel in June 1854. He then commanded a division in the war with Persia in 1856. Returning to Bombay in May 1857 after the Sepoy Rebellion had broken out, he was given command of a column of 1,000 men and sent to the relief of the British garrisons at Cawnpore and Lucknow. He marched the 126 miles from Allahabad to Cawnpore in nine days at the hottest time of the year, fighting and winning three battles on the way and defeating 5,000 rebels at Cawnpore on July 16, 1857. He then beat an army of 4,000 rebels at Bithur on August 16. Reinforced by Sir James Outram, the combined force of 3,000 men advanced on Lucknow, September 19, and relieved it on the 25th, only to become besieged itself until relieved seven weeks later. Now aged sixty-two and weakened by his months of strenuous campaigning, Havelock contracted dysentery and died at Lucknow, November 24, 1857.

A brilliant and determined commander and planner, Havelock earned his promotions through merit, not purchase or position, and when, after forty-two years service in the army, he got his great chance, he was ready for it.

John Hawkwood

1321?–1394

Born in County Essex, England, son of a successful tanner, Gilbert de Hawkwood, John embarked on a military career in 1340 and fought with the English army in France during the Hundred Years War (1337–1453), where he served as an archer at Crécy, August 25, 1346, and Poitiers, September 19, 1356, after which he was knighted.

By 1359 Hawkwood was earning his living commanding a troop of freelancers in Gascony, raiding and pillaging. The following year he went to Italy, stopping by Avignon long enough to levy a "contribution" from Pope Innocent VI. Hawkwood spent the rest of his life in Italy, serving a succession of popes, nobles, and city-states, competing with other *condottieri* (mercenaries) but most uniformly loyal to Florence, although he led the forces of Pisa against Florence in 1364. At times he was successful, as when outnumbered two to one, he defeated Count Landau on June 2, 1372, and took him prisoner, or as at Castagnaro, where, in March 1387, he defeated the Veronese decisively; at other times he was not, as in June 1369, when German mercenaries defeated him near Arezzo and took him prisoner. He was ransomed by the Pisans, however, testifying to how much they valued his services. He is supposed to have once responded archly to a friar who wished him peace, "I live by war and peace would undo me!" He died at Florence and his bones were later returned to England.

Hawkwood was a good organizer and a brave soldier who welded his men into one of Europe's earliest regular armies.

Henry IV, King of France

1553–1610

Born at Pau, in Béarn, Henry was descended through his father from King Louis IX and next in succession to the throne of France, after the children of Henry II. He went to court at the age of four and into the army at sixteen.

Henry's first battle was in 1570 at Arnay-le-Duc, where he distinguished himself. In 1572, upon the death of his mother, he became King Henry III of Navarre. After the St. Bartholomew Massacre (August 24, 1572) he aligned himself with the Protestants against the King of France, but eventually they became reconciled and Henry of France designated Navarre his successor upon his death in 1589. But first Protestant Henry IV had to secure his kingdom from the Catholics, backed by Spain. At Arques, September 31, 1589, with only 8,000 men, Henry defeated a Catholic army of 24,000 by luring them into a skillful ambush. At Ivry on March 14, 1590, Henry inflicted 4,000 casualties compared with his 500 by employing a double line of arquebusiers, front rank kneeling, rear rank standing, combined with a vigorous cavalry charge. When Henry renounced his Protestant faith in 1593, resistance to his rule disappeared and he entered Paris in March 1594. He was assassinated by a religious fanatic in 1610.

Henry was a courageous and resourceful commander who improvised brilliantly on the battlefield. As king, he founded a military academy, established the artillery as a regular corps, strengthened his frontier defenses, and regularized pay scales in his army.

Henry V, King of England

1387–1422

Born at Monmouth, eldest son of Henry IV, as the adolescent Prince of Wales, Henry campaigned successfully against Welsh rebels, 1402–1407.

On ascending to the throne in March 1413, Henry attempted to secure by negotiation what he thought was his by inheritance—the crown of France. When this failed, he sailed for France in April 1415 with an army of 12,000 men. At Agincourt Castle on the morning of October 25, 1415, a French army of 30,000 attacked Henry, who, reminiscent of **Edward III** at Crécy, deployed his men in three groups in a narrow defile between woods. When they had advanced to within half a mile of the French, Henry's archers deployed to the front, and when the French attacked, bunched up between the woods on their flanks, the English arrows caused havoc among them. At least 5,000 French nobles died at Agincourt compared with 13 English men-at-arms and 100 footmen. Henry did not follow this victory up, but in 1417 he returned to France and conquered Normandy. By the Treaty of Troyes in 1420, Charles VI of France gave Henry his daughter in marriage and recognized Henry as his successor, but Henry died before the crown could be conferred upon him.

Immortalized by Shakespeare as the insouciant Prince Hal in *Henry IV, Part II* and the soldier king of *Henry V,* the historical Henry was an able and brave commander, from the age of fifteen. His victories at Agincourt and in Normandy have inspired Englishmen for over 500 years.

Heraclius, Byzantine Emperor

575?–641

Born in Cappadocia (modern Turkey) or North Africa—authorities disagree—Heraclius was of Armenian origin and his father was Byzantine viceroy in North Africa when the tyrant Phocas usurped the crown in 602.

Fed up with Phocas's tyranny, Heraclius led his father's fleet to Constantinople, overthrew Phocas, and had himself installed as emperor in October 610. Heraclius found the empire in disarray, the Slavs and Avars threatening its remaining European territories while the Persians were conquering its eastern lands. Heraclius bought off the Slavs, and when he was ready, he attacked the Persians, first at the Battle of Issus in October 622 and then at Halys in the spring of 623. He then turned to Media (central Iran), where he spent the winter, and in the spring of 624 he invaded Persia itself, defeating the Persians at the Sarus River in the fall of 625. Ignoring a Persian-Avar siege of Constantinople (June–August 626), Heraclius continued his campaign, finally routing the Persians near Nineveh in December 627. Following peace, Heraclius turned to strengthening the empire's military forces, initiating a system of *themes,* or provincial armies under the command of the local governor. Worn-out in the last years of his life, he was unable to prevent the Arabs from seizing Egypt and Syria.

A brilliant strategist and battlefield tactician, Heraclius founded the Byzantine military system that was to endure for 400 years.

Henry Heth

1825–1899

Born in Virginia, Heth was offered an appointment to the U.S. Naval Academy in 1842, but refused and went to West Point instead, where he graduated thirty-eighth out of thirty-eight in the Class of 1846.

Heth saw action in the Mexican War at Matamoros, and Tamaulipas and fought Indians on the frontier afterward, earning promotion to captain for heroism at the Battle of Ash Hollow in 1855, and served with **Joseph E. Johnston** in the expedition against the Mormons, 1857–1858. In April 1861 he resigned from the U.S. Army to accept a captaincy in the CSA and later that year commanded the 45th Virginia as a colonel. Promoted to brigadier general in January 1862, he served for a time in the west under **Kirby Smith,** he was assigned a brigade under **A. P. Hill** and succeeded him at Chancellorsville (May 2–4, 1863), where he was wounded. Promoted to major general May 24, his division was the first of **R. E. Lee's** units engaged at Gettysburg (July 1), where Heth was wounded again and put out of action. He was back in command at Bristoe Station (October 14, 1863) and he commanded his division at Spotsylvania (May 1864), Bethesda Church (May–June), and Cold Harbor (June 3–12, 1864). He fought with distinction during the siege of Petersburg and briefly (February–March 1865) commanded Lee's III Corps, before surrendering with him at Appomattox. After the war he engaged in business and for a time was an Indian agent.

Heth was a brave and reliable commander, the only officer whom Lee is known to have called by his first name.

Hideyoshi Toyotomi

1537–1598

Born in Owari Province near modern Nagoya, Hideyoshi came from humble origins at a time in Japanese history when the lack of hegemony among the warring clans created an environment wherein an ambitious and talented man could rise if he backed the right *daimyo* (baron) in the struggle for power.

Hideyoshi joined Oda Nobunaga's (1534–1582) army as a common soldier and by pure ability rose to be one of his most trusted generals and earned himself a fiefdom. Hideyoshi's tactical ability helped Oda win control of the Japanese central provinces. Hideyoshi realized the value of firearms, introduced by Europeans in 1542, as well as large, nonsamurai armies used in real battles instead of the ritual warfare that had characterized Japanese battles up to that time.

When Oda was assassinated by a renegade general in 1582, Hideyoshi avenged his patron and by 1590, through judicious alliances and battlefield victories, had established himself as the most powerful military leader in Japan. He realized the value of European technology and trade, but when he'd gotten what he wanted, he expelled the Europeans in 1587. Hideyoshi then turned his attention to China, which he planned to conquer by first taking Korea. In 1592 his armies landed in Pusan and by July had captured P'yŏngyang, a march of 200 miles in three weeks. But in July 1592 Admiral **Yi Sung Shin** destroyed his fleet and in October Chinese reinforcements forced the Japanese back upon Pusan, which they held during peace negotiations. In 1597, however, Hideyoshi broke out of the Pusan perimeter, and despite Chinese intervention a second time, he maintained the initiative until once again the Korean navy destroyed the Japanese fleet. His lines of communication with Japan effectively cut, Hideyoshi was forced to withdraw. He died suddenly in September 1598.

Hideyoshi's rise from the peasantry to unifier and dictator of medieval, socially stratified Japan is one of the more spectacular achievements of history. He was an accomplished tactician and politician and a man of tremendous energy who did everything on a grand scale.

Ambrose Powell Hill

1825–1865

Born in Culpeper, Virginia, A. P. Hill graduated one year late and fifteenth out of thirty-eight in the West Point class of 1847. He served in the Mexican War in 1847 and the Seminole campaigns of 1849–1850 and 1853–1855. He resigned from the army in March 1861 to accept the colonelcy of the 13th Virginia Infantry.

Hill was promoted to brigadier general in February 1862 and major general in May. He fought with distinction under **Longstreet** in the Peninsular Campaign. In July 1862 his division was transferred to reinforce **Stonewall Jackson's** army. At Second Manassas (Bull Run) (August 29 and 30, 1862), his division held the left of Jackson's line under repeated heavy attacks, and at Sharpsburg (Antietam; September), his arrival on the field from Harper's Ferry prevented a Union breakthrough on the Confederate right.

At Fredericksburg (December 13, 1862), the Union forces broke through Hill's lines, but were repulsed after heavy fighting. Wounded at Chancellorsville, Hill got Jackson's corps after the latter's death and was promoted to lieutenant general May 23, 1863. He directed the fighting at Gettysburg on the first day (July 1, 1863), but at the Wilderness (May 1964) he was taken ill and this may account for his poor performance on May 7, when he was outflanked and saved by the arrival of Longstreet. In March 1865, he fell sick again, and on April 2, returning to the front, he was killed.

Hill was an aggressive, sometimes impetuous, but reliable commander who always had the confidence and loyalty of his men. Both **R. E. Lee** and Jackson called for him as they lay dying.

Daniel Harvey Hill

1821–1889

Born in South Carolina, Hill graduated twenty-eighth of fifty-six in the West Point class of 1842, a class that produced fifteen generals during the Civil War.

Hill fought in the Mexican War, earning a brevet promotion to captain for gallantry at Churubusco, a brevet to major after Chapultepec, and a sword of honor from South Carolina for his service in the war. He resigned from the army in 1849 to teach and in 1859 he was

appointed superintendent of the North Carolina Military Institute. At the outbreak of the Civil War he was appointed colonel of the 1st North Carolina, was promoted to brigadier general in September 1861, and major general in March 1862. He subsequently fought in the Peninsular Campaign, Second Manassas (Bull Run), South Mountain, and Sharpsburg (Antietam; September 1862). **R. E. Lee** blamed him for losing the copy of his battle plan for the Sharpsburg Campaign that fell into Union hands, but Hill denied responsibility. Hill also publicly criticized Lee for his attack at Malvern Hill (July 1, 1862). "It was not war, it was murder," he said. Named lieutenant general in July 1863, he fought brilliantly at Chickamauga (September 19–20, 1863), but afterward accused his superior, Braxton Bragg, of incompetence during the battle. Jefferson Davis refused Hill's promotion to lieutenant general and removed him from command until the very end of the war.

Hill's outspoken criticism of his superiors may have been insubordinate, but he was a clear-sighted tactician who could fight, and he called the shots as he saw them.

Paul von Hindenburg

1847–1934

Born in Poznan, Poland, to an old *Junker* family, Hindenburg was trained in the Prussian Cadet Corps. He fought in the wars against Austria (1866) and France (1870), winning the Iron Cross for bravery at the battle of Königgrätz in 1866.

By 1904, Hindenburg was commanding a corps. He retired in 1911, but was recalled for World War I and given command of the 8th Army on the Eastern Front with **Erich Ludendorff** as his chief of staff. At Tannenburg, August 26–29, 1914, Hindenburg, in one of the most spectacular German victories of the war, defeated a Russian army twice the size of his own. He secured another victory at the Masurian Lakes in September, and that November he was promoted to the rank of field marshal and given supreme command in the east. In 1916 he was made chief of the general staff with Ludendorff as his operations deputy. Based on his victories in the east and ending the stalemate at Verdun, his leadership of the GS looked promising at first, but as the war ground on, Hindenburg's stubborn all-out offensives bled Germany white, and after the failure of his drive at the Second Battle of the Marne in July 1918, German strength had run out. As president of the Weimar Republic in 1933, he was manipulated by the Nazis into appointing Hitler chancellor.

The success of the Hindenburg-Ludendorff team was due to Hindenburg's steadying influence on Ludendorff's genius. Hindenburg was the personification of the Prussian ideals of duty, honor, and total dedication to the state.

Samuel Houston

1793–1863

Born near Lexington, Virginia, son of a veteran of the Revolution who made a career of the army, Houston spent his youth in Tennessee, including some years among the Cherokee.

During the War of 1812, Houston served with **Andrew Jackson** during his campaign against the Creeks, and at Horseshoe Bend, Alabama (March 28, 1814), he distinguished himself in action and was wounded. Houston stayed in the army after the war but resigned in 1818 to enter law. After some success in politics, he was practicing law in Nacogdoches, Texas, when the Texan Revolution began in October 1835. The following March he was appointed to command the Texan forces. At first this army consisted of only 400 men, but after the fall of the Alamo (March 6, 1836), its ranks swelled to 750 volunteers. Houston labored to train his men and stay out of reach of the victorious Mexicans until he was ready to fight. On April 20, both armies, about equal in strength, faced each other on the San Jacinto River. When Mexican general Santa Ana was reinforced by 500 men on the twenty-first, Houston mounted a surprise attack. The battle lasted fifteen minutes. Houston lost six men killed and twenty-five wounded, including himself; the Mexicans were totally defeated and Santa Ana captured. Houston later served as president of the Texas Republic and helped bring it into the Union. Governor of Texas in 1861, he refused to join the Confederacy and was forced to resign, but he rejected Lincoln's offer of federal troops to restore him to office, and at his death he still owned a dozen slaves.

Sam Houston was a charismatic and determined individual whose self-confidence bordered on vanity, but he commanded respect. As a soldier, he refused battle until he was ready, and then he hit the enemy hard.

Sam Houston

J

Andrew Jackson

1767–1845

Born in the backwoods settlement of Waxhaw, South Carolina, the son of a man who emigrated from Ireland in 1765, Jackson found himself orphaned and alone in the world by the age of fourteen.

During the American Revolution, Jackson and his brother Robert were captured by the British at the Battle of Hanging Rock in 1780 and interned. In 1787 Jackson, having studied law on his own, was licensed to practice in North Carolina. Migrating to Tennessee Territory, he became the state's first U.S. congressman when it was admitted to the Union in 1796, and in 1797 was elected to the Senate. In 1802 he was elected major general of the Tennessee Militia on a tie-breaking vote. Between then and the outbreak of the War of 1812, he lived the life of a country gentleman, maintaining his militia commission as his only public office. Sent to fight the Creek Indians in Mississippi Territory, Jackson led his force of short-term volunteers by river and through trackless wilderness in a campaign that culminated in storming the Indians' fortified camp at Horseshoe Bend, Alabama, on March

27, 1814. He emerged from this campaign with a commission as major general in the U.S. Army and the enduring nickname "Old Hickory." He next traveled down the Mississippi to New Orleans to repel an expected British invasion. On January 8, 1815, at Chalmette, Louisiana, his ragtag force of militiamen from Kentucky and Tennessee joined by creoles, Negroes, and some local pirates, killed 2,000 veteran British troops and their commander, Sir Edward Pakenham, at a cost of thirteen dead on their own side. As a two-term president of the United States, Jackson proved a shrewd, tenacious, and very effective politician.

A strong-willed man who believed in direct action, Jackson possessed the boundless self-confidence of the self-made man who is afraid of nothing. Possessing a high order of intelligence, sound tactical instinct, and a complete understanding of the men he commanded, Jackson got a motley crew of backwoodsmen to stand up to and destroy a veteran European army at New Orleans. It has been said of this victory that it "created a president, a party, and a tradition."

Thomas Jonathan Jackson

1824–1863

Born at Clarksburg in what is now the state of West Virginia, Jackson graduated seventeenth of fifty-nine in his West Point class of 1846.

Commissioned in the artillery, Jackson saw ac-

tion during the Mexican War at Vera Cruz, Cerro Gordo, and Chapultepec, where his bravery earned him brevet promotions to major and a commendation from General **Winfield Scott**. In

80

1852 he resigned from the army to accept the professorship of artillery tactics and natural philosophy at the Virginia Military Institute. He was not an inspired teacher. In April 1861 he was commissioned a colonel in the CSA and promoted to brigadier general in June. Commanding a brigade at First Manassas (Bull Run) (July 21, 1861), he earned the name "Stonewall" when General **Bernard Bee** rallied his men, saying, "There is Jackson standing like a stone wall." It is possible Bee meant this as a criticism because Jackson was not moving to his support at the time. Promoted to major general in October 1861, Jackson was given command in the Shenandoah Valley district of Virginia. In the spring of 1862 he mounted a brilliant campaign in the valley, diverting and beating a federal army of 60,000 men with only 16,000 of his own. In cooperating with **R. E. Lee** in the defense of Richmond, Jackson found himself at a disadvantage in terrain he did not know well. But at Second Manassas, he marched his men fifty-one miles in two days to destroy the federal depot there and then, on August 30–31, held Pope's army at bay until **Longstreet** arrived to drive it

back. After capturing 12,500 federals at Harper's Ferry on September 15, 1862, Jackson marched to Sharpsburg (Antietam) in time to plunge into the bloody fight there on the seventeenth. Promoted to lieutenant general in October 1862, he commanded a corps at Fredericksburg (December 13, 1862). At Chancellorsville on the night of May 1–2, 1863, he marched undetected behind the Union XI Corps, completely routing them in a surprise attack on the morning of May 2. That night, returning from the front, he was accidentally shot by one of his own men and died on May 10.

"I know not how to replace him," Lee wrote after Jackson's death. Jackson was an audacious, aggressive, and tenacious commander who, when he was in full possession of himself (lack of sleep fogged his mind) and knew his ground, moved with lightning speed to strike his enemy with powerful, fully coordinated attacks. His men called him "Old Jack" and were proud of their sobriquet as "Jackson's foot cavalry." He and Lee understood each other perfectly, and had Jackson lived, it is a fair bet the south might have won its independence on the battlefield.

Joan of Arc [Jeanne d'Arc, "The Maid of Orléans"]

1412–1431

Born at Domremy in the duchy of Bar, France, Joan led the life of a French peasant girl until the age of thirteen, when she claimed to have had a series of "visions" from various Catholic saints who told her to go to the aid of the King of France, then at war with the English.

Joan was so persistent and persuasive that in 1429 Charles VII gave her a role in the relief of the siege of Orléans. During the fighting Joan was wounded. When the English divided their forces among garrisons in the Loire Valley, the French, their morale bolstered by Joan's leadership, recaptured them. On June 19, 1429, her

army defeated the English at Patay and drove them from the valley. The French peasantry, inspired by these victories, rose against the English and in July Joan captured Troyes, Châlons, and Rheims. Joan was at Charles's side when he was crowned at Rheims on July 18, 1429. Repulsed in an attack on Paris in September, Joan was wounded again. Leading a force to the relief of Compiègne on May 23, 1430, she was captured by the Burgundians, turned over to the English, convicted of heresy, and burned at the stake in Rouen on May 30, 1431. Why Charles did not intervene to save her is a mystery.

Free Library of Philadelphia

Joan of Arc

Joan believed her inspiration was divine and was able thereby to inspire men to action. Modest and intelligent, Joan was fearless in battle and the boost her victories gave French morale enabled them to secure a truce some years after her death. Joan was canonized by the Catholic Church in 1920.

Joseph-Jacques-Césaire Joffre

1852–1931

Born in Rivesaltes in the eastern Pyrenees; Joffre's early education was in mathematics and engineering.

Joffre served in the Franco-Prussian War of 1870 but did not enter the army as a career officer until 1872. In the years before World War I he served overseas as an engineer officer, where he saw action in Indochina, China, and Africa. Promoted to major general in 1905, in 1914 he was chief of the general staff, and at the outbreak of World War I he became commander of all the French armies. In August and early September 1914, in the face of the imminent collapse of the French army, he calmly disposed his forces to meet the German onslaught, stopping their advance at the Marne, September 5–9. After the Marne, Joffre was a hero to the French people, but disillusionment with his leadership began to set in by the following year. Shocked by the heavy casualties, he called off the unsuccessful offensives at Champagne and Artois in 1915. In December 1916 he was relieved as a result of the high casualties sustained at Verdun and the Somme.

As an engineer, Joffre failed to appreciate the full nature of the trench warfare that developed on the Western Front in 1915 and 1916, and the Germans surprised him at Verdun. But while Joffre was unimaginative, he had one great, saving grace in that he could remain unperturbed in the face of disaster when everybody else was losing his head. This saved the French in the crisis of August 1914.

John of Austria [Don Juan de Austria]

1547–1578

Born the natural son of the Spanish emperor Charles V by Barbara Blomberg, the daughter of a rich citizen of Regensburg, he was first raised by humble foster parents living near Madrid under the name Gerónimo. In 1554 he was given into the care of a Spanish noble family. Charles recognized him in his will, and when he died John's half brother, Philip II, brought him to court and gave him the name Don Juan de Austria.

In 1568 John was given command of a squadron of thirty-three galleys to operate against Algerian pirates, which he did successfully. On October 7, 1571, in command of over 200 galleys and other vessels, John met the Turkish fleet at Lepanto and destroyed it, killing or capturing 35,000 men and freeing 15,000 Christian galley slaves. His success apparently engendered the jealousy of Philip, but in 1576 John was appointed governor-general of the Netherlands, where a revolt under **William of Orange** was having some success. Frustrated in negotiations with the Dutch, he resumed the war, capturing Namur in 1577, and reinforced by **Farnese,** John defeated the Dutch at Gembloux the following January. Denied further support by Philip, he was unable to exploit his successes. Frustrated by Philip's indifference, and his health weakened, John died of typhus in October.

John was a man of vaulting ambition but a chivalrous and charismatic commander whose energy and accomplishments went unrewarded, possibly out of Philip's unfounded fear that John wanted the throne for himself.

Albert Sidney Johnston

1803–1862

Born in Mason County, Kentucky, son of a doctor and grandson of a Revolutionary War veteran, Johnston graduated eighth in the West Point Class of 1826.

Johnston served in the Black Hawk War in 1832, but resigned from the army in 1834. He joined the Army of Texas in 1836, was appointed its commander in January 1837, and in December 1838 was made secretary of war for the Republic of Texas. He resigned in 1840 and returned to Kentucky. He served under **Zachary Taylor** during the Mexican War and saw action at Monterrey. He stayed in the army and in 1855 was appointed colonel of the 2nd U.S. Calvary; in 1857, as a brevet brigadier general, he led the expedition against the Mormons in Utah. In April 1861 he was appointed full general in the CSA and given command of the Western Department. Outnumbered, lacking equipment, his army suffered a string of defeats in early 1862 that forced Johnston to withdraw to Corinth, Mississippi, where, with **Beauregard,** he prepared to attack **Grant** at Shiloh Church with 40,000 men before his army of 42,000 men could be reinforced. He struck at dawn on April 6, 1862, obtaining complete surprise and driving Grant back to the Tennessee River in disorder. At about two P.M. Johnston was hit by a bullet in the leg and, refusing medical attention because he thought the wound minor, bled to death from a severed artery.

An experienced and sagacious commander, Johnston's loss on the verge of what might have been a great victory was a staggering blow to the Confederacy.

Joseph E. Johnston

1807–1891

Born in Prince Edward County, near Farmville, Virginia, Johnston graduated thirteenth of forty-six in his West Point class of 1829.

He served with distinction in the Second Seminole War in 1836 and 1838, being twice wounded in skirmishes. As a captain, he marched with **Winfield Scott** to Mexico and was wounded twice at Cerro Gordo and a third time at Chapultepec, ending the war a brevet colonel. He served in the Mormon Expedition of 1857–1858 and promoted to brigadier general in 1860, he was concurrently appointed quartermaster of the army. In April 1861 he resigned from the U.S. Army and in May was appointed a brigadier general in the CSA. In command of troops at Harper's Ferry in July 1861, he skillfully withdrew his command under the noses of a superior federal army to reinforce **Beauregard** at Manassas (Bull Run), where his leadership helped win the battle. Facing McClellan on the peninsula, he was wounded at Fair Oaks (May 31, 1862) and replaced by **R. E. Lee**. When his orders were not followed at Vicksburg, the entire garrison there was lost. Defending Atlanta against Sherman in 1864, he was forced back upon the city by superior forces although he stopped Sherman at Kenesaw (June 27, 1864). He was relieved of command by Jefferson Davis in July 1864, ostensibly for his failure to stop Sherman. After the war he served a term in congress and was commissioner of railroads under President Cleveland.

Johnston fought every battle outnumbered, but he was better on the defensive than on the attack. Feisty and quarrelsome, he exasperated his superiors but was admired by his subordinates.

John Paul Jones

1747–1792

Born John Paul in Kirkcudbrightshire, Scotland, Jones was apprenticed to a shipbuilder. Released from his apprenticeship early because his employer went bankrupt, by age nineteen Jones was first mate on a slaver trading between Africa and Jamaica. Jones's seamanship asserted itself, and in 1760 he was master of his own ship trading in the West Indies.

On the second voyage in December 1773, Jones killed a mutinous seaman. Since a previous incident at sea had earned him a bad reputation in Tobago, he fled to America and changed his name, hoping to get a fair trial when things blew over. What he got was a commission in the fledgling U.S. Navy in 1775 and command of the *Providence* in 1776, with which he took sixteen prizes. Commanding the *Ranger* (eighteen guns, 140 men) in 1777, he raided the Scottish coast and captured another seven prizes including the sloop *Drake* (twenty guns) after a one-hour battle on April 24, 1778. On the night of September 23, 1779, commanding the decrepit *Bonhomme Richard* (forty-two guns), Jones attacked the *Serapis* (fifty guns) off Flamborough Head in the most famous naval engagement of the war—and one of the most famous in all American naval history. He lashed his own vessel to the *Serapis* and while the British guns ravaged his ship from below, he captured the *Serapis* from topside. Tradition has it that when asked to surrender by the captain of the *Serapis*, Jones replied disdainfully, "I have not yet begun to fight." In 1787 Jones was voted a gold medal by Congress. In 1913 his remains were brought from Paris and enshrined at the U.S. Naval Academy in Annapolis, Maryland.

A hard, tough seaman with a huge ego, an ex-slaver and adventurer, Jones was also a resolute and brilliant naval commander who, according to the inscription on his tomb, "gave our navy its earliest traditions of heroism and victory."

Chief Joseph [In-mut-too-yah-lat-lat]

1840?–1904

Born in the Walloway Valley of Oregon, son of a Cayuse father and a Nez Percé mother, Joseph's Indian name meant "thunder coming from the water up over the land."

Upon his father's death in the early 1870s, Joseph became chief of a Nez Percé faction that had refused to subscribe to a treaty of 1863 that ceded large portions of their land to the U.S. government and confined them to reservations. In 1877 Washington decided to enforce the treaty, at first by negotiation, but when renegades massacred twenty whites in revenge for purported outrages, the army moved in. Joseph, who was drawn into the war against his will, knew he could never defeat the U.S. Army, so with fewer than 200 warriors, he sought refuge in Canada. After defeating one force in a desperate fight at Big Hole River in Montana on August 9, 1877, Joseph skillfully eluded powerful pursuing columns in a thousand-mile trek that ended in the Bear Paw Mountains, thirty miles short of his goal, where, on September 30, 1877, his camp was surrounded by 600 soldiers under the command of General **Nelson A. Miles**. Joseph held out for five days and surrendered only to relieve

Chief Joseph

the suffering of his people, 431 souls including 87 warriors, half of whom were wounded.

Joseph was a brilliant small-unit tactician and a man of great personal courage and integrity. He never condoned the usual outrages that characterized Indian warfare. His case is a tragic example of how arrogant governments crush those who refuse to fit in.

Judas Maccabaeus or Judah Maccabee

d. 160 B.C.

The third son of the priest, Mattahias of Modin, little is known of Judas's early life. While the actual meaning of the name "Maccabaeus" is disputed, it might connote something like "hammerer," and derive from the way he conducted his military campaigns.

Judas's father exhorted him on his deathbed to continue the revolt he had begun against the anti-Jewish persecutions of the Syrian-Greek monarch Antiochus IV Epiphanes in 167 B.C. At first Judas chose to engage Antiochus' Macedonian commanders using guerrilla tactics, which were successful in confusing and unbalancing them. In 165 Judas escalated the conflict and conducted a successful campaign in Emmaus, in the northwest of Judea, where he outmaneuvered and outfought several enemy armies over a broad area. In 164 he recaptured Jerusalem and rededicated the Temple, and this is commemorated by Jews today in the ceremony of Hanukkah. Judas suffered his first serious setback in 162, when he was defeated by Lysias at Ben Zecharia. Lysias had been appointed regent upon Antiochus' death in 163 and, needing time to secure his hold on the throne, agreed to peace on terms very favorable to the Jews. This did not last long after Lysias was overthrown. In 161 Judas defeated Nicanor at Adassa and signed a treaty with Rome, but was killed at Elasa before help could arrive.

For more than 2,000 years Jews and Christians have drawn inspiration from Judas's defense of freedom.

K

Philip Kearny

1815–1862

Born into a wealthy New York City family and a millionaire by the time he was twenty-one, Kearny always wanted a career as a soldier.

In 1836 Kearny applied for a commission in the U.S. Army and was appointed a second lieutenant of dragoons on March 8, 1837. After service on the frontier, he was sent to France to study cavalry tactics and in 1840 saw action with the Chasseurs d'Afrique in Algeria. Although he resigned his commission in 1846, he was recalled for the Mexican War and lost his left arm at Churubusco (August 20, 1847). He fought Indians in California after the war but resigned again in 1851. He served with the French in the Italian War of 1859 and was the first American to receive the Cross of the Legion of Honor for gallantry at Magenta and Solferino. In May 1861

he was appointed brigadier general and commander of the 1st New Jersey Brigade. He served in the Peninsula Campaign and fought at Williamsburg, Fair Oaks, and Second Manassas (Bull Run), where he commanded a division as a major general. On September 1, 1862, Kearny was riding on a reconnaissance when he was shot dead at Chantilly, Virginia. **Robert E. Lee** had Kearny's body shipped through the Union lines under a flag of truce and later returned his horse, saddle, and sword to Mrs. Kearny.

Kearny never had to don a uniform or put one back on again after losing his arm in Mexico, but a valiant soldier and a natural leader, he was drawn to the sound of the guns. **Winfield Scott** called him "the bravest man I ever knew."

Albrecht Kesselring

1885–1960

Born into a middle-class Bavarian family, Kesselring was commissioned in the artillery in 1906.

Kesselring emerged from World War I a captain of artillery and stayed in the army after the war, where he distinguished himself in a number of staff posts. In 1935 he was transferred into the German air force with the rank of major general. He commanded the air forces in Poland in 1939 and in France in 1940. Misled by German intelligence, he supported Göring's misguided emphasis on the bombing of British civilian targets instead of defeating the Royal Air Force. But

between June and December 1941, Kesselring commanded the German air forces in Russia with great skill. Created a field marshal and appointed to command in the Mediterranean in 1942, he fought a brilliant delaying action against the Allies during the invasion of Italy in early 1944, exacting from them the maximum in casualties for the least gain in territory. He managed to hold the Allies in the northern Apennines until March 1945, when Hitler made him commander in chief, west. He was sentenced to death for war crimes—on a very broad interpretation of the doctrine of command responsibility—but this was commuted to life in prison; he was released in 1952.

Nicknamed "Smiling Al" for his indomitable optimism in the face of tremendous odds, Kes-selring was nevertheless a battlefield realist. While he was an able commander of Germany's air forces, it was as a ground commander in Italy that he showed superb skills in the defensive role.

Ernest J. King

1878–1956

Born in Ohio, King graduated fourth out of sixty-seven in his Naval Academy class of 1901. For the next forty years King made no secret about his ambition to someday be chief of naval operations.

King saw service during the Spanish-American War as a midshipman and he ended World War I a junior captain with a Navy Cross. In 1922 he volunteered for submarine service, and although he never qualified, he did command the New London Sub Base. At age forty-nine he qualified as a pilot and was given command of the carrier *Lexington,* which earned him promotion to rear admiral in 1932. Promoted to vice admiral in 1938, King was awaiting retirement when appointed to command the Atlantic Fleet early in 1941. Here he gained President Roosevelt's confidence and in March 1942 was at last appointed CNO. Throughout the war as CNO and a member of both the joint and combined chiefs of staff, King played a major role in shaping Allied strategy while building the U.S. Navy into the most powerful in the world. He insisted that the Allies not ignore Japan in their "Germany first" policy, thus probably shortening the war considerably.

King could be arrogant and he was outspoken, but he succeeded on professional merit alone. He had a lot to be arrogant about, but a party lover and womanizer, he was indifferent to public opinion and often tangled with his civilian superiors. He encouraged his reputation for toughness and was particularly delighted when a friend gave him a miniature blowtorch "for shaving."

Thomas C. Kinkaid

1888–1972

Son of a career naval officer, Kinkaid graduated 136th out of 201 in his Naval Academy class of 1908.

While he saw no action in World War I, Kinkaid was a lieutenant commander and gunnery officer on the newly commissioned battleship *Arizona* when the war ended in 1918. With quiet competence, Kinkaid filled a number of sea and shore commands between the wars, becoming a captain in 1937 and a rear admiral in November 1941, when he was given command of Cruiser Division Six, then at Pearl Harbor. He arrived there just five days after the Japanese attack. He fought his division at the Battle of the Coral Sea (May 4–8, 1942), Midway (June 2–5), Guadalcanal (August 7), the Eastern Solomons (August 22–25), and the Santa Cruz Islands (October 25–28). His flagship, the *Enterprise,* was struck repeatedly during these last two campaigns. Kinkaid commanded the naval force that retook the Aleutians in January 1943 and in June he was promoted to vice admiral. In November Kincaid was given command of the Seventh Fleet under **Douglas MacArthur**. His fleet supported the Philippine landings on Leyte in October 1944 and then defended the beachheads on October 25,

1944. In January 1945 he participated in the Lingayen Gulf landings. Kincaid was promoted to full admiral in April 1945.

Although combat command came to Kincaid late in his career, he proved a highly competent commander who could delegate responsibility in times of crisis. He won the respect of Mac-Arthur, which was no mean feat.

Horatio Herbert Kitchener, 1st Earl Kitchener

1850–1916

Born near Bally Longford, County Kerry, Ireland, Kitchener graduated from the Royal Military Academy in 1871 with a commission in the Royal Engineers.

Kitchener first saw action as a volunteer cadet with the French during the Franco-Prussian War of 1870–1871. Transferred to the cavalry, he served with distinction in the Nile Expeditionary Force sent to relieve **Gordon** at Khartoum in 1884-1885. Appointed to command the Egyptian army in 1892, in 1896 he embarked on the campaign to reoccupy the Sudan. He proceeded methodically and ruthlessly, defeating the Mahdist forces on the Atbara River on April 8, 1898. At Omdurman, with 26,000 men, Kitchener defeated 40,000 dervishes at the cost of only 500 of his own men killed to 10,000 of theirs. At Omdurman, the machine gun proved its usefulness. Appointed to command in South Africa in November 1900, Kitchener's superior strength and harsh tactics wore down the Boer insurgents and he returned to England a national hero in 1902. At the outbreak of World War I, he foresaw that victory would be won only with a very large, highly trained army. His outspokenness so upset his overly optimistic colleagues that in 1916 he was removed as secretary of state for war and sent on a mission to Russia. On the night of June 5, 1916, he went down with his ship when it struck a mine.

Kitchener drove himself as mercilessly as he did his enemies. He understood logistics in war and he was almost alone in realizing the terrible cost of victory in World War I.

Henry Knox

1750–1806

Born in Boston, son of a shipmaster, at the age of twenty-one Knox opened "The London Book-Store," from which he made a respectable living before the Revolution.

Knox enlisted in the militia at the age of eighteen, and on March 5, 1770, he was a witness to the Boston Massacre, where he tried to restrain the British troops from firing on the mob. On November 17, 1775, **Washington** appointed Knox colonel of the Continental Artillery Regiment, a unit with no cannon. At Knox's urging, Washington authorized him to remove the guns from Fort Ticonderoga at the head of Lake Champlain in what is today New York State and bring them to Boston. Knox reached the fort on December 5, 1775, and selected about fifty guns for removal. The manhandling of these guns, including three siege mortars weighing a ton each, through the snowy Berkshire Mountains to Boston was one of the great feats of the American Revolution. Knox spurred on his teamsters by a natural talent for leading men and his command of profanity, which was prolific. Knox's guns enabled Washington to force the British evacuation of Boston early in 1776. Knox knew virtually nothing about artillery, but he learned. At Trenton, December 25–26, 1776, he distinguished himself and was promoted to brigadier general, December 27. Knox fought at Princeton in January 1777, Brandywine in September, Germantown in October, and Monmouth, June 28, 1778. At Yorktown Washington said of Knox that "the resources of his genius supplied the deficit of means." Knox was promoted to major general on November 15, 1781. He was appointed secretary of war in 1785.

Known as the "Gargantuan hero" of the Revolution because of his courage and enterprise but also because of his physical size (he weighed over 300 pounds in 1783), Knox was a natural leader who inspired others with his own optimism and self-confidence.

Henry Knox

Free Library of Philadelphia

Ivan Stepanovich Konev [Koniev]

1897–1973

Born into a peasant family in the area known as Kirov Oblast, Konev was drafted into the imperial Russian army in 1916 and saw action in Galicia.

Konev joined the Red Army in 1918, and by the end of the civil war that followed the Bolshevik Revolution, he was a corps political commissar. He participated in the suppression of the Kronstadt naval mutiny of 1921. He became a regular army officer in 1924 and graduated from the Soviet military academy in 1926. In 1934 he completed training at the Frunze Military Academy. He survived the purge of 1937–1938 to

become a member of the Central Committee in 1939. In January 1941 he was commanding the North Caucasus Military District and led the Nineteenth Army against the Germans around Smolensk in September 1941. He then became commander of the Western Front. He was replaced by **Zhukov** in October and sent to the Kalinin Front. In 1943 he was given command of the 2nd Ukrainian Front, where he won fame during the Soviet offensive of 1943–1944. While Stalin gave Zhukov the honor of capturing Berlin, Konev took Prague and was called to Zhukov's assistance in the face of stiff German resistance at Berlin. In 1944 Konev was made a marshal of the Soviet Union. He was twice cited as a Hero of the Soviet Union.

Although overshadowed by Zhukov, Konev was one of the most highly praised and deco-rated Russian generals of WWII. Stalin may have encouraged the rivalry between the two men to keep Konev in his place, not for lack of confidence in his generalship.

Otto Kretschmer

1912–

Known as the "tonnage king" because he sank so much Allied shipping during World War II, Kretschmer was in a British prisoner-of-war camp when he was awarded Germany's highest decoration for bravery, the Knight's Cross with Oak Leaves and Swords.

While commanding the submarines *U-23* and *U-99* during the first eighteen months of WWII, Kretschmer sank 300,000 tons of Allied shipping, including three British destroyers. His tactic was to penetrate a convoy and then launch torpedoes from a close-in but highly vulnerable position. After expending all his torpedoes attacking a convoy south of Iceland on March 17, 1941, Kretschmer's *U-99* was on the surface headed for its base when it was spotted by the convoy's escort of five destroyers and two corvettes. The *U-99* dived immediately but was damaged and forced to the surface by a pattern of depth charges released by the destroyer *Walker*. Under fire from the guns of another destroyer, the *U-99* sank rapidly. Kretschmer and all but two of his crew were rescued and spent the rest of the war as prisoners of the British. After the war Kretschmer reached the rank of rear admiral in the West German navy.

Kretschmer's daring and skill made him one of the most successful submariners of any navy in WWII. After the war he was able to meet the man who sank him, Captain Donald Macintyre, and the two became friends.

Walter Krueger

1881–1967

Born in Germany, Krueger came to the U.S. when he was eight years old. He dropped out of high school to enlist as a volunteer in the Spanish-American War, where he served in the Philippines as an infantry private, rising to the rank of second lieutenant.

During WW I Krueger served with the American Expeditionary Force in France, rising to command the fledgling Tank Corps. He earned both the Distinguished Service Cross and the Distinguished Service Medal in France. He ended the war a colonel, but in 1919 reverted to his permanent rank of captain. Between wars he earned a solid reputation as a planner, teacher, and troop commander. At the outbreak of WW II he was a lieutenant general commanding the Third Army with Dwight Eisenhower as his chief of staff. At **Douglas MacArthur's** request, he was given command of the Sixth Army in February 1943, which was then forming in Australia and was to be MacArthur's primary ground combat force in the Southwest Pacific. Nearly sixty-three when he received this command, Krueger led troops in twenty major operations before the end of the war. During the New Guinea Campaign of 1944 his units were spread out in six different locations along a 500-mile section of coastline, but Krueger maintained effective command and control of their operations. He was promoted to full general in March 1945.

Krueger was a careful planner whose caution saved lives. MacArthur wrote of him that he was "swift and sure in the attack, tenacious and determined in defense, modest and restrained in victory."

Kublai Khan [Khubilai, Qubilai, Qan]

1215–1294

The fourth son of Tolui, youngest son of **Genghis Khan,** Kublai was the great khan's favorite grandson, endeared to him by his qualities of strength, intelligence, and bravery. As a boy, Kublai accompanied his father on his military campaigns.

When Kublai's older brother, Mangu, became khan in 1251, he entrusted Kublai with the administration of the Chinese territories in the eastern part of the Mongol empire. Mangu expected Kublai to conquer the southern Chinese Sung dynasty whose capital was at Hangchow, but instead he conducted a campaign against the western province of Szechwan, whose capital he took in 1252, after which he conquered Yunnan Province. In 1257 Mangu undertook the conquest of Sung China himself, but died in 1259. Elected khan in June 1260, Kublai first dealt with his rebellious brother, Arik Buka. After a five-year siege, 1268–1273, Kublai captured the Sung cities of Hsiang-yang and Fan-ch'eng. His trusted subordinate, Bayan, captured Hangchow in 1276 and destroyed the remnants of the Sung at the naval battle of Canton in 1279. Despite reverses afterward, most notably his invasions of Japan in 1274 and 1281, at the time of Kublai's death the Mongol empire stretched from Korea to Arabia and into eastern Poland.

Vigorous, shrewd, and pragmatic, Kublai Khan was a determined and resourceful leader. By 1290 as many as 58 million Chinese were under Mongol rule. His defeats in Japan were due as much to the weather as to the fanaticism of the Japanese.

L

Marquis de Lafayette

1757–1834

Born Marie-Joseph-Paul-Yves-Roch-Gilbert du Motier, by the age of thirteen, with both parents and his grandfather dead, Lafayette was an orphan and heir to a vast fortune. Although he entered the army in 1771, he had little real military experience before joining the American Revolution.

In June 1777, at his own expense, Lafayette outfitted a ship to take him to America, where he offered his sword to the Continental Congress. Not yet twenty, he agreed to serve without pay and, on July 21, 1777, was commissioned a major general without command. **Washington,** however, liked Lafayette, and at Brandywine, September 11, 1777, the French nobleman was slightly wounded checking the British advance. At Gloucester, New Jersey, in November, leading a reconnaissance of about 300 men, he defeated a larger force of Hessians. On Washington's recommendation, Lafayette was given command of a division of light troops, and he commanded two brigades at Newport in 1778. He returned to France in 1779, where he laid the groundwork for sending a French army to serve in America. In Virginia in the summer of 1781, Lafayette proved an able tactician, and at the siege of Yorktown he commanded a division. Although he lost his fortune in the French Revolution, he never asked the U.S. to reimburse the expenses (estimated at $200,000) he incurred fighting for American liberty.

A mere stripling in 1777, Lafayette possessed "bravery and military ardor," in Washington's words, and this, combined with intelligence and a willingness to learn, made a man of the boy.

Jean Lannes

1769–1809

Son of a farmer in Gascony, Lannes was taught to read and write by his brother, a priest, and was apprenticed at one time to a dyer but volunteered for the army in 1792.

Lannes fought in Spain, where he was first wounded, and commissioned. He commanded a brigade under **Napoleon** in Italy in 1796–1797, where he distinguished himself in several battles, sustaining three wounds at Arcole, November 15–17, 1796. At the siege of Acre in May 1799, he was wounded again and left for dead on the field but recovered in time to be wounded at Abukir in July. For Acre he was promoted to command a division. He received Napoleon's praise for fighting his outnumbered division at Marengo in June of 1800. In May 1804 he was elevated to marshal of the empire. He played a key role at Austerlitz (December 2, 1805) and Jena (October 14, 1806). Wounded severely at Pultusk in December 1806, he did not rejoin the army until June 1807. In 1808 and 1809, he fought in Spain. At Ratisbon on April 23, 1809, he led his troops by seizing a ladder and shouting, "I was a grenadier before I was a marshal" and scaling the wall. On May 21, 1809, At Aspern-Essling on the Danube, protecting the French withdrawal, Lannes had both legs mangled by a cannonball and died nine days later. Napoleon is said to have wept when he heard of his death.

Wounded at least ten times in sixty battles, Lannes was best in the forefront of an assault, leading by personal example, but he encouraged his staff to avoid unnecessary heroics. Napoleon said of him that Lannes "was a swordsman when I found him and a paladin when I lost him."

Jean de Lattre de Tassigny

1889–1952

Lattre was born at Mouilleron-en-Pareds (Vendée) and graduated from the St. Cyr military academy in 1911.

Lattre began World War I in the cavalry and ended it commanding an infantry battalion. He was wounded four times fighting on the Western Front. He fought against **Abd-el-Krim** in Morocco, where he was wounded again. In 1938 he was chief of staff of the Fifth Army and as a major general commanded the 14th Division against **Guderian** in May 1940. Under Lattre's command the division held together until the armistice in June, when he moved into the free zone of Vichy France. When the Germans occupied Vichy in November 1942, Lattre resisted and was sentenced to ten years in jail. He escaped and reached North Africa in October 1943, where he

was given the French First Army and then led it in the invasion of southern France in August 1944. At Toulon and Marseilles his troops took 50,000 prisoners at the cost of 1,500 of their own killed. He helped eliminate the German Nineteenth Army at Colmar during January and February 1945. On May 8, 1945, in Berlin, Lattre signed Germany's final capitulation on behalf of France. In 1951–1952 he organized the campaign to recapture most of northern Vietnam lost to the Viet Minh in October 1950, but in December 1951 Lattre fell sick and returned to France, dying in Paris in January 1952.

Lattre was a tough and flamboyant leader whose resistance to the German takeover of Vichy inspired the French people and gave them a patriot to rally them.

Thomas Edward Lawrence

1888–1935

The second of five illegitimate sons of Sir Thomas Chapman, Lawrence was born in Wales and educated at Oxford, and spent the years just before World War I doing archaeological work in the Middle East.

At the outbreak of WWI, Lawrence was commissioned in military intelligence. Promoted to captain, he was sent to serve the emir Faisal's army as political and liaison officer in the Arab revolt against the Turks. In July 1917, leading a

force of Huwaitat tribesmen, Lawrence captured the port of Aqaba, which became Faisal's base of operations in cooperation with British forces in Palestine. For this deed Lawrence was decorated and promoted to Major. Captured by the Turks in November, Lawrence soon escaped and in January 1918 participated in the battle at Tafila for which he was again decorated and promoted to lieutenant colonel. Lawrence used his influence to bind the Arabs to the British war effort in

Egypt and Palestine and he exploited their ability as guerrillas to tie down 25,000 Turks who would otherwise have been available for conventional operations. After the war he fled the notoriety he earned in the desert, enlisting first in the Royal Air Force and then the Royal Tank Corps under assumed names. He was killed in a motorcycle accident in 1935.

If Lawrence was not the actual leader of Arab armies that his admirers portray, he empathized with and understood the Arabs and it was his vision and grasp of strategy as well as guerrilla tactics that enabled Faisal's army to achieve solid victories.

Jacques Leclerc

1902–1947

Born in Picardy as Philippe, Vicomte de Hautecloque, Leclerc graduated from St. Cyr in 1924 and was a captain when war broke out in 1939.

Wounded and taken prisoner during the battle for France, Leclerc escaped to England and offered his services to **De Gaulle** under his assumed name, to avoid German reprisals against his family still in France. Appointed commander in French Equatorial Africa, in December 1942 he led a column 1,500 miles across the Sahara from Chad to link up with the British Eighth Army in Libya, destroying enemy outposts along the way. This was a great feat of organizational and logistical skill, especially since much of Leclerc's equipment had to be transported 1,000 miles up the Congo River to Fort Lamy in the Chad. In addition, Leclerc had to train his men to endure the hardships of desert campaigning. Leclerc was subsequently given command of the French 2nd Armored Division, which he led in the invasion of Normandy. His troops led the dash for Paris after the Normandy breakout and Leclerc accepted the surrender of the city in the name of the provisional government. In June 1945 he was sent to Indochina, where he adopted harsh measures against the Viet Minh insurgents that resulted in his recall in 1946. Appointed inspector general of the French troops in North Africa, he was killed in an air crash in November 1947.

Leclerc was a simple and modest man who combined great fighting spirit with prudence, and his leadership in Africa did much to restore faith in the French Army.

Fitzhugh Lee

1835–1905

Born in Fairfax County, Virginia, not far from the city of Alexandria, Fitzhugh Lee's father was an elder brother of **Robert E. Lee**. Fitzhugh graduated forty-fifth of forty-nine in his West Point class of 1856.

As a second lieutenant with the 2nd U.S. Cavalry in Texas, Fitzhugh was wounded twice fighting Indians. He was an instructor at West Point when the Civil War broke out. In May 1861 he was appointed a first lieutenant in the CSA and served at First Manassas (July 1861) as a staff officer. In August 1861 he was made lieutenant colonel of the 1st Virginia Cavalry and in July 1862 he was promoted to brigadier general. He commanded a brigade at Second Manassas (Bull Run; August 1862), fought at South Mountain, Sharpsburg (Antietam), Chancellorsville, and Gettysburg. At Kelly's Ford on March 17, 1863, he held off a much larger force of Union cavalry. Promoted to major general in August 1863 and given command of the Cavalry Division, Army of Northern Virginia, he fought with distinction at Spotsylvania Court House (May 1864), had three horses shot out from under him at Winchester (September 1864), and was seriously wounded. After the war he turned to farming, remarking that up to then he had drawn his corn from the quartermaster but now had to draw it "from the obstinate soil." In 1885 he was elected governor of Virginia. He was American consul in Cuba from 1896 to 1898. Appointed a major general of volunteers in 1898, he commanded the VII Corps in Cuba. In 1901 he retired as a brigadier general.

"Fitz" Lee was a dashing and capable cavalryman and an astute tactician.

Fitzhugh Lee

National Archives

Henry Lee

1756–1818

Born near Dumfries, Virginia, Henry Lee graduated from Pinceton in 1773. Admitted to the Middle Temple to study law, he was preparing to leave for England when the American Revolution broke out.

Appointed captain in a regiment of Virginia cavalry in June 1776, in April 1777 his unit joined **Washington's** main army. He distinguished himself in action at Spread Eagle Tavern near Valley Forge in January 1778, and for this was promoted to major in April. As commander of "Lee's Legion," a force of cavalry and infantry that he used skillfully in guerrilla operations in New York, he earned the thanks of Congress and a special medal. Promoted to lieutenant colonel and sent south, in January 1781 he joined **Greene** in South Carolina, where his legion consistently distinguished itself in action. He shattered the Tories at Haw River, North Carolina (February 1781); fought gallantly at Guilford Court House, North Carolina (March 1781); Fort Watson, South Carolina, in April; Forts Motte and Grandy, South Carolina, in May; Augusta and Ninety-Six, Georgia, in May and June; and Eutaw Springs, South Carolina, on September 8, 1781. He was at Yorktown when

Cornwallis surrendered on October 19, 1781. In 1794 Washington gave him command of an army of 15,000 troops to quell the Whiskey Rebellion in Pennsylvania, which he did without the loss of life. In Congress in 1799, it was Lee who called Washington "first in war, first in peace, and first in the hearts of his countrymen." Going to the aid of a friend during a riot in Baltimore in 1812, Lee was badly injured. He spent the few remaining years of his life in sickness and poverty.

Nicknamed "Light-Horse Harry," Henry Lee was a brilliant tactician and a fearless commander who consistently maneuvered his legion of infantry and cavalry with consummate skill. Remembered today as the father of **Robert E. Lee,** his third son, Henry Lee was an accomplished and valiant soldier in his own right.

Robert Edward Lee

1807–1870

Third son of the Revolutionary War hero **Henry Lee,** Robert Edward was born at Stratford, the Lee estate in Westmoreland County, Virginia. He graduated number two in the West Point class of 1829, without a single demerit.

Commissioned in the engineers, Lee spent the years before 1847 engaged in fortification, surveying, and harbor work, rising to the grade of captain in 1838. In August 1847 he joined the American Expeditionary Force at Buena Vista, Mexico. Transferred to Vera Cruz, he served on the staff of **Winfield Scott** and was slightly wounded at Chapultepec on September 13, 1847. He emerged from the war a brevet colonel. In 1852 he was appointed superintendent at West Point. In March 1855 he was appointed lieutenant colonel of the 2nd U.S. Cavalry in Texas. He commanded the regiment in person from March 1856 to October 1857, and from February 1860 to February 1861; in 1859 he commanded the troops who put down John Brown's insurrection at Harper's Ferry. On March 16, 1861, he was made colonel of the 1st U.S. Cavalry. When Virginia voted to secede from the Union, Lee resigned from the U.S. Army and, on April 23, 1861, accepted command of the state's forces. In August he was appointed to the rank of general as military adviser to Confederate president Jefferson Davis. When General **Joseph E. Johnston** was wounded in May 1862, Lee assumed command before Richmond. For the next thirty-four months Lee and his Army of Northern Virginia fought a series of the most difficult and bloody campaigns in history. Lee's battles and his lieutenants have become household names in America and his exploits are studied around the world. After the war he served as president of Washington College (now Washington and Lee) in Lexington, Virginia.

Robert E. Lee never commanded men in combat before May 1862, in his fifty-fifth year; he never had a field command before going to Texas in 1856. Between April 1861 and May 1862 his duties did not allow him to show what he could do with an army, and in his campaign against McClellan around Richmond in the spring and early summer of 1862, he and his staff were getting themselves sorted out. But at Second Manassas (Bull Run) in late August 1862, Lee's qualities of audacity, aggressiveness, and tactical genius began to show. He was an attacker and a fighter. Utterly contemptuous of his personal safety and comfort, Lee suffered the hardships of his soldiers. He always subordinated himself to the civilian authority of his government. Constantly outnumbered two or three to one, Lee was ground down and exhausted by his opponents. Lee was not a great strategist, and while he fought brilliantly to defend the front door of the Confederacy, the Union armies got at him finally through its back door. At times he was too lenient with his subordinates, especially **James Longstreet,** and perhaps he was too aggressive considering his limited manpower, but he saw it as his duty to fight on until victory, or he was ordered to stop, or until he could fight no more. Although he led the army that attempted to break the Union, today he is one of the most respected figures in the military pantheon of the reunited United States.

Le Loi

1385–1433

Born into a prominent landholding family of Lam Son village, Thanh Hoa Province, Vietnam, Le Loi served in the imperial bureaucracy until Chinese rule was reimposed on Vietnam in 1407. Resigning, he returned to Lam Son to organize armed resistance against the Chinese.

Known for his courage, honesty, and fairness, Le Loi attracted a considerable following in the mountains of his native province. Other nationalist groups rose up against the Chinese occupation, but Le Loi's gradually became the most effective. His strategy was to attack isolated Chinese outposts and ambush their supply columns, withdrawing before reinforcements could arrive. He also stirred up the local population through a masterful anti-Chinese propaganda campaign, and his troops were under strict orders never to exploit or mistreat the local people. Nevertheless, Le Loi was often defeated and once would have been captured, had it not been for the sacrifice of a loyal subordinate. In September 1426 he defeated a major Chinese army just west of Hanoi, and at Chi Lang, September 18, 1427, he inflicted a decisive defeat on the Chinese that forced them to sue for peace. Le Loi treated his Chinese prisoners (said to number 20,000) with kindness and, upon the signing of an armistice, let them return home. After the withdrawal of the Chinese, Le Loi established himself as emperor and the dynasty he founded lasted until 1788.

Five hundred years before Mao and Ho Chi Minh, Le Loi mastered the principles of "unconventional" war in Vietnam.

Curtis E. Lemay

1906—1990

A native of Ohio and son of a laborer, Lemay left college early to join the National Guard, receiving his pilot's wings in 1929.

As early as 1936 Lemay had concluded that bombers would have a decisive effect on any future war and in 1937 he joined the 305th Bombardment Group, with which he trained as a navigator. He was one of the first to fly the B-17. As a lieutenant colonel, he commanded the 305th in England in 1942. To prove that bombers could fly level over their targets long enough to drop their bombs accurately, he personally led raids against the enemy. Soon his men doubled the number of bombs placed on their targets. In August 1943 he led the famed "shuttle" bombing raid against Regensburg, Germany, and was promoted to brigadier general in September, major general in March 1944. Sent to the China-Burma-India Theater in August 1944, he was given the 21st Bomber Command based on Guam in January 1945. From there his stripped-down B-29s, flying at low-level altitudes, devastated targets in Japan. After the war Lemay commanded the Strategic Air Command. Promoted to full general in 1951, he was chiefly responsible for building the strong bomber-force deterrent of the Cold War years.

From 1961 to 1965 he was air-force chief of staff.

Lemay faced every problem head-on. No armchair theorist, he risked his own skin to prove his points. For him, the moral issue in war was how to win at the least cost to America. He knew how to motivate men to fight for him.

Leonidas of Sparta

d. 480 B.C.

The son of the Spartan king Anaxandridas, Leonidas ascended to the throne in 490 B.C., upon the demise of his two elder brothers, who left no issue.

When in 480 the Persian king Xerxes invaded Greece with an army of 100,000, Leonidas led a small force to hold the strategic pass of Thermopylae in eastern Greece, between Mt. Oeta and the Gulf of Maliakós, near the modern town of Lamia. His detachment numbered about 4,000 and consisted of 300 Spartans and men from other Greek cities. Meanwhile the main Greek army retreated beyond the Isthmus of Corinth, leaving Leonidas to delay the Persians until reinforcements could be sent. Leonidas considered retreat out of the question for himself, but he offered the other Greeks a chance to withdraw.

About 700 Thespians decided to stay. The historian Herodotus wrote that the Spartan Dieneces, when informed that the Persian arrows would fly so thickly as to blot out the sun, replied, "Good, then we will have our battle in the shade!" Leonidas held the pass for three days, until a traitor led the Persians by a path through the mountains to get behind the Greeks. The Greeks fought to the last man. It is said that Xerxes lost 20,000 men, including two brothers. The Persians were defeated at Platea the following July and withdrew from Greece.

Several monuments were erected over the graves of the Greeks who died at Thermopylae, one bearing the famous lines: "Go tell the Spartans, you who read: We took their orders, and are dead."

Lin Piao

1908?–1971

Born Lin Yu-yung in Ungkung, Hupeh Province, Central China, son of a poor artisan, Lin graduated from the Whampoa Military Academy in 1926. There he changed his name to Piao, "Tiger Cat."

Lin attained the rank of colonel in 1927 for his service against the warlords in southern China, but in August 1927 he defected to the communists with his regiment. He was given command

of the I Red Army Corps in January 1932. Using brilliant guerrilla tactics, Lin was able to avoid decisive defeat by Chiang Kai-shek's overwhelmingly larger forces. Lin's corps led the "Long March," in 1934–1935, a 6,500-mile trek to safety in Shensi Province in northeast-central China, where Mao Tse-tung set up his headquarters. In 1937 Lin commanded the 115th Division of the Eighth Route Army against the Japanese and, on September 25, 1937, ambushed and wiped out a Japanese brigade at Pingxing Pass, proving that with proper leadership, his men could defeat a modern military force. Seriously wounded at Pingxing, Lin spent four years recuperating in Russia. In January 1949 he took Peking from the Nationalists. By 1969 he was identified as Mao's successor. He died in a plane crash in 1971, reportedly fleeing in the wake of a failed coup.

Lin was a humane commander who believed in keeping his casualties low, but he was a bold and determined fighter. He told his men, "Pay for articles purchased from the peasants and establish latrines well beyond people's houses."

James A. Logan

1826–1886

A native of Jackson County, Illinois, Logan served as a lieutenant in the Mexican War, after which he practiced law and served in the Illinois Legislature. He was elected to the U.S. Congress as a Democrat in 1858 and reelected in 1860.

Logan fought at First Manassas (Bull Run; July 1861) as a private in a Michigan regiment. In September he was appointed colonel of the 31st Illinois. He fought under **Grant** at Belmont (November 1861), where he had a horse shot out from under him, and at Forts Donelson and Henry (February 1862), where he was wounded. Promoted to brigadier general, he led a division at Vicksburg, and promoted to major general in November 1863, he was given the XV Corps in the Army of Tennessee. In July 1864 he took command of the Army of Tennessee but was relieved by **Sherman,** who considered his attention to logistics deficient. At the Grand Review held in Washington after the war, however, he was honored to lead the Army of Tennessee again. Logan became a Republican after the war and it was he who conceived the idea of Memorial Day and inaugurated it, May 30, 1868. He was ever attentive to the welfare of the Union veterans.

Sherman considered Logan "perfect in combat" but not so meticulous in the details of army administration, and he mistrusted his political activities (he took leave to campaign for Lincoln in the election of 1860). Rutherford B. Hayes called him "clearly the most eminent and distinguished of the volunteer soldiers."

James Longstreet

1821–1904

Born in South Carolina, son of a farmer, Longstreet was raised in Georgia and graduated fifty-fourth of sixty-two in his West Point class of 1842.

During the Mexican War Longstreet served first with General **Taylor** at Monterey and then with General **Scott** during the expedition to Mexico City. He was wounded at Chapultepec in September 1847 and won two brevet promotions for heroism during the war; he was made major in the regular army in 1858. He resigned from the U.S. Army to accept a commission as a brigadier general, CSA, in June 1861. He commanded a brigade at First Manassas (Bull Run) (July 1861). He commanded a division at Yorktown and led five divisions to relieve **Jackson** at Second Manassas (August 1862). He fought at

South Mountain and Sharpsburg (Antietam; September 1862) and was promoted to lieutenant general in October; he led his corps at Fredericksburg in December. At Gettysburg he advised maneuver instead of a frontal attack against **Meade,** but **R. E. Lee** insisted he strike directly against the Union Army on Cemetery Ridge on July 2 and 3, 1863, which failed to dislodge Meade's army, as Longstreet feared. He fought brilliantly at the Wilderness in May 1864, where he was wounded severely. He surrendered with Lee at Appomattox. After the war he became a Republican and was minister to Turkey (1880) and held other political appointments.

Longstreet was a cautious planner, but once battle was joined, a ferocious opponent; he was an ideal corps commander. He preferred a defensive to Lee's offensive strategy and his actions at Gettysburg are still hotly debated. His criticism of Lee after the war earned him much hatred in the South.

Lysander

d. 395 B.C.

Raised in poverty and subject to rigid Spartan discipline; details of Lysander's early life are obscure.

Lysander is first noted in history when he was appointed admiral of the fleet in 408, during the Spartan League's war with Athens (the Peloponnesian War, 431–404). Lysander's first move was to establish a base in Ephesus and then he made friends with the Persian satrap, Cyrus the Younger, the son of King Darius II. Lysander's appointment came at a time when the Peloponnesian fleet had been demoralized by a series of defeats and the quarrels of previous commanders with their Persian allies. With Persian aid, Lysander built a fleet of ninety ships manned by mercenary rowers attracted by high wages, and he established a network of personal supporters to rule in occupied areas. In 407 he defeated the Athenians at Notium, a port on the southwest coast of Asia Minor. In August 405 Lysander moved to threaten the Athenian supply line through the Dardanelles. At Aegospotami, a small town on the Dardanelles, he caught 171 Athenian ships on the beach and destroyed all but a few. The 3,000 Athenians taken prisoner were put to the sword. Lysander than blockaded Piraeus, Athens's harbor, and in April 404, the city surrendered. Lysander's career after the war was uneven. He was killed suppressing a revolt in Boetia.

Lysander was a harsh victor and irresponsible in his appointment of subordinates, but personally he was incorruptible. Athens was the supreme naval power in the world until its fleet was destroyed at Aegospotami, one of the most decisive naval victories in history.

M

Arthur MacArthur

1845–1912

When he failed to obtain an appointment to West Point during the Civil War, in August 1862 MacArthur volunteered for service in the 24th Wisconsin Volunteers.

MacArthur served throughout the war as an officer in the 24th Wisconsin, rising from lieutenant to full colonel and regimental commander by the age of twenty. During the war he was wounded several times and twice promoted for gallantry under fire. At Missionary Ridge (November 25, 1863) he led his regiment to the crest and personally planted its colors there, for which he received the Medal of Honor in June 1890. Discharged in June 1865, he came back into the army as a second lieutenant in 1866. In May 1869, as a captain in the 36th Infantry, he was placed on the inactive list but was recalled in July 1870 and assigned to the 13th Infantry. He held this grade and served in this regiment, mostly on frontier duty, for the next twenty years. He did not regain his wartime rank of lieutenant colonel until 1896. In May 1898 he was commissioned a brigadier general of volunteers and sent to the Philippines in command of the 1st Brigade, 2nd Division, VIII Corps, where he took part in the occupation of Manila. He played an important role in the pacification of the Philippines, combining aggressive military operations against the guerrillas with humane civic action programs. He was promoted to major general in the regular army in 1900 and lieutenant general in 1906. He retired

Arthur MacArthur

from active service in 1909 and died in the middle of a speech at a reunion of the 24th Wisconsin in Milwaukee on September 5, 1912.

Like **"Light-Horse Harry" Lee,** Arthur MacArthur was a splendid soldier in his own right who has been overshadowed by an illustrious son. Arthur was an intrepid and gallant combat commander who had a natural aptitude for the military profession. Promoted to high rank after many years of selfless service in obscure posts, he stood out in the small group of professionals who led the U.S. Army into the 20th century.

Douglas MacArthur

1880–1964

The third son of **Arthur MacArthur,** Douglas was born in Little Rock, Arkansas, and graduated first in his West Point class of 1903.

MacArthur went straight to the Philippines from West Point. He served as an aide to his father on a tour of Asia in 1905–1906, which he referred to as the "most important preparation of my entire life." In 1906 he was appointed an aide to President Theodore Roosevelt and in 1913 was assigned to the general staff. He won the Medal of Honor during the Vera Cruz expedition of 1914. He helped organize the 42nd Division upon the United States' entry into World War I in 1917, and in the fall of 1917, he went to France as a colonel and division chief of staff. He was at Aisne-Marne in July and August 1918, commanded a brigade at Saint-Mihiel in September and Meuse-Argonne in October and November, and ended the war a brigadier general in command of the division. He was wounded twice and earned numerous decorations for heroism. In 1919 he was appointed superintendent of the Military Academy and in 1925 was promoted to major general. He was appointed chief of staff of the army in 1930. In 1935 President Franklin Roosevelt sent him to the Philippines as military adviser to the commonwealth. MacArthur retired in 1937, but in July 1941 he was recalled as a lieutenant general and given command in the Far East. He led the hopeless defense of the Philippines against the Japanese, December 1941–March 1942, before he was ordered to Australia. He was awarded a second Medal of Honor for the defense of the Philippines. In April 1942 he was made commander of the Allied forces in the Southwest Pacific, when he undertook the reconquest of New Guinea and the Philippines. He presided at the Japanese surrender at Tokyo Bay on September 2, 1945. He then became supreme commander of the occupation forces in Japan and as such virtually remolded Japanese society. He became commander of the United Nations forces fighting in Korea in July 1950 and launched the brilliant counterattack at Inchon September 15, 1950, which resulted in the complete defeat of the North Korean army. Surprised by the Chinese invasion in the winter of 1950, he was relieved by President Truman in April 1951 after making bellicose statements conflicting with Truman's policy on the conduct of the war in Korea. After a brief tour making speeches against Truman's conduct of the Korean War, MacArthur retired into relative obscurity for the rest of his life.

A complicated and contradictory personality, Douglas MacArthur was either loved or hated. He was brilliant as an innovative superintendent at West Point, an aggressive supreme commander in the Pacific, and America's proconsul in Japan. But he was unprepared in the Philippines and Korea and his insubordination ended his military career under a cloud. He was a very brave soldier, as his many decorations attest. His campaigns during World War II were brilliantly executed, bold, and achieved at a low cost in the lives of his men. All in all, he was one of history's greatest commanders, but what irked many people about him was that he knew it and always acted the part.

Ranald S. Mackenzie

1840–1889

Son of Commodore Alexander S. Mackenzie, Ranald was born in New York and brought up in New Jersey. He graduated first of twenty-eight in his West Point class of 1862.

As a brand-new second lieutenant of engineers, Mackenzie went straight into combat from West Point and was wounded at Second Manassas (Bull Run). He was at Fredricksburg, Chancellorsville, Gettysburg, the Wilderness, Spotsylvania, Cedar Creek, and Petersburg. He was wounded five times and ended the war at age twenty-five a major general of volunteers commanding the 2nd Brigade, 1st Division, VI Corps. In later life he was known among the Indians as "Bad Hand" because two fingers on his right hand were shot off during the war. Mackenzie stayed in the army after the war, first as colonel of the 41st Infantry along the Texas frontier, then as commander of the 24th Infantry, and in 1871 he was appointed to command the 4th Cavalry Regiment, where he led long-range patrols against the Comanches and Kiowas. In 1872–1873, marching against the Kickapoos and Apaches, Mackenzie conducted a 150-mile raid into Mexico, at least tacitly approved by his superiors, to destroy the Indians' base of operations. Pursued by Mexican cavalry, he successfully withdrew his command with only two casualties. Mackenzie realized that killing Indians was not as important a part of subduing them as destroying their supplies and horse herds, and until he was promoted to higher command in 1883, he pursued a successful policy of swift and decisive raids that placed sure retribution and relentless pressure upon the Indians. He died in a madhouse, perhaps from the effects of brain damage sustained in an accident in 1875.

Grant wrote of Mackenzie that he succeeded in command "upon his own merit and without influence," and a contemporary newspaperman wrote that "he was always prompt in the saddle and never tangled his spurs in the maze of endless red tape." Add to this that he was an exacting and austere man who shared every hardship in the field with his men.

Carl Gustav Emil von Mannerheim

1867–1951

Born at Vilnäs, near Turku, Finland, Mannerheim joined the Russian army in 1889 (Finland was part of czarist Russia at the time).

Mannerheim fought in the Russo-Japanese War of 1904–1905 and commanded a corps as a lieutenant general under the czar in World War I, but after the Russian Revolution, he returned to Finland. He became a national hero for fighting the Bolsheviks and helping Finland secure its independence from Russia in 1918. As chairman of the Finnish defense council he strengthened the border defenses against the Russians, so that when the Soviets hurled a million-man invasion army against the Finns in November 1939, Mannerheim's much smaller forces stopped them. Using small, highly mobile units, Mannerheim's army chopped the poorly led, ill-equipped Russians to pieces, killing 27,500 of them at the Battle of Suomussalmi, December 1939-January 1940, while losing only 900 of his own men. The Russians lost perhaps 200,000 more men when they counterattacked in February 1940, but by sheer weight of numbers they forced the Finns to capitulate. In June 1941, Finland allied herself with Germany, and as part of a combined force, Mannerheim took back the territory conquered by the Russians. In September 1944 Finland signed a unilateral truce with the Soviet Union and Mannerheim became president of the Finnish Republic.

Mannerheim was a master of mobile warfare who also understood defensive tactics and modern army administration.

Fritz Erich von Manstein

1887–1973

Born in Berlin, son of General Eduard von Lewinski, Manstein was raised in the family of General George von Manstein following his father's death. His uncle was **Paul von Hindenberg**.

Severely wounded early in World War I, Manstein served the rest of the war in staff positions. A major general at the outbreak of World War II, he proposed a brilliant "left hook" strategy for the invasion of France: a surprise armored attack through the Ardennes followed by a drive to trap the Allies against the coast, which worked brilliantly, despite some reservations in the high command. As commander of the LVI Panzer Corps in Russia, he advanced 200 miles in four days, June 22–26, 1941, and as commander of the Eleventh Army, he captured Sevastopol after

a 250-day siege. If his advice had been followed at Stalingrad, some of the German Sixth Army trapped there might have been saved, but its commander, Paulus, hesitated and Hitler's interference sealed its doom. Manstein advocated luring the Russians into prepared positions and cutting them off, but Hitler dictated no retreat and the two clashed often. He managed a brilliant fighting withdrawal in southern Russia until he was relieved by Hitler in March 1944. Although convicted, primarily on Soviet insistence, of war crimes in 1949, Manstein's sentence was reduced and he was released in 1953.

Manstein, who had the courage, rare in Nazi Germany, to disagree with Hitler, was also a master of maneuver warfare.

Marcus Aurelius

121–180

Born into a patrician Roman family, Marcus Aurelius is remembered today chiefly as a Stoic philosopher—his *Meditations* may still be read for pleasure—and an especially enlightened emperor, but he was also a very successful soldier.

After serving three times as consul, Marcus served the emperor Antoninus Pius faithfully until his death in March 161, whereupon Marcus declared himself emperor with his foster brother, Lucius Verus, co-emperor. His first military campaign was against the Parthians in 162,

but actual operations were conducted by Verus or his principal field commander, Cassidus. In 167 Marcus again took the field, this time in person against the Germans, who were ravaging the Danube frontier. Marcus forced them to accept an armistice in 168. Verus died in 169 and the Germans crossed the Danube again. This time Marcus took the field for three years, decisively defeating the Marcomanni and Quadi tribes. While in Germany, news reached Marcus that Cassidus, commanding in Asia, had revolted. As he was preparing to take an army to Egypt to suppress the revolt in 175, word was received that Cassidus's troops had killed him. Marcus then undertook an extensive tour of the eastern provinces. In 178 he took the field against the Germans again. The campaign was going very well when Marcus became ill and died at Vindobona (Vienna).

Marcus Aurelius was a determined and tenacious commander, a skilled tactician and administrator who knew the value of good planning.

Francis Marion

1732–1795

Born in South Carolina, Marion was a small, frail child, whose education was rudimentary. He began his adult life as a planter on his family's modest estate.

As a militia lieutenant in an expedition against the Cherokee Indians in June 1761, Marion was picked to lead a sortie to break up a suspected ambush; this he accomplished, with a detachment of thirty men, twenty-one of whom were wounded in the engagement. In June 1775 he was named captain in the 2nd South Carolina Regiment, eventually taking command as a lieutenant colonel in September 1778. He fought gallantly in the unsuccessful assault on Savannah in October 1779, but with the surrender of Charleston in May 1780, Marion began his career as a guerrilla. He was pursued for seven hours through twenty-six miles of swamp by **Banastre Tarleton,** who finally gave up the chase, muttering, "The devil himself could not catch him!" Marion then established a base of operations in South Carolina and from there conducted raids against British positions and troops. At Eutaw Springs, September 8, 1781, the militia under his command fought so well that **Greene** wrote to Congress that they "gained much honor by their firmness," a high compliment for revolutionary militia. At Fair Lawn on August 29, 1782, he fought his last action, ambushing a troop of 200 dragoons sent to surprise him.

Known as the "Swamp Fox," Marion had a natural genius for unconventional warfare. He was ruthless in the attack. But he also had the professional standards of a regular soldier and could subordinate his operations to an overall strategy.

John Churchill, Duke of Marlborough

1650–1722

Born at Ashe in Devonshire, England, the son of an obscure squire, Marlborough was commissioned an ensign in the Foot Guards in 1667.

Marlborough served with distinction under James II, becoming a baron in 1685 and rising to the rank of lieutenant general. Marlborough supported William and Mary in the Revolution of 1688 and was created Earl of Marlborough by them, but he fell out of favor and was even briefly imprisoned in 1692. Gradually regaining William's confidence, he was returned to military command in 1700, and when Anne became queen in 1702, he was given command of the troops fighting in France in the War of the Spanish Succession. At the battles of Blenheim (August 13, 1704) and Ramillies (May 23, 1706), Marlborough achieved stunning victories, inflicting upon the French and Bavarians a total of

53,000 killed, wounded, and captured to 16,000 of his own. Blenheim was second only to Waterloo in its triumph. At Malplaquet (September 17, 1709), Marlborough forced a well-led French army to withdraw simply by attacking when other generals would have given up. But England began to weary of the war, and no longer on good terms with Queen Anne's government, he was recalled in 1710 and accused of corruption. George I restored him to his military offices, but his health declining, Marlborough died of a stroke in June 1722.

Ambitious and arrogant, Marlborough made many enemies who were jealous of his power. Called "Corporal John" by his men because of his concern for their welfare, Marlborough was one of England's greatest soldiers. A brilliant tactician, administrator, and diplomat, he led his Dutch and German allies to victory. His record as an undefeated general remains unbroken. Sir Winston Churchill was one of Marlborough's direct descendants.

Charles Martel

690?–741

The illegitimate son of Pepin II and a noblewoman, Alpaide, Charles did not receive his nickname—Martel ("Hammer")—until long after his death.

When Pepin died in 714 while his legitimate heirs were still children, Charles took control of the Frankish kingdoms. He fought his father's widow, Plectrude, and her supporters, defeating them decisively at Vichy in 718, after which he was accepted as ruler of all the Frankish regions. His first priority was to protect southern France against incursions from the Moors, who had conquered Spain in 711 and were now raiding across the Pyrenees into France. The Moors captured the city of Narbonne in 719, were driven back, returned in 725–726, and in 732, under 'Abd ar-Rahmān, the governor of Spain, burned

Bordeaux and laid waste to Aquitaine. In early October 732, Charles confronted the Moors somewhere between Tours and Poitiers. Charles's army of infantrymen was formed into a square. The Moorish cavalry wildly charged the square in a series of attacks that lasted several days, but they were all beaten off, and when 'Abd ar-Rahmān was killed, the Moors withdrew. After this, Charles developed the cavalry as his primary offensive arm. Charles checked the Moors again at Valence in 737, and Lyons in 739.

Aside from checking the Moorish invasion of France, Charles established the cavalryman in European warfare, which led to the class of elite mounted knights who dominated medieval France.

André Masséna

1758–1817

Orphaned early in life, Masséna worked in an uncle's soap factory until the age of thirteen, when he ran away to sea.

In 1775, Masséna enlisted in the French

army's Royal Italian Regiment, rising to the rank of sergeant major in 1784. Discharged in 1789, he became a grocer and possibly a smuggler. He returned to the army via the National Guard in

1791, and by 1793, as a general of division, he played a prominent part in the Italian Campaign under **Napoleon,** who called him "the darling child of victory." In June and September 1799, he won the important battles of Zurich, inflicting such a defeat on the Russo-Austrian force invading Switzerland from Italy that the Russians withdrew from the alliance against France. By holding the Austrians and the British in Italy in 1800, he gave Napoleon time to prepare for his victory at Marengo in June. He was made a marshal of France in May 1804. In 1809, after an undistinguished campaign in Italy, he performed brilliantly at Aspern-Essling on May 21–22, covering Napoleon's retreat, and at Wagram in July he commanded the weak French left, successfully holding off the Austrians while Napoleon crushed the Austrians' left and center. Masséna's campaign in Portugal in 1810–1811 was a failure, and weary and sick, he was relieved. He remained neutral in 1815 and was not with Napoleon at Waterloo.

Masséna was an instinctive general and his titles were given as combat honors. While he loved fast women and a quick franc, his courage was absolute and he was never discouraged in combat.

Maurice of Nassau

1567–1625

Second son of William I, Maurice spent his early childhood in Germany and by the age of eighteen, had studied both at Heidelberg and Leiden universities.

Appointed the president of the council of state of the United Provinces upon the assassination of his father in July 1584, the following year Maurice succeeded his father as stadholder (governor) of the provinces of Holland and Zealand; by 1591 he was also governor of Utrecht, Overijssel, and Gelderland Provinces and captain general and admiral general of the Dutch forces. A student of Roman warfare, he applied what he had learned from books to the siegecraft and troop maneuvers of his day, which were not that much advanced over what the Romans knew. He created a large standing army of paid, long-term, locally recruited professionals trained and disciplined to high standards; he hired the great mathematician Simon Stevin as a military engineer; he sent his engineers and senior officers to study the science of war at the University of Leiden; and he developed a strong cavalry arm. With the capture of Breda in 1590, Maurice commenced a series of brilliant victories against the occupying Spanish forces, culminating in the one-sided victories at Turnhout in January 1597 and Nieuport in July 1600. He inherited the title of Prince of Orange in 1618. His younger brother, Henry, carried on the struggle against Spain after his death.

An innovative, intelligent, and aggressive soldier far ahead of his times, Maurice laid the foundation for an independent Holland.

George Gordon Meade

1815–1872

Born in Cádiz, Spain, son of a U.S. naval agent, Meade graduated nineteenth of fifty-six in his West Point class of 1835.

Commissioned a second lieutenant in the 3rd Artillery, he served a year in Florida during the Seminole War and then resigned his commission in October 1836 when he went to work for the railroad. In May 1842 he came back into the army as a second lieutenant of topographical engineers. He served in Mexico and was at Palo Alto, Resaca de la Palma, Monterey, and Vera Cruz. In 1850 he saw service again in Florida against the Seminoles. He spent the years before the Civil War engaged in topographical and engineering work. In August 1861, he was made brigadier general of volunteers and commanded a Pennsylvania brigade. He was severely wounded at Frayser's Farm (June 30, 1862) and fought at Second Manassas (Bull Run) in August 1862 and Sharpsburg (Antietam) in September,

where he temporarily commanded the I Corps of the Army of the Potomac. In November he was made a major general of volunteers and commanded the V Corps at Fredericksburg in December 1862. He was at Chancellorsville in May 1863. On June 28, 1863, he was named to replace Hooker in command of the Army of the Potomac. He protested this selection but followed orders and three days later turned back **R. E. Lee** at Gettysburg. From March 1864 to the end of the war, when **Grant,** as commander of all the Union forces, took the field with Meade's army, Meade's work was confined to the tactical arena. On November 6, 1872, weakened by his old war wounds, he died from pneumonia.

Meade was a steadfast and loyal officer whose tenacity at Gettysburg, after only three days in command of the Army of the Potomac, secured a victory that was pivotal to the success of the Union cause.

Frank D. Merrill

1903–1955

Born in Hopkinson, Massachusetts, Merrill enlisted in the army in 1922 and rose to the rank of staff sergeant before being accepted at West Point, where he was commissioned in the cavalry in 1929.

In 1938 Merrill was sent to the U.S. embassy in Tokyo, where he studied Japanese and learned Chinese dialects. When World War II broke out, he was in Burma, on a mission for General **Douglas MacArthur**. He remained in Rangoon and joined Lieutenant General **Stilwell**'s forces in March 1942. He retreated with Stilwell into India in May 1942 and, in October 1943, was given command of the 5037th Provisional Regiment,

the only U.S. infantry unit then on the Asian mainland. The 5037th, dubbed "Merrill's Marauders," was modeled after **Orde Wingate's** Chindits to fight in the jungles behind Japanese lines. Promoted to brigadier general in November 1943, in February 1944 Merrill led his men from Ledo in India on a 100-mile march to cut the Japanese supply lines at Maingkwan in northern Burma, on the Chindwin River. Cooperating with Stilwell's Chinese forces, Merrill's men killed 650 Japanese at the cost to themselves of 7 dead and 37 wounded. From April–July 1944 Merrill was hospitalized, but returned to direct the final assault on the Japanese at

Myitkyina in August. He ended the war a major general.

Merrill trained and organized and then led his men on a punishing but ultimately successful 100-day jungle campaign. Heart trouble and malaria, not the enemy, laid him low.

Wesley Merritt

1834–1910

Originally a law student, Merritt entered the U.S. Military Academy in 1855, graduating twenty-two out of forty-one in the Class of 1860 with a commission in the dragoons.

After brief service on the frontier, Merritt spent the first two years of the Civil War a staff officer, until on June 29, 1863, he was promoted from captain to brigadier general of volunteers. In command of the reserve cavalry brigade at Gettysburg (July 1–3, 1863), he received a brevet promotion to major in the regulars for bravery in that battle. Between then and April 1865, he participated in no fewer than thirty battles and skirmishes, rising to command a cavalry division and then the cavalry corps of both the Army of the Shenandoah and the Army of the Potomac. He received five brevet promotions during the war, ending it as a major general of volunteers. He remained in the army after the war, fighting Indians on the frontier as lieutenant colonel of the 9th Cavalry in 1866 and colonel of the 5th Cavalry, which he commanded from 1876 to 1879. In 1882 he became superintendent at West Point and a brigadier general of regulars in 1887. Promoted to major general in 1895, in 1898 he commanded the Philippine expedition. He accepted the surrender of Manila with Admiral **Dewey** in August 1898. He retired in 1900.

With over forty years of active service, Merritt was one of the solid, competent, widely experienced, and distinguished but personally modest senior officers who led the U.S. Army into the twentieth century and world prominence.

Nelson A. Miles

1839–1925

Born on his father's farm near Westminster, Massachusetts, as a young man Miles worked in a crockery store in Boston while he studied military subjects on his own.

At the outbreak of the Civil War, Miles recruited a company of volunteers that was assigned to the 22nd Massachusetts Regiment. He was wounded and cited for gallantry at Fair Oaks, Virginia, May 31–June 1, 1862, after which he was appointed lieutenant colonel of the 61st New York. At Sharpsburg (Antietam), September 17, 1862, when the 61st's colonel was wounded, he assumed command of the regiment on the field and became its commander on September 30. He was shot at Fredericksburg in December, where he was again cited for gallantry; desperately holding the line against the advancing Confederates at Chancellorsville on May 3, 1863, he was shot from his horse (in 1892 he received the Medal of Honor for valor in this action); and was wounded again at Petersburg in 1864. He ended the war a major general of volunteers in command of the II Corps of the Army of the Potomac—at the age of twenty-six. Ap-

Free Library of Philadelphia

Nelson A. Miles

pointed colonel of the 40th Infantry in 1866, he was transferred to the 5th Infantry in 1869. On the frontier, he fought the Cheyennes, Kiowas, and Comanches in Texas in 1874–1875; the Sioux in Montana in 1876; the Nez Percé and the Bannocks in 1877; the Apaches in 1885–1887; and the Sioux again during the Ghost Dance uprising in 1890–1891. Appointed brigadier general in the regular army in 1880, he was made major general in 1890, commander in chief of the army in 1895, and lieutenant general in 1901. He retired in 1903.

A natural soldier, Miles attained high leadership through great personal courage and demonstrated ability.

Miltiades

549?–488 B.C.

Born into an aristocratic Athenian family, Miltiades' career prior to the Persian invasion of 490 was spent engaged in a series of political/military adventures, including a period of service under the Persian king Darius I.

In July 490, with a Persian fleet already under way to punish Athens for its support of the Ionian revolt against Persia, Miltiades, because of his experience with the Persian army, was elected one of ten generals appointed to oppose them. A Greek army of about 11,000 men (including a 1,000-man contingent from neighboring Platea) marched the twenty-six miles to Marathon, where they blocked the road to Athens as an army of 20,000 Persians disembarked from their ships. The rest of the army, perhaps another 20,000 men, sailed on for Athens, which they expected to find undefended. Realizing what was happening, Miltiades argued for an immediate attack. Miltiades' argument prevailed and he was given tactical command of the Greek army. With his center deliberately weakened to reinforce his wings, Miltiades attacked, drawing the Persians into the center and enveloping them with his wings. About 200 Greeks were killed to 6,500 Persians; the survivors fled in their ships. The Greeks then force-marched back to Athens in time to thwart the planned seaborne invasion. Wounded in an attack on Paros in 489, Miltiades died of his wounds in 488.

At Marathon, Miltiades executed a perfect "double envelopment" to win one of the most decisive battles in history.

Walther Model

1891–1945

The son of a music instructor, Model started his military career in 1909 and, as a captain on the Western Front in World War I, won the Iron Cross.

Model stayed in the army after the war, and when Hitler came to power in Germany, he joined the Nazi party and remained loyal to Hitler until the end. He served as chief of staff of the IV Panzer Corps in Poland in 1939 and was chief of staff of the Sixteenth Army in France in 1940. In October 1941, commanding the 3rd Panzer Division in Russia, he led the drive that encircled vast numbers of Russian troops around Kiev. He was given command of the Ninth Army in January 1942. Known as "Hitler's fireman," Model was switched from sector to sector during the Russian counterattacks of 1943–1944. Promoted to field marshal in March 1944, he succeeded in temporarily stabilizing the front on the East Prussian border. Transferred to the Western Front in August 1944, his quick reaction defeated the British airborne forces at Arnhem on September 17. His Army Group B launched the Ardennes Offensive in December 1944. Forced back into the Ruhr, Model surrendered 300,000 men in April 1945. Having said two years before, when Paulus surrendered the Sixth Army at Stalingrad, that it would be "unthinkable" for a field marshal to capitulate, he shot himself on April 21, 1945.

Model was an aggressive and skillful commander who inspired his subordinates to fierce resistance. He had the traditional "balls to the wall" attitude of the cavalryman.

Sir Charles Carmichael Monro

1860–1929

Born at sea aboard the SS *Maid of Judah,* Monro came from an old Scottish family of distinguished physicians. He graduated from Sandhurst in 1879.

In 1897 Monro saw service in India, and during the Boer War in South Africa, he participated in the march to Pretoria and saw action at Poplar Grove on March 7, 1900, and Dreifontein on March 10, 1900. Based on his combat experience in India and South Africa, he was responsible for the evolution of new infantry fire tactics, and reformed the methods of teaching marksmanship in the British army. Promoted to major general in 1910, he led a division to France in August 1914. His division fought at Mons in August 1914, the Marne in September, and the First Battle of Ypres in October. When an enemy shell killed nearly all the staff officers of his division on October 31, he survived with only slight wounds. In October 1915 he was sent out to command the expeditionary force at Gallipoli that had been stymied there with severe losses. Within days of his arrival he saw that the Allied position there was hopeless and recommended a complete withdrawal. Between December 8, 1915, and January 9, 1916, the entire British force was withdrawn, the final 35,000 men under the noses of the unsuspecting Turks on the night of January 8–9, 1916. He served in India after the war and retired in 1920.

Monro was deliberate, cool, and determined in action. His masterful withdrawal of the Allied force from Gallipoli was one of the greatest feats of the war.

Louis-Joseph, Marquis de Montcalm

1712–1759

Born in Nîmes, France, of an impoverished noble family, Montcalm entered the army at the age of fifteen.

Montcalm distinguished himself in action during the War of the Austrian Succession (1740–1748), during which he received six wounds, five of them from saber slashes while rallying his men under the walls of Piacenza, Italy, June 16, 1746. Promoted to major general in 1756, he was sent to Canada to defend the colony against the British during the French and Indian (Seven Years) War. Obstructed by the royal governor, who resented his authority, Montcalm fought outnumbered and with indifferent supplies, his operations hampered by unpredictable Indian allies and the sheer difficulty of moving troops through the trackless North American wilderness. At no time did he ever directly command more than 4,500 regular troops. By gaining local superiority, he captured Fort Oswego in July 1756 and Fort William Henry in August 1757. When his Indians ran amok and began to slaughter the surrendered garrison at Fort William Henry, Montcalm physically intervened to save those he could. At Fort Ticonderoga (Fort Carillon), in July 1758, he held off 15,000 British and provincial troops with only about 3,600 men. Inexorably, the British forced Montcalm back upon Quebec. On September 13, 1759, British general **James Wolfe** besieged Quebec with about 4,800 men. Montcalm attacked with 4,500 troops. Both commanders were mortally wounded and the city surrendered the next day.

An officer of high personal bravery and integrity, Montcalm fought a splendid defensive campaign against a superior enemy.

Raimondo Montecuccoli

1609–1680

Born near Modena, Italy, son of an Italian noble family, Montecuccoli entered the Austrian service in 1629 as an ensign in a dragoon regiment.

Montecuccoli fought at Breitenfeld (September 1631) against **Gustavus Adolphus,** and at Nördlingen (September 6, 1634) he won promotion to colonel for leading a cavalry charge through a breach in a wall. Captured in 1639, he spent his time until release studying mathematics, the art of war, and other subjects. He won distinction fighting the Swedes at Triebel in August 1647. In 1648 he was made general of cavalry, and field marshal in 1658. From 1658 to 1660 he campaigned successfully against the Swedes, and on August 1, 1664, his much smaller army won a decisive victory over the Turks at the Raab River. During the early phase of the Dutch War of 1672–1678, he fought against **Turenne,** pushing the French back across the Rhine and into Alsace after the latter was killed in July 1675.

Driven back himself when **Condé** succeeded Turenne in command of the French army, Montecuccoli kept his force intact. He retired in December 1675.

Montecuccoli was a brilliant battlefield commander, a military reformer, and a military theorist whose books were widely read in their day. An advocate of firepower, he introduced a lighter musket, instituted tighter fire discipline among his troops, and systematized the entire organization of the Austrian army. He coined the saying "For war you need three things, 1) Money. 2) Money. 3) Money."

Simon de Montfort

1165–1218

Born near Rambouillet in the north of France southwest of Paris, de Montfort's early life is obscure.

In 1202 Simon set off on the Fourth Crusade. He wound up going to the Holy Land on his own while the rest of the "crusaders" sacked the port city of Zadara on the Adriatic and then Constantinople as the result of fast business deals with the Venetians and the son of a deposed Byzantine emperor. Back in France, Simon led a crusade against the Albigensian heretics between 1208 and 1213, slaughtering them with great abandon while enriching himself. In 1213 Pedro II of Aragon allied himself with the heretics under Raymond VI of Toulouse and with an army of 4,000 knights and 30,000 infantry besieged Simon's fortress at Muret, garrisoned with only 700 men. With only 900 horsemen, Simon joined the garrison. Luring the attackers inside the castle walls where the garrison engaged their attention, Simon and his horsemen pretended to abandon the place only to circle around the Aragonese army, surprising and smashing a large detachment. When the main body came up, 600 of Simon's horse attacked their center while the remainder under Simon attacked their rear. The Spanish force broke and fled, leaving Pedro dead on the field. Simon then routed Raymond's army! He was killed besieging Toulouse in June 1218.

Simon's cruelty and greed were matched by his boldness and personal courage in battle. Instead of running at Murat, he stayed to win one of history's most one-sided victories.

Bernard Law Montgomery

1887–1976

Born in London, Montgomery grew up in Tasmania, attended St. Paul's School in London, and graduated from Sandhurst in 1908 with a commission in the Royal Warwickshire Regiment.

Montgomery ended World War I a lieutenant colonel with a wound and a D.S.O. for leadership at the First Battle of Ypres. At the outbreak of World War II he was a division commander. In the retreat to Dunkirk (June 1940) he commanded his corps' rear guard and was knighted for his conduct. In July 1942, he was named commander of the Eighth Army in Egypt. His defeat of **Rommel**'s army at el-Alamein, October 23–November 4, 1942, drove the Germans out of Egypt. For this victory he was promoted to full general. He commanded the Eighth Army in Tunisia, Sicily, and Italy before returning to

National Archives

Bernard Law Montgomery (left, shaking hands)

England in December 1943 to prepare the 21st Army Group for the invasion of Europe. He directed the British Second and the U. S. First Armies at Normandy, June 6, 1944. He was promoted to field marshal in September 1944. While his attack at Arnhem in September 1944 was a failure, at the Battle of the Bulge (December 16, 1944–January 15, 1945) his troops restored the northern shoulder of the line and crossed the Rhine, March 23, 1945. He was deputy supreme allied commander, Europe, from 1951 to 1958, when he retired.

Montgomery was a careful and thorough planner who inspired the men under him, and while opinionated and brusque, which offended many and made him very hard to get along with, he was certainly one of World War II's greatest commanders.

Daniel Morgan

1736–1802

Probably born in New Jersey, first cousin of Daniel Boone, Morgan left home at the age of seventeen to seek his fortune.

In 1755 he joined Braddock's ill-fated army as a teamster on its march to capture Fort Duquesne on the site of modern Pittsburgh. During this campaign he got to know **George Washington**. In 1756 he was sentenced to receive 500 lashes for striking a British officer. In later life he joked that he "owed" the British one stripe, because the drummer had miscounted. In 1773 and 1775 he fought Indians. In June 1775 he was commissioned captain of one of two Virginia rifle companies and joined Washington at Boston. He accompanied **Arnold** to Quebec and in the abortive assault on the city, December 31, 1775, led the attack after Arnold was wounded. As a colonel, his regiment of sharpshooters played a decisive role at the Battle of Saratoga in 1777. Citing ill health, he retired in 1779, but was recalled in 1780, appointed brigadier general, and eventually sent to serve under **Greene** in the south. At Cowpens, January 17, 1781, his decisive victory over **Tarleton** has been called an "American Cannae" because Morgan executed a perfect double envelopment of the British force, killing over 100 men and capturing more than 800 at a loss of only 12 of his own killed and 60 wounded. For this victory Morgan was awarded a gold medal by Congress. In February 1781 he resigned again. After the Revolution Morgan became a prosperous landowner and served a term in Congress.

Known as "Old Wagoner" and "Old Dan," Morgan was a stout and active man despite his frequent complaints of ill health. He was also a resolute soldier with a natural talent for command of men in war.

Naitonal Archives

Daniel Morgan

Henry Morgan

1635?–1688

Born in Wales, Morgan was kidnapped at Bristol when a boy and sold as a servant in Barbados, from where he made his way to Jamaica and became a buccaneer.

Morgan is first mentioned commanding a ship during the British expedition of 1666 against Curaçao in the Netherlands Antilles. In 1668, under orders from the governor of Jamaica, Morgan performed a reconnaissance against the Spanish in Cuba. He sent word back that the Spanish were assembling an expedition against Jamaica. With 400 men and no artillery, Morgan then sailed to Portobelo on the east coast of Panama, where on June 26, 1668, he launched an attack against its three forts, which he took after heavy fighting. The city fell and Morgan's men plundered the place. Morgan was lightly censured for having exceeded his commission by attacking the town. In January 1671, with 1,400 men in seven ships and some boats, he landed at the Chagres River on the east coast of Panama and marched overland to a site about seven miles east of where the modern Panama City now stands, where he attacked a Spanish force of 3,000 infantry and cavalry. After a two-hour fight the Spanish ranks broke, leaving 600 dead on the field. Morgan then burned the city. According to the commission granted by the governor of Jamaica in 1670, Morgan's men were to be paid by plunder, so they plundered. Appointed lieutenant governor of Jamaica in 1674, he lived in quiet respectability until his death.

Morgan's accomplishments and skill as an irregular commander have been obscured by his cruelty and rapaciousness. With few resources and a handful of men, he did great service for England in the Caribbean, but since he profited immensely from his risks, some who have never faced a Spanish blade have since called him a mere pirate.

John Hunt Morgan

1825–1864

Born in Alabama but raised in Kentucky, Morgan saw action at Buena Vista in the Mexican War. A prosperous businessman, he organized a militia company, the Lexington Rifles, in 1857.

In September 1861, Morgan joined the Confederate Army as a scout. He fought at Shiloh in April 1862 and for his conduct there was given a regiment. In the summer of 1862 he commenced his career as a raider. On July 4, with 800 men, he began a 1,000-mile raid through Kentucky, during which he captured over 1,200 federals at the cost of only 100 of his own men. In October, with 1,800 men, he captured Lexington. In December, with 4,000 men, he rode back into Tennessee, capturing 1,880 federals at the cost to him of only 2 men killed and 21 wounded. In the summer of 1863, at the head of about 2,400 men, he was authorized to raid into Kentucky, but contrary to orders, crossed into Indiana. For three weeks he caused panic in Indiana and Ohio, raiding into the suburbs of Cincinnati the night of July 13–14. Spending up to twenty-one hours in the saddle throughout this expedition, his men covered fifty to sixty miles a day. Captured July 26, in November he escaped and rejoined his army. On September 3, 1864, he was surprised and killed at Greenville, Tennessee.

Severely criticized for his Ohio raid, Morgan was at his best when he moved quickly, fought hard, and kept his enemy off balance, which is what raiders are supposed to do.

John Singleton Mosby

1833–1916

Born in Powhatan County, Virginia, Mosby entered the University of Virginia in 1849. While there, he was sentenced to six months in jail and a $1,000 fine for shooting a bully.

At the outbreak of the Civil War, Mosby enlisted as a private in the 1st Virginia Cavalry. He was at First Manassas (Bull Run), and during the Peninsula, Second Manassas, and Sharpsburg (Antietam) Campaigns, he was attached to General **J.E.B. Stuart's** staff. On January 2, 1863, he was authorized to commence independent partisan operations in Loudoun County, Virginia. He started with only nine men, but by the end of the war he was a colonel commanding eight companies of rangers mustered into the Confederate service as the 43rd Battalion of Virginia Cavalry. On March 9, 1863, with only 29 men, he penetrated the Union lines at Fairfax Court

House, only a few miles outside Washington, capturing Union general Edwin Stoughton— whom he awakened with a rude slap on the butt—and 100 men and horses without being discovered. Mosby moved so freely throughout northern Virginia that the area became known as "Mosby's Confederacy." He disbanded his command at Salem, Virginia, April 21, 1865, rather than surrender it. After the war he practiced law, supported **Grant** (for which he earned the enmity of many Southerners), and was U.S. consul at Hong Kong, 1878–1885.

Mosby was a bold and fearless but extremely intelligent guerrilla fighter. Grant called him "able and thoroughly honest and truthful." After the war he got on with his life.

John Singleton Mosby

Louis Mountbatten

1900–1979

Related to the royal family, Mountbatten graduated from the Royal Naval College first of seventy-two in his class of 1916.

Mountbatten spent World War I at sea, ending as a lieutenant aboard a coastal torpedo boat. As captain of the destroyer, H.M.S. *Kelly* in 1939–1941, he was torpedoed twice and mined once before his ship was sunk by dive-bombers off Crete in May 1941. He was a courageous and resourceful seaman, even if his ship-handling skills left something to be desired—he nearly capsized the *Kelly* and once almost rammed another destroyer. Made head of Combined Oper-ations in April 1942, he planned the disastrous Dieppe raid of August 1942, which taught him that Britain's amphibious capability needed improvement, which he set about doing. His work in this area bore fruit during the Normandy invasion of June 1944, but in August 1943 he became supreme allied commander for South-east Asia. In this position he established a good working relationship with **William Slim** and handled the delicate complexities of fighting a determined enemy in a secondary theater of the war. After the war he became the last viceroy of India, an assignment he handled with remarkable aplomb. Along with his grandson and a local Irish lad, he was murdered by Irish terrorists when a bomb destroyed his yacht, August 27, 1979.

Mountbatten learned from his mistakes and throughout his life he remained undaunted by any challenge, handling very difficult assignments with consummate skill.

N

Nāder Shāh (Nader Khān)

1688–1747

Born a Turkoman tribesman, Nāder may have earned his living as a bandit before becoming the governor of Khorasan.

After the assassination of Shah Hussein in 1726, the resulting confusion in Persia enabled the Ottoman Turks to occupy Persian territories from Russian Georgia to Hamadān in western Iran. As the chief military strategist for Tahmāsp II, the uncrowned shāh, Nāder waged an extremely successful campaign against the Turks, smashing them at Hamadān in 1730, driving them out of Hamadān and then going on to occupy Iraq and Azerbaijan. By 1732 Nāder was so powerful in Persia that he deposed Tahmāsp and installed an infant son, whom he deposed in 1736 in favor of himself as shāh. Next he conquered Afghanistan, and in 1738, after a nine-month siege, took Kandahār, a city garrisoned by 80,000 men behind walls thirty feet thick. With 50,000 men, he then set out on an invasion of Mongol India, forcing Kabul to surrender in September 1738 and advancing through the Khyber Pass. At Karnal, seventy-five miles north of Delhi, he was met by an Indian army of 300,000 men with 2,000 elephants, which he defeated by a skillful combination of maneuver and musket fire. He returned home with an indemnity of 700 million rupees, the Mogul throne, and the crown jewels. He defeated the Turks again but was murdered by his own bodyguards in 1747.

Nāder's thirst for conquest was abetted by his genius for military organization and discipline, which enabled him to defeat armies six times the size of his own.

Charles James Napier

1782–1853

Born at Whitehall, London, Napier grew up in Ireland. Commissioned at age twelve, he did not serve until 1799.

As major in the 50th Foot, Napier commanded the 1st Battalion at Corunna, Spain, January 16, 1809, where he was wounded five times—leg broken, beaten with a musket butt, a bayonet in the back, a saber cut on the head, and ribs broken by a musket ball. He was captured and later released. He returned to Spain in 1810 to fight under **Wellington** and was wounded again at Busacco (September 27, 1810). Commanding the 102nd Foot, he fought in America in 1813. He missed Waterloo but entered Paris with the allies. Promoted to major general in 1837, he went to India in 1841. He was sent to command in the Sind, now a province in Pakistan, where the local emirs were outraged over an ultimatum to accept a treaty with the British. In February 1843, Baluchi warriors stormed the residency at Hyderābād. Napier, with twelve guns and 2,200 men, only 500 of them Europeans, met the Baluchi army of eighteen guns and 20,000 men at Miani on the Falaili

River, February 17, 1843. The battle lasted two hours. At the critical moment Napier ordered his cavalry to charge upon the Baluchi right, smashing through and attacking from the rear while Napier led his infantry in a charge that broke the enemy's line. Napier lost 20 officers and 250 men killed, the Baluchis at least 6,000.

Napier was an austere, fearless, and aggressive commander who took good care of his soldiers. He has been called "a prescient general, a beneficent governor, a just man."

Napoleon I (Bonaparte)

1769–1821

Born of Italian parents on the island of Corsica, son of a lawyer, Napoleon graduated forty-two of fifty-one at the Paris Military Academy in 1785.

Napoleon began his military career a lieutenant of artillery. He supported the Jacobins during the French Revolution. Commanding the artillery against the British and royalist troops at the siege of Toulon (September–December 1793), he suffered a bayonet wound in close fighting. In October 1795 his cannon dispersed rebels, thus saving the revolutionary government, and he was rewarded with command of the army in Italy. Between March 2, 1796, and May 12, 1797, Napoleon moved quickly, attacked the enemy simultaneously and aggressively, keeping the Italo-Austrian forces arrayed against him off balance and unable to support one another. In June 1798, he landed in Egypt with 40,000 men. He had overrun the country by August. He defeated an Anglo-Turkish army at Abukir in July 1799. Responding to the political crisis at home, in October he carried out the coup of 18 Brumaire (November 9, 1799), installing himself as the ruler of France. Going to the relief of **Masséna** at Genoa, Napoleon crossed the Alps in May 1800. On June 14, 1800, he defeated the Austrians at Marengo, which led to the peace of Luneville in February 1801. Appointed consul for life in May 1802, he crowned himself emperor on December 4, 1804. During the next decade Napoleon fought no fewer than twenty-five major battles in Europe, most of which he won; captured both Moscow and Vienna; and fought Russians, Prussians, Bavarians, and Austrians. These campaigns cost the French dearly. Ill and exhausted, his marshals in revolt, Napoleon was forced to abdicate the throne of France on April 11, 1814. Exiled to the island of Elba in the Mediterranean in May 1814, he returned to France, March 1, 1815. His army—the Grande Armée—rallied to him. After achieving some success during the opening phase of the Waterloo Campaign of June 1815, on June 18, Napoleon, with 72,000 men, attacked **Wellington** with 68,000. Unable to break Wellington before **Blücher**'s 83,000 Prussians joined forces with him, the French lost 30,000 men at Waterloo. On June 21, Napoleon abdicated again and was exiled this time to the island of St. Helena in the South Atlantic, 1,200 miles from the west coast of Africa, where he died on May 5, 1821.

Between the time of the caesars and Adolph Hitler, no man dominated Europe as Napoleon did. Napoleon waged war with his brains and his guts. He mastered the rules of war so well that he could break them when his instinct told him the occasion was right. He went after the enemy army to destroy it, which he did by using speed, mass, firepower, and maneuver: turning a flank to threaten the rear; against combined armies, he split them up and defeated them separately, as he almost did at Waterloo. He took care to arrange for reserves, to secure his flanks and his lines of communications. While he overreached himself and was worn down by his enemies, today most of those enemies are forgotten, but Napoleon is not.

Narses

480?–574

Born in Persarmenia (that part of Armenia ceded to Persia in 384), Narses was a eunuch in the court of the Byzantine emperor Justinian I. He was a favorite of the Empress Theodora.

Narses rose to the highest rank in the imperial court. In 532, he helped suppress a revolt against Justinian by plying the disaffected populace with generous bribes. In 535, as imperial commissioner in Alexandria, he avoided another revolt by installing Justinian's candidate for governor. In 538 he was made imperial treasurer and then sent to Italy to assist **Belisarius** against the Ostrogoths. The two generals did not get along and this led to the Goths' capture of Milan. Recalled to Constantinople in 539, Narses campaigned in the Balkans before returning to Italy in 551 at the head of an army of about 30,000 men. In June 552 he defeated the Goths at Busta Gallorum (Taginae), in the Apennines, near modern Gubbio, killing their leader, Totila, and 6,000 of his men. In 553, he defeated another army at Mons Lactarius, near Salerno. In 554 his army of 18,000 defeated 30,000 Franks near Capua. Attacked by phalanxes, Narses drew his lines into a curve so his archers could deliver their arrows into the backs of the Franks while his center came up and smashed into the barbarian mass. Recalled by Justin II in 567, he preferred to remain in Italy.

Narses's destruction of the barbarian armies in Italy was due to his superior tactical skill, while his affability and generosity earned him great popularity among his troops.

Horatio Nelson

1758–1805

Born at Burnham Thorpe, Norfolk, England, the son of a clergyman, Nelson became a midshipman in the Royal Navy under his uncle in 1770.

After service in the Arctic, the West Indies, and the American Revolution, Nelson was commanding his own ship in the West Indies when he was put on half pay (retired) in 1787. Recalled when war broke out with France in February 1793, Nelson was given the HMS *Agamemnon* (sixty-four guns). During the siege of the Corsican port of Calvi in August 1794, Nelson lost his right eye when hit by a stone splinter. He was knighted and promoted to rear admiral for service against the Spanish during the battle off Cape St. Vincent in February 1797. In July, during an attack on the Spanish seaport of Santa Cruz de Tenerife, he was shot through the right elbow and his arm was amputated. At Abukir Bay in August 1798, at the mouth of the Nile River, he surprised the French fleet that had transported **Napoleon's** army to Egypt and destroyed it, thus giving the British control of the Mediterranean. For this victory, in which he was again wounded, struck in the forehead by a shot, Nelson was created a baron. For his service in support of the kingdom of Naples against Napoleon in 1799–1800, the King of Naples made him Duke of Bronte. In July 1801, Nelson was promoted to vice admiral and made second in command of the Baltic fleet. At the Battle of Copenhagen, April 1, 1801, when signaled by the fleet commander to withdraw, Nelson put the telescope to his blind eye and exclaimed that he saw no such signal! In the bitter four-hour engagement that followed, he defeated the Danish fleet and forced an armistice. For this victory he was created a viscount. In April 1805, commanding the Mediterranean fleet, Nelson commenced the search for the French fleet that resulted in the Battle of Trafalgar on October 21. "England expects that every man will do his duty," he signaled before engaging. He attacked the French center in a two-column formation. One French vessel was sunk and seventeen captured, to no English losses. Wounded by a marksman's musketball as his flagship, HMS *Victory* engaged the French flagship *Bucentaure,* Nelson died three hours later. This victory totally smashed Napoleon's sea power.

Superficially, Nelson seems the ideal hero for a bodice ripper: a dashing, handsome nobleman and a lover (based on his adulterous love affair with Lady Hamilton). But Nelson was one of the greatest sea commanders in history. He was a brilliant naval tactician who kept his wits under fire and reacted quickly to take advantage of every opportunity. He knew his men and he made sure they knew what he expected of them. His style of leadership has become known as the "Nelson touch."

Michel Ney, Duc d'Elchingen, Prince de La Moskova

1769–1815

Born in Alsace, the son of a cooper, Ney enlisted in the 5th Hussars in 1788 and by 1792 had reached the rank of sergeant major.

New was commissioned a lieutenant in October 1792. He was wounded at Maastricht in December 1794 and fought at Opladen in 1795 and Altenkirchen in 1796. In August 1796 he was promoted to general of brigade. In March 1799 he was made general of division. Up to this time he had been wounded four times. In May 1804 he was created a marshal of France. In the campaign of 1805 he commanded the VI Corps. His brilliant victory at Elchingen led to the surrender of the Austrians at Ulm. In the pursuit of the Prussians after Jena in 1806, he captured 36,000 men. In 1808 he was made Duke of Elchingen. He fought in Spain under **Masséna** in 1810 and won some victories, but Masséna had to relieve him in March 1811 for insubordination. In the invasion of Russia in 1812 he led the III Corps with distinction. At Kowno Bridge on December 13, 1812, he held off the Russians for four hours with a musket and a rear guard of 100 men. He was wounded again at Lützen in May 1813. After the fall of Paris on March 31, 1814, he urged Napoleon to abdicate. He then pledged his loyalty to Louis XVIII, but when Napoleon returned in March 1815, Ney rallied to him. At Waterloo his gallant but hopeless cavalry charges against the British deprived the infantry of its cavalry support. After the war the Bourbons had him shot.

Ney's record was erratic. He was best commanding a corps because he tended to lose control of larger formations. But no marshal was braver and in battle he inspired others with his epic courage. At his execution he gave the firing squad the order to shoot.

O

David Ochterlony

1758–1825

Born in Boston, Ochterlony went to India as a cadet in the Bengal army of the East India Company in 1777. In 1778 he was made a lieutenant in the 24th Bengal native infantry.

Ochterlony distinguished himself in the arduous campaign against the Franco-Indian army during the Second Mysore War of 1780–1784. At Gúdalúr in 1783 Ochterlony was wounded and captured. In 1796 he was promoted to captain; major in 1800; lieutenant colonel in 1803. He fought at Koel in August 1803 and Delhi in September. From October 7 to 16, 1804, Ochterlony conducted a desperate defense at Delhi with a handful of men against an army of 20,000. Help arrived just as the enemy was breaching the walls. He was promoted to major general in June 1814. During the opening campaign of the Gurkha War of 1814–1816, Ochterlony's column of 6,000 men and sixteen guns was the only one to achieve its objectives. He led his men through steep mountain defiles, blasting a road for his guns, reducing the Gurkha strongholds one by one. In April 1815, after a vicious battle on a ledge with 2,000-foot precipices on each side, he defeated the Gurkhas. When their government refused to ratify the peace treaty, Ochterlony took the field once more. On February 14, 1816, struggling up a steep, unguarded mountain path with one brigade, he flanked the Gurkhas and at the village of Magwampur, twenty miles from Katmandu, repulsed their attack, killing 800 men. Reprimanded by the governor-general for supporting the lawful claim of the young Raja of Bharatpur to his throne, Ochterlony resigned in protest after nearly fifty years of service.

Ochterlony was a decisive and energetic commander who endured with his men the hardships of fighting a determined enemy on some of the most rugged ground in the world. His real-life accomplishments are the stuff of romantic legend and his obscurity today is totally undeserved.

Richard Nugent O'Connor

1889–1981

Commissioned in the Cameronians (Scottish Rifles), he was commanding a division in Palestine when he was promoted to command the Western Desert Force (later the Eighth Army).

In December 1940, as Italian Marshal Graziani was dug in around Sidi Barrani in northwestern Egypt, O'Connor devised an original and daring plan to defeat him. He infiltrated a small force of 36,000 men behind the Italian positions and at dawn on December 9, 1940, caught them completely by surprise. He completely smashed Graziani, capturing 38,000 Italians and seventy-two tanks. On January 3, 1941, O'Connor's forces took the fortress of Bardia in the Gulf of Sallum, inflicting 40,000 casualties on the Italians and capturing 128 more tanks. At Tobruk on January 21, advancing behind an artillery barrage, he took that town and another

25,000 Italians. With the Italian army on the run, O'Connor made for the coast to cut them off, which he did at Beda Fomm February 5–7, taking 20,000 prisoners, 120 tanks, 216 guns, and 1,500 trucks. In preparation for an invasion of Greece under orders from Churchill, O'Connor's force was broken up, but when German General **Rommel** arrived in North Africa, O'Connor was called back to the front. While on a forward reconnaissance April 6, 1941, he was captured by the Germans and interned in Italy, but he escaped in time to lead the VIII Corps in Normandy.

O'Connor's motto was "offensive action wherever possible." His command style was to move constantly among his troops, urging them on. His capture was a stroke of bad luck for the British.

Osceola

1800–1838

Born in a Creek village on the Tallapoosa River in Georgia, his stepfather was a Scottish trader, William Powell, but Osceola was not a half-breed, as some have asserted.

In 1808 Osceola and his mother moved to Florida, where they lived among the Seminoles and Osceola fought against the U.S. in the War of 1812 and First Seminole War (1817–1818). In 1832 he was living peacefully near Fort King, Florida. With other chiefs, he opposed the Removal Bill of 1830, which proposed removing the Seminoles to lands across the Mississippi. In 1835 he was arrested for refusing to sign the treaty by which the Indians would have accepted removal. It is said he showed his displeasure by plunging his knife into the paper. Feigning acceptance, he was released shortly afterward. On December 28, 1835, he precipitated the Second Seminole War by murdering Indian agent Wiley Thompson and a Seminole chief, Emathla, who had signed the treaty. Next he annihilated a 150-man column of regulars in the Wahoo Swamp. Pursued by an 800-man force, he was wounded and took refuge in the swamp, where, with his Indian followers and escaped slaves, he conducted a successful guerrilla war against the whites. Arrested while under a flag of truce on October 21, 1837, he was confined at Fort Moultrie near Charleston, South Carolina, where he died January 30, 1838.

A master of guerrilla tactics, Osceola resisted the U.S. Army for two years. His conduct was no more dishonorable than that of the U.S. government.

P

George S. Patton

1885–1945

Born in California, grandson of a Confederate officer who died of wounds received at Winchester in 1864, Patton grew up in comfortable circumstances. He took five years to get through West Point, graduating 46 of 103 in the class of 1909.

A natural athlete and superb horseman, representing the U.S. at the Olympic Games of 1912, he placed fifth in the military pentathlon. In 1916 he accompanied **Pershing** to Mexico, personally killing three of Pancho Villa's bodyguards in a gunfight. Upon the U.S. entry into World War I, he went to France in May 1917; as a lieutenant colonel he commanded the 304th Tank Brigade in the Saint-Mihiel Offensive (September 12–14, 1918), and in the Meuse-Argonne, on September 26, 1918, he was wounded and put out of action for the rest of the war. In April 1941, as a major general, he was given command of the 2nd Armored Division, and of the I Armored Corps in January 1942. In November he directed the amphibious operations at Casablanca. In March 1943 he took command of the II Corps, which he rebuilt after its defeat at the Kasserine Pass. He led the Seventh Army in the invasion of Sicily in July 1943. In

March 1944 Patton was transferred to command of the Third Army in England, which he led brilliantly in the pursuit of the Germans after the Normandy breakout. During the Battle of the Bulge in December 1944, in one of the most spectacular maneuvers of the war, he wheeled his army to shore up the southern shoulder of the Bulge and broke through to relieve the defenders of Bastogne. Patton reached the Rhine in March 1945. In April he was promoted to full general. On December 9, 1945, he broke his neck in an automobile accident and died twelve days later.

A profane, flamboyant, outspoken, and often mawkishly sentimental man, Patton was possibly the best battlefield commander of World War II. He understood how to integrate armor, infantry, artillery, and airpower into an invincible battlefield combination, and he knew how to use it, instinctively striking the enemy at the right time and in the right place to keep him constantly off balance. Patton was bold and audacious but a meticulous planner, and while he drove his men beyond normal limits, he gave them pride and confidence in themselves and what they could do.

John Pelham

1838–1863

Born on his grandfather's plantation in what is today Calhoun County, Alabama, Pelham entered West Point in July 1856 but resigned in April 1861 to join the Confederate Army.

Commissioned in the artillery, he was at First Manassas (Bull Run) and in November 1861 General **Stuart** recommended Pelham organize a battery of horse artillery. This unit was the nucleus of the famous Stuart Horse Artillery, whose fame attracted to its ranks volunteers from the Confederacy and foreign nations. Pelham worked his guns at Yorktown and in the Seven Days Battles. Promoted to major in August 1862, at Second Manassas, his guns saved **Jackson's** rear from a surprise attack, and at Sharpsburg (Antietam) he successfully defended a key position in the Confederate lines. At Fredericksburg in December 1862, he held up the Union advance against the Confederate right for two hours with only two guns, despite twenty-four cannon concentrated against him. Refusing repeated orders to withdraw, he quit only when out of ammunition. At Kelly's Ford, Virginia, on March 17, 1863, temporarily detached from his guns, he joined the fight as a cavalryman and, struck by a shell fragment while directing a column, died a short while later. Stuart named his daughter Virginia Pelham, in honor of the gallant major.

Pelham combined dashing courage with sound tactical skill. He kept up with the fast-moving cavalry and in battle moved his guns quickly and unexpectedly to deliver devastating fire on the enemy when it was needed most.

John Pelham

Oliver Hazard Perry

1785–1819

Born at Rocky Brook, South Kingstown, Rhode Island, Perry was appointed midshipman on his father's ship, *General Greene,* in April 1799. His younger brother, Matthew, also a seaman of renown, would open Japan to the West in 1854.

During the war with Tripoli (1800–1805) he served in the Mediterranean from 1802 to 1806 on the *Adams* and the *Constellation.* He served in the West Indies during the naval war with France and in 1807 was appointed permanent lieutenant. At the outbreak of the War of 1812, he offered his services at Washington, which resulted in his being given command of the naval forces on Lake Erie. He made his headquarters at Erie, Pennsylvania. In May he participated in the capture of Fort George, where he demonstrated great coolness and valor under fire. By August 1813, successfully overcoming vast logistical obstacles, he had assembled a fleet of ten small vessels mounting fifty-four guns, the largest of which were his flagship, the *Lawrence* (twenty guns) and the *Niagara,* each of 480 tons. At 11:45 A.M., September 10, 1813, flying a battle flag inscribed "Don't Give Up the Ship," he engaged the British fleet, which was about evenly matched with his own. The battle lasted until three P.M. When the *Lawrence* was knocked out of action, Perry transferred to the *Niagara,* and about fifteen minutes later the British surrendered. Perry lost twenty-seven killed and ninety-six wounded to forty-one killed and ninety-four wounded for the British, but with this victory the U.S. controlled Lake Erie and validated its claim to the northwest. Perry announced his victory with the message "We have met the enemy and they are ours." In a postwar duel with marine Captain John Heath in which neither man was injured, Perry refused to fire after receiving Heath's shot. Perry died of yellow fever during a diplomatic mission to South America.

Perry was a charismatic leader who could make quick decisions and take the responsibility for them. The building and manning of his fleet on Lake Erie was a logistical and organizational miracle.

John J. Pershing

1860–1948

Born in Laclede, Missouri; Pershing's first military experience was in June 1864, when Confederate partisans pillaged and terrorized his neighbors. After teaching school for a while, Pershing entered West Point in 1882, graduating thirty of seventy-seven in his class.

After service with the cavalry in the west, in 1891 he was assigned as professor of military science and tactics at the University of Nebraska, where in 1893 he earned a law degree. In 1895–1896, he served with the all-black 10th Cavalry, where he earned his nickname, "Black Jack." In June 1897 he was sent to West Point as a tactical instructor. During the Spanish-American War in 1898, he led the 10th Cavalry with distinction in the battles around Santiago. Sent to the Philippines and promoted to captain in 1901, he fought the Moros with tenacity, but he was humane with them in his government. His conduct in the Philippines so impressed President Theodore Roosevelt that in 1903 he recommended him for promotion from captain to brigadier general (over 862 officers senior to him), and this was confirmed in 1906. In 1916 he commanded the punitive expedition against Pancho Villa in Mexico. In May 1917, he was chosen to head the American Expeditionary Force (AEF) going to France to assist the Allies in World War I. Pershing argued for and got an independent AEF in France. He directed it in three major

General John J. Pershing

offensives: Aisne-Marne in July–August 1918; Saint-Mihiel (September); and Meuse-Argonne (September–November 1918). In July 1919 he was appointed general of the armies of the United States, and army chief of staff in 1921. He retired in 1924.

Pershing created the modern American army and tested it in France in 1918. The first of the truly modern generals himself, many of the great generals of World War II earned their spurs under Pershing. He was a master of tactics from cavalry troop to two-million-man army, but he also appreciated the value of logistics, person-

nel, and firepower, the sinews of modern war. Austere, distant, a strict disciplinarian, Pershing was meticulously honest and fair and he understood how to get the best out of his men.

Peter I [Peter the Great]

1672–1725

Born in Moscow, the only son of Czar Alexis's second marriage, Peter came to the throne in 1689 after a period as coczar under the regency of his half sister, Sophia.

Peter early developed an interest in military affairs, raising and training two guards regiments while still in his teens. He deposed Sophia in 1689 and in 1695 got his first taste of action fighting the Turks at Azov. Realizing Russia lacked adequate naval forces, Peter built a modern navy, sending representatives to Western European countries to study shipbuilding and navigation. In 1697, Peter went abroad himself—unprecedented for a czar—to Holland, England, Germany, and Austria, where he was impressed by Western technology. In league with Poland and Saxony, he attacked the Swedes

at Narva in November 1700 and was badly defeated. He remodeled his army on Western patterns, and under Marshal Shermemetev in 1702, it achieved some small victories against the Swedes. In August 1704 Peter captured Narva, and at Poltava on July 8, 1709, he destroyed the army of Swedish King Charles XII, who fled the field with only 1,800 men. Forced to cede the port of Azov to the Turks in 1711, Peter's naval forces crushed the Swedes at Hangö in July 1714, giving Russia naval superiority in the Baltic. It is said Peter died from a cold caught rescuing soldiers from a river.

Peter was an organizational genius and a genuine reformer who learned from his mistakes and picked reliable subordinates to advise him.

James J. Pettigrew

1828–1863

When Pettigrew, a brilliant scholar, graduated from the University of North Carolina at the age of only nineteen, President Polk appointed him assistant professor at the Naval Observatory in Washington.

In 1849 Pettigrew studied law and afterward practiced in South Carolina, where he was also active in politics. In 1860, he became colonel of the 1st Regiment of Rifles of Charleston. At the outbreak of the Civil War, he enlisted as a private in the Hampton Legion and, in May 1861, was

elected colonel of the 12th North Carolina Volunteers. Recommended for promotion to brigadier general by President Davis, Pettigrew returned the commission on the grounds that he was not qualified, but his friends persuaded him to accept. At Seven Pines he was bayonetted and captured but later exchanged. In May 1863, he was ordered to take his brigade to Gettysburg with **R. E. Lee**'s army, where it was part of **Heth's** division. When Heth was wounded on July 1, Pettigrew took command of the division and led it in **Pickett**'s Charge on July 3, during which he reached the stone wall at the crest of Cemetery Ridge, where he was wounded in the hand. He was one of the last off the field that day. He commanded the rear guard during the retreat into Virginia and on the night of July 14, 1863, was wounded in a skirmish with federal cavalry and died three days later.

Brave, modest, and capable, Pettigrew is a fine example of an age when it was believed that generals should lead their men from the front.

Philip II of Macedon

382–336 B.C.

Son of Amyntas II, Philip spent some years as a youth in Thebes, where he received military training under the famous general **Epaminondas**.

Philip became regent of Macedonia in 359 when his older brother, Perdikkas, was killed in battle. He guarded the throne well for his nephew, Amyntas. In 358 he agreed to an Athenian proposal that he recapture their colony of Amphipolis on the coast of western Thrace in return for control of the city of Pydna, on the western shore of the Gulf of Salonika. Amphipolis controlled the gold and silver mines in that region, so Philip just kept it and used the money to build up his army. Between 355 and 338 Philip consolidated his power. At Chaeronea in 338, with 32,000 men, he defeated an Athenian-Theban army of 50,000, which gave him undisputed control of Greece and resulted in the creation of the Hellenic League of Greek states with himself as chairman. Philip was assassinated in 336 while preparing for an invasion of Persia.

Philip completely reorganized the Macedonian army, converting it from an aristocratic structure of feudal nobles into a truly national army by allowing free commoners into its ranks (this also weakened the power of his nobles). He integrated the field operations of infantry (heavy and light) with cavalry and siege weapons (artillery). He trained his men rigorously, so under his personal command, it was one of the most mobile, efficient fighting machines in history.

Francisco Pizarro

1470–1541

Born in Trujillo, Estremadura, Spain, the illegitimate son of a small landholder, Pizarro served with some distinction in Italy before migrating to the New World in 1509 to seek his fortune. Most authorities agree he was illiterate.

Pizarro accompanied Alonso de Ojeda on his expedition to Colombia in 1510, and was with Balboa when he discovered the Pacific in 1513. In 1519 he settled in Panama. Inspired by the conquests of **Cortéz,** in 1524 he explored along the Pacific coast of South America as far as Guayaquil in modern Ecuador, searching for gold. On March 10, 1526, he signed an agreement with Diego de Almagro and Father Hernando de Luque to conquer Peru, and in 1528 he returned to Spain to obtain a royal charter for the purpose, which Charles V gave him on July 26, 1529. In early January 1531, with 180 men and twenty-seven horses in three ships, accompanied also by his half brothers and a cousin, he set sail from Panama for Peru. On November 15, 1532, at the Inca city of Cajamarca, 370 miles northwest of modern Lima, Pizarro seized Atahualpa, the Inca emperor, and held him for ransom—with his small force an act of breathtaking audacity, but it worked. When it was paid—enough gold to fill his cell—Pizarro had him strangled. In 1533 he seized the Inca capital of Cuzco, 350 miles southeast of Lima, which he founded in 1535. Internal dissensions then racked Pizarro's company, and in 1538, after putting down a revolt by Almagro, he had him executed. Almagro's son assassinated Pizarro at his home in Lima on June 26, 1541.

Audacious and courageous in an age when those qualities were common currency among men of his background, Pizarro was also a man of inflexible determination and direct methods. Instead of exploiting internal dissension among the Incas, as Cortéz did with the Aztecs of Mexico, he simply seized their leader and killed him. Illiterate but no bumpkin, he got what he wanted from the Spanish court. Perfidious and murderous, Pizarro was nevertheless generous with his friends and lived abstemiously himself. Re-

Francisco Pizarro

viled today for how he brought vast wealth into the Spanish coffers, his royal masters spent it with a clear conscience.

Pompey (Pompey the Great)

106–48 B.C.

Son of the Roman general Pompeius Strabo, under whom he served in the Socii War of 91–88.

Pompey first came to prominence through his support of Lucius Cornelius Sulla, raising three legions to support his march on Rome in 83, and securing Sicily and Africa for him in 81–80. Sulla rewarded him with the title *Magnus,* "The Great," and a triumphal parade through the streets of Rome, despite Pompey's age, only twenty-four at the time. After Sulla's death in 78, the senate gave Pompey several commissions, including suppressing the rebel proconsul Lepidus, in Spain, helping defeat **Spartacus** in the Third Servile War (71), and in 67 the job of ridding the seas of pirates. These pirates had 1,000 ships and had taken 400 cities, but within a year Pompey, using the extraordinary powers granted to him to raise a fleet and conduct operations, had swept them from the sea. He took 20,000 prisoners, most of whom he resettled peacefully in Greece. Pompey then secured Rome's territories in the East and in 59 became a member of a triumvirate that included **Julius**

Caesar and M. Lucinius Crassus. In 53, when Crassus was killed fighting the Parthians, Pompey and Caesar came into opposition. Defeated by Caesar in Greece at Pharsalus in 48, Pompey fled to Egypt, where he was assassinated.

Pompey's early career on land and sea was brilliant and showed him as an enterprising and resourceful commander more than a match for Rome's enemies. But as Caesar's star rose, aided by his battle-hardened army fresh from Gaul, Pompey's fell.

Pontiac

1720?–1769

Son of a Chippewa mother and an Ottawa father; not much is known of Pontiac until the French and Indian War, when, in 1755, it is likely he was among the Indians who defeated British General Edward Braddock near what is today Pittsburgh.

A longtime ally of the French, when Pontiac discovered the British had taken Quebec, he switched to their side and supported them when they took Detroit in 1760, but this alliance was short-lived. Motivated either by threats of British encroachments upon Indian lands or a rumor that the French were about to reinvade, in April 1763, at a meeting near Detroit, he persuaded the Great Lakes tribes to declare war on the British. On May 7, 1763, he personally led the attack on Detroit, which failed because the garrison had been warned of the uprising. Nevertheless, the Indians besieged the place until October 30. During the siege, when he occupied the homes of French residents, he issued them bills of credit. On July 31, his men repulsed a sortie from the fort at Bloody Ridge, killing 60 of the 250 British soldiers engaged. Pontiac attacked all the British outposts simultaneously so they could not reinforce each other. Only three, including Detroit, held out. Defeated by strong relief columns, Pontiac agreed to peace in July 1766. In April 1769, he was murdered by another Indian, possibly at British instigation.

Pontiac's uprising was well organized and well led, according to a sound strategic plan. His five-month siege of Detroit was unparalleled in the history of Indian warfare.

David Porter

1780–1843

Son of a naval officer of the American Revolution, Porter was commissioned a midshipman on the frigate *Constellation* in January 1798.

During the Quasi War with France, Porter saw action against the French frigate *Insurgente*, which he was given to command as a prize, and in 1799 he was promoted to lieutenant and given command of the schooner *Enterprise*. As a captain commanding the *Essex* in July 1812, he captured many prizes in the South Atlantic and the Pacific. Forced to surrender after a five-hour battle off Valparaiso in February 1814, he signaled, "We have been unfortunate but not disgraced." Commanding the West Indies Squadron in 1823, he fought pirates, and when the Spanish arrested one of his officers on shore near Fajarado, Puerto Rico, in November 1824, Porter got him released by threatening a bombardment. Recalled as the result of a Spanish protest and suspended from command for six months, Porter resigned. He then accepted the position of commander of the Mexican navy in August 1826. In 1830 he was appointed U.S. consul general in Algiers. He was serving as U.S. minister to Turkey when he died of yellow fever in March 1843.

Porter was decisive, direct, and aggressive, qualities that seem to have run in his family. His cruise in the South Atlantic and the Pacific during the War of 1812 was a remarkable feat of seamanship and tactical skill that caused great damage to British shipping in the region.

David Dixon Porter

1813–1891

Son of **David Porter,** David Dixon served in the Mexican navy under his father and in 1828 was captured in action against the Spanish but soon released. He entered the U.S. Navy as a midshipman in 1829.

As a lieutenant in the Mexican War, he led an assault against the fort at Tabasco on June 16, 1847, and for gallantry in this action was given command of the steamer *Spitfire,* his first command. After blockade duty early in the Civil War, Porter played a prominent role in the capture of New Orleans in April 1862, and was commended for his support by **Farragut** when the latter ran the batteries at Vicksburg in June. In October, Porter was chosen to command the Mississippi Squadron as acting rear admiral. From then until July 1863, Porter cooperated with **Grant**'s army in the campaign to take Vicksburg, providing vital transportation, logistical, and naval gunfire support. Both Grant and **Sherman** expressed their thanks for this service, and on July 4, 1863, Porter was promoted to permanent rear admiral, skipping captain and commodore. After further service along the Mississippi and its tributaries, including the failed Red River Campaign, March–May 1864, Porter took command of the North Atlantic Blockading Squadron in October 1864. When he died in 1891, a full admiral, he had served over sixty-two years on active duty.

With little formal education, Porter rose to the top of the navy through natural ability. Resourceful and energetic, he was generous to his subordinates but blunt with his superiors.

Edward Preble

1761–1807

Born in Portland, Maine (then part of Massachusetts and called Falmouth), Preble was commissioned a midshipman in the Massachusetts navy in 1780 and sailed aboard the frigate *Protector.*

While serving on the *Protector,* Preble participated in two bloody naval battles with British ships and was captured and imprisoned in 1781 after the second engagement. Appointed first lieutenant of the sloop *Winthrop* in 1782, he distinguished himself by capturing the loyalist privateer *Merriam* under the guns of Fort George at Castine, Maine. After the Revolution, Preble was a merchant seaman, but with the outbreak of the Quasi War with France in 1798, he was commissioned captain of the frigate *Essex,* and in command of this vessel, he was the first to show American flag beyond the Cape of Good F Appointed to command the third squadr' to the Mediterranean during the Tripol' in 1803, he blockaded the port of Tripoli. His force consisted of the USS *Constitution* (forty-four guns) and several smaller ships with a total complement of 1,060 officers and men. Tripoli was defended by forts, many gunboats, and 25,000 men. The fighting with the ships in the harbor was desperate, but Preble was not able to take the town.

Preble was a decisive and vigorous commander and a harsh disciplinarian, but he earned the respect and admiration of his men. He believed in delegating responsibility to promising officers, like **Decatur,** to whom he was role model and teacher.

Andries Pretorius

1798–1853

Born near Graaf Reinert in the Cape Colony, by 1838 Pretorius had established himself as a landowner and a prosperous farmer in the region. He moved to Port Natal in 1838 and, shortly after his arrival in November, was elected commandant general of the people's council.

In February 1838 the Boer leader Piet Retief and his party had been massacred by the Zulu chief Dingane, and Pretorius was commissioned to lead an expedition against him. At the head of a column of 464 mounted riflemen, Pretorius camped along the Buffalo River (known afterward as the Blood River) on the night of December 15, 1838. The following day he was attacked by approximately 10,000 Zulu warriors. For two hours the Zulu regiments attacked the Boers behind their wagons but were never able to get

within thirty feet of the laager. A surprise cavalry sortie broke the Zulus and they fled, leaving 3,000 dead behind. Four Boers were wounded, including Pretorius. In the 1840s Pretorius opposed British efforts to make Natal a crown colony. He defeated a British force at Congela in May 1842, besieged Durban for a month (May–June 1842), but eventually was forced to smart under British rule. Pretorius led the uprising of 1848, and although he was defeated at Boomplaats in August, he secured British recognition of the independence of the Transvaal in 1852.

A decisive commander, Pretorius nevertheless made his decisions in consultation with his subordinates. His victory on the Blood River is still commemorated by South African Boers.

Lewis B. Puller

1898–1971

Born at West Point, Virginia, Puller dropped out of the Virginia Military Institute in 1918 to enlist in the marines for combat duty in World War I. Instead, he trained recruits at Parris Island, South Carolina.

Puller was commissioned in 1919, but almost immediately placed on the inactive list due to postwar cutbacks. He then came back on active

duty as a corporal and served with the Gendarmerie d'Haïti until 1924. Between 1928 and 1932, Puller, now a lieutenant, served two tours in Nicaragua, fighting guerrillas and earning two Navy Crosses. In 1933 he commanded the "Horse Marines" —a contingent of mounted Marines—guarding American property at Peking. At the outbreak of World War II, Puller was commanding the 1st Battalion, 7th Marines. In September 1942 the 7th Marines fought on Guadalcanal, where Puller won his third Navy Cross. Of thirty-seven medals and nineteen commendations given to the 7th Marines for action on Guadalcanal, Puller's battalion won twenty-eight medals and fifteen commendations. He won his fourth Navy Cross in January 1944 for heroism at Cape Gloucester, New Britain. Commanding the 1st Marine Regiment in Korea, Puller won his fifth Navy Cross (and the army's Distinguished Service Cross) for heroism during the retreat from the Chosin Reservoir in the winter of 1950.

He was promoted to brigadier general in January 1951, major general in 1953, and lieutenant general upon his retirement in November 1955.

Nicknamed "Chesty" for the way he threw out his barrel chest, Puller was a blunt and outspoken combat commander who carried his own pack, ate with his men, walked where they walked—and killed enemy soldiers. "Paperwork will ruin any military force," he once said. He was especially respected by his junior officers and enlisted people. In **Napoleon's** army, men like Puller could wind up with a marshal's baton.

R

Red Cloud [Mahpiua Luta]

1822–1909

Born into the Oglala Sioux tribe on Blue Creek in the present state of Nebraska, Red Cloud early earned himself the reputation of a warrior in fighting against neighboring tribes, accumulating a record of eighty acts of individual courage during these engagements.

Red Cloud opposed the Bozeman Trail, which had been constructed through Sioux hunting lands in 1862–1863 to reach the goldfields of Colorado and Montana. When Red Cloud learned in 1865 that the government intended to build a military road along the trail and establish a series of forts along its length, he declared war. At the head of about 2,000 Sioux and Cheyenne warriors he besieged Forts Reno, Phill Kearny, and C. F. Smith in Wyoming and Montana while mounting attacks against relief parties. The most famous of these was the Fetterman Massacre on December 21, 1866, when he wiped out a detachment of eighty men under the command of Captain William Fetterman. In August 1867 his men participated in the Hayfield and Wagon Box fights. In the latter engagement (August 2) he was repulsed by only thirty-two soldiers armed with repeating rifles. In April 1868, Red Cloud signed the Treaty of Fort Laramie, whereby the army agreed to abandon the forts and close the North Platte area to white settlement while Red Cloud promised not to fight anymore. Red Cloud kept his promise and in later life won concessions from the government by persuasive argument.

Personally fearless and a good battlefield tactician, Red Cloud realized that the Indian people could never prevent through war the encroachment of whites upon their lands.

Richard I ["The Lion Hearted"]

1157–1199

The third son of Henry II and Eleanor of Aquitaine, Richard earned a solid reputation as a young military commander in campaigns against rebellious French barons.

When Richard ascended to the thrones of England and Normandy in 1189, he determined to recapture the city of Jerusalem from the Saracens. Richard set out for the Holy Land in 1190. He stormed Messina to force Sicilian cooperation and next conquered Cyprus, which he used as an advanced base. He landed at Acre in June 1191. The city had been under siege by the Crusaders for two years; in July, Richard forced its capitulation. In September he led his army of 50,000 men along the coast, accompanied by his fleet offshore, toward Jerusalem. Richard enforced strict discipline upon his men during the march, and his careful logistical preparations ensured that they were well supplied along the way, thus avoiding the fate of another Crusader army, which, at Hittin, in July 1187, was crushed by **Saladin**. Richard's column never broke despite repeated attacks by the Saracens, until, at Arsuf on September 7, 1191, he turned and killed 7,000 of them at the cost of only 700 of his own men. But unable to take Jerusalem, Richard concluded a truce with Saladin in September 1192. Held for ransom by Leopold of Austria on his way home in 1194, he went to England for a few months upon his release, the only time he set foot there during his reign. During the siege of Châluz in April 1199, Richard was wounded by a crossbow bolt and died a short time later.

An indifferent king, Richard was a brilliant tactician and administrator, one of the best commanders of his day.

Matthew B. Ridgway

1895–1993

Born to the army at Fort Monroe, Virginia, where his father, a colonel of artillery, was stationed, Ridgway graduated from West Point in 1917, but saw no combat during World War I.

Between world wars, Ridgway served in China, Nicaragua, and the Philippines. In 1942 he was selected to command the 82nd Infantry Division with the mission of converting it to an airborne unit. On July 9–10, 1943, the division was dropped behind the lines on Sicily, and while poor coordination caused the paratroopers to be dropped haphazardly, the operation badly confused the German and Italian commanders. Ridgway jumped with the 2nd Battalion of the 505th Parachute Regiment at Normandy, June 5, 1944, where the division achieved is objective but sustained 46 percent casualties. Ridgway's units also achieved their objectives in the disastrous Market-Garden operation in Holland in September 1944. He commanded the XVIII Airborne Corps during the Battle of the Bulge in December 1944 and was promoted to lieutenant general in June 1945. When General **Walton Walker** was killed in Korea in December 1950, Ridgway replaced him as commander of the Eighth Army. With his forces badly chewed up by the Chinese communists, Ridgway stabilized his lines south of Seoul in January 1951, when he launched a counteroffensive that by the end of February had driven the enemy beyond the 38th parallel. When **Douglas MacArthur** was relieved in April 1951, Ridgway succeeded him as supreme commander. As chief of staff of the army, Ridgway, with considerable foresight, advised President Eisenhower against involvement in Indochina.

Ridgway has been described as brilliant, highly principled, nonpolitical, and courageous. He was a pioneer in airborne operations and a proponent of the doctrine of "flexible response" to Cold War threats as opposed to nuclear "massive retaliation." In combat he was always in the forward positions. In Korea his staff claimed three ways of doing business, "the right way, the wrong way, and the Ridgway."

Frederick Roberts

1832–1914

Born at Cawnpore (now Kanpur), India, the son of General Abraham Roberts, Frederick graduated from Sandhurst in 1847 and then attended the East India Company's college at Addiscombe. In 1851 he joined the Bengal Artillery.

Roberts served under his father on the Northwest Frontier. During the Indian Mutiny he saw much action, winning the Victoria Cross for valor in a skirmish in January 1858. Except for service in Ethiopia in 1867–1868, Roberts was involved in Indian affairs until his permanent return to England in 1893. During the Second Afghan War (1878–1880), Roberts became a national hero when his forces took Kabul in October 1879 and then marched 300 miles over the mountains to relieve Kandahār, where he smashed the Afghan army and ended the war (September 1, 1880). In 1885 Roberts was appointed commander in chief in India. Created a field marshal in 1895, Roberts commanded the army in Ireland. In December 1899, he was appointed to command in South Africa. With **Kitchener** as his chief of staff, Roberts adopted a strategy of attacking the major Boer strongholds instead of defending scattered garrisons, and in May 1900 he took Johannesburg and in June Pretoria. Recalled to England in December 1900, from 1901 to 1904 he was commander in chief of the army. Appointed to command the Indian troops sent to France to fight in World War I, he died of pneumonia at the age of eighty-two en route to the front.

Roberts was a determined fighter and skillful professional soldier who won his battles with few losses.

Jean-Baptiste-Donatien de Vimeur, Comte de Rochambeau

1725–1807

Born at Vendôme of an ancient French family, Rochambeau was being prepared for the church but changed careers at age seventeen and joined the army.

Commissioned in the cavalry, he fought with distinction during the War of the Austrian Succession (1740–1748), rising to the rank of colonel by the age of twenty-two. During the Seven Years War (1756–1763) he was wounded several times and promoted to brigadier general. Promoted to lieutenant general in 1780, he was given command of the force being sent to support **Washington**. In July, speaking no English, he landed at Newport, Rhode Island, with 5,500 men, having left 2,000 behind at Brest because the French navy was short of transports. His instructions were to place himself under Washington's orders, and this he did. Waiting for reinforcements, Rochambeau joined Washington in blockading New York City. After conferring with Washington, it was decided that the two armies should cooperate in attacking Cornwallis, who had occupied Yorktown in August 1781. Reinforced by 4,000 troops brought from Haiti by **De Grasse,** the Franco-American army besieged Cornwallis at Yorktown in September. Bottled up by the French fleet and without hope of raising the siege, Cornwallis surrendered, October 19, 1781. In a final gesture of respect, when Cornwallis's deputy attempted to surrender to Rochambeau, he directed the officer to Washington.

Rochambeau made the Franco-American alliance work. He was a modest man, a good judge of character, and a thorough and experienced professional soldier, ideal qualities in an ally.

John Rodgers

1773?–1838

Born near modern Havre de Grace, Maryland, son of a militia captain in the American Revolution, Rodgers was apprenticed to a Baltimore shipmaster trading with France and the West Indies. By the age of twenty he was master of his own ship, the *Jane.*

During the Quasi War with France in 1798, he served as a lieutenant on the *Constellation* and participated in the capture of the frigate *Insurgente*. In March 1799, he was promoted to captain, the first under the new Constitution to be advanced to that grade. Between 1802 and 1806 he served in the Mediterranean against the Barbary pirates and with the blockading fleet off Tripoli. Three times he commanded the squadron there, which entitled him to the honorary title of commodore. He took a hard line in the peace negotiations with the Tripolitans. At the outbreak of the War of 1812, he was the senior officer in the U.S. Navy. Commanding the forty-four-gun frigate *President*, he was wounded during an engagement with the British frigate *Belvidera* when a gun exploded and broke his leg. During August–September 1814 he led a small detachment of sailors in the defense of Washington, and at Baltimore his men played a decisive role in the defense of the inner harbor. He was acting secretary of the navy in 1823.

Frank and independent, Rodgers was a methodical, disciplined and stern commander. He was ahead of his times as the first to advance the strategy of fleet operations at sea instead of the spectacular individual actions of his more junior contemporaries.

Konstantin Konstantinovich Rokossovsky

1896–1968

Born of Polish stock, Rokossovsky was drafted into the Russian imperial army during World War I, and joined the Red Guard during the October Revolution of 1917.

Rokossovsky fought with the Bolshevik forces during the Russian Civil War. Between wars he was promoted in the Red Army and the Communist party, and although he rose to command the V Corps stationed in Manchuria, he was arrested during Stalin's purge of the officer corps in August 1937, charged with spying for the Japanese and the Poles. Reinstated in March 1940, he commanded the IX Mechanized Corps during the German invasion of 1941. During November–December 1941, commanding the Sixteenth Army, he gained distinction fighting the German advance on Moscow. In 1942 he commanded the Don Front at Stalingrad. The forces under his command encircled the German Sixth Army at Stalingrad in November 1942, and on January 31, 1943, it surrendered to him. One of Marshal **Zhukov's** trusted subordinates, Rokossovsky commanded the Central Front during the Battle of Kursk in July 1943, and in June 1944 his forces on the First Byelorussian Front drove into Poland and to the outskirts of Warsaw. His forces captured Danzig in April 1945. After the war he served in the Polish government for several years.

Rokossovsky's victory at Stalingrad was one of the turning points of World War II. Although he was criticized for not supporting the Warsaw uprising of July 1944, that was a political decision made in Moscow.

Erwin Johannes Eugen Rommel

1891–1944

Born at Heidenheim, near Ulm, Germany, Rommel was commissioned a lieutenant in 1912 and during World War I served with distinction on several fronts, was wounded three times, and earned the *Pour le Mérite* for valor at Caporetto, Italy, in 1917.

As a colonel in 1939, Rommel was assigned to command Hitler's Bodyguard Battalion. On leaving this post, he requested and received the command of the 7th Panzer Division, which he led with audacity and skill in France, May–June 1940. In February 1941, now a lieutenant general, Rommel was given command of the German Expeditionary Force sent to North Africa to bail out the Italians. For the next eighteen months he conducted a series of rapid, fluid attacks, adroitly exploiting every battlefield opportunity to thrust his Afrika Korps into the guts of the British Eighth Army, driving it back into the Nile delta. This campaign earned him the nickname "Desert Fox" and promotion to field marshal in June 1942. But as his supply lines lengthened, those of the British shortened, and unable to break through the defenses at el-Alamein, he was driven back by **Montgomery's** offensive there in October 1942. In March 1943, Rommel was recalled and in May the remnants of his army surrendered. Rommel was given command of Army Group B in northern France in December 1943. With characteristic energy and foresight, he set about strengthening the channel defenses in Normandy. Rommel wanted to deploy a forward defense in Normandy, to destroy any invaders on the beaches, but he was overruled. Without Panzer reserves, there was not much he could do to stop the Allied invasion of June 6, 1944. Rommel was recuperating from severe wounds on July 20, 1944, when the abortive assassination attempt against Hitler took place. Rommel was implicated in the plot, but to avoid scandal, Hitler gave him the option of suicide instead of a public trial and the execution of his staff and family. He took his own life on October 19, 1944.

While Rommel, unlike other German generals, did not command the vast armies in the

Erwin Rommel

National Archives

titanic struggles of WWII, he understood the principles of mobile warfare, concentrating his forces to achieve local superiority at the proper moment, leading his men from the front to inspire and control them, instantly exploiting every opportunity the fluid battlefield offered. And unlike so many other generals who served Hitler, he was an apolitical, dedicated professional soldier who dealt fairly with his enemies. British General **Claude Auchinleck** said of Rommel after his death, "I salute him as a soldier and a man and deplore the shameful manner of his death."

Karl Rudolf Gerd von Rundstedt

1875–1953

Born into an aristocratic Prussian family, Rundstedt briefly commanded the 22nd Reserve Division at the Battle of the Marne in September 1914 before being transferred to staff assignments.

Although Rundstedt deplored the ruthlessness of the Nazis and was openly critical of them, he approved of their military programs. He retired from the army a colonel general (full general) in 1938. Called back for the invasion of Poland, he commanded Army Group South. In 1940 his Army Group A developed a devastating surprise attack that turned the Battle of France by striking through the Ardennes, and in July he was promoted to field marshal. In the spring of 1941 he commanded Army Group South during the invasion of Russia. When Hitler refused his request to allow a tactical withdrawal of some of his units, Rundstedt resigned. In March 1942 he was recalled and given command in the West. Here he clashed with **Rommel** over the defense of the Normandy coast, but in any event, Hitler refused to commit the reserves after the June 6, 1944, landings. When Rundstedt asked Hitler to allow him to withdraw to the Seine to establish a defensive line in eastern France, he was replaced. Rundstedt was called back to direct the Ardennes counteroffensive in December 1944—which he thought was futile. He surrendered in May 1945.

Rundstedt was a skilled commander both tactically and strategically and he got on well with his younger officers, but his Prussian code of honor would not allow him to defy Hitler.

Michel Adriaanszoon de Ruyter

1607–1676

Born at Flushing, the Netherlands, de Ruyter went to sea at the age of nine and worked his way up to captain of a Dutch merchant ship before he was twenty.

De Ruyter's first military command at sea was against the Spanish in 1641, where he distinguished himself in battle off Cape St. Vincent. With the outbreak of war with England in 1652, he accepted a naval commission and, having proven himself in several fierce engagements, was promoted to vice admiral in 1653. During the next thirteen years, de Ruyter fought against French privateers, Barbary pirates, the Swedes, and the English. At the Four Days Battle (June 11–14, 1666) off the mouth of the Thames River, he fought off repeated English attacks. Defeated by a surprise sally from the Thames River at North Foreland on July 25, 1666, he led his own audacious surprise raid against the English in June 1667, attacking up the Thames to within twenty miles of London itself. This action so devastated the English fleet that peace was concluded within a month. In the Third Dutch War of 1672–1674, de Ruyter frustrated Anglo-French invasion plans and broke their blockade of the Dutch coast. Wounded in action against the French at the battle of Messina, off the Gulf of Augusta on April 22, 1676, he died of wounds at Syracuse a few days later.

One of history's greatest admirals, de Ruyter's victories at sea ensured the survival of the Dutch republic on land. His daring, ferocity, and superb seamanship enabled him consistently to outmaneuver and defeat the larger fleets sent against him.

S

Laurent Gouvion Saint-Cyr

1764–1830

Born at Toul, the son of a middle-class family, Saint-Cyr supported the revolution; in 1792 he joined a Parisian battalion, and by 1794 had risen to command a division.

In Germany and Italy he displayed much tactical skill. At Bierbach on May 9, 1800, he defeated the Austrians, and again, at Castelfranco di Veneto in November 1805, he captured an entire Austrian corps. In Spain he ran afoul of **Napoleon** for being too slow to take Gerona in June 1809 and was relieved by **Augereau.** Outraged, he quit his post and Napoleon exiled him to his estates until 1812, when he was given command of the VI Corps for the invasion of Russia. Although wounded at the battle of Polotsk, August 17–18, 1812, he continued to command, and saved the day. On August 27, Napoleon made him a marshal of France. Wounded again at the Second Battle of Polotsk in October, he had to relinquish his command. Forced to surrender at Dresden in 1813, he was repatriated in June 1814, but he refused to join Napoleon for Waterloo. After the war he served the Bourbons with distinction, reorganizing the French army and establishing a general staff. Although he called for the court-martial of **Ney,** he voted for acquittal and later he helped restore many of his old comrades.

Nicknamed "the Owl" for his intellectualism, Saint-Cyr fought his battles like chess games, well-planned thrusts into his enemy's guts. He was a brilliant organizer but distant from his troops and sometimes insubordinate.

Saladin

1138–1193

Born at Tikrit, Iraq, of Kurdish stock, Saladin (Salāh ad-Dīn, "Honor of the Faith") grew up in Damascus. In 1163 he went with his uncle, Shirquh, in the army he led against the Egyptians on behalf of Nureddin, his Turko-Syrian master.

Saladin distinguished himself in Egypt. Although defeated by a combined Frankish-Egyptian force at Cairo in April 1164, Shirquh eventually drove the Franks out and established himself as vizier in January 1169. When Shirquh died later in 1169, Saladin succeeded him as vizier. Saladin's rule was both fair and effective. He restored the caliph's army, built a navy, and secured Egypt's frontiers. In 1174, with the death of Nureddin, Saladin extended his conquests, eventually coming again into conflict with the Franks. Defeated at Ramleh in 1177, Saladin marched into Palestine in 1187 at the head of 20,000 men. He was met at Hattin on July 4, 1187 by an army under Guy of Lusignan and Raymond of Tripoli. Saladin defeated them and on October 2 he captured Jerusalem. In 1189 Guy of Lusignan, who had been released after Saladin captured him, besieged Acre. In the spring of 1191 **Richard I** took Acre, defeated Saladin at Arsuf, but was unable to take Jerusalem. The Third Crusade ended in an uneasy truce. Saladin returned to Damascus, where he died after a short illness on March 4, 1193.

Saladin was a resourceful and intelligent commander who was chivalrous to his enemies in victory, traits that gained him a grudging respect from men like Richard. He was a practical, generous, and shrewd ruler who lived piously according to the abstemious tenets of his Muslim faith.

José de San Martín

1778–1850

Born at Yapeyú, near the northern frontier of Argentina, to an aristocratic Spanish family, San Martín and his parents returned to Spain in 1785, and in 1790 he entered the Spanish army.

San Martín fought against the French in the Peninsular Wars (1808–1812), rising to the rank of lieutenant colonel, but learning of the independence movement in his native Argentina, he returned there in 1812. Realizing the key to independence was defeating the Spanish forces in Peru, but lacking the naval force to get there by sea, San Martín resolved to attack overland, through Chile. Between 1814 and 1817 he assembled and trained an Argentine-Chilean republican army at Mendoza, in western Argentina. In January–February 1817, he led a force of 3,000 infantry, 700 cavalry, and twenty-one guns across the Andes. On February 12, he defeated a 2,000-man Spanish force at Chacabuco, entered Santiago de Chile, and se-

cured the de facto independence of Chile. On March 16, 1818, a 9,000-man Spanish force from Peru defeated San Martín at Cancha-Rayada, but he regrouped and in April drove the Spanish back into Peru with heavy losses. With the help of the British Admiral **Thomas Cochrane,** the Spanish fleet was bottled up in their Chilean ports, and on July 9, 1821, San Martín captured Lima. The Spanish retreated into the highlands where they were too strong for San Martín, so in 1822 he merged his army with **Simón Bolívar**'s. Unable to work with Bolívar (the precise nature of their disagreement is not clear), San Martín resigned and returned to Europe.

San Martín was a thoroughly professional, completely selfless soldier, honest and dedicated. He gave up his command rather than allow his personal disagreements with Bolívar to hamstring the independence movement.

Hermann Maurice, Comte de Saxe

1696–1750

Born in Goslar, Germany, the first of 354 known illegitimate children of Augustus II, Elector of Saxony and King of Poland, Saxe was sent into a Saxon infantry regiment at the age of twelve.

Saxe served under Prince **Eugène of Savoy,** learning the fundamentals of infantry training and musketry. In 1709 he was at the Battle of Malplaquet under the **Duke of Marlborough** and

Eugène. In 1719 his father purchased for him the command of a German regiment in the French service. He was made a lieutenant general for his service during the War of the Polish Succession (1733–1738) during which he fought against Prince Eugène and his own brother. In 1741, during the War of the Austrian Succession (1740–1748), he captured the city of Prague. In

1743 he was made a marshal of France. In May 1745 he led an army of 70,000 against Tournai, which was being defended by 50,000 English troops. On May 10 he took 50,000 men to block a relief force at Fontenoy. So ill he had to be carried into battle, Saxe rallied his men when an allied attack broke the French line, and directing withering musket volleys and artillery fire, repulsed it. Saxe died at his château, some say as the result of a duel, others say from overexercise after "interviewing" a troupe of eight young actresses.

Saxe was enterprising, fearless, and a peerless master of tactics. He realized the importance of training and was receptive to new technology in weapons. He revived the practice of cadence marching, which had been lost since the Romans.

John M. Schofield

1831–1906

Born in Chautauqua County, New York, son of a Baptist minister, Schofield was raised in Illinois. After working as a surveyor and a teacher, he entered West Point in 1849 and graduated seventh of fifty-two in his class of 1853.

Commissioned in the 1st Artillery, at the outbreak of the Civil War Schofield accepted a commission as major in the 1st Missouri Volunteer Infantry. He was at the Battle of Wilson's Creek, Missouri, August 10, 1861, where he won the Medal of Honor for leading his regiment in a charge. In November he was promoted to brigadier general of volunteers. After service in Missouri, he was appointed major general in May 1863 and in February 1864 took command of the XXIII Corps, and fought under **Sherman**. At the Battle of Franklin (November 30, 1864), he defeated Hood and for this action was promoted to brigadier general in the regular army. His corps was then moved to North Carolina, where he remained until the end of the war. In 1865–1866 he went to France as a confidential agent for the State Department to deal with Mexican affairs. He served briefly as secretary of war in 1868–1869; was superintendent at West Point, 1876–1881; commanding general of the army, 1888–1895; and retired as a lieutenant general in November 1895.

As a corps commander, Schofield proved himself a capable combat leader. While acting secretary of war, he dealt capably with a series of complex problems involving reconstruction and army reorganization. Neither a flamboyant nor self-promoting person, his long and solid record of service is often overlooked.

Philip John Schuyler

1733–1804

Schuyler was born at Albany, New York, of an old and prosperous Dutch family. At the age of seventeen he was first struck by an episode of the rheumatic gout that would plague him the rest of his life.

In 1755 Schuyler commanded a company of militia in the British expedition against Crown Point during the French and Indian War. He fought at Lake George on September 8, 1755, and in the spring of 1756 he accompanied the expedition that relieved Fort Oswego. He resigned his commission in 1757 but in 1758 served as a commissary officer with the rank of major in the expedition against Forts Ticonderoga and Frontenac. In 1759–1760 he worked in the depot at Albany, provisioning the British forces. After the war Schuyler went into business and politics, and in June 1775, was appointed commander of the Northern Department as a major general under **Washington**. He organized and led the expedition against Canada in 1775 but relinquished command because of illness in 1776. His logistical skills were responsible for its early success, but in 1777 he was wrongly reprimanded by Congress for its failure. Reinstated, Schuyler conducted an intelligent delaying action against Burgoyne, but in August 1777 he was relieved of his post over the loss of Fort Ticonderoga. Schuyler requested a court-martial and was acquitted of the charge of incompetence in 1778. He resigned his commission in April 1779. Schuyler spent the remainder of his life serving with distinction in various public offices.

A master logistician and a sound military strategist, Schuyler was a victim of the vicious political backstabbing that plagued military operations during the American Revolution.

Scipio Africanus Major [Publius Cornelius]

236?–183 B.C.

Son of the general Publius Cornelius Scipio and descended from the patrician branch of the Cornelian family, Scipio first saw action with his father during the Second Punic War at the Battle of Ticinus in November 218, where it is said he saved his father's life when **Hannibal** defeated the Roman army.

Scipio fought at Cannae in August 216 and was one of the few Roman officers to survive that disaster. In 213 he was appointed to command in Spain, and in 206 at Ilipa, north of Seville, with an army of 48,000 men he defeated a combined Carthaginian army of 70,000 under Hasdrubal, thus securing Spain for Rome. In 204 he invaded Africa with an army of 35,000 and was so successful that in 203 the Carthaginians recalled **Hannibal** from Italy. They met at the Battle of Zama in October 202, Scipio with about 43,000 men, Hannibal with 48,000. Hannibal was weak in cavalry and many of his infantrymen were newly raised levies. Caught between the Roman legions and their cavalry, his army collapsed, leaving 20,000 dead on the field to Scipio's 1,500. Scipio was granted the surname Africanus for this victory. Accused of accepting bribes from the Syrian king Antiochus III in 185, he reminded the people at his trial that that very day, October 19, was the anniversary of his victory at Zama, the charges were dropped, and the people marched to the capitol to pray for more men like Scipio Africanus.

A brilliant tactician and strategist, Scipio was a charismatic leader who inspired confidence in others.

Winfield Scott

1786–1866

Born near Petersburg, Virginia, Scott read law after dropping out of college in 1805. In 1807 he enlisted in a Petersburg cavalry troop and in May 1808 was appointed a captain of artillery.

Incensed at the conduct of his superior, General Wilkinson, Scott made some intemperate remarks about his loyalty and was suspended from the army for a year in 1809. But in 1812, as war with Britain loomed, he was called back, promoted to lieutenant colonel, and sent to the Niagara frontier, where he distinguished himself in several sharp actions. On March 9, 1814, he was promoted to brigadier general. He trained his brigade assiduously. The results were seen when he crossed into Canada and at Chippewa, July 4–5, with a force of 1,100, defeated a larger British force, and again, at Lundy's Lane, on July 25, where although severely wounded, he carried the field. Between the War of 1812 and 1841 when Scott was appointed commanding general of the U.S. Army, he served with distinction in a number of difficult and exacting military and diplomatic assignments. As commander of the army, Scott initiated a number of humane reforms in discipline practices and revised its infantry tactics. When the Mexican War broke out, Scott endorsed **Zachary Taylor** to command the expeditionary force, but he was ordered to Mexico, landing his army at Vera Cruz in March 1847. During the next six months his small army of 10,000 men fought five major battles and in September captured Mexico City. After the war he was defeated in his bid for the presidency in 1852 on the Whig ticket, but in 1855 Congress promoted him to lieutenant general, only the second American up to that time to hold that rank since Washington. Although a Virginian, Scott remained loyal to the Union in 1861. Seeing the Civil War coming, several times he warned that forts and armories in the South should be fortified, and his strategic vision for winning the war once it came, although rejected, eventually proved correct. In November 1861 Scott retired. He died at West Point, New York, on May 29, 1866.

Winfield Scott

A physically large man (he stood 6'5'' and weighed 230 pounds when still a teenager), Scott was an imposing presence, particularly in battle. Nicknamed "Old Fuss and Feathers" for his insistence on military discipline, Scott was a deeply religious, humane man. His penchant for making powerful enemies delayed some promotions and defeated his political ambitions, but Scott's only real failure during the fifty years he served his country was not getting elected its president. He was one of the greatest American generals.

John Sedgwick

1813–1864

Born in Connecticut, grandson of an officer in the American Revolution, Sedgwick taught school before entering the U.S. Military Academy, where he graduated twenty-five of fifty in his Class of 1837.

Commissioned in the artillery, Sedgwick saw service in the Seminole War and on the Canadian border. At the outbreak of the Mexican War in 1846, he joined General **Taylor's** army in northern Mexico. Transferred to **Scott's** army at Vera Cruz, he won brevet promotions to captain and major for heroism at Churubusco and Chapultepec. As a major in the regular army, he participated in the Mormon expedition of 1857–1858 and fought Kiowas and Comanches during 1858–1860. Appointed a brigadier general of volunteers in August 1861, he led a brigade at Glendale, Virginia, during the Peninsular Campaign on July 30, 1862, where he was wounded. Promoted to major general in July 1862, at Sharpsburg (Antietam), he was wounded again, and at Chancellorsville, he commanded the VI Corps of the Army of the Potomac. He force-marched his corps to Gettysburg and arrived there on the second day of the battle (July 2, 1863). He led the corps into the fighting at the Wilderness in the spring of 1864, and at Spotsylvania, on May 9, 1864, while directing the emplacement of artillery, he was killed by a sharpshooter.

Nicknamed "Uncle John" by his men, Sedg-

John Sedgwick

Free Library of Philadelphia

wick was a strict disciplinarian who won the respect and affection of his men by leading them to victory on the battlefield.

Raphael Semmes

1809–1877

Born in Charles County, Maryland, Semmes was raised in Georgetown, District of Columbia, and appointed a midshipman in the U.S. Navy in

1826, although he did not attain his lieutenancy until February 1837.

During the Mexican War, Semmes was on

shore at Vera Cruz with the naval artillery. He accompanied **Scott's** army inland on special duty, where he was several times cited for gallantry. On "awaiting orders" status for long periods after the war, Semmes practiced law between sea tours and in 1855 was promoted to commander. He resigned in February 1861 and in April was given command of the CSS *Sumter,* a packet steamer he refitted as a commerce raider. He put to sea in June and, before he was forced to lay the *Sumter* up for repairs and discharge her crew in April 1862, captured or destroyed eighteen Northern vessels. He was then ordered to take command of the English-built steam bark *Enrica,* rechristened CSS *Alabama* on August 24, 1862. During the next twenty-two months Semmes, with a mostly English crew, sailed over 30,000 miles, destroying or capturing fifty-five Union ships and sinking the man-of-war USS *Hatteras* (January 11, 1863) in a night engagement. Semmes rescued all the Union sailors. At 10:57 A.M., June 19, 1864, the *Alabama* engaged the *Kearsarge* off the port of Cherbourg and at 12:24 P.M. the *Alabama* sank. Semmes escaped and returned to the Confederacy, where as a rear admiral he was put in charge of the James River Squadron. When Richmond was evacuated in 1865, Semmes formed his men into a naval brigade and surrendered with **Johnston's** army in North Carolina on May 1, 1865.

Semmes was a gallant, chivalrous sea dog. His cruise in the *Alabama* was a remarkable feat of seamanship.

Friedrich Wilhelm Freiherr von Seydlitz

1721–1773

Born near Kleve, Germany, son of a cavalry officer, Seydlitz as a youth demonstrated an extraordinary ability as a horseman, and in 1740 was commissioned in the cavalry.

Taken prisoner by the Austrians at the Battle of Chotusice, Czechoslovakia, in 1742, Seydlitz was exchanged shortly afterward. His performance as a cavalryman had been noted by **Frederick the Great,** however, and in 1753 the king gave him command of the 8th Cuirassiers, which, through rigorous training, Seydlitz turned into a model regiment. Because he was menaced by many enemies during the Seven Years War (1756–1763), Frederick was forced to develop the art of mobile warfare and maneuver, and his cavalry played an important role in these tactics. Seydlitz distinguished himself in this style of warfare at Prague in May 1757, and at Kolín, Czechoslovakia, in June, when the Austrians broke Frederick's line and Seydlitz's cavalry provided a rear guard that saved the army. At Rossbach, Germany, in November 1757, Seydlitz's charge at a critical moment enabled Frederick's army of only 21,000 men to defeat the Franco-Austrian army of 64,000 troops. At Zorndorf (Sarbinowo), in Poland, in August 1758, smashing into the Russian flank, Seydlitz decided the battle. He saved Frederick again at Hochkirch, Germany, in October, by leading a breakout after the Prussians had been surrounded. Seydlitz was badly wounded at Kunersdorf (Kunowice) in August 1759, but at Freiburg, on October 29, 1762, Seydlitz led a combined force of infantry and cavalry to defeat the Austrians in the last battle of the war.

Seydlitz was an up-and-at-'em fighter who was the first in every charge, but his rigid training and strict discipline enabled him to keep good control of his horsemen in battle.

William R. Shafter

1835–1906

Born in Kalamazoo County, Michigan, Shafter was attending seminary when the Civil War broke out, and he volunteered for service in the 7th Michigan Infantry.

At the Battle of Fair Oaks (Seven Pines), May 31–June 1, 1862, Shafter was wounded but refused to leave the field, and for his gallantry was promoted to lieutenant colonel of volunteers. In 1895 he was awarded the Medal of Honor for this engagement. Shafter ended the war a brevet brigadier general of volunteers. After the war he was assigned to the 24th Infantry (Colored) and served along the Rio Grande in Texas, where he fought Indians. In 1875 he commanded an expedition that mapped and explored the Staked Plains of Texas, covering more than 2,500 arduous miles in the process. In 1879 he was given command of the 1st Infantry (Colored). He was promoted to brigadier general in 1897 and major general of volunteers in 1898, at the outbreak of the Spanish-American War. He commanded the V Corps of over 16,000 men that sailed for Cuba in June 1898. Weighing over 300 pounds and nearly sixty-three years old, Shafter suffered in the humid heat of Cuba. His army depleted from tropical diseases, short of supplies, and in need of reinforcement, Shafter refused to mount the direct assault on the fortifications of Santiago demanded by the newspapers and some of his own officers. Instead, he negotiated with the garrison commander, and after the Spanish fleet had been destroyed, terms were concluded on July 17, 1898. Shafter retired as a major general on July 1, 1901.

Shafter's conduct on the frontier was exemplary, but he never received the recognition he deserved for it. Given less than two months to train and prepare his corps for Cuba, its shortcomings were not his fault. Gruff, fat, and disheveled, he was viciously ridiculed by the press for "inaction" in Cuba, but he did not allow this criticism, which he never bothered to answer, to goad him into sacrificing the lives of his men.

Shaka

1787?–1828

Illegitimate son of a petty Zulu king, Shaka (from *iShaka*, the name of an intestinal parasite) grew up in disgrace and exile until taken in by Dingiswayo, king of the Mtetwa. Later in life he exacted hideous revenge on those who had rejected him as a boy.

As a young man, Shaka demonstrated a talent for warfare and Dingiswayo rewarded him with his own regiment, the *iziCwe*, which he trained in the use of new tactics and weapons of his own devising. This included heavier shields and a short stabbing spear used as the Romans did their short swords. He trained his men rigorously, until they could march barefoot fifty miles in a day. He also developed the famed "buffalo" battle tactic, where a strong center of his line (the "chest") would engage the enemy closely while the wings ("horns") surrounded them. He employed his men ruthlessly in a form of warfare hitherto unknown among his people, sparing no one who opposed him. When Dingiswayo was killed in 1818, Shaka stepped in. By 1822 he had ruthlessly conquered a domain of 11,500 square miles with an army of 20,000. By the time of his death in 1828, he had built the Zulus into a nation of 250,000 people and could field an army of 40,000 warriors. It is estimated that he killed two million people in the process and made refugees of countless others. As his power increased, Shaka used it capriciously, rewarding people one moment and ordering mass executions the next. On September 23, 1828, Shaka was assassinated by his half brothers, and he died badly.

Shaka was not the kind of man one invites over for tea, but had he been born in Europe, with his vision, determination, and character, doubtless he would have left an indelible mark on history.

Robert Gould Shaw

1837–1863

Robert Gould Shaw

The son of a rich Boston abolitionist family, Shaw left Harvard University in his third year in 1859 and moved to New York. When the Civil War broke out he accepted a commission in the 2nd Massachusetts Volunteers, fighting with his regiment at Sharpsburg (Antietam) in September 1862 and rising to the rank of captain.

In January 1863, Massachusetts Governor Andrew got permission from Washington to raise a regiment of free black men for the Union Army. The regiment was designated the 54th Massachusetts Colored Regiment and Shaw was asked to command it. Shaw, who sincerely believed black men could make good soldiers, accepted the offer, and by May he had organized, equipped, and trained the regiment. Lewis Douglass, son of Frederick Douglass, was regimental sergeant major, and his brother, Charles R., was also enlisted. After mustering into the federal service, the 54th was sent to South Carolina. Shaw requested that his regiment be given combat duty and in July this was granted. In action on James Island on July 16, the 54th lost forty-six men. On July 18 the 54th was transported to Morris Island and Shaw was offered the chance to lead an assault on Confederate Battery Wagner. At 7:45 P.M. he led his regiment across the beach. At the top of the parapet, Shaw was killed. The 54th lost 272 out of the 650 men engaged. Supporting white regiments suffered equally heavy losses. The battery was never taken. Shaw was buried with his men in a mass grave on the beach. They are all still there.

Unlike so many who want others to sacrifice for their pet cause, Shaw gave the last full measure of devotion to his, and his men gave theirs to him, and together they showed what brave men could do.

Philip H. Sheridan

1831–1888

Born in Albany, New York, Sheridan was raised in Ohio. Despite a one-year disciplinary suspension, he graduated thirty-four of forty-nine in his West Point class of 1853.

Assigned to the 1st Infantry, Sheridan served along the Rio Grande and then fought Indians with the 4th Infantry in the northwest. At the outbreak of the Civil War he was appointed a captain in the 13th Infantry, where he served as quartermaster and commissary for Union troops in Missouri and Mississippi. Appointed colonel of the 2nd Michigan Cavalry on May 25, 1862, he was promoted to brigadier general for distinguished service in a raid at Boonesville, Mississippi, where he actually commanded a brigade. He then commanded a division at Perryville, Kentucky, on October 8, 1862, where he showed great courage and skill. For his service at Stone's River, Tennessee, on December 31, 1862, he was promoted to major general. He fought at Chickamauga, and at Chattanooga on November 24–25, 1863, his men stormed Missionary Ridge and broke the Confederate line. Appointed to command the 10,000-man cavalry corps of the Army of the Potomac in April 1864, he fought at Wilderness and Spotsylvania, Cold Harbor, and in May conducted his celebrated raid around Richmond, destroying Confederate stores and communications. In August he began his campaign of destruction in the Shenandoah Valley and at Cedar Creek, October 19, 1864, performed his famous ride of twenty miles from Winchester to the battlefield, where he rallied his troops and turned defeat into victory. For this feat he was promoted to major general in the regular army. Subsequently he did signal service at Petersburg and blocking **R. E. Lee's** retreat from Appomattox. In May 1865 he was sent to Texas and, after Reconstruction duty, fought Indians. In March 1869 he was appointed lieutenant general, and in November 1883 succeeded **Sherman** as commanding general of the army. In June 1888, only two months before his death, Sheridan was promoted to full general.

Sheridan was not a great strategist and had only two rules of tactical warfare: attack and pursue. Under fire he was cool and self-possessed, but he always saw to the welfare of his troops. He was outspoken and once remarked, "If I owned both Hell and Texas, I'd rent out Texas and live in Hell."

William Tecumseh Sherman

1820–1891

Born at Lancaster, Ohio, Sherman graduated sixth of forty-two in his West Point class of 1840.

Commissioned in the artillery, Sherman served in the Second Seminole War in 1840–1842. During the Mexican War he saw no action. He resigned his commission in 1853 and went into banking. From 1859 to 1861 he was superintendent of Alexandria Military Academy in Louisiana (now Louisiana State). At the outbreak of the Civil War, Sherman was appointed colonel of the 13th Infantry and he commanded a brigade at First Manassas (Bull Run) in July 1861. In August he was promoted to brigadier general of volunteers and sent to Kentucky, but he overestimated the strength of the enemy and earned the enmity of the press, which resulted in the rumor that he was having a nervous breakdown and led to his relief. Sherman wound up under **Grant** and at Forts Henry and Donelson and at Shiloh, April 6, 1862, wounded but refusing to leave the field, he had four horses shot out from under him. Promoted to major general in May, he commanded Grant's XV Corps in the final stages of the Vicksburg Campaign. Grant's strategic plan for 1864 called for Sherman to lead three combined armies against **Joseph Johnston** at Atlanta.

In May 1864 he launched his drive toward Atlanta with a force of 100,000 men. Atlanta fell on September 1 after four months of sharp fighting and skillful maneuvering on Sherman's part. On November 15, with 62,000 men, Sherman began his famous "march to the sea," which ended with the capture of Savannah on December 21. He then maneuvered through the Carolinas, receiving Johnston's surrender at Durham Station, North Carolina, April 26, 1865. Promoted to lieutenant general in July 1866, Sherman was promoted to full general and given command of the U.S. Army in March 1869, which post he held until his retirement in 1883.

Sherman is known as the first "modern" general principally because of his policy of bringing the war home to the civilian population during his famous march from Atlanta to Savannah, although the wanton destruction of private property that occurred was not done under his orders. Sherman was a highly intelligent battlefield commander, quick thinking and imaginative, a superb administrator and logistician, and, in this latter aspect, definitely very modern in his approach to warfare.

Otto Skorzeny

1908–1975

Born in Vienna, Austria, and educated as an engineer, Skorzeny operated his own business before Austria was annexed by Germany in 1938.

As an officer in the SS *Das Reich* Division, Skorzeny fought in France and the Low Countries in the spring of 1940 and the invasion of Russia in 1941. Wounded that winter, he was sent back to Germany to recuperate and then was given the task of recruiting commando units for clandestine operations. On September 12, 1943, he led an airborne force of ninety men by glider onto a landing zone beside the hotel in the Appenines where Mussolini was being held prisoner. Skorzeny freed him in four minutes without firing a shot. In October 1944 he captured first Milos Horthy (Operation Mickey Mouse), son of Hungarian regent Miklós Horthy, and then Horthy himself (Operation Panzerfaust), to prevent the surrender of Hungary to the Russians. During the Ardennes Offensive in December 1944, he infiltrated special English-speaking units behind American lines. Transferred back to the infantry, he commanded a 15,000-man division defending an Oder River crossing (January–February 1945), until recalled to organize the defense of the Alpine Redoubt. Acquitted of war crimes in 1945, Skorzeny settled in Spain, where he died at Madrid.

A man of great personal courage and high

Otto Skorzeny

National Archives

intelligence, Skorzeny was a master of unconventional warfare, considered the most dangerous man in Europe during World War II.

William Joseph Slim

1891–1970

Born in Bristol, England, Slim joined the Royal Warwickshire Regiment as a private at the outbreak of World War I.

Commissioned a second lieutenant, Slim fought with his regiment at Gallipoli in 1915, where he was wounded. He was wounded again in fighting in Mesopotamia in 1916. His postwar service included the 6th Gurkha Rifles. As a major in the 1920s, Slim had such difficulty making ends meet on his army pay that he wrote adventure fiction for the pulp magazines under an assumed name. At the beginning of World War II he commanded the 10th Indian Brigade in North Africa, where he was wounded again. In 1941 he commanded the 10th Indian Division in Iraq, Syria, and Iran, and in March 1942 was given command of the I Burmese Corps. He held his troops together during the disastrous retreat into India and gave the Japanese their first major defeat in this theater at Arakan in February 1944. Afterward Slim directed the liberation of northern Burma, which cost the Japanese 65,000 men. In 1945 he launched the British counteroffensive in Burma, capturing Rangoon May 2. Slim was made a full general in July 1945 and field marshal in January 1949. From 1953 to 1960 he was governor-general in Australia.

The lantern-jawed Slim's operations in Burma were a masterpiece of timing and strategy. Known as "Bill," he infused new energy and confidence into his men after their retreat into India and then led them aggressively back into Burma against a veteran enemy occupying some of the most rugged terrain on earth.

Holland M. Smith

1882–1967

Born at Hatchechubbee, Alabama, he declined an appointment to the U.S. Naval Academy because his parents feared he might succumb to "Yankee ideology" while there. Instead he went to law school and practiced before securing a commission as a second lieutenant in the marine corps in 1905.

Smith participated in expeditions to Nicaragua and Santo Domingo in 1916 and during World War I he received the *Croix de Guerre* at the Battle of Belleau Wood. Smith ended the war a major. He was promoted to brigadier general in August 1939 and given command of the 1st Marine Brigade, which he trained rigorously in amphibious landing techniques. In 1941 he was given command of the 1st Marine Division and promoted to major general in October. In June 1943 he assumed command of the V Amphibious Corps. He participated in the landings at Makin and Tarawa in November 1943, and at Saipan in June 1944, as a lieutenant general in command of the invasion, he relieved the commander of the army's 27th Division for failure to act aggressively. This resulted in a controversy that would follow Smith the rest of his life. He led the operations at Tinian and Iwo Jima in 1945. He retired in August 1946, a full general.

Nicknamed "Howlin' Mad" because of his short temper, Smith was the father of amphibious warfare, laying the groundwork for the success of American landing operations during WWII. He developed the basic methods for organizing and equipping troops for rapid embarkation. Smith believed heavy preinvasion bombardments and swift assaults shortened the battle and saved lives, and when he didn't get this kind of support, he didn't mind letting people know about it.

Oliver P. Smith

1893–1977

Born in Menard, Texas, Smith graduated from the University of California and in May 1917 was commissioned in the marine corps.

Smith saw no action during World War I. He remained on active duty after the war. He did not see combat in World War II until March 1944, when he assumed command of the 5th Marines, then in action in New Britain. At Peleliu, September 15, 1944, he commanded the shore operations the first day of the landing from an antitank ditch. As a brigadier general, he served on the Tenth Army staff during the Okinawa Campaign. In July 1950 he took command of the 1st Marine Division and led it ashore at the Inchon landing on September 15, 1950. His men captured Seoul, September 25. He led it ashore at Wŏnsan, on the east coast of Korea, October 26, 1950 and by November 2 had advanced beyond the Chosin Reservoir toward the Yalu. Attacked by eight Chinese communist divisions, Smith organized a brilliant fighting withdrawal, bringing back all his equipment and wounded (4,400 men). When asked by a reporter if he was retreating, he was quoted as saying, "Retreat Hell, we're just attacking in another direction." Later Smith commanded the IX Corps for a time. He retired a full general in September 1955.

Caught in one of America's worst military debacles, Smith was careful not to divide his forces and to secure his supply route. His seventy-eight-mile fighting withdrawal from the Chosin Reservoir to Wŏnsan has become an epic of endurance and bravery.

Horace Lockwood Smith-Dorrien

1858–1930

Son of a physician, Smith-Dorrien graduated from Sandhurst in 1877 and was appointed a lieutenant in the 95th Foot.

Smith-Dorrien's first combat was during the Zulu War of 1879, and at Isandhlawana on January 22, 1879, he was one of only five officers to survive the massacre. He fought in Egypt in 1882 and again in 1884 and he commanded the 13th Sudanese Battalion at Omdurman, September 2, 1898. He commanded the 29th Brigade in South Africa during the Boer War and in 1901 was promoted to major general. In France in World War I he commanded the II Corps of the British Expeditionary Force, which suffered the brunt of the German offensive at Mons, August 23, 1914. Withdrawing from that engagement, his troops exhausted and the Germans close behind them, he decided against orders to turn and fight at Le Cateau. Despite taking 7,800 casualties, Smith-Dorrien's corps held and the German pressure was relieved. His corps fought at the Marne in September 1914 and First Ypres, October 30–November 24, 1914. In 1915 Smith-Dorrien was given command of the Second Army. At the Second Battle of Ypres in April 1915, he had a serious disagreement with General French, BEF commander, arguing that the army should withdraw to a more tenable position closer to Ypres itself. French refused to listen and relieved Smith-Dorrien on May 6, 1915. The Second Army was subsequently withdrawn. He died in an auto accident, August 12, 1930.

Smith-Dorrien was a brave and resourceful field commander. His relief in 1915 deprived the British of a very able officer.

Jan Sobieski [John III, King of Poland]

1629–1696

Born near Lvov, Poland, son of the commander of the Cracow fortress, he was at Beresteczko on July 1, 1651, when John II Casimir with 34,000 Poles defeated an army of 200,000 Cossacks and Tartars.

In 1655, when Poland came under Swedish domination, Sobieski first supported and then helped drive the Swedes out. After further service against the Cossacks and Tartars, he was appointed field commander of the Polish army in 1665 and commander in chief in 1668. During the Turkish invasion of 1672 he won a series of battles that forced the enemy to withdraw. In November 1673, upon the death of King Michael, Sobieski rushed to Warsaw with 6,000 veterans and, on May 21, 1674, was proclaimed king. In 1675 and again in 1676 Sobieski repulsed two more Turkish invasions. In March 1683 Sobieski signed a defensive treaty with Austria. When 150,000 Turks besieged 15,000 Austrians in Vienna during July–September, Sobieski with 30,000 Poles marched 220 miles in fifteen days to join with German and Austrian forces just west of the city. On September 12 he attacked, personally leading the cavalry charge on the Turkish commander's headquarters that broke the Turkish army.

A man of great energy and ability, an excellent strategist and tactician, and a superb leader of men, Sobieski personally freed Poland from Turkish and Tartar domination. His march to the relief of Vienna, his finest hour, was one of the more remarkable, if lesser known feats of history.

Nicholas-Jean de Dieu Soult

1769–1851

Son of a notary, Soult enlisted as a private in the Bourbon army in 1785. He rose rapidly in rank, from lieutenant in 1791 to brigade commander in 1794 and division commander in April 1799.

Serving in Italy in 1800 under **Masséna,** Soult was wounded and captured but soon exchanged. In 1804 he was on **Napoleon's** first list of marshals. At Austerlitz on December 2, 1805, it was Soult's corps that seized the Pratzen Heights, cutting the allies in two and routing their left wing. He commanded the right at Jena, October 14, 1806, and at Eylau on February 8, 1807, he held against great odds. In Spain and Portugal between 1809 and 1812, Soult was beaten by **Wellington** at Oporto, May 12, 1809, but redeemed himself at Ocaña in November, defeating a Spanish army of 53,000 with only 30,000 Frenchmen. Recalled to France in January 1813, he brought with him a collection of historic canvases in his baggage (Soult was a looter with good taste). He returned to Spain in July to oppose Wellington. In command of a beaten, ragamuffin army, Soult reequipped it and reinvigorated his men. Forced back into France, defeated again and again, he rallied his army until he surrendered at Toulouse in April 10, 1814. He came to Napoleon in 1815 and was his chief of staff at Waterloo, a job for which he was not fitted. At Queen Victoria's coronation in 1838, Wellington grabbed his arm and said, "I have you at last!"

Intelligent and calm, Soult trained his men with care. He fought gallantly if cautiously in Spain. A hard and avaricious man, Soult nevertheless served France honorably in later life.

Spartacus

d. 71 B.C.

A Thracian by birth, Spartacus may have served in the Roman army at one time and deserted, was captured, and sold as a slave. In 73 he was a member of the gladiatorial school at Capua run by Gnaeus Lentulus Batiatus.

What is certain is that in 73 Spartacus, along with seventy other gladiators, escaped from the school and fled to the slopes of Mount Vesuvius. With the assistance of two lieutenants, Celts known as Crixus and Oenomaos, Spartacus raised a band of desperate fugitives consisting of escaped slaves and brigands. When a hastily raised force of 3,000 levies attempted to confine the rebels to their mountain fastness, Spartacus and his men descended upon them and put them to flight. When confronted by an army under Publius Varinius, Spartacus defeated him in several engagements and took control of al-most all of southern Italy. His ranks swelled by success, Spartacus soon had an army of between 70,000 and 90,000 men. In 72 Spartacus defeated four legions sent against him. His plan was to cross the Alps to freedom. After reaching Modena, however, Spartacus' men voted to return to Italy for plunder. He threatened Rome, and when his attempt to leave Italy for Sicily failed, in the spring of 71 he broke through the Roman lines and made a stand in Calabria, where he was killed, his army defeated, and 6,000 survivors crucified.

Spartacus almost achieved one of the greatest breakouts in history but was defeated only by internal dissension in his army. He has been a powerful symbol for oppressed people ever since.

Raymond A. Spruance

1886–1969

Born in Baltimore, Maryland, Spruance entered the U.S. Naval Academy in 1903 and graduated with the Class of 1906, one year early. He saw no action during World War I.

Between wars Spruance developed extraordinary skills as a ship commander and a student of naval strategy and tactics. He believed that a line officer's place was at sea and he sought sea duty, although he was susceptible to seasickness. Spruance never cultivated friends in high places, but in 1939 he was promoted to rear admiral and given command of the 10th Naval District. In August 1941 he was given command of a heavy cruiser division in the Pacific, where he participated in the first U.S. carrier raids of the war, including the **Doolittle** raid against Tokyo. Although not an aviator, Spruance com-manded one of two carrier task forces opposing the Japanese at Midway (June 3–6, 1942), sinking four enemy carriers. Promoted to vice admiral in 1943, he directed the capture of the Gilberts, the Marshalls, and Truk in the Carolines. Made full admiral in March 1944, he destroyed Japanese naval aviation (450 planes in one day) at the Battle of the Philippine Sea in June, although the Japanese fleet escaped. In April 1945, directing the Fifth Fleet at Okinawa, his flagship, the *Indianapolis,* was hit by a kamikaze. Spruance retired in 1948. He was ambassador to the Philippines, 1952–1955.

Spruance planned carefully to deliver overwhelming force swiftly. He was unperturbable under fire, always unassuming, and encouraged initiative in his subordinates.

John Stark

1728–1822

Born at Londonderry, New Hampshire, Stark grew up on the frontier of his day, where hunting, fishing, and fighting Indians were a way of life.

During the French and Indian War, Stark saw much service with Rogers' Rangers, where he rose to the rank of captain. In January 1757, while on a scouting party to Lake Champlain, his men were engaged in an all-night march followed by an all-day fight with an enemy patrol. Afterward he walked forty miles through heavy snow to bring help for his wounded. In 1758 and 1759 he participated in the expeditions against Ticonderoga and Crown Point. On April 23, 1775, he led the 1st New Hampshire Regiment at Bunker Hill, where he told them, "Boys, aim at their waistbands!" He fought at Trenton and Princeton, but passed over for promotion, he resigned in March 1777 and returned to his home. When Burgoyne invaded New York, the New Hampshire general court selected Stark to raise a brigade and within three weeks he had enlisted 1,400 men, with whom he marched to the aid of Vermont. At Bennington on August 16, 1777, Stark's brigade overwhelmed a British contingent of 800 German mercenaries—with a few British regulars, Tories, and Indians attached—under the command of Lieutenant Colonel Friedrich Baum. Stark reportedly told his men, "Beat them or my wife sleeps a widow tonight." The Germans lost 207 killed and 700 captured to very slight loss for the Americans. After the war Stark retired to his farm, where he lived the rest of his days in peace.

Stark may have been lucky at Bennington and he was certainly insubordinate at times, but he could handle his men and his victory at Bennington gave the American cause a great boost.

James B. Steedman

1817–1883

Born in Northumberland County, Pennsylvania, Steedman was orphaned as a child. He served in the Texan army, was active in Ohio politics, and participated in the Gold Rush of 1849. He was appointed public printer under Buchanan in 1857.

Steedman was appointed colonel of the 14th Ohio Volunteer Infantry in April 1861, and although he was nominated for brigadier general in August, his confirmation was delayed by politics (he had published an article in the *Toledo Times* favorable to secession) until July 1862. At the Battle of Chickamauga, September 20, 1863, Steedman was commanding the 1st Division, Reserve Corps, Army of the Cumberland, when the Union right was driven back and the army's commanders fled to Chattanooga, thinking all was lost and leaving Major General **George H.** **Thomas** and his XIV Corps alone on the field. Steedman led his division through heavy fire to relieve Thomas's beleaguered troops. In twenty minutes he lost one fifth of his strength. His horse shot out from under him and badly bruised in the fall, Steedman grabbed up the colors of one of his regiments and led the attack in person. Before starting off, he turned to an aide and asked him to be sure that in his obituary they spelled his name *Steedman,* not *Steadman.* In April 1864 he was appointed a major general of volunteers. In later life he was active in public affairs and practiced journalism.

Steedman possessed great physical size and strength and was an aggressive, determined, fearless individual who relished responsibility and was at his best in great emergencies.

Joseph W. Stilwell

1883–1946

Born at Palatka, Florida; Stilwell's father, believing the discipline would be good for him, arranged an appointment to the U.S. Military Academy. Stilwell graduated 32 of 124 in his class of 1904.

Stilwell's first assignment as a lieutenant was in the Philippines, where he fought guerrillas for fourteen months. During World War I he served with British and French units and American intelligence. Before World War II, Stilwell served a total of ten years in China in various assignments, learning the languages and the country. While an instructor at Fort Benning, he earned the nickname "Vinegar Joe" because of the acerbic tongue-lashings he gave his students. Promoted to brigadier general in 1939, Stilwell was a lieutenant general in 1942 when he was sent back to China as chief of staff to Chaing Kaishek. He also got command of all U.S. forces in the China-Burma-India (CBI) Theater and the Chinese 5th and 6th Armies. Caught in Burma when it fell to the Japanese in May 1942, Stilwell and his staff were forced to walk out to India to avoid capture. Although Stilwell was promoted to full general in 1944, Chaing refused the recommendation that he appoint Stilwell to overall command of Chinese forces and demanded instead that he be recalled. Stilwell then commanded the Tenth Army on Okinawa. He died of stomach cancer in San Francisco in 1946.

Stilwell was a soldier, not a diplomat. He openly despised Chaing for his defensive psychology, calling him "Peanut." The CBI had low

General Joseph W. Stilwell

National Archives

priority for supplies and equipment and no one man could possibly have coped with all of Stilwell's responsibilities at the same time. He believed the Chinese soldier, if properly trained and equipped, was equal to his task and he kept the Chinese army in the war in Burma. Stilwell said of those who criticized his service in China, "I've done my best and stood up for American interests. To hell with them."

James Ewell Brown Stuart

1833–1864

Born in Patrick County, Virginia, the son of a Virginia congressman, Stuart attended Emory and Henry College for two years before entering the U.S. Military Academy in 1850, graduating thirteen of forty-six in the Class of 1854.

Stuart served for a while in Texas and then in Kansas. While in Washington in October 1859, he accompanied **R. E. Lee** to Harper's Ferry during John Brown's raid. At the outbreak of the Civil War, he resigned his commission and accepted a captaincy of Confederate Cavalry on May 24, 1861. At First Manassas (Bull Run) he protected the Confederate left. In June 1862 he was promoted to brigadier general and on June 11 conducted his famous ride around McClellan's army on the Virginia peninsula with the loss of only one man. Promoted to major general in July, Stuart took command of the cavalry division of Lee's army. At Second Manassas in August he supported **Jackson** and, on October 9, led his celebrated raid to Chambersburg, Pennsylvania. At Chancellorsville on May 3, 1863,

Stuart took command of Jackson's corps after the latter was wounded and handled it skillfully. Some have accused him of being off "joyriding" during the Gettysburg Campaign and it is possible he interpreted Lee's orders too liberally and thus deprived him of badly needed intelligence on **Meade's** movements. Subsequently, he never failed Lee again. On May 11, 1864, in a skirmish with **Sheridan's** troopers at Yellow Tavern, near Richmond, Stuart was wounded and died the next day.

Nicknamed "Jeb," Stuart organized his staff and trained his men in a very professional manner, preferring to live in the field with them. He was flamboyant and conspicuous everywhere he went, and although deeply religious, he loved music and dancing, but never allowed drinking or swearing in his presence. At Chancellorsville he proved he could handle a corps command. But Stuart was always the ideal cavalryman, daring, resourceful, intelligent.

Frederick Charles Doveton Sturdee

1859–1925

Born at Charlton, Kent, the eldest son of a Royal Navy captain, Sturdee went to sea as a midshipman in July 1873.

Sturdee saw service in Egypt in 1882, for which he was decorated. During the years before World War I he saw much sea service and shore assignments. He commanded the battleship *New Zealand* in the Channel fleet before being promoted to admiral in September 1908. Appointed commander in chief in the South Atlantic and South Pacific in 1914, Sturdee reached Port Stanley in the Falkland Islands on December 7, 1914. The following morning the

German squadron under the command of Admiral Maximilian von Spee, consisting of the armored cruisers *Scharnhorst* and *Gneisenau*, four light cruisers, and two colliers, was sighted. Sturdee's squadron consisted of the battle cruisers *Inflexible* and *Invincible* and five cruisers. Sturdee gave the order to raise steam and then "went down to a good breakfast." In the running sea fight that followed, von Spee and his two sons were killed and all the German vessels but the light cruiser *Dresden* were sunk. Sturdee commanded the 4th Battle Squadron at Jutland on May 31, 1916. He was promoted to full admiral in 1917 and admiral of the fleet in 1921.

Sturdee was a thoroughly professional naval officer who rose to the highest command through hard work, devotion to the service, and his own considerable merits. He was unperturbable under fire. His defeat of von Spee was one of the most complete British naval victories of the war.

Louis Gabriel Suchet

1770–1826

Born at Lyons, the son of a rich silk manufacturer, Suchet joined the cavalry of the National Guard in 1791 and in September 1793 was elected lieutenant colonel of his battalion, which he led in the siege of Toulon.

Suchet served in Italy in 1795–1797, being twice wounded. In 1798 he was promoted to brigade commander and the next year division commander. In the 1805 campaign he served under **Soult** and **Lannes** and his division fought with distinction at Ulm, Hollabrunn, Austerlitz, Jena, and Pultusk. In 1807 he succeeded **Masséna** in command of the V Corps. In 1809 Suchet was given command of the III Corps in Spain, which he restored to a state of combat readiness. With great wisdom and diplomacy, he also fulfilled his duty as governor of Aragon, which gave him a secure base of operations. In three years he captured 77,000 prisoners and 1,400 guns, and in July 1811 **Napoleon** made him a marshal of France, the only French general to win his baton in Spain. In 1813–1814, because of French defeats elsewhere, Suchet withdrew his command, still undefeated, from Spain. Although he rallied to Napoleon in 1815, his peerage was restored to him in 1819.

Napoleon said that if he had had two Suchets, he could have kept Spain. When word of his death reached Spain, priests at the cathedral in Saragossa said mass for him. Suchet was a brave, aggressive fighter and a man of great integrity. His humane and evenhanded governorship of Aragon demonstrated his skill as an administrator.

Pierre-André de Suffren Saint-Tropez

1729–1788

Born in Aix-en-Provence, the younger son of the Marquis de Saint-Tropez, Suffren entered the French navy as a midshipman in October 1743.

Suffren saw his first action at the Battle of Toulon in February 1744. In the Battle of Cape Finisterre in October 1747, he was captured. He was captured again at the Battle of Lagos in August 1759. In the service of the Knights of Malta, he fought Muslim pirates, 1763–1767. During the American Revolution, Suffren served in the Caribbean and North America. Early in 1781 he was sent to protect French interests in India. By keeping his fleet constantly at sea, Suffren ensured that the British fleet was kept from supporting their land forces. This led to his famous rivalry with the British commander in Indian waters, Edward Hughes. Between February 17, 1782, and June 20, 1783, Suffren and Hughes engaged in five battles. Suffren won three and the engagement off Trincomalee in September 1782 was a draw but could have been a victory had his subordinates been more aggressive. With the end of hostilities in July 1783, Suffren stopped at Capetown on the way home, where he was honored by the British naval officers. Suffren died in a duel with the Prince de Mirepoix, who was angry because Suffren had refused to reinstate two of his relatives whom he had dismissed for misconduct.

Suffren was a tenacious and bold fighter and a fine naval tactician and seaman who also showed a good grasp of strategy in his campaign in India.

Süleyman I ["The Magnificent"]

1494–1566

The only son of Sultan Selim I, Süleyman got his early training in statecraft under the tutelage of his grandfather, Bayazid II, whom Selim I forced to abdicate in 1512. Süleyman succeeded his father in 1520.

Süleyman continued the expansion of the Ottoman empire undertaken by his father, marching first into Western Europe. In 1521 he captured Belgrade. From June to December 1522 he besieged Rhodes, the stronghold of the Knights of St. John. After sustaining over 50,000 casualties, Süleyman conducted a negotiated evacuation. The residents who wished to remain were allowed to keep their civil rights and were given a five-year remission of taxes. In August 1526, with about 80,000 men, Süleyman engaged King Louis of Hungary on the plain of Mohács, along the Danube. The Hungarians had about 12,000 cavalry and 13,000 infantry. At first Louis was successful in breaking through the first two Turkish lines, but exhaustion and Süleyman's artillery broke the Hungarians, and Louis and 15,000 of his men fell. Süleyman's sieges of Vienna in 1529 to 1530 and 1532 failed but the victory of his fleet at Preveza in September 1538 gave him naval control in the Mediterranean. In 1555 he concluded his long-standing war with Persia by the Treaty of Amasia. He was unsuccessful in his siege of Malta in 1565, where the Knights of St. John moved after their expulsion from Rhodes. Although he annexed Hungary in 1541, there was no peace, and in August 1566, Süleyman, now seventy-two, personally led his army into Hungary with Vienna as his goal. At Szigetvár in southern Hungary, Süleyman was stopped by about 3,000 defenders under Miklós Zrínyi. On September 8, 1566, after lighting the fuses to the magazines, Zrínyi and his men charged out in one last desperate sortie, determined to break through or take as many besiegers with them as they could. The detonating magazines killed all the defenders and hundreds of Turks, too. But Süleyman had already died on the night of September 5–6.

Süleyman was a remarkable commander, bold, aggressive, and ruthless when he had to be, but he also knew when to negotiate for what he wanted. He believed in delegating power to his vassals and none served him better than Admiral Khayr ad-Dīn Barbarossa.

Lucius Cornelius Sulla

138?–78 B.C.

Son of a poor patrician family, Sulla was forced as a young man to live in rented quarters because he was so impoverished. Apparently his stepmother and a wealthy inamorato left him property and money when they died.

In 107 B.C. Sulla went to Libya where he distinguished himself by the capture of the Numidian rebel, Jugurtha. He fought against the Germans in 105–101 and was appointed governor of Cilicia in southern Turkey in 92. He distinguished himself during the Social Wars in 91–88, so that in 88 he was given command of the army sent to Greece to suppress Mithridates, King of Pontus, a region on the southern shore of the Black Sea. An effort to replace him failed when Sulla marched on Rome, the first time a Roman army had done such a thing, and executed the tribune P. Sulpicius Rufus. At Chaerona in 86, with about 30,000 men, Sulla met Mithridates' general, Archelaus, with about 110,000 men. In the first known use of field fortifications, Sulla dug entrenchments on his flanks and erected palisades along his front, placing his legions in squares inside. Sulla repulsed the Mithridatic cavalry and chariot attacks and then counterattacked with his own cavalry and infantry, routing Archelaus completely. Sulla used the same tactics at Orchomenus in 85. Meanwhile Rome had been seized by democrats who had instituted a reign of terror. With 40,000 veterans, Sulla overthrew them in 82. With himself as dictator, he restored the senate and instituted other reforms, retiring to his estates in Campania.

Sulla was a vigorous and ruthless man who loved wine and sensory pleasures, but he was also a brilliant and innovative battlefield tactician who consistently kept his head in the face of overwhelming odds.

Aleksandr Vasilyevich Suvorov

1730–1800

Born in Moscow, son of an army officer, Suvorov enlisted in a Guards regiment in 1745 and by 1751 had risen to the rank of sergeant.

Commissioned in 1754, Suvorov fought with distinction during the Seven Years War (1756–1763), rising to the rank of colonel by war's end. He was promoted to major general for his service during the Polish Civil War in 1768. In 1775 he put down a Cossack revolt. Suvorov distinguished himself during the Russo-Turkish Wars of 1768–1774 and 1787–1792 and during the Polish revolt of 1793–1794. For capturing Warsaw in November 1794, Suvorov was promoted to field marshal. Forced into retirement upon the death of Catherine the Great in 1796, he was recalled in 1798 to command an Austro-Russian army to expel the French from Italy. He defeated the French at Cassano in April 1799 and took Milan and Turin. At Trebbia in June he inflicted a partial defeat on the French and on August 15 at the Battle of Novi defeated the French under Joubert, who was killed in the battle. As he was pursuing the French toward Genoa, Suvorov was ordered to Switzerland. Despite an epic march through the Alps, he arrived too late to save the Russian army from **Masséna** at Zurich, and in January 1800, Czar Paul recalled him to St. Petersburg in disgrace; he died there in May.

Suvorov was a tireless adversary who pushed himself and his men relentlessly. He spared neither his soldiers nor his enemies. Crude and unsophisticated, he was the perfect match for his soldiers, whom he trained painstakingly. Although he is regarded by some as a general without a science, Suvorov's campaign in Italy was the one bright spot in the allied coalition against France in 1798–1800.

T

Tamerlane [Timur Lenk]

1336–1405

Born at Kesh, about fifty miles south of Samarkand, Tamerlane, the name by which he is known in the West, is a corruption of the Persian *Timur Lenk,* or "Timur the Lame," because he was lame. A Tartar, not a Mongol, Tamerlane nevertheless declared himself a descendant of **Genghis Khan** and claimed his conquests were restoring Genghis's empire.

After a series of intrigues, rebellions, and murders, Tamerlane ascended the throne at Samarkand in 1369. During the next thirty years he campaigned from the Caspian and the banks of the Ural and the Volga rivers in the west and northwest to Iran and Syria to the south and southwest, and into India. Tamerlane's conquests were marked by their ferocity and slaughter. In 1390, at the head of 100,000 men, Tamerlane invaded Russia to dispose of the khanate of the Golden Horde, the Mongol empire so-called because of the magnificence of its capital on the Volga River. At the Battle of the Steppes, somewhere east of the Volga, he achieved a narrow victory at the cost of 30,000 men. But at the Battle of the Terek in 1395 he defeated the Mongols and ravished southern Russia and the Ukraine, advancing as far as Moscow. In 1398 he invaded India and, after sacking Delhi, abruptly went home. In 1400 he slaughtered 20,000 at Damascus and in 1401 massacred the inhabitants of Baghdad. He was starting out on an invasion of China when he died in January 1405.

Tamerlane's campaigns were great raids for plunder and his quest to conquer insatiable, but no commander could lead armies through such vast territories as he did without considerable organizational and tactical skill, not to mention superhuman personal endurance and determination.

Banastre Tarleton

1754–1833

Born in Liverpool, son of a wealthy family, Tarleton was educated at the University of Liverpool and Oxford before his father purchased him a cornet's commission in the king's Dragoon Guards in April 1775.

In May 1776 Tarleton participated in Sir Henry Clinton's unsuccessful expedition to Charleston, South Carolina, and later he served under Clinton in New York and New Jersey. In 1778 he was promoted to lieutenant colonel and named commander of the British Legion, which consisted of several troops of dragoons recruited in the colonies. In 1780 he was attached to Clinton's army at Charleston. At the Battle of Waxhaw, South Carolina, on May 29, 1780, he earned the nickname "Bloody Ban" when he bayonetted Americans attempting to surrender. This act was also dubbed "Tarleton's Quarter"—*no* quarter. At Cowpens, January 17, 1781, Tarleton was beaten by **Daniel Morgan,** but at Tarent's

Tavern, North Carolina, on February 1, 1781, he was victorious. At the Battle of Guilford Court House on March 15, he lost two fingers in action with the British advance guard and was wounded again, leading a cavalry charge at the end of the battle. During a sharp skirmish at Gloucester, Virginia, on October 3, 1781, Tarleton was almost captured. He surrendered with Cornwallis at Yorktown and was afterward paroled to England. He was promoted to major general in October 1794 and full general in January 1812.

Ruthless and vindictive as a man, Tarleton commanded with vigor, dash, and daring, at his best in the charge and melee.

Maxwell D. Taylor

1901–1987

Born in Keytesville, Missouri, son of a railroad attorney, at the age of five Taylor told his parents that he wanted to go to West Point, which he did, graduating fourth in the class of 1922. His classmates included **Joseph Collins, Matthew Ridgway,** and **Omar Bradley;** the superintendent was **Douglas MacArthur.**

Between wars Taylor perfected his command of languages, becoming fluent in French and Spanish; in 1935 he was assigned to the embassy in Tokyo to learn Japanese. A lieutenant colonel when the U.S. entered World War II, Taylor helped Ridgway convert the 82nd Infantry Division into an airborne unit. Taylor did not jump into Sicily with the division, but prior to the invasion of Italy, he and one other officer were sent behind the lines to Rome, to assess the possibility of an airborne landing supported by antifascist forces. Taylor recommended against the operation and it was aborted at only the last minute. As commander of the 101st Airborne Division, Taylor jumped with his men into France on the night of June 6, 1944, becoming the first American general to fight in France in WWII. With his troops scattered upon landing, Taylor rallied those he could and went on to capture his objectives. The division lost one third of its men before being pulled out of Normandy. Taylor jumped with his men into Holland in Operation Market-Garden in September 1944. Back in the U.S. when the Battle of the Bulge started, Taylor rejoined the division on December 27, 1944, and led it to the end of the war. After the war he served as superintendent at West Point; commander, Eighth Army in Korea; and was chief of staff of the army until his retirement in 1959. He was called back to be chairman of the joint chiefs of staff and then ambassador to South Vietnam in June 1964.

Taylor was an early exponent of "vertical envelopment" by paratroopers, so much so that he bet his life on the tactic by parachuting into combat with his men. Later, he advocated "flexible response" versus "massive retaliation" in the Cold War, and although his strategy for winning in Vietnam—limited U.S. forces in a counterinsurgency role—failed, so did everybody else's.

Zachary Taylor

1784–1850

Born in Orange County, Virginia, but raised in Louisville, Kentucky, in 1808 President Jefferson appointed Taylor a lieutenant in the 7th Infantry.

Promoted to captain in 1810, during the War of 1812 Taylor served in Indiana Territory, where on September 4, 1812, he successfully defended Fort Harrison against an attack by 400 Indians, for which he was brevetted to the rank of major. He served in the Black Hawk War in 1832 and fought Seminoles in Florida, where on December 25, 1837, he won a great victory at Lake Okeechobee. In 1838 he was brevetted to brigadier general. In May 1845 Taylor was ordered to Texas in anticipation of trouble with Mexico upon the annexation of Texas into the U.S. In January 1846, with 4,000 men, he was ordered to the mouth of the Rio Grande, where he built a fort opposite the Mexican town of Matamoros. Attacked by Mexicans, Taylor did not wait for a declaration of war but attacked them at Palo Alto and defeated a force three times the size of his own. On May 9, 1846, he won another victory at Resaca de la Palma. On the twenty-first of September he attacked Monterey, which he took after three days of assaults. On February 22–23, he defeated a Mexican army of 20,000 troops under Santa Ana at Buena Vista, ending the war in the north. Taylor was elected the twelfth president of the U.S. on the Whig ticket in 1848. He died of heatstroke July 9, 1850.

Nicknamed "Old Rough and Ready," Taylor was a blunt and rugged individual, and although personally modest, he was a brave and resourceful battlefield commander.

Tecumseh [Tikamthe, Tecumtha]

1768–1813

Born near modern Springfield, Ohio, the son of a Creek mother and a Shawnee father, Tecumseh had already won the reputation of a warrior by the time he reached manhood.

Tecumseh fought white settlers in a number of raids and skirmishes during the American Revolution and he was at Fallen Timbers when the Indians were defeated by **Anthony Wayne** on August 20, 1794. Later he and his brother, Tenskwatawa ("The Prophet") settled their people on the Wabash River at the junction of the Tippecanoe. Tecumseh argued with great force and eloquence against the sale of Indian lands to whites. He achieved some success in confederating the tribes against the encroachments of whites. In this he was supported by the British in Canada. In 1811, while he was away from Tippecanoe recruiting for his confederation, William Henry Harrison, governor of Indiana, precipitated the Battle of Tippecanoe in which the Indians under Tenskwatawa were defeated and Tecumseh's confederation began to fall apart. At the outbreak of the War of 1812, Tecumseh led his few remaining followers to Canada, where the British made him a brigadier general. Tecumseh fought under the British in a number of battles. At the Thames on October 5, 1813, covering the retreat of Brigadier General Henry Proctor's army, Tecumseh was killed.

Harrison called Tecumseh an "uncommon genius." Tecumseh never practiced the horrors that characterized Indian warfare in his day and his word was respected by everyone. A brilliant orator and man of principle, Tecumseh had good reason not to trust whites, betrayed as his people were by the Americans and abandoned by the British.

Alfred H. Terry

1827–1890

Born in Hartford, Connecticut, Terry attended Yale Law School in 1848 and was a county superior court clerk until the outbreak of the Civil War.

Appointed colonel of the 2nd Connecticut Militia, Terry led his regiment at First Manassas (Bull Run), and when the regiment was discharged on the expiration of its three months' service, he raised the 7th Connecticut Volunteers for three years of service. He participated in the capture of Port Royal, South Carolina, in November 1861 and the siege of Fort Pulaski, Georgia, in April 1862. On April 25, Terry was appointed brigadier general of volunteers and major general in August 1864. On January 15, 1865, after General. B. F. Butler had failed, Terry took Fort Fisher, North Carolina, and the port city of Wilmington, thus closing the last port open to Confederate blockade runners. For this he was appointed a brigadier general in the regular army without ever having served as a regular. In 1866 he assumed command of the Department of Dakota with headquarters at St. Paul and then Fort Snelling, Minnesota. He took personal command of the forces deployed to the Yellowstone–Big Horn region of Montana in the summer of 1876. When **Custer**'s command was decimated at the Little Big Horn on June 25, 1876, Terry tacitly accepted responsibility for Custer having exceeded his orders. Terry was promoted to major general in 1886 and retired in 1888.

Terry studied well the art of war firsthand. He cooperated well with others but fully accepted responsibility.

Themistocles

524?–460? B.C.

Born at Athens, the son of a middle-class family, Themistocles fought at Marathon and was elected chief magistrate of Athens in 493.

Themistocles was a forceful advocate of Athenian naval power. In 483 he persuaded the Athenians to build 100 triremes (three-tired warships) with revenue from state-owned silver mines while at the same time building a naval base at the Athenian port of Piraeus. When the Persians renewed their war with Greece in 480, Athens had the largest navy in Greece. As the Persian army marched on Athens (it was taken in September) the Greek navy battled the Persian fleet indecisively at Artemisium, off the island of Euboea. In September 480, with the entire Greek army aboard his ships (some 6,000 infantrymen), Themistocles massed his ships in a narrow strait off the northeast coast of Salamis, a small island near Piraeus. He realized that in the narrow confines of the strait his ships could use their maneuverability to great advantage. He enticed the Persians to attack him there by sending them a false message that the Greeks were in disorder and ready to flee. On September 23, 480, the Persian fleet of 500 vessels attacked the Greeks. The battle lasted seven hours, the Greek infantrymen fighting across the decks of the ships. The Greeks lost 40 ships to the Persians' 250 or more. A few years later Themistocles fell out of favor and was ostracized. He spent the rest of his life an exile in Persia.

A man of great strategic vision, Themistocles rose to high command and influence on his ability and courage alone.

George H. Thomas

1816–1870

Born in Southampton County, Virginia, Thomas graduated twelve of forty-two in his West Point class of 1840. His classmates included **William T. Sherman** and **Richard Ewell**.

Assigned to the 3rd Artillery, Thomas saw action against the Seminoles in Florida. He fought with **Taylor**'s army in Mexico and was brevetted to captain and major for gallantry in action at Monterrey and Buena Vista. While serving in the 2nd Cavalry in Texas, he was wounded in the face by an Indian arrow. In the 2nd Cavalry, **A. S. Johnston** was his colonel, **R. E. Lee** his lieutenant colonel, and **William Hardee** was the other major. At the outbreak of the Civil War Thomas stayed with the Union. He was appointed colonel of the 2nd Cavalry in May 1861 and brigadier general of volunteers in August. In November he took command of the 1st Division of the Army of the Ohio and won a decisive action at Mill Springs, Kentucky, on January 19, 1862. He was promoted to major general in April. He commanded the XIV Corps of the Army of the Cumberland at Stones River in December 1862. At the Battle of Chickamauga, on September 20, 1863, when half the Union Army fled in disorder, Thomas remained on the field all day, his line bent like a horseshoe but unbroken. For his stand that day, which saved the Army of the Cumberland, he was known ever afterward as "the Rock of Chickamauga." Thomas commanded the Army of the Cumberland during the siege of Chattanooga, assuring **Grant,** "We will hold the town till we starve." He served under Sherman in the Atlanta Campaign and, sent west to counter Confederate General Hood's army, defeated him decisively at Nashville, December 15–16, 1864. For this service he was promoted to major general in the regular army. In 1868 President

George H. Thomas

Free Library of Philadelphia

Johnson recommended Thomas for promotion to brevet lieutenant general and full general, but he declined this as too great an honor.

Known as "Old Tom" as a cadet, "Slow Trot" as an instructor at West Point, and later "Pap Thomas" by the soldiers in the Army of the Cumberland, Thomas was a deliberate and fastidious officer, but he was also modest and disdainful of military glory. He was a brilliant commander whose solid achievements have been obscured by the careers of his more flamboyant contemporaries.

Thutmose III

1504–1450 B.C.

The son of Thutmose II by a concubine named Isis, Thutmose III ascended the throne when his father died in 1491, but actual control of the government was exercised by a regency under his aunt, Hatshepsut, who died about 1472.

During Hatsheput's regency the vassal states of Palestine and Syria threw off Egyptian rule. The Palestinian-Syrian coalition consisted of about 300 rebellious princes under the King of Kadesh. Almost annually for the next twenty years, Thutmose conducted a military campaign somewhere in western Asia. His greatest feat, and the first recorded battle in history, took place outside the fortress city of Megiddo near Mount Carmel. At the head of about 10,000 men, he forced the Megiddo Pass and enveloped the princes' army, personally leading the northern wing in his own chariot. The surviving troops took refuge in the city, which fell after a seven-month siege. The record of this particular exploit was carved in some detail on the walls of the temple at Karnak. By the end of his reign, Thutmose had extended Egyptian rule into Palestine and Syria and parts of modern Turkey and prompted the Babylonian, Hittite, and Assyrian monarchs to pay tribute. Thutmose appointed men loyal to himself to rule the conquered territories and he assured their continued loyalty by taking their families hostage. His sarcophagus and mummy, discovered in 1881, and are on display in Cairo.

Thutmose was a talented, aggressive, and determined general and an extremely able governor.

Tiberius Julius Caesar Augustus

42 B.C.–37 A.D.

Born at Rome, the son of Tiberius Claudius Nero, one of **Julius Caesar's** officers, Tiberius was introduced to public life at the age of nine, when he gave his father's funeral eulogy. He held several high government offices (quaestor, praetor, consul) before he was legally old enough to occupy them.

He fought in Spain before being sent to Armenia in 20 B.C., where he restored the vassal King of Rome, after which he served as governor of transalpine Gaul. In 15 B.C. he went with his brother, Drusus, to subjugate the Germans on the Rhine and in 11 B.C. he carried out a successful campaign against the Pannonians (modern Hungary and Yugoslavia). In 6 B.C. he retired to Rhodes, with the grudging permission of the Emperor Augustus, who considered Tiberius an indispensable military commander. He returned to Rome in 2 A.D., leading armies into Germany and Illyria on the eastern Adriatic coast. His victory there somewhat alleviated the loss of Varus and his legions in Germany (9 A.D.). At his victory banquet Tiberius spared the life of Bato, the defeated Illyrian leader, out of respect for his chivalry on the battlefield. At the death of Augustus in 14 A.D., Tiberius assumed the throne as Augustus's designated successor. As emperor, Tiberius preserved the republican forms of government, effected reforms in finance, and strengthened defense. As he preferred diplomacy to war, his reign marked the beginning of the *Pax Romana*, which lasted 200 years. Never a very popular ruler, in his later years Tiberius ruled from the island of Capri, where he retired in 23 A.D. Barricaded on Capri, fearful of his enemies, Tiberius's last years were marred by conspiracies, trials, and executions. He was succeeded by his nephew Caligula.

An extremely capable soldier and administrator, Tiberius was modest and industrious in his early career and as emperor he followed policies of great benefit to Rome. His inscrutability and personal coldness were no doubt exacerbated by a disastrous family life, including a scheming mother and a forced marriage to Julia, daughter of Augustus.

Johann Tserclaes Tilly

1559–1632

Born near Nivelle in Brabant, Belgium; Tilly's father was exiled during the persecutions of **Toledo,** the Duke of Alva in the Spanish Netherlands, and was educated at Liege and Cologne.

The family made peace with the regime in 1574 and Tilly served in the army of **Farnese,** Duke of Parma, as a foot soldier at the siege of Antwerp and in the French religious wars, where he distinguished himself by his bravery. He then took service with the Austrian imperial army and fought the Turks, rising to the rank of field marshal in 1605. In 1610 he entered the service of Maximilian of Bavaria, head of the Catholic League. In 1620 he became commander of Maximilian's field forces. At Höchst, June 20, 1622, he inflicted a defeat on Christian of Brunswick when he caught his army attempting to cross the Main River. Tilly took Heidelberg on September 19. In 1625, the Danes invaded Germany and Tilly took the field in cooperation with **Wallenstein**. At Lutter, August 24–27, 1626, Tilly inflicted a great defeat on the Danes, but at Magdeburg on May 20th, 1631, his troops ran amok and sacked the city despite Tilly's personal efforts to save some prominent landmarks. Tilly was subsequently defeated by **Gustavus Adolphus** of Sweden at Breitenfeld in September and fell back into Bavaria. While attempting to defend crossings on the River Lech in April 1632, Tilly was wounded and died at Ingolstadt April 30, 1632.

Although Tilly was constantly subjected to political difficulties during the Thirty Years War, his men, trained to his ideal of the "ragged soldier with a bright musket," were responsible for the successes the Catholic League did achieve during the war.

Josip Broz Tito

1892–1980

Born near Zagreb in Croatia, seventh son of a peasant, Tito was conscripted into the Austro-Hungarian army during World War I. Wounded and captured by the Russians in April 1915, he escaped in 1917 and participated in the Bolshevik Revolution.

After fighting against the White Russians, Tito returned to Croatia in 1920, where he was active in the outlawed Yugoslav Communist party, becoming its general secretary in 1937. Tito opposed his country's entry into World War II, but upon Hitler's invasion of Yugoslavia in April 1941, he organized a partisan network to fight them, adopting the *nom de guerre* "Tito," which he later took as his legal surname. By September 1941 he had forced the Germans out of Serbia. Taking advantage of internal dissensions between Tito and the royalist partisans, the Germans recaptured most of the lost territory by December, forcing Tito into Bosnia and Montenegro. From the mountains Tito waged a classic guerrilla war. The Germans mounted a vigorous antiguerrilla campaign supported by artillery, armor, and airpower. Tito survived the operations of 1942–1943, breaking out of encirclements and narrowly avoiding capture in May 1944 when paratroopers were dropped near his headquarters. Heavily supported by the Allies, Tito's forces joined up with the British Eighth Army at Trieste in May 1945. In 1949 Tito, then prime minister of Yugoslavia, broke with Moscow and for the rest of his life pursued his own course of accommodation with the West.

Tito was a courageous fighting man who seized power at the risk of his own life and it was his determined leadership and strength of character alone that held Yugoslavia together until his death. His guerrilla war against the Germans, although marred by the atrocities common to such fighting, remains one of the most brilliantly executed and successful in history.

Marshal Josip Tito

National Archives

Heihachirō Togō

1848–1934

Born in Kagoshima Prefecture, Japan, Togo first saw action during a British bombardment of Kagoshima, August 15–16, 1868. He participated in the naval actions that led to the overthrow of the Tokugawa shogunate.

Togo entered the imperial navy as a cadet in 1871 and was sent to Britain as a naval student, where he trained aboard British ships, circumnavigating the globe as an ordinary seaman on the *Hampshire* in 1875. After studying mathematics at Cambridge and observing ship construction, Togo returned to Japan in 1878. In 1894,

commanding the cruiser *Naniwa*, he sank the British transport *Kaosheng* as it was transporting Chinese troops to Korea. Promoted to rear admiral in 1895, he commanded the combined fleet in the Russo-Japanese War in 1904–1905. At Tsushima Strait between the East China Sea and Sea of Japan on May 27, 1905, Togo destroyed the Russian fleet under Admiral Rozhdestvenski, sinking or capturing eight battleships, seven cruisers, and four destroyers to the loss of only three Japanese torpedo boats. Togo served as chief of the naval general staff,

1905–1909, and was promoted to fleet admiral in 1913.

Dour, taciturn, and cautious, Togo took risks when necessary. His victory at Tsushima, where he used a maneuver called "crossing the T"—turning his ships in succession, exposing each in turn to the fire of an enemy while masking his own supporting fire—was one of the most decisive since Trafalgar and earned him the title of "the Nelson of Japan."

Álvarez de Toledo, Duke of Alva

1507–1582

Born at Piedrahita into one of the most distinguished families of Spain, Toledo served in the army of Charles V in France at the age of fourteen.

In 1531 Toledo fought against the Turks, was promoted to general in 1533, and distinguished himself at the siege of Tunis in 1535. In 1546 he joined Charles in Germany and led his army to victory over dissident German Protestants at Mühlberg on April 24, 1547, one of the first major battles where cavalry armed with pistols played an important role. Upon the abdication of Charles in 1556 and subsequent ascendancy of Philip II, Toledo was appointed Spanish commander in Italy, where by maneuver he compelled the pope to accept a truce in 1557. In August 1567 he was sent to the Spanish Netherlands to suppress political and religious unrest, which he did with excessive cruelty. When **William of Orange** and his brother, Louis of Nassau, invaded Holland, Toledo defeated Louis at Jemmingen on July 21, 1568, and then beat William at Jodoigne in October, forcing him into France. In 1572 William and Louis led another invasion. When Haarlem fell after a seven-month siege in July 1573, Toledo butchered the garrison to a man. Unable to recapture the northern part of Holland, Toledo requested recall to Spain. In 1580 Toledo conquered Portugal for Philip but died in Lisbon in December 1582.

A man of inflexible purpose, Toledo was a strict disciplinarian who enforced high standards of training and order among his troops. He also had a good understanding of logistics and was in the forefront of the tactical development of firearms in the Spanish army.

François-Dominique Toussaint Louverture

1743–1803

Born a slave in French Saint-Domingue, as the western or French part of the island of Hispaniola that is now called Haiti was then known, Touissant was fortunate to have a kindly master who taught him French and allowed him time to read extensively. Reportedly, his favorite readings were of the campaigns of **Caesar** and **Alexander**.

During the great slave revolt of August 1791, Toussaint led his master to safety and then, at the head of 600 former slaves, made his way to Santo Domingo, as the eastern or the Spanish side of the island (which became the Dominican Republic in 1844) was then called, where he organized resistance against the French as a colonel in the Spanish army. Assisted by French deserters, he built his band into a disciplined force of 4,000 men. In 1794, when France abolished slavery, Toussaint returned to Saint-Domingue, rescued the French governor, and declared his loyalty to France as a free citizen. But in 1798 Toussaint expelled the French officials and attacked the Spanish, so that by 1801 he controlled all of Hispaniola. In January 1802 **Napoleon** sent an army of 23,000 under General Charles Leclerc to Haiti with a letter to Toussaint promising freedom for his people. Not fooled, Toussaint resisted, but lured into Leclerc's headquarters under the pretense of negotiations, he was arrested and sent to France, where he died in prison in April 1803. His army weakened by disease, Leclerc himself died in November 1802 and the rebellion continued. The Haitians declared their independence in 1803.

A tough, tenacious, and charismatic leader, Toussaint rose from nothing by virtue of his extraordinary intelligence, all of this after he'd reached the age of fifty.

Lucian K. Truscott, Jr.

1895–1965

Born at Chatfield, Texas, son of a country doctor, Truscott was teaching school in Oklahoma when the United States entered World War I. On August 15, 1917, he was commissioned a second lieutenant in the 17th Cavalry. In December he became a first lieutenant.

Truscott accompanied the 17th Cavalry to Hawaii in 1919 and in 1920 he was promoted to captain. After a series of schools, cavalry and armor assignments, Truscott was promoted to full colonel in December 1941. In May 1942, as a brigadier general, he formed a special task force of rangers for the raid on Dieppe in August. Although the raid was a failure, Truscott's men performed well. In October he was promoted to major general and participated in the North Africa landings in November. He commanded the 3rd Infantry Division during the Sicily Campaign and then led it ashore at Salerno, September 18, 1943. He led the division ashore at Anzio on January 22, 1944, and as commander of the VI Corps, took part in the breakout there and the capture of Rome in June. Truscott led the VI Corps in the invasion of southern France in August 1944, leading it in a brilliant victory over the German Nineteenth Army, capturing over 32,000 men. Promoted to lieutenant general in September, Truscott commanded the Fifth Army in Italy until the end of the war. He retired in 1947 and was promoted to full general in 1954.

Truscott was said to have had **Patton**'s charisma, **Bradley's** soundness, and Eisenhower's diplomacy. He was honest, loyal, and courageous, straightforward and direct in his leadership style, and aggressive in combat.

Henri de La Tour d'Auvergne, Vicomte de Turenne

1611–1675

Born at Sedan, nephew of **Maurice of Nassau,** and raised a Protestant, Turenne entered his uncle's army as a private soldier in 1625.

After attaining the rank of captain, Turenne entered the French service in 1627 and was given a regiment in 1630. He fought against the Spanish and served in Italy. Turenne was created a marshal of France in 1643 and sent to fight the Germans. Reinforced by **Condé,** the French army forced the Germans out of the Rhineland, and although defeated at Mergentheim on May 2, 1645, they came back to win at Nördlingen in

August. Then ensued a war of maneuver that was concluded at the Truce of Ulm in 1647. When Turenne's German cavalry mutinied, shortly afterward, he convinced them to rejoin the French service. In 1648 Turenne joined forces with a Swedish army to defeat the Austrians at Zumarschausen on May 17. He supported Louis XIV against his old friend Condé and defeated him at Gien in April 1652, again in July, and with British support, beat him decisively at Dunkirk, June 14, 1658. In 1660 Louis made him marshal general. During the invasion of Holland in 1672, Turenne commanded a column (Condé, who had become reconciled with Louis, commanded another). Sent into Westphalia in September 1672 with only about 20,000 men, Turenne skillfully outmaneuvered the larger combined army commanded by **Montecuccoli** and Frederick William of Brandenburg. Frederick sued for peace in 1673. In 1674 the reinforced German coalition threatened France again and Turenne was ordered to defend Alsace. After a series of brilliant and daring maneuvers, Turenne smashed the enemy army at Turckheim in January 1675. On July 27, 1675, while making a reconnaissance at Sasbach, Turenne was killed by a cannonball.

Fighting outnumbered, using the terrain features to his advantage, Turenne constantly put his opponents at a disadvantage at a relatively small cost to his own soldiers.

Emory Upton

1839–1881

Born near Batavia, New York, Upton attended one semester at Oberlin College before entering the U.S. Military Academy, graduating eight of forty-five in the class of 1861.

Commissioned a second lieutenant in the 4th Artillery, Upton trained recruits until assigned to the 1st Division staff in McDowell's army, where he was wounded at First Manassas (Bull Run), on July 21, 1861. In the Peninsula Campaign of April–July 1862, he served with Battery D, 2nd Artillery. He was at South Mountain and Sharpsburg (Antietam) in September 1862, and at Fredericksburg, Chancellorsville, and Gettysburg in 1863. At Spotsylvania on May 10, 1864, he was promoted to brigadier general on the spot by General **Grant** for gallantry in leading an assault on the Confederate works (Bloody Angle). He fought at Cold Harbor and Petersburg before being transferred to the Shenandoah Valley, where at the Third Battle of Winchester, on September 19, 1864, he took command of the 1st Division, VI Corps, when its commander was killed; although wounded himself, he continued to lead his men from a stretcher. As a major general leading the 4th Cavalry Division at Selma, Alabama, on April 2, 1865, he broke through the city's fortifications and captured it. After the war Upton briefly reverted to his permanent rank of captain before being appointed lieutenant colonel of the 25th Infantry. From 1870 to 1875 he was commandant of cadets and instructor of tactics at West Point. From 1875 to 1877 he toured the world, observing foreign armies. Suffering from the ravages of a brain tumor, Upton resigned March 14, 1881, and shot himself the next day.

Upton was a resourceful, energetic, skillful, and brave battlefield commander, a strict disciplinarian who drilled his men incessantly, and a man who took nothing for granted. After the war he became the army's leading tactician. He believed in readiness, but his views did not come into vogue until long after his death.

V

Alexander A. Vandegrift

1887–1973

Born at Charlottesville, Virginia, Vandegrift attended the University of Virginia before enlisting in the marine corps in 1908. In 1909 he was commissioned a second lieutenant.

Although Vandegrift missed action in World War I, he participated in operations in Nicaragua in 1912 and Veracruz, Mexico, in 1914. In Haiti in 1915, he served under Colonel **Smedley Butler,** and back there again in 1919, he pursued and captured the Caco bandit chieftain Charlemagne Peralté. Promoted to brigadier general in 1940, Vandegrift took command of the 1st Marine Division in March 1942 and in June he took it to the South Pacific, where on August 7 he led it ashore at Guadalcanal in the first American amphibious operation of World War II. Vandegrift's objective was to seize and hold the Japanese airstrip, which he did, his Marines renaming it Henderson Field, in honor of Major Lofton P. Henderson. For the next four months, in the face of a severe shortage of supplies and replacements and the ravages of tropical diseases, the 1st Marine Division held the field against fanatical Japanese attacks. Vandegrift was awarded the Medal of Honor for his leadership during this campaign. In November 1943 he participated in the landings at Bougainville, after which he became the eighteenth commandant of the marine corps, earning his fourth star in April 1945. He retired in 1947.

Vandegrift's tenacious stand on Guadalcanal gave the U.S. its first offensive victory in the Pacific.

James A. Van Fleet

1892–1992

Born in Coytesville, New Jersey, Van Fleet graduated from West Point in the Class of 1915.

During World War I, Van Fleet went to France with the 6th Infantry Division, where he commanded the 17th Machine Gun Battalion in the Meuse-Argonne Offensive, September–November 1918, during which he was wounded. As a colonel commanding the 8th Infantry Regiment of the 4th Infantry Division, he led his regiment ashore in Normandy on D-Day, June 6, 1944. Promoted to brigadier general, he commanded the 4th Infantry Division for a short time before taking over the 90th Division in **Patton's** Third Army. During October–December 1944, the 90th crossed the Moselle River despite heavy casualties and helped capture Metz. Promoted to major general in November, Van Fleet led his division in the Battle of the Bulge (December 1944–January 1945). At war's end he had earned three Distinguished Service Crosses. Promoted to lieutenant general in 1947, in April 1951 Van Fleet took command of the Eighth Army in Korea, holding it until January 1953. Under his leadership, the Eighth Army pushed the communists behind the 38th parallel and stabilized the front line until the end of the war.

Van Fleet openly denounced the political decision to accept static warfare in Korea and he identified closely with the authoritarian government of Syngman Rhee. He retired as a four-star general in April 1953.

Van Fleet used maneuver and firepower (air and artillery) on the battlefield, believing the aim of war is to destroy the enemy, but his outspokenness on these matters did not go down well with his military and political superiors.

Sébastien Le Prestre de Vauban

1633–1707

Born near Avallon in Burgundy, Vauban enlisted as a youth in the rebel **Prince of Condé's** army, where he soon displayed a talent for laying out fortifications. In 1653, while defending the towns in the Argonne, Vauban was captured by Louis XIV's forces, pardoned, and commissioned in the army.

After the successful capture of Stenay on May 3, 1655, Vauban, who was wounded twice during the siege, was appointed king's engineer. For the next twenty years he served Louis XIV in this capacity. During the Dutch War of 1672–1678, he was promoted to infantry brigadier for his successful siege of Maastricht (June 5–30, 1673). Vauban was again wounded in action at Valenciennes in 1656, and Montmédy in 1675. At the siege of Charleroi in 1693, he commanded an infantry division for the first time. When not on campaign, Vauban built or redesigned a total of 160 fortresses for Louis. He developed siegecraft to a science in the king's service, using a system of parallel trenches advanced under the cover of artillery, and he designed a system of defense-in-depth using semidetached bastions and towers. He was the first to use ricochet fire against a fortress, a system of gunnery that skipped cannonballs over parapets, and he invented the socket bayonet to replace the plug version then in use. The socket bayonet permitted muskets to be fired while the bayonet was attached and this had a far-ranging effect on the infantry organization and tactics of the day. Vauban wrote extensively, not only on military matters but on river navigation, forestry, and land reclamation.

Possibly the greatest military engineer in history, Vauban was no armchair theorist but put his ideas to the test in the field, which earned him four combat wounds during his career. He used ammunition and siege tactics to reduce fortified places, sparing the lives of his men.

W

Jonathan M. Wainwright

1881–1953

Born at Walla Walla, Washington, Wainwright was descended from a long line of American soldiers. He graduated 25 of 78 in his West Point class of 1906.

Wainwright saw his first action with the 1st Cavalry Regiment in the Philippines against the Moro rebels. He served with the 82nd Division in France in 1918, where he participated in the Saint-Mihiel and Meuse-Argonne Offensives. Promoted to brigadier general in 1938 and major general in 1940, Wainwright was sent to the Philippines in command of U.S. infantry troops; there, in September 1941, he became **Douglas MacArthur's** senior field commander. Wainwright was commanding the North Luzon Defense Force north of Manila when the Japanese Fourteenth Army invaded the Philippines on December 10, 1941. With no airpower and raw troops under his command, Wainwright conducted a fighting withdrawal into the relative safety of the Bataan peninsula, abandoning Manila, which had been declared an open city on December 26. After President Roosevelt ordered MacArthur to Australia in March 1942, Wainwright took command in the Philippines. On April 9 he abandoned Bataan for the island fortress of Corregidor, where, with no possibility of relief, he held out until May 6. The Japanese eventually moved Wainwright to a prisoner camp in Manchuria, where he was released by Russian troops in August 1945. Although beaten and humiliated by the Japanese, he maintained his soldierly dignity throughout his captivity. Much to his surprise, he returned a hero and was awarded the Medal of Honor by President Truman. He retired from the army in 1947.

Jonathan M. Wainwright

If Wainwright overestimated the Japanese, they underestimated him and his motley Amer-Filipino forces. With no hope of reinforcement, resupply, or relief of any kind, Wainwright fought the Japanese for five months, giving the American people a badly needed symbol of heroic resistance in the face of hopeless odds. His last message from Corregidor, announcing the surrender, began with the famous words, "With head bowed in sadness but not in shame . . ."

Walton H. Walker

1889–1950

Born in Belton, Texas, the son of a real-estate agent, Walter attended Virginia Military Institute before going to the U.S. Military Academy, where he graduated in the Class of 1912.

Walker participated in the American expedition to Vera Cruz in 1914. During World War I he served with the 13th Machine Gun Battalion and fought in the Saint-Mihiel and Meuse-Argonne Offensives, winning two Silver Stars for gallantry under fire. During the 1930s Walker served with the 15th Infantry in China. In 1941 he commanded the 36th Infantry, and in July, promoted to brigadier general, he commanded the 3rd Armored Brigade; as a major general, he commanded the 3rd Armored Division and, in February 1942, the IV Armored Corps. In early 1944, the IV Corps was redesignated the XX Corps and sent to England. In August 1944 it was committed to battle in France, where Walker led it courageously in deep, slashing attacks that took so much ground so quickly it became known as the "Ghost Corps." Walker earned the Distinguished Service Cross for gallantry crossing the Seine. In 1948 he went to Tokyo to command the Eighth Army, a command sadly depleted by peacetime cutbacks and full of inexperienced soldiers. When the Korean War erupted in June 1950, the Eighth Army, hopelessly outnumbered by the well-equipped North Korean forces, was routed. Walker fought a tenacious delaying action, finally stabilizing his lines in the hills around the South Korean city of Pusan. "There must be no further yielding," he told his men. "From now on let every man stand or die." Walker's men held for six weeks, giving **Douglas MacArthur** time to execute his landing at Inchon in September 1950. When the Chinese communists intervened in November 1950, Walker again conducted a tenacious fighting withdrawal. He was killed in an accident near Seoul on December 23, 1950.

Known as "Bulldog" after his tenacious and aggressive style, Walker once said of himself, "All my life I've been a soldier and nothing else." His stand at Pusan is a classic example of defending along interior lines, shifting forces as needed to meet enemy attacks. Wary of Chinese intervention, Walker advanced into North Korea too cautiously for MacArthur, but events proved Walker right.

William Wallace

1270?–1305

Born in Renfrewshire in the west of Scotland; not much is known about Wallace's youth except that he became an outlaw after killing an English sheriff.

Wallace led a small band in guerrilla attacks on English officials until the Rising of 1297, when he emerged as the rebel leader. King **Edward I** sent an army against the Scots that Wallace soundly defeated at Stirling Bridge on September 11, 1297, after which he drove the English out of Scotland. Wallace then carried the war into England, as far south as Newcastle. Edward, campaigning in France, concluded a truce and hurried back to England, where, with an army of 25,000 men, he invaded Scotland. Wallace fell back before Edward, laying waste the countryside to deny the English provisions. At Falkirk on July 22, 1298, the Scots fought valiantly, but deserted by his noble cavalrymen, Wallace and his infantry could not withstand the

English cavalry and archers alone. Wallace escaped and for the next few years returned to guerrilla warfare. Betrayed to the English by a former supporter, Wallace was convicted of treason and executed on August 23, 1305. As a warning to other rebels, his head was impaled on London Bridge and parts of his body were displayed at castles in Scotland. The effect was just the opposite of what was intended, and revolt broke out anew in 1306 under **Robert Bruce**.

A man of true personal valor and considerable tactical and leadership skill, Wallace never had the support of the Scottish nobility, which betrayed him at Falkirk, leaving the field without striking a single blow. Wallace subsequently became a symbol to generations of Scottish nationalists and inspired the verses by Robert Burns that begin:

Scots, wha hae wi' Wallace bled,
Scots, wham Bruce has aften led,
Welcome to your gory bed
Or to victorie!

Albrecht Eusebius Wenzel von Wallenstein

1583–1634

Born into a noble family at Hermanitz in Bohemia, Wallenstein's first military service was in the Hapsburg army, in their war against Hungary in 1604.

In 1606, to ensure himself a place at the Hapsburg court, Wallenstein converted to Catholicism. In 1609 he married a rich widow, and upon her death in 1614, he became a very wealthy man. In 1617 Wallenstein raised his own mercenary force to fight in Italy, and when the Bohemian nobles rebelled against the emperor elect Ferdinand in 1618, Wallenstein raised and led his own cavalry regiment against them. In 1625 Ferdinand made him Duke of Friedland. Wallenstein turned his duchy into an arsenal and recruiting depot and bound his senior officers to him through personal financial interests. In 1625 he was named commander in the war against German and Danish Protestant invaders and by 1627, in cooperation with **Tilly,** had conquered all of continental Denmark. Now one of the greatest and most powerful figures in the empire, Wallenstein began to act like a king himself, conducting negotiations on his own, forcing Ferdinand to dismiss him on August 13, 1630. When **Gustavus Adolphus** invaded later that year, Ferdinand called Wallenstein back. Wallenstein and Gustavus met at Lützen on November 16, 1632, and although Wallenstein was forced to withdraw with heavy casualties, Gustavus was killed. With the threat of Gustavus removed, Wallenstein's power began to ebb, and on February 25, 1634, he was assassinated by some of his own officers.

Wallenstein did not scruple to take advantage of every opportunity to make money, but he was an able field commander who used his fortune to raise armies to fight Ferdinand's battles for him.

Gouverneur K. Warren

1830–1882

Born at Cold Spring, New York, just across the Hudson from West Point, Warren entered the Military Academy at the age of sixteen with the admonition to graduate not lower than second in his class, which he did, number two of forty-four in the Class of 1850.

Commissioned in the Corps of Topographical Engineers, Warren saw his first action in the Sioux expedition of 1855. At the outbreak of the Civil War, he accepted an appointment as lieutenant colonel of the 5th New York in May 1861 and fought at Big Bethel in June. He was wounded at Gaines' Mill on June 27. He fought at Second Manassas (Bull Run) in August 1862 and was promoted to brigadier general of volunteers in September; he fought at Fredericksburg in December 1862 and was promoted to major general of volunteers in June 1863. At Gettysburg on the second day, he observed that Little Round Top, the key to the Union Army's line, was undefended. Warren rushed to commandeer men and a battery of artillery and led them to the hilltop, where he was wounded again. Subsequently he commanded the II Corps of the Army of the Potomac until March 1864, and then the V Corps at the Wilderness, Spotsylvania, and Cold Harbor. At Five Forks, on April 1, 1865, when Warren's men did not move as quickly as General **Phil Sheridan** wished, he relieved Warren. Although Warren remained in the army after the war, he never rose higher than lieutenant colonel of engineers, his career ruined by Sheridan's imputations of dilatory personal leadership. Warren spent the rest of his life trying to clear his name. A court of inquiry was not impaneled until 1879, and Warren died before its decision exonerating him could be published.

Warren's initiative at Gettysburg may have saved the Union Army and the Union cause itself from defeat. Sheridan's summary relief of this valiant and competent commander was a great injustice.

George Washington

1732–1799

Born at Bridges Creek in Westmoreland County, Virginia, Washington received little formal education before entering public life in 1748 as surveyor of the Fairfax property in Virginia.

In 1753 Governor Dinwiddie of Virginia sent Washington on a mission to ascertain French activity in the Ohio Valley and, after his return in January 1754, appointed him lieutenant colonel of the Virginia Militia. In April, at the head of two companies of militia, he led an expedition to Fort Duquesne (modern Pittsburgh) to dislodge the French garrison reportedly building a fort there. On May 28 he defeated a force of French and Indians at Great Meadows but was surrounded and forced to surrender at Fort Necessity on July 3, 1754. He accompanied British General Edward Braddock on his ill-fated march to Fort Duquesne and played a prominent role in keeping the army together after Braddock was killed in the ambush on the Monongahela, July 9, 1755. Washington accompanied the Forbes expedition of 1758 that captured Fort Duquesne and in 1759 resigned his militia commission and resumed the life of a Virginia gentleman at Mount Vernon. In August 1774, Washington was appointed a delegate to the first Continental

Congress and in June 1775, as war with Great Britain loomed, was selected commander in chief of the Continental Army. From June 1775 to December 23, 1783, Washington commanded this army and, after the French alliance of 1778, the combined forces of France and America. Washington's army never amounted to much more than 35,000 men, of which he never had more than 10,000 under his direct command. In the New York Campaign of August–November 1776, Washington was badly defeated, but his attacks at Trenton, December 25–26, 1776, and Princeton, January 3, 1777, were brilliant counterstrokes. Detaching troops to counter Burgoyne's offensive from Canada, he held his army together despite defeats at Brandywine in September 1777 and Germantown in October and the ordeal of the winter at Valley Forge that began in December 1777. In coordination with French General **Rochambeau,** he planned and executed the Yorktown Campaign that forced British General Cornwallis's surrender October 19, 1781. After the war Washington served two terms as president in 1789 and 1792, but refused a third term.

A man of stupendous character and fortitude, George Washington was at his best in a disaster. His years as commander of the American army were characterized by lack of support from the public and the states, and an impotent and interfering Congress. Despite this, Washington held his army together in the face of a series of bitter defeats by the British. He also survived cabals by his own officers to replace him. No other man could have done all this. As Lafayette remarked, Washington *was* the American Revolution. Perhaps the best insight into Washington's character is that in November 1783, when his officers initiated a move to make him king, he refused.

Anthony Wayne

1745–1796

Born at Waynesboro, Pennsylvania, Wayne began public life as a surveyor and land agent and later manager of his father's tannery.

When the American Revolution began, Wayne raised a regiment of volunteers and was appointed its colonel. He was wounded at Three Rivers in June 1776 on the expedition to Canada; commanded the defense of Ticonderoga in February 1777; fought at Brandywine, September 1777; Germantown in October, where he was wounded again; and spent the winter of 1777–1778 at Valley Forge. At Stony Point, New York, on July 16, 1779, Wayne achieved one of the outstanding American victories of the war. Commanding 1,350 men, he stormed the fort, the northernmost British post on the Hudson River, killing or capturing the entire garrison of 624 men and taking all their stores. He served under Lafayette in the Yorktown Campaign and ended the war a brevet major general. Recalled to command the army in 1792, Wayne was dispatched to quell an Indian uprising in the area of present-day Ohio after a previous expedition had ended in failure. He trained his troops rigorously, and on August 20, 1794, at Fallen Timbers on the Maumee River near present-day Toledo, he defeated the Indians decisively. He died of a fever while inspecting frontier posts in December 1796.

Nicknamed "Mad Anthony" after his ferociousness in battle, Wayne was a coolheaded and resourceful commander who learned his business in the hard school of actual combat operations.

Anthony Wayne

Free Library of Philadelphia

Arthur Wellesley, 1st Duke of Wellington ◦

1769–1852

Born Arthur Wesley (the family changed its name to Wellesley in 1798), Arthur was educated at Eton and a French military academy at Angers, after which he was commissioned in the 73rd Foot in March 1787.

Young Arthur was considered the dullard of the family, and a career in the army in those days was considered an appropriate hiding place for wellborn but poor and not very bright young gentlemen. As an aide to the lord lieutenant of Ireland from 1787 to 1793, Wellington languished until his father purchased the lieutenant colonelcy of the 33rd Foot for him. He led his regiment capably in Flanders in 1794, where he learned firsthand how badly organized the army was. In 1796 he took his regiment to India. There, Wellington distinguished himself in a number of actions, culminating at Assaye, on September 23, 1803, where with only 7,000 men (only 1,800 British) and 22 guns, he defeated the Mahratta army of 40,000 with 100 guns. In April 1808, now a lieutenant general, Wellington sailed for Portugal with an army of 17,000 men. He conducted himself well, but due to a scandal precipitated when his superiors, Burrard and Dalrymple, allowed the French army under Junot to return to France in English ships, he was recalled to stand trial. Cleared of wrongdoing, Wellington returned to Spain in 1809 in sole command of an army of 23,000 men. Always outnumbered, he fought a brilliant defensive campaign in Spain and Portugal, ruining the reputations of several of **Napoleon's** marshals. On June 28, 1813, at Vitoria, Wellington decisively defeated Joseph Bonaparte and afterward steadily pushed the French back to Toulouse, which he took just as news of Napoleon's abdication arrived. Upon Napoleon's return from Elba in March 1815, Wellington was given command of the allied army assembling in the Netherlands. During the Waterloo Campaign, Wellington at first mistook Napoleon's line of advance and at Waterloo was caught by surprise and outnumbered on June 18, 1815. Taking advantage of the terrain, he held on despite desperate assaults by the French until relieved by the Prussians under **Blücher**. Wellington went on to have a brilliant career as a statesman, serving as prime minister, 1828–1830.

Nicknamed "Nosey" and the "Iron Duke," Wellington was respected more than loved by his men. Although he could plan his campaigns meticulously, he was most of all an improviser who claimed he made his plans of "rope," so if things went wrong, he could simply tie a "knot" and carry on. He employed his infantry intelligently, taking advantage of terrain and firepower, and was careful always to husband the lives of his men. Wellington despised politics and politicians and he always spoke bluntly and to the point, but he was a realist who knew the value of compromise and cooperation and he displayed these qualities during his long political career. Austere on campaign, he could be jovial and hospitable at other times. Those who knew him well testified that his famous composure would sometimes crumble when he was informed of the deaths of friends and soldiers.

Joseph Wheeler

1836–1906

Born near Augusta, Georgia, Wheeler entered the U.S. Military Academy in 1854, graduating nineteenth of twenty-two in the class of 1859.

Upon graduation Wheeler was commissioned a second lieutenant of dragoons and saw service in New Mexico, where it is said he earned his nickname, "Fightin' Joe," in a skirmish with Indians. Upon the outbreak of the Civil War, he resigned his commission to join the Confederacy on April 22, 1861. Offered the command of the 19th Alabama Infantry, he led this regiment at Shiloh, April 6–7, 1862, and in July was placed in command of the cavalry of the Army of the Mississippi. He conducted two celebrated cavalry raids during the war, one from October 1–9, 1863, during the Chattanooga Campaign, and the other August 10–September 10, 1864, dur-

ing the Atlanta Campaign. On the Chattanooga raid the damage Wheeler did to Union Army logistics and communications was very serious although it cost him many casualties. He ended the war a twenty-eight-year-old lieutenant general, wounded three times, the survivor of 200 engagements and 800 skirmishes. He served in the U.S. Congress as a representative from Alabama from 1885 to 1900. During the Spanish-American War he was appointed a major general of volunteers and participated in the engagement at Las Guásimas, June 1898, and San Juan Hill, July 1, where in all the excitement apparently he forgot what war he was in and is said to have yelled, "We got the damn Yankees on the run again!" He then commanded a brigade in the Philippines before retiring as a brigadier general in the regular army on September 10, 1900.

While he lacked the dash and flair of **Forrest** and **Stuart,** Wheeler was a steady, capable field commander. He became a symbol of national reconciliation after the war.

William I ("The Conqueror")

1027–1087

Born at Falaise, the illegitimate son of Robert, Duke of Normandy, William succeeded to his father's dukedom at the age of seven. At Val-lès-Dunes, near Caen, in 1047, with the aid of King Henry I, William defeated his rebellious barons and secured his authority.

While visiting King Edward of England in 1051, William apparently received (or thought he had) Edward's promise to make him King of England upon his death. William also claimed that Harold Godwinson, Earl of Essex, swore an oath to support his claim to the throne of England during a visit to France in 1064. But when Edward died in January 1066, it was Harold, not William, who was crowned king. On September 28, 1066, William landed at Pevensey, Sussex, at the head of an army of 30,000 men, determined to stake his claim by force. At a spot about eight miles northwest of Hastings, the Norman army met the Anglo-Saxons at dawn on October 14, 1066. At first, fighting uphill against Harold's smaller army, William did not do well. When, however, a group of Anglo-Saxons momentarily left their commanding positions to pursue a body of retreating Normans, William saw his chance. He threw aside his helmet so his men could see him and personally led a charge against the Anglo-Saxon infantry. When Harold was killed, the Anglo-Saxon army collapsed, and on Christmas Day, 1066, William was crowned King of England. William spent the rest of his days fighting rebels in England and France and repulsing a Danish invasion of England. He died of injuries when thrown from his horse while fighting against King Philip I of France.

A thorough and capable but harsh commander and ruler, William led by personal example. While his quarrel with Harold over the English throne was in itself a petty dynastic one, the resultant fusion of Anglo-Saxon and Norman cultures established a new feudal order in England that was a turning point in world history.

Orde C. Wingate

1903–1944

Born at Nainital, India, son of an army officer, Wingate was educated at Charterhouse and the Royal Military Academy at Woolwich, receiving a commission as a second lieutenant of artillery in 1923.

Between 1928 and 1933 Wingate served on the Abyssinian frontier and late in 1936 he was sent to Palestine, a country with which he became fascinated. He identified closely with the Zionists, made friends with many Jewish leaders, and helped organize Jewish defense units for counterterrorist operations against the Arabs. On one such mission in 1938 he was wounded. One of his students was **Moshe Dayan**. At the outbreak of World War II, Wingate was sent to Khartoum to assist the Ethiopians against the

Italians. From January to May 1941 he led a guerrilla force that caused the Italian garrisons considerable difficulty. Depressed, physically ill, he attempted suicide while in Egypt in June 1941. After recuperating in England, Wingate went to India, where he was sent on a reconnaissance into Burma. Subsequently, Wingate, now a major general, proposed forming an organization to carry out guerrilla missions behind Japanese lines. This unit, the 77th Indian Infantry Brigade, or "Chindits" (from *Chinthe*, the mythical figures that guard Burmese temple doors), entered Burma in February 1943, 3,000 strong. When it emerged a month later, the men sick, hungry, exhausted, only about 600 of the 2,200 survivors were fit for further duty. These were not handpicked men, just ordinary British and Gurkha infantrymen, but they had proved the Japanese soldier was not the master of the Burmese jungles. The Chindits returned to Burma in February 1944 as part of a large-scale Allied invasion, employed more in a conventional than a behind-the-lines role. They took heavy casualties but contributed to the overall success of the invasion. Wingate was not there to welcome them back. He had been killed in an air crash in Assam on March 24, 1944.

Orde Wingate was an outspoken eccentric with little respect for his superiors, not the kind of officer who makes a good subordinate. But he

Orde C. Wingate

was also charismatic, innovative, energetic, and a brilliant leader of unconventional forces. Comparisons with **"Chinese" Gordon** and **T. E. Lawrence** are inevitable and probably not far off the mark.

James Wolfe

1727–1759

Born at Westerhan, Kent, the son of Lieutenant General Edward Wolfe of the Royal Marines, James was commissioned in the 44th Foot, his father's regiment, at the age of thirteen. In March 1742, he transferred to the 12th Foot.

Wolfe was a thin, sickly lad who later in life developed tuberculosis, but what he lacked in physical stamina, he made up for in spirit. He fought at Dettingen, Germany (June 27, 1743),

where his regiment suffered the heaviest casualties of any present, and during the Jacobite rebellion in Scotland, was at Falkirk in January 1746 and Culloden in April. In 1750 he became lieutenant colonel of the 20th Foot, which through training and discipline he turned into a model infantry regiment. In 1757 Wolfe came to the attention of British Prime Minister William Pitt, who named him one of three brigadiers in the force sent to capture the French fortress of Louisbourg on Cape Breton Island. On June 8, 1758, Wolfe led his men ashore in the face of heavy fire and took the French positions at bayonet point. In June 1759, now an acting major general in command of 9,000 men, he returned to Canada for the assault on Quebec. The French garrison under **Montcalm** numbered 16,000 (but only 2,000 regulars) and at first refused to meet the British. By August, Wolfe was down to only 5,000 effectives. On the night of September 12, 1759, he slipped past the French batteries and scaled the cliffs above the St. Lawrence River. By daybreak he had 4,500 men on the plain before the city. Montcalm decided to engage. At forty paces the French line was shattered by a volley from the English troops and then collapsed under a bayonet charge. Early in the action Wolfe's wrist was smashed by a musketball, a second ball struck him in the body, and a third killed him, but not before he learned the attack had succeeded. Quebec surrendered on September 18 and Canada the next year.

Wolfe was fearless, full of self-confidence, and eager for responsibility. While he was impetuous and often tactless in criticizing his superiors, he was an ardent student of the military profession. When informed that Wolfe's conduct was "unpredictable," King George II reportedly replied, "Mad, is he? Then I hope he will bite some of my other generals!"

James Wolfe

Free Library of Philadelphia

John E. Wool

1784–1869

Born at Newburgh, New York, son of a heelmaker, Wool was raised by his grandfather near Troy and apprenticed to an innkeeper. His formal education ended at the country-school level.

In 1807 Wool joined the militia, and at the outbreak of the War of 1812, he became a captain in the 13th Infantry Regiment. He was wounded at Queenstown Heights on October 13, 1812, and brevetted a lieutenant colonel for gallantry at the Battle of Plattsburgh in September 1814. After the war he stayed in the army and was made a colonel and inspector general in 1816, a grade he held until 1841. At the outbreak of the Mexican War, Wool was sent to the Ohio Valley to recruit volunteers and in August 1846 he arrived in Texas, to join the army of **Zachary**

Taylor. With his command of 1,400 men, Wool marched 900 miles into Mexico, joining Taylor at Saltillo. The march was arduous, and along the way Wool's men had to build roads and bridges as well as scale mountains. Wool distinguished himself at Buena Vista, February 22–23, 1847, and when Taylor returned to the States, Wool commanded the occupation forces in northern Mexico. From 1854 to 1857 he served in California, dealing successfully with hostile Indians and recalcitrant settlers. At the outbreak of the Civil War his timely reinforcement of Fort Monroe saved the post for the Union, and on May 15, 1862, he captured Norfolk. His last duty involved suppressing the New York draft riots in July 1863. Wool retired a major general in the regular army, August 1, 1863.

Wool was a strict disciplinarian but a gallant and able field commander. As inspector general of the army, he worked for modernization in all branches, particularly the artillery. Wool distinguished himself in three wars—the War of 1812, the Mexican War, and the Civil War—during the latter conflict at an age when ordinary men think only of retirement.

Xenophon

430?–350 B.C.

Born in Athens, the son of a wealthy aristocrat, Xenophon was a disciple of Socrates as a young man.

In 401 a Boetian friend, Proxenus, invited Xenophon to join a contingent of Greek mercenaries commanded by the Spartan general Clearchus, to serve under Cyrus the Younger in his war against his brother, Artaxerxes II, King of Persia. Attracted by the possibility of wealth and adventure, Xenophon joined the expedition as a soldier without rank. At the Battle of Cunaxa, near Babylon, Cyrus, with about 65,000 men, met Artaxerxes, who had 100,000 men. The Greek mercenaries, about 13,000 strong, defeated Artaxerxes' left wing, but Cyrus on the other side of the field was killed and his army disintegrated. The Greeks held their ground and Artaxerxes agreed that they could go home unmolested. He even gave them a guide, the satrap Tissaphernes, to show them the way to the sea. Tissaphernes lured Clearchus and his senior officers to a banquet and had them all murdered.

Leaderless, the Greeks elected new generals, one of whom was Xenophon. During the next five months Xenophon led his men 1,500 miles through the wilds of Armenia to the Greek colony of Trapezus on the Black Sea, fighting the barbarian hill tribes almost every step of the way. About 6,000 Greeks made it. Later Xenophon wrote about the ordeal in his *Anabasis,* or *The March Upcountry,* one of the greatest military histories ever written. In his later career Xenophon was a prolific author, writing books on the life of Socrates, government and finance, household management, hunting and horsemanship, and a history of Greece.

After the assassination of Clearchus and his officers, when Greek morale was at its lowest, Xenophon stood up boldly and rallied his comrades, denouncing surrender to the Persians and arguing for the election of new generals. The Greeks took heed and wisely elected him one of their leaders.

Y

Isoroku Yamamoto

1884–1943

Born into the Takano family in Niigata Prefecture, Japan, Yamamoto took the last name of the family that adopted him. He graduated from the naval academy in 1904 and was wounded at the Battle of Tsushima in 1905, losing two fingers on his left hand.

In 1919 Yamamoto studied at Harvard University and in 1923–1924 he toured the U.S. and Europe. He was naval attaché in Washington, D.C., from 1925 to 1928, and then headed the Japanese delegation to the London Naval Conference in 1934–1935. Yamamoto opposed the ultranationalist Japanese army faction that wanted to attack the U.S., and at least partly for his own protection from a possible assassination attempt, he was made commander of the combined fleet in 1939. Yamamoto was responsible for planning the spectacular successes that marked the first few months of Japan's war with the U.S. Knowing that Japan could never sustain a prolonged struggle with the Americans, he favored a quick knockout punch followed by negotiations once Japan had the upper hand. The attack on Pearl Harbor was not an unqualified success because the American carriers were at sea on December 7, 1941, but that was not Yamamoto's fault. At Midway in June 1942, Yamamoto's overly complicated plan confused his commanders, and during the Solomons Campaign in 1943, he committed his resources piecemeal. A contributing factor to these failures was the fact that American codebreakers were onto the Japanese movements and it was this intelligence coup that enabled a flight of P-38 Light-

Isoroku Yamamoto

ning fighters to shoot Yamamoto's plane down while he was on an inspection tour of Japanese forces in the Solomons on April 18, 1943.

Yamamoto was a very perceptive strategist and a very capable naval commander, as proved by the stunning success of Japanese arms during the first six months of World War II. It will never be known if he could have recovered his failures at Midway and the Solomons, but once he was gone, the Japanese had no one of his stature with which to replace him.

Tomoyuki Yamashita

1885–1946

Born in Kochi Prefecture, Japan, the son of a country doctor, Yamashita graduated from the military academy in 1906 and was commissioned in the infantry.

In the years before World War II Yamashita made powerful enemies in the Japanese army first, by championing a proposed cut in its size in 1929, and then, on the eve of Japan's attack on America, by urging delay until a thorough modernization of the air and ground forces could be effected. Nevertheless, in December 1941 he was given command of the Twenty-fifth Army, which on December 8, 1941, he led in an invasion of Malaya. Opposed by about 90,000 British and Commonwealth troops, in seventy days Yamashita's force of only 35,000 men pushed the British back 650 miles into Singapore. He outflanked the British by advancing through jungle terrain they considered impassable, used bicycles and abandoned vehicles to move troops, and successfully employed his armor in country the British thought unsuited for it. By February 1, 1942, with only 30,000 men, Yamashita faced 85,000 British troops in Singapore. He decided to bluff the British and on February 8 landed two divisions on the island; on February 15, the garrison surrendered. In all, Yamashita took 130,000 prisoners during this short campaign. Jealous of his success, the Japanese high command relegated him to Manchuria until July 1944, when he was sent to command the 14th Army Area in the Philippines. Yamashita resisted the American invasion as best he could, declaring Manila an open city and retreating into the hills. Unfortunately, Japanese marines disobeyed his orders to evacuate the city, and dug

Tomoyuki Yamashita

National Archives

in, committing horrible atrocities upon the civilian population before they were killed to the last man. Yamashita surrendered in September 1945, was tried for war crimes, and executed on February 23, 1946.

A brilliant and daring field commander, Yamashita inflicted one of the worst defeats on British arms in history. His task of defending the Philippines was impossible from the beginning.

While his men may have committed war crimes in Malaya for which he could have borne much responsibility, his trial for the Manila atrocities was an act of revenge because they were committed against his orders after direct contact with the marines had been broken.

Yi Sun Shin

1545–1598

Not much is known about Yi's early life. He steps onto the stage of history during the Japanese invasion of Korea in 1592.

Appointed to the admiralship of the Cholla provincial navy in 1592, Yi is credited with developing the first armored seagoing vessels in history. Known as "turtle ships" after their configuration, Yi's warships measured about 100 feet in length, were propelled by oars, and manned by a crew of about 160. Covered by awllike iron studs and armed with cannon, they could be used to ram and blast their way through an enemy fleet. The first was launched on March 27, 1592. At the battle of the Yellow Sea in July, they sank fifty-nine Japanese ships and prevented the landing of reinforcements for the invaders. Relieved of his command in 1597 for refusing to obey an order he considered foolish, Yi was reinstated after his successor's incompetence precipitated a disastrous naval defeat in July. Reconstituting his fleet, Admiral Yi attacked the Japanese at the Battle of Chinhae Bay (Pusan Harbor), November 18, 1598. More than 200 enemy ships were sunk and the Japanese fleet dispersed, but Yi himself was killed by an enemy marksman. Their lines of communication cut, the Japanese sued for peace and evacuated Korea that December.

The comparison of Yi at Chinhae with **Nelson** at Trafalgar is inevitable. Koreans today revere the memory of Yi as much for the beautiful poetry he wrote as for his valor, technological originality, organizational ability, and perseverance in adversity.

Z

Georgy Zhukov

1896–1974

Born into a Russian peasant family near Moscow, Zhukov was drafted into the Czarist army in 1911, where eventually he was promoted to NCO rank in a dragoon regiment.

In 1918 Zhukov joined the Red Army and became a member of the Communist party in 1919. In 1939, commanding five brigades of armor in the 1st Army Group along the Mongolian-Manchurian border, Zhukov achieved notable success repelling troops of the Japanese Sixth Army, for which he was awarded the Order of Lenin. In January 1941, as chief of the general staff, Zhukov advocated withdrawing from Kiev in the face of the advancing Germans, which earned him Stalin's displeasure and reassignment to Leningrad. Here and at Moscow during October–November 1941, he conducted a superb defensive campaign and then a successful counterattack early in 1942. As deputy supreme commander he ordered the defense of Sta-lingrad in August 1942, which resulted in the destruction of the German Sixth Army. In 1943 Zhukov directed a vast counteroffensive all across the Russian Front. He personally led the attack on Berlin that began on April 16, 1945, and ended on May 8, when the German high command surrendered. After the war Zhukov's popularity caused him to fall out of favor with Stalin. He was restored on Stalin's death in 1953 only to fall out again under Khrushchev. He emerged from the political shadows in the mid-1960s and in 1971 was given the Order of Lenin for the sixth time.

Zhukov commanded more men in fiercer fighting than anyone since the Mongols invaded Europe. While he won his battlefield successes with an expenditure of life that would not have been tolerated in a democracy, that was the Russian way of war and it worked.

Jan Žižka

1376?–1424

Born at Trocnov, Bohemia, the son of a minor noble, Žižka was brought up in the court of Wenceslaus (Vaclav) IV, where during the intermittent civil strife that plagued Wenceslaus's reign, Žižka lost an eye in battle.

Žižka fought with Poland in its war with the Teutonic Knights and was at the Battle of Grünwald in 1410. Afterward, in Prague, Žižka became a supporter of the religious reformer John Huss against the Catholics. During an armistice between the factions, Žižka traveled to the Hussite fortress of Tábor, near Ústí, where he developed his unique battlefield tactics. Using large armored horse-drawn wagons with loopholes, Žižka's infantry advanced into enemy territory screened by units of light cavalry. With his wagons laagered and chained together, protected by pikemen, cannon, crossbowmen, and handgunners, his formations were impregnable against cavalry and infantry. At Prague on July

20, 1419, he so decisively defeated the forces of Sigismund, King of Hungary, that they had to withdraw from Bohemia. Žižka repulsed Sigismund twice more in 1421, but at the siege of Rába he lost his other eye. Undeterred by his blindness, Žižka again defeated Sigismund's army at Německý Brod on January 10, 1422. The following year he suppressed dissident factions within the Hussite movement. Given command of the combined Hussite army for an invasion of Moravia, he died of plague at Pribyslav on October 11, 1424.

A tireless drillmaster and commander of undeniable bravery, Žižka also understood the difference between tactical defense (his laager formations) and strategic offense (employing them to win wars). That he could still retain command and fight successful battles after losing his sight marks him as one of the most remarkable generals in history.

Bibliography

Sachchidananda Bhattacharya. *A Dictionary of Indian History*. New York: George Braziller, 1967.

Frederic Boase. *Modern English Biography*. London: Frank Cass & Co., Ltd., 1965.

Mark M. Boatner, III. *The Civil War Dictionary*. New York: Vintage Books, 1987

———. *Encyclopedia of the American Revolution*. New York: David McKay Co., 1969.

Peter Burchard. *One Gallant Rush*. New York: St. Martin's Press, 1965.

Joan Comay. *Who's Who in the Old Testament*. New York: Holt, Rinehart and Winston, 1971.

John Canning. *100 Great Lives of Antiquity*. Bungay, Suffolk, England: Methuen, 1985.

Owen Connelly. *Historical Dictionary of Napoleonic France, 1799–1815*. Westport, CT: Greenwood Press, 1985.

S. A. Cook, et al. *The Cambridge Ancient History*, Vol. 9, *The Roman Republic 133–44 B.C.* Cambridge, England: Cambridge University Press, 1971.

Current Biography. New York: The H. W. Wilson Co., 1944, 1945, 1951, 1954, 1972, 1988, 1991.

Dictionary of American Biography. New York: Charles Scribner's Sons, 1928–1936, 1944, 1958, 1973, 1974.

Dictionary of American Military Biography. Westport, CT: Greenwood Press, 1984.

Dictionary of National Biography. New York: Oxford University Press, 1912–1981.

William J. Duiker. *Historical Dictionary of Vietnam*. Metuchen, NJ: Scarecrow Press, 1989.

R. Ernest and Trevor N. Dupuy. *The Encyclopedia of Military History*. New York: Harper and Row, 1970.

Trevor N. Dupuy, et al. *The Harper Encyclopedia of Military Biography*. New York: HarperCollins, 1992.

John R. Elting. *The Super-Strategists*. New York: Charles Scribner's Sons, 1985.

———. *Swords Around a Throne*. New York: The Free Press, 1988.

Ainslie T. Embree. *Encyclopedia of Asian History*. New York: Charles Scribner's Sons, 1988.

Encyclopedia Americana. Danbury, CT: Grolier Inc., 1984.

Encyclopedia Britannica. Encyclopaedia Britannica, Inc., London & New York, 1920 ed.

Herbert A. Giles. *A Chinese Biographical Dictionary*. New York: Paragon Book Gallery, Ltd., 1971.

Aryeh Grabolis. *The Illustrated Encyclopedia of Medieval Civilization*. New York: Mayflower Books, 1980.

Holger H. Herwig and Neil M. Heyman. *Biographical Dictionary of World War I*. Westport, CT: Greenwood Press, 1982.

Brian Hook. *The Cambridge Encyclopedia of China*. Cambridge, England: Cambridge University Press, 1982.

Seiichi Iwao, ed. (Burton Watson, transl.). *Biographical Dictionary of Japanese History*. Kodansha International, Ltd., 1978.

Harry Judge. *Oxford Illustrated Encyclopedia*, Vol. 3, *World History from Earliest Times to 1800*. New York: Oxford University Press, 1988.

Alexander P. Kazhdan. *The Oxford Dictionary of Byzantium*. New York: Oxford University Press, 1991.

John Keegan and Andrew Wheatcroft. *Who's Who in Military History from 1453 to the Present Day*. New York: William Morrow & Co., Inc., 1976.

George C. Kohn. *Dictionary of Wars*. New York: Facts on File, 1986.

Isaac Landman. *The Universal Jewish Encyclopedia*. New York: Universal Jewish Encyclopedia Co., 1939-1948.

Peter Macdonald. *Giap. The Victor in Vietnam*. New York: W. W. Norton & Co., 1993.

David Mason. *Who's Who in World War II*. Boston: Little, Brown and Company, 1978.

Donald R. Morris. *The Washing of the Spears*. New York: Simon & Schuster, 1965.

The McGraw-Hill Encyclopedia of World Biography. New York: McGraw-Hill, 1973, 1987, 1988.

The National Cyclopedia of American Biography. Clifton, NJ: James T. White & Co, 1977.

New Catholic Encyclopedia. New York: McGraw-Hill, 1967.

The New Century Classical Handbook. New York: Appleton-Century-Crofts, 1962.

Nguyen Van Thai and Nguyen Van Mung. *A Short*

History of Vietnam. Saigon: The Times Publishing Co., 1958.

Edgar Leon Newman. *Historical Dictionary of France from the 1815 Restoration to the Second Empire.* Westport, CT: Greenwood Press, 1987.

Political Profiles: The Kennedy Years. New York: Facts on File, 1976.

Political Profiles: The Nixon/Ford Years. New York: Facts on File, 1979.

Norman Polman and Thomas B. Allen. *World War II: America at War, 1941–1945.* New York: Random House, 1991.

William H. Prescott. *History of the Conquest of Mexico and History of the Conquest of Peru.* New York: The Modern Library.

Ilan Rachum. *The Renaissance: An Illustrated Encyclopedia.* New York: Mayflower Books, 1979.

Edwin Riddell. *Lives of the Stuart Age, 1603–1714.* New York: Barnes & Noble Books, 1976.

Heinrich E. Schulz, et al. *Who Was Who in the USSR.* Metuchen, NJ: Scarecrow Press, 1972.

Louis L. Snyder. *Snyder's Historical Guide to World War II.* Westport, CT: Greenwood Press, 1982.

Harry G. Summers, Jr. *Vietnam War Almanac.* New York: Facts on File, 1985.

Joseph R. Strayer. *Dictionary of the Middle Ages.* New York: Charles Scribner's Sons, 1982–1989.

Daniel Thrapp. *Encyclopedia of Frontier Biography.* Spokane, WA: Arthur H. Clark, 1990.

Alice Rains Trulock. *In the Hands of Providence.* Chapel Hill, NC: The University of North Carolina Press, 1992.

Denis Warner. *Certain Victory How Hanoi Won the War.* Kansas City: Sheed Andrews and McMeel, 1977.

Webster's New Geographical Dictionary. Springfield, MA: G. & C. Merriman Co., 1977.

Geoffrey Wigoder. *Dictionary of Jewish Biography.* New York: Simon & Schuster, 1991.

Peter Young. *The World Almanac of World War II.* New York: Bison Books, 1981.